DEADLY INHERITANCE

Murder, intrigue and marriage in the Welsh Marches of old...

When Sir Geoffrey's unpopular brother, Henry, is murdered, he unwillingly inherits Goodrich Castle in the Welsh Marches. Immediately, his sister pushes him towards a marriage that will provide an heir and stability for the family. But when Geoffrey survives attempts on his own life, he wonders whether they are linked to Henry's death, to his potential brides, or even to the rumoured murder of the Duchess of Normandy, as a Welsh revolt against the English looms.

DEADLY INHERITANCE

Simon Beaufort

Severn House Large Print
London & New York

This first large print edition published 2011
in Great Britain and the USA by
SEVERN HOUSE PUBLISHERS LTD of
9-15 High Street, Sutton, Surrey, SM1 1DF.
First world regular print edition published 2009 by
Severn House Publishers Ltd., London and New York.

British Library Cataloguing in Publication Data

Beaufort, Simon.
  Deadly inheritance.
  1. Mappestone, Geoffrey, Sir (Fictitious character)--
  Fiction. 2. Inheritance and succession--Welsh Borders
  (England and Wales)--Fiction. 3. Great Britain--History--
  Norman period, 1066-1154--Fiction. 4. Detective and
  mystery stories. 5. Large type books.
  I. Title
  823.9'14-dc22

  ISBN-13: 978-0-7278-7908-0

Severn House Publishers support The Forest Stewardship Council
[FSC], the leading international forest certification organisation. All
our titles that are printed on Greenpeace-approved FSC-certified paper
carry the FSC logo.

Printed and bound in Great Britain by the
MPG Books Group, Bodmin, Cornwall.

For
Barry Hunt
and
Cathy Rose

Prologue

Goodrich, Herefordshire, September 1102

Henry Mappestone was drunk. He had finished off two jugs of wine, reaching the point where he no longer bothered with a goblet. It was easier to upend the jug, and if some spilt, so be it: his sister Joan had made astute investments, so he had plenty of money to spend.

When Henry thought about his sister and her husband, his flushed face broke into a sneer. He hated them both. Goodrich Castle and its lands were *his* – he had inherited them when his older brothers died. But it was Joan and Olivier who had made them profitable. It was good to be wealthy after many lean years, but Henry resented the way that Joan pursed her lips when he – the lord of the manor – enjoyed his wine or hit a labourer. In fact, he was of a mind to throw her and Olivier out altogether.

But then he would be obliged to run the estate himself, and, unlike Olivier, Henry could not read – he would have to hire a clerk to keep the accounts and the man would surely cheat him. Henry scowled. No, Joan and Olivier would have to stay, as much as it infuriated him.

It was late, and most people were in bed. It was

harvest, so servants and masters alike were exhausted from gathering crops. Everyone was forced to lend a hand, even Henry. He was tired, too, but he did not feel like sleeping. He seldom did; Joan said it was because his innards were pickled. But there were times when he thought the only way to survive until dawn was to drink.

He lurched unsteadily across the hall, treading on fingers and toes as he waded through weary bodies on straw pallets. But no one dared complain. It had only been an hour or so since Henry had punched Torva – Goodrich's steward – and no one else wanted to attract his attention. Henry wished he had not hit Torva so hard, because he was sure that he had broken his own hand in doing so.

Henry reached the door, then staggered across the bailey towards the stables. Animals would be better company than peasants with their resentful, fear-filled glances, and, like most Normans, Henry liked horses. He especially liked the spirited palfrey called Dun. He reeled inside the stable, trying to see in the moonlight. He slapped Dun on the rump, then cursed at the searing pain in his knuckles. He leant against the wall, cradling his hand to his chest.

He shouted for the groom, Jervil, who slept in the loft. When he appeared, Henry tried to kick him, but Jervil melted into the darkness. Henry was incensed. How dare he slink away when summoned by his master! But then there was a shadow beside him. Jervil knew his place.

'Get me some wine,' Henry snapped, easing into Dun's stall. The horse had seemed lame

8

earlier, and he wanted to check it.

But the shadow did not reply, and Henry suddenly felt something hot near his liver. He was suddenly gripped by a deep, searing ache, and he slid down the wall and into the straw. When he reached for his stomach, his hand met a protruding dagger. He raised his hand to where silver moonlight slanted in through the door; it dripped black with blood. He felt light-headed, and then people he knew started to walk in front of him in a silent procession.

First was his wife, who had died the previous year, her face now no more than a blur; she carried their two little sons, who had died of fever that spring. His brothers were there, too – the two older ones, with the younger Geoffrey behind them. Henry did not remember being told that Geoffrey was dead, but perhaps he had died on Crusade. Joan followed Geoffrey, and Henry saw that she was laughing at him, mocking him. Had she thrust the weapon into him, or was it someone else? Henry did not know, but the knowledge that he was dying enraged him. He screamed at the ghosts and shadows, cursing them until his last breath.

Normandy, Spring 1103

The Duchess was dying, and no one could help her. She lay in the great bed in the Duke's chamber, eyes closed and deathly pale, under the heap of furs. The people who watched her last moments did so in silence. The priests had finished their prayers, and all attention was on the breath that hissed softly past her bloodless lips.

At her side was the Duke of Normandy, his face a mask of anguish as he clutched her cold, white fingers. The Duke had fallen in love with Sibylla de Conversano the first time he had seen her, and it was cruel that she should be snatched from him after only two years of marriage. She had recently given him a son, and her physicians said that it was complications from the birth that had led to her decline.

Behind the Duke was his mistress, Agnes Giffard. Unfortunately for Agnes, Sibylla was extremely popular, and few had condoned the Duke breaking his wedding vows while his wife was confined by her pregnancy. Agnes met the hostile glares with an unrepentant pout. Perhaps the Duke would marry *her* once he was free of Sibylla; *then* these sanctimonious pigs would pay for slighting her. She rested her hand on her son's shoulder. Poor Walter was a skinny, unprepossessing youth, cursed with his dead father's dull wits. He beamed at her, so she pinched him, to remind him that he should not grin at deathbeds – not when people were watching.

At the back of the chamber, politely keeping their distance, were the well-wishers. These included Lord Baderon, who, with estates in both Normandy and England, owed allegiance to the Duke as well as to his brother, King Henry of England. Baderon was deeply worried: the gentle, kind Sibylla was far better than her husband at keeping peace and dispensing justice. What would happen to his estates when she was gone?

The Duchess sighed, and one of the priests began to pray again. A tear rolled down the Duke's cheek, and a physician stepped forward to lay a comforting hand on his shoulder. Sibylla was dead.

One

Goodrich Castle, Spring 1103

The grave was already hard to find. Snow and rain had flattened the mound of earth, and the cross was listing so heavily that it was all but lost among the weeds. Sir Geoffrey Mappestone would not have been sure that he had the right place, were it not for the other tombs nearby. His mother's was there, mottled with lichen, next to his father's, which was grander and newer. And nearby were his brothers – Walter and Stephen. His sister Enide should have been there, too, but she had been lost in the River Wye and her body never found, although Geoffrey and Joan had erected a cross anyway.

He bent to straighten Henry's cross, fighting with the nettles that enmeshed it. When it was more or less upright, he stood back, noting that none of his family's graves were very well tended. His father had been a foul-tempered tyrant, unloved by his children or tenants; his mother had been equally formidable, and even fifteen years in the ground had not mellowed the memories of those who had known her. Their six children had been cast in their mould, although Geoffrey hoped that two decades away from

13

their influence had left him a better man, while a happy marriage and encroaching middle age had softened his sister Joan.

'A sorry sight,' said the parish priest, Father Adrian, coming to stand next to Geoffrey. 'All of them, except your father, dead well before three score years and ten.'

'Aye,' agreed Geoffrey's old comrade-in-arms, Will Helbye. 'It *was* a war-like family. Only you and Joan are left.'

Geoffrey sighed. He did not need reminding that all his kin had met violent ends. He turned to the priest. 'What happened to Henry? I know he was found with a knife in him. If he was killed by some vengeful neighbour or servant, I should know. I do not want the same to happen to Joan.'

'Or to you,' mused Father Adrian. 'You have been soldiering these last twenty years, but now that you have inherited Goodrich and its villages, farms and woods, you will be obliged to spend time here.'

Geoffrey said nothing, but doubted that he would stay long. He had assumed Goodrich would be dull, full of occupants obsessed with cattle and crops, but it had transpired to be rather turbulent, thanks to the two powerful nobles in the region. Lord Baderon owned manors to the west, which he was giving to those of his knights who took Welsh brides; this, he claimed, would build alliances between Wales and England and thus prevent a Celtic invasion. Meanwhile, fitz-Norman, who, as Constable of the Forest, ruled the tracts of woodland to the south and east,

14

believed Baderon's marriages potentially united the Welsh at England's expense. The two disliked each other, and Goodrich was caught in the middle.

'Henry was stabbed while you and I were fighting the King's war,' said Helbye. 'You were not here, and could not have prevented it happening.'

Geoffrey nodded absently – the King's war, and the part he had been forced to play in it, still rankled. He had returned from the Holy Land when his father was dying, but had been prevented from returning there when the King had demanded he help put down a rebellion. It had taken several months, during which Geoffrey's liege lord, Prince Tancred, became so angry his repeated summonses were ignored that he had dismissed Geoffrey from his service. The King had offered a post, but Geoffrey disliked the monarch's sly ways and had refused it, instead spending three months travelling around England until he found himself again at Goodrich.

'I would like to visit the Holy Land,' said Father Adrian wistfully. Then he coolly regarded Geoffrey's surcoat with its faded Crusader's cross. 'However, *I* would go as a pilgrim, not as a knight who slaughters everyone he meets.'

'The Crusaders who liberated Jerusalem – who carry the honoured title of *Jerosolimitani* – are assured a place in Heaven,' objected Helbye, stung. He was a veteran of countless battles at Geoffrey's side, and was proud of his role in wresting the Holy Land from its previous occupants. 'Our mission was a holy one, blessed by God.'

'It was an excuse for bloodshed and looting,' countered Father Adrian. Geoffrey had witnessed enough incidents to make him question the sanctity of the Crusade, too, but he said nothing.

'You cannot have a Crusade without bloodshed and looting,' said Helbye, bemused by the priest's attitude. 'What would be the point?'

Father Adrian grimaced, declining to argue against such rigidly held convictions. Instead, he addressed Geoffrey. 'Will you return to the Holy Land? If so, you should abandon your armour and go as a penitent, to atone for the crimes you committed on your first visit.'

Geoffrey was unable to keep the bitterness from his voice. 'I doubt I will ever return. The King has seen to that.'

Helbye was sympathetic. 'Write to Tancred again. His anger will not last forever. I wish I could go, too, but my fighting days are over.'

'His should be, too,' said Father Adrian, as though Geoffrey were not there. 'He is not yet four and thirty, but has dedicated his life to killing. It is time he stopped spilling blood and concentrated on his soul. He does not have long to do it, if his siblings are anything to go by.'

'Which takes us back to Henry,' prompted Geoffrey.

'It happened last September,' said Father Adrian, relenting with a sigh. 'It was a terrible harvest – you have seen for yourself that the granaries are almost empty, and it is not yet Easter. The disaster was a combination of bad

16

weather and the war with Robert de Bellême. Folk were afraid to reap their crops – or Bellême set the fields alight.'

'It was a great day for England when the King exiled Bellême,' declared Helbye. 'I am proud of the role we played in getting rid of him.'

Father Adrian nodded before continuing. 'Like every able-bodied man, Henry had been helping with the threshing. He was tired – as were we all – but instead of going to bed, he turned to wine.'

'My wife says he did that a lot,' added Helbye. 'Henry always liked wine, but he became greedy for it last year.'

'Why?' asked Geoffrey. 'Was he grieving for his children?'

Father Adrian released a startled laugh. 'He had no affection for them, or for his wife! They were too much like him – selfish, greedy and violent. He intended to start a new family with another woman.'

'Did he have anyone in mind?' asked Geoffrey, wondering what lady would be fool enough to consider marrying a man with Henry's unsavoury reputation.

Adrian nodded. 'He wanted Isabel, Lord fitz-Norman's youngest daughter.'

Geoffrey was astonished. 'Surely she was too ambitious a prize? The Constable of the Forest controls a vast region. There must have been better marriages than Henry of Goodrich.'

'The Constable *is* a powerful man,' agreed Father Adrian. 'The forest's boundaries stretch from the River Severn to Monmouth, and from Chepstow to Rosse.'

'I know its size,' said Geoffrey, wondering why the priest chose to explain facts that he had known since boyhood. 'But why would Henry think he stood a chance of winning Isabel?'

'Oh, that is easy,' said Father Adrian carelessly. 'She was carrying his child.'

Goodrich Castle guarded the ford of the River Wye on the Gloucester-to-Monmouth road. Like most castles erected following the Conquest in 1066, it comprised a tower-topped motte and an earthwork-enclosed bailey. In Goodrich's case, the earthworks included a dry moat around its east, south and west sides, while the north made use of the steep, natural slope that ran down to the river.

The stone tower was the strongest part of the castle, with only one way inside: wooden steps from the bailey to the first floor. In the event of an attack, the stairs could be hauled inside, making access more difficult for invaders. The tower had four floors. The lowest was a vaulted chamber used for storage, the first comprised the hall, and the top two contained bedchambers and offices. The roof was battlemented, allowing archers and lookouts to be stationed there.

In Geoffrey's youth, the tower had been a grim place. Its walls were thick and cold, and his father had not believed in fires unless the weather was particularly foul. Consequently, it had been dank, dismal and uninviting, even on warm days. Wet dogs, stinking floor coverings and spilt food made it reek, and Geoffrey recalled inventing excuses to avoid being in it.

But Joan had changed things. Braziers lit even the most distant corners of the hall, and there was always a fire in the hearth. Its floor was swept after every meal, tapestries adorned the walls and the furniture was comfortable. It seemed a totally different place.

That evening Geoffrey watched her as she sewed in the lamplight. She was tall and strong, with an unsmiling face and flecks of grey in her thick brown hair. She ruled Goodrich with firm efficiency, and Geoffrey was happy to let her continue, although he knew that he should take some responsibility for the lands that were now his. Sitting next to her, strumming on a harp, was her husband, Sir Olivier d'Alençon. He was resplendent in a blue tunic with elegantly embroidered hems and cuffs, and his black hair was neatly trimmed. He was far smaller than Joan, and it never failed to amaze Geoffrey that his burly, gruff sister should lavish her affections on such a puny specimen. It astonished him even more that the feelings were reciprocated.

Like Joan, Geoffrey was tall and well built, although a life of fighting meant that he had remained lean, while she was tending towards fat. He was clean-shaven and his brown hair was cut short. He was unusual for a knight, in that he could read and write; his mother had wanted him to join the Church, but he had rebelled, so his father had sent him for knightly training instead. He had been in the Duke of Normandy's service, and then a commander for the ambitious Lord Tancred. Now, for the first time since winning his spurs, he was part of no man's army, although it was not a freedom that he relished. As he listened to Olivier playing a song often sung by Crusaders, he wished with all his heart that Tancred had not dismissed him.

Cautiously – for Joan had a terrible temper – Geoffrey broached the subject of their brother's plans for the Constable's daughter. She was unrepentant for neglecting to mention them, which annoyed him: if Henry *had* impregnated fitzNorman's daughter, then it was possible that fitzNorman considered Henry – and his kin – an enemy, and Geoffrey did not like the notion that powerful men harboured grudges about which he was blithely unaware.

'Henry may have been murdered by fitzNorman or his men,' he said irritably. 'I am sure the Constable had more ambitious plans for his daughter than the likes of Henry.'

'You have done this ever since you arrived,' said Joan, setting down her sewing to glare at him. 'Underestimate the value of our estates. Besides this castle and its demesne, we have manors in Herefordshire *and* Gloucestershire. Henry might not have warranted fitzNorman's *eldest* daughter, but the youngest was not beyond his sights.'

'Is it true that she carried his child?' Geoffrey asked, unconvinced but loath to argue. 'How did that happen?'

Olivier gave a giggle, which quickly turned into a cough when his wife scowled.

'How do you *think* it happened?' Joan demanded. 'Surely you have not been away from female company *that* long?'

'I meant was Isabel happy with Henry as a suitor?' said Geoffrey, striving for patience.

'Isabel detested Henry,' volunteered Olivier. He shrugged when Joan turned furious eyes on him. 'Geoffrey will find out from someone else if we do not tell him. Ergo, we should answer his questions lest he starts interrogating the wrong people.'

Geoffrey was immediately suspicious. 'What do you mean? What *wrong people*?'

Joan glared at her husband. 'I thought we had agreed the less said, the better.'

'If Geoffrey wants to look into Henry's death, we cannot stop him,' said Olivier. 'Kings and princes have employed him to investigate far more dangerous matters. Tell him what he wants to know.'

Joan sighed loudly. 'It is not *him* I am worried about. It is Goodrich. Several people had cause to want Henry dead, and I do not want him accusing them of murder. He could do a great deal of damage by interfering.'

'He could,' acknowledged Olivier. 'We have Baderon poised on one side, fitzNorman on the other, and we are trapped in the middle.'

'I have done my best to salve the wounds inflicted by our father and brother,' Joan said, 'but this is an uneasy region. Baderon is a decent man, but he is so determined to have peace with the Welsh that he infuriates the English.'

'He always sides with them in disputes,' agreed Olivier. 'And this business of marrying his knights to Welsh ladies is causing resentment.'

21

'Meanwhile, fitzNorman is a senseless oaf,' Joan declared uncompromisingly. 'He applies harsh laws to the royal forests ruthlessly – peasants forbidden to gather firewood, or catch game – it is impractical in hard times.'

'And times *are* hard right now,' nodded Olivier. 'We had a poor harvest followed by a fierce winter. People are starving, and the King comes to the forest so rarely that he would not miss the odd duck or deer.'

'What did fitzNorman say when he discovered what Henry had done to Isabel?' asked Geoffrey, thinking that the seduction of a daughter was a good motive for murder.

'That he was happy to secure an alliance with Goodrich,' said Joan. 'He said we provide a friendly buffer between him and Baderon. Unfortunately, he was angry at the way Henry went about it.'

'Ralph de Bicanofre was none too pleased, either,' said Olivier. He turned to Geoffrey. 'Bicanofre is the little manor to the south of Goodrich, and its heir, Ralph, wanted to marry Isabel himself: he was incensed when Henry deflowered her.'

'Baderon was offended by Henry, as well,' added Joan. 'He, too, wanted Goodrich as a buffer, and there was talk of Henry marrying *his* daughter. Henry would not have her, but I suspect Baderon had not given up hope.'

'So,' summarized Geoffrey. 'Two of the richest men in the region – Baderon and fitzNorman – were angered by Henry's relationship with Isabel, as was Ralph. Any of them – or their retainers – might have murdered Henry.'

'They are not the only ones,' said Joan gloomily. 'Henry did a lot of damage by burning our Welsh neighbours' grain stores, too.'

Geoffrey was appalled. 'He fired their granaries?'

Joan nodded. 'Caerdig of Llan Martin is the only Welsh lord friendly to us now. The rest say *our* corn should be used to compensate them – and they have a point. It is only a matter of time before hunger leads them to attack us.'

'Welsh harvests were even worse than English ones,' said Olivier. 'But you already know that.'

Geoffrey nodded. 'The Welsh Prince Iorwerth summoned his warriors to fight for Bellême against the King last summer, although he then changed sides. But the war kept men from their farms.'

'And now they are paying the price,' said Joan. 'By the time the men returned home, rains had ruined the crops. Many Welsh villages only harvested a fraction of the grain they need. So, the situation is delicate. I know you want to bring Henry's killer to justice, but we cannot afford a feud with Baderon or fitzNorman – and we certainly must not give the Welsh a reason for attacking us.'

'I will be discreet,' said Geoffrey, unwilling to let the matter drop. Henry was his brother, and if one Mappestone could be slain, then so could another.

Joan gave a disbelieving snort. 'You will not! Your idea of discretion is to ask questions at the end of a sword. Henry is dead, Geoff, and no good can come of looking into his end.'

Geoffrey stared into the flames. Was she right? *Was* it best to maintain the tenuous truces between Goodrich and its neighbours at all costs? He had seen what happened to manors owned by warring lords, and knew that it was not only the owners who suffered: the peasantry were victims, too. Perhaps Joan was right to preserve stability at the expense of letting her brother's killer go free. Or did she have another reason for wanting the murder forgotten? Everyone agreed that Henry had been a tyrant, and few tears had been shed when he died. Perhaps she already knew who killed him, and her motive to keep Geoffrey from investigating was not to avert a war, but to protect the killer.

Joan changed the subject when Geoffrey made no reply, unaware that he had reached a decision. He would not rest easy until he understood why his brother had been murdered, and Joan's urging him to forget the matter only made him more determined to learn what had happened.

The following morning Geoffrey threw open the window shutters in the room that had been his father's. In the foreground meadows stretched to the River Wye, divided into neat fields of wheat, oats and barley. In the distance hills were dotted white with sheep. The great brown-green mass of the forest lay to the south and east, a vast tangle of trees and scrub, broken by the occasional path.

A bowl of water had been left in the garderobe

for his morning ablutions, but there was a layer of ice across the top and he did not feel like washing in it. He scraped a dagger across his cheeks a couple of times, then glanced at the shelves holding his few clothes. The shelves concealed an entrance to a passageway that wound through the castle's foundations before emerging in the woods. Joan's description of relations between Goodrich and its neighbours had been unsettling, and he realized that he might be obliged to defend the castle. He knew that he should make himself familiar with potential escape or foray routes, but the tunnel was cramped, pitch-black and airless, and his irrational but paralyzing horror of dark underground places meant that he had not yet plucked up the courage to open the hidden door. Unwilling to address his fears, he turned his attention to his clothes.

Joan objected to Geoffrey wearing full armour around the estate, claiming it made him look eager to fight, and he supposed that he should make an effort to adapt to civilian life. He opted for the outfit of a knight at ease: a light mail vest under a long, belted tunic and sturdy oxhide boots. The tunic was brown. Despite Joan's efforts to encourage him to don brighter, more fashionable colours, after twenty years of practical military attire, it was difficult to change.

When he reached the hall, breakfast had already been served and the tables and benches cleared away. He supposed he should rise earlier in future, so as not to be seen as someone who spent half the day in bed while his people

25

worked. He grabbed bread and ale from Peter the cook, and sat with Joan near the hearth while she mended a basket. Olivier perched nearby, studying the accounts.

'I meant to tell you yesterday that I received a message from Roger – my fellow knight from the Holy Land,' Geoffrey said. 'He is coming to visit.'

'Really?' said Olivier, pleased. He liked the bluff, northern knight, and they spent a great deal of time trying to impress each other with battle tales. Roger's stories were grossly exaggerated, but there was more truth in them than Olivier's: the little knight had never raised a sword in anger.

Joan was less enamoured of a man whose idea of a good time was drinking vast quantities of ale and annoying the local women. When those pastimes were unavailable, Roger looted and raided for any man who would pay him.

'He will not stay long,' added Geoffrey quickly, seeing Joan's disapproving frown.

'Helbye thinks you should ask Prince Tancred to be reinstated,' said Joan, clearly worried about what might happen with two restless *Jerosolimitani* in residence.

Geoffrey stared at the flames in the hearth. 'There is nothing I would like more, but Tancred's last letter made it clear that will never happen. I spent too long following the orders of the King, and no prince wants a knight who accepts commissions from another master.'

'Tell him you did not accept them readily,' said Olivier. 'The King *forced* you to remain in

England – and you did it to help Joan. Surely he will understand?'

'He considers my loyalty compromised,' said Geoffrey, recalling Tancred's scathing words. 'And there is also the matter of my former squire, Durand.'

'Durand,' said Joan, scowling. 'The King's spy. But what does he have to do with your predicament? I know Tancred charged you to turn him into a warrior, but surely you told him the task was impossible?'

Unfortunately, Durand's feckless, cowardly dishonesty was irrelevant to Tancred, which left only the bald fact that Geoffrey had failed in his commission. That, combined with his long absence following the King's bidding, had destroyed their friendship; Geoffrey knew there was no point travelling to the Holy Land to put forward his case in person. He reached inside his tunic and pulled out the last letter he had received from Tancred. Olivier read it, then passed it back without a word. Joan raised questioning eyebrows. Unlike her husband and brother, she was illiterate.

'Tancred says Geoffrey had no right to obey King Henry's orders, and says he will never trust him again,' summarized Olivier. 'He thinks Geoffrey should have ensured Durand returned to the Holy Land rather than joining the King's service, because he had talents Tancred wanted to harvest himself. He also says that if Geoff sets foot in his lands again, he will be executed as a traitor.'

Joan gaped. 'But I thought you were friends.'

27

'So did I,' said Geoffrey shortly. He was still bewildered by the bitter tenor of Tancred's words, as he had loved Tancred as a brother. He had assumed that the Prince would understand his desire to help his sister, so he was shocked by the petty, mean-spirited response. He was also bemused by the importance Tancred affixed to Durand, whom Tancred had earlier despised.

'Then I suppose you must live with it,' said Olivier. 'You can either accept the post the King offered or stay here. Another pair of hands is always useful.'

Not for the first time, the reality of the situation hit Geoffrey. He longed to be away from Goodrich's drudgery, but he had nowhere else to go. He did not want to sell his martial skills to the highest bidder, like other knights, because he did not want to fight for a cause in which he did not believe. The alternative was to become a royal agent – but he did not like the King, and accepting his commission would be akin to selling his soul to the Devil. Glumly, Geoffrey stood and left the hall.

Geoffrey spent the day riding through forest and steep-sided valleys. His black-and-white dog loped at his side and his horse cantered gamely along remote tracks. By sunset he was less gloomy, and he arrived at Goodrich in time for the evening meal. Tables and benches were arranged in the hall for the servants, while Geoffrey joined Joan and Olivier in a niche near the hearth. Afterwards they went to the solar on the upper floor, leaving the hall to the servants.

A fire filled the chamber with welcoming warmth, and, tired from his exercise, Geoffrey began to feel sleepy.

'What happened to Durand?' asked Olivier, strumming a harp-like instrument from Turkey that Geoffrey had given him. 'The last we heard, he was accused of a serious theft. The King is unlikely to hang a squire for stealing, as he might a peasant, but I anticipate he was heavily fined?'

Geoffrey shook his head. 'God knows how, but not only did Durand escape punishment, he inveigled himself a post in the King's household. He is now a senior clerk.'

Joan was astonished. 'I thought he would have been sent back to Tancred in disgrace.'

'Durand did not want to return to Tancred, because Tancred would have forced him to train as a soldier. He decided to make his fortune in England – and he has done just that. He writes occasionally, describing his progress.' Although Geoffrey had not liked his old squire – a feeling wholly reciprocated – it was difficult not to admire his capacity to make the best of a bad situation. 'It is a pity he was dishonest; I miss his resourcefulness and intelligence.'

'What of Bale?' asked Olivier. 'The man I found to replace Durand? How is he?'

Geoffrey leant down to scratch his dog's head, loath to answer. Bale was not up to the task, but Geoffrey did not want to offend Olivier by saying so.

'I would like to know what actually happened when Henry died in the stables,' he said instead.

'I *could* ask other people, but I would rather hear it from you.'

'Very well,' said Joan with a long-suffering sigh. 'What do you want to know?'

'You have already said you do not know who killed him, so I will settle for hearing what happened when you found his body.'

'I discovered him the next morning,' obliged Olivier, pulling his legs up on to the seat of his chair when Geoffrey's dog stood and shook itself. The animal had a tendency to bite. 'When I first saw him, with the dagger in his stomach, I assumed someone had killed him. But I have since reconsidered. Now, I think he killed himself.'

Joan glared at the dog when it moved towards her. Prudently, it backed off, flopping down again at Geoffrey's side. 'At the time, I believed he had been murdered by a Bristol merchant, but was later proved wrong. Now I do not know what happened – nor do I want to.'

'It was suicide,' pressed Olivier. 'Henry was deep in his cups, and became overwhelmed with self-pity.'

'Do not look sceptical, Geoff,' admonished Joan. 'Henry was violent, surly and selfish, and no one liked him. He often felt sorry for himself. Moreover, if he was alive now, you would be fighting each other.'

She was right about Henry's aggression: he and Geoffrey had fought constantly as boys, and Henry had carried the feud into adulthood. Geoffrey was unconvinced by Olivier's theory, however. 'Henry was not the kind of man to inflict

30

harm on himself. He was more likely to vent his anger on others.'

'I agree with you,' said Joan. 'I believe he was murdered, too. But I also think it will do no good to investigate.'

'Turning a blind eye to murder is tantamount to inviting the culprit to strike again,' argued Geoffrey. 'Or, if the culprit is a villager, telling him it is acceptable to kill his overlords.'

'I was tempted to kill Henry myself on occasion,' snapped Joan. 'And there is not one of our servants, villagers or neighbours who did not feel the same way. Unless someone confesses, we will never know.'

Geoffrey regarded her steadily. 'Then are you happy with this state of affairs?'

She met his eyes. 'Yes. Most people were relieved when he died, including me. It is easier to manage the estate without him. And, of course, you benefited, too.'

'There was a rumour that *you* killed him, because he stood between you and Goodrich,' supplied Olivier.

Geoffrey had known it was only a matter of time before fingers pointed at him as the man who had gained most from Henry's death. 'I have dozens of witnesses who will testify that I did not slip off for a few days to murder my brother. Besides, I never wanted to inherit Goodrich.'

'We know,' said Joan gently. 'And we have done our best to quell the rumours.'

'Jervil did not mean any harm by his comments,' said Olivier. He slapped his hands over his mouth in alarm. 'Damn!'

'Who is Jervil?' asked Geoffrey.

'Our groom,' replied Joan, glaring at her husband. 'The accusation that you killed Henry originated with him, because he thought no one else would have the courage. He meant it as a compliment.'

'Some compliment,' muttered Geoffrey. 'No wonder people run when they see me coming!'

'That is nothing to do with Jervil,' said Joan. 'That is because Father Adrian has been telling them about the Fall of Jerusalem and the slaughter that followed. He says only the most vicious, hardened and ruthless soldiers survived – and Helbye says nothing to contradict him.'

'Helbye tells people what they want to hear,' ventured Olivier. 'They are more interested in tales of terror and death than in stories of mercy and forbearance.'

'I will speak to him,' said Geoffrey, reaching for his sword and buckling it around his waist. It was an instinctive action, and he barely realized he was doing it.

Joan eyed it disapprovingly. 'You will not improve your reputation if you walk around armed like a Saracen. You do not need a sword to speak to your friends, surely?'

Given what had happened to Henry, Geoffrey was not so sure.

'You must marry soon,' said Joan, as they sat in the solar the next evening. Geoffrey had spoken to Helbye that morning, but had been unable to persuade the old warrior not to portray him as a bloodthirsty brute. Then Helbye's wife had given them a large jug of her strong ale, and sensible conversation went out the window. Geoffrey still felt dizzy, even after sleeping most of the afternoon, and he was barely listening. He nodded absently at what he thought had been a question.

'That was easy,' said Olivier. 'I thought he would object.'

'He just agreed,' said Joan, pleased. 'You saw him nod.'

Geoffrey glanced up and wondered what he had done. 'Marry?' he asked, forcing his muddled wits to concentrate before he found himself in deep water.

'Goodrich needs an heir,' said Joan, making it sound like it was his fault it did not have one. 'And the sooner you make a start, the better. If you die without one, the estate will pass to Baderon, our overlord. But fitzNorman will counterclaim, because part of Goodrich lies in the forest.'

'And Wulfric de Bicanofre will become involved, too,' added Olivier. 'Some of the manors we own were once under his lordship – before the Conqueror divided them up.'

'The only way to prevent a dispute is to provide heirs,' said Joan. 'At the moment you are the only thing standing between our neighbours and extra land. You should marry – to protect yourself, if for no other reason.'

'Later,' replied Geoffrey tiredly.

Joan scowled. 'No, soon. Within a month.'

Geoffrey gaped at her. *'A month?'*

'It is the price you pay when you inherit an estate that is strategically important and wealthy. There are several candidates to choose from.'

'Henry did not marry within a month of inheriting Goodrich,' Geoffrey pointed out resentfully.

'He started thinking about it, though. As we said, he set his heart on Isabel fitzNorman – much good it did him.' Joan's eyes lit up. 'Are you interested in her? She would certainly be the best, and an alliance with fitzNorman would solve numerous problems.'

'After what Henry did to her?' asked Geoffrey uneasily. 'I doubt she will be very keen.'

'She did dislike Henry,' agreed Olivier. 'But her father is a practical man who knows good value when he sees it.'

'Speaking of which, did you speak to Helbye about stopping his tales of slaughter?' asked Joan. 'You will have greater value, and will be easier to sell, if people think you are polite and gentle.'

'*Sell*?' echoed Geoffrey, horrified. 'I am not an animal.'

'You are a commodity,' countered Olivier. 'Much like Baderon's prize ram, which is the envy of the region. Both represent a way to greater wealth.'

'Lord!' breathed Geoffrey, shocked.

'You said you wanted to be appraised of all the details surrounding Henry's death,' said Joan tartly. 'And his wedding plans were certainly a factor: it is possible he was killed because some-one thought he was looking in the wrong direction. Like you, he had six heiresses to choose from. FitzNorman was furious at what happened to his daughter, but, even so, Isabel would be my first choice. He is Constable of the Forest, and a favourite of the King.'

'Then Isabel is out,' said Geoffrey firmly. 'I do not want to attract the King's attention. Besides, if fitzNorman did kill Henry, he may believe that what worked for one brother will work for another. I do not want to be stabbed when he decides I am not appropriate for his daughter.'

'He has a sister,' said Joan tentatively. 'Margaret – a gentle woman with a sizeable dowry...'

'How old a sister?' asked Geoffrey suspiciously.

Joan was dismissive. 'That does not matter. Since she is a widow, she knows her duties and will require little training.'

'No,' said Geoffrey. 'For the same reasons as Isabel.'

Joan pursed her lips. 'Then there is Hilde, Baderon's daughter. He would not normally be interested in us, but he has been ordered to secure peace in the region, and combining his estates with ours would certainly keep fitz-Norman quiet.'

'He has already tied three of his daughters – and several of his knights – to useful alliances, and is looking for a match for his son Hugh, as well as Hilde,' added Olivier.

'I will not marry Hugh,' said Geoffrey flippantly.

Joan ignored him. 'Baderon offered Hilde to

us once. He may be prepared to do so again.'

'Why did Henry refuse her?' asked Geoffrey warily.

'He wanted someone pretty,' said Olivier bluntly. 'And someone ... well, someone who does not behave like a man. I can see his point: Hilde seems just as happy wielding a battleaxe as a needle.'

'There are rumours that she may be barren,' Joan continued. 'In which case, she will not suit our needs at all. But people have unkind tongues, and the rumour may have arisen because she is older than her sisters and not yet wed. I shall make enquiries.'

'Did Henry refuse Hilde *politely* when she was offered?' asked Geoffrey uncomfortably.

Joan looked furtive. 'Comments were made by both parties, which ended with her leaving in a rage. It was unfortunate, and I later berated him for not being more tactful.'

Geoffrey sighed. 'So Baderon – and Hilde – had a reason to kill Henry, too? Because he refused her in an unpleasant manner?'

'Possibly,' hedged Joan.

'Then I do not want her, either. I cannot marry a woman who may have murdered my brother. It would be rash, to say the least.'

Joan was becoming exasperated. 'Then what about Wulfric de Bicanofre's daughter – Douce?'

'Did Henry refuse her, too?'

'He pointed out that he could do better.'

'God's teeth!' muttered Geoffrey. 'Is there any woman whom Henry has not offended?'

'Well, there is Wulfric's older daughter,' said Joan. 'Eleanor. But you will not want her.'

'Why not?'

'Just trust me,' replied Joan. 'There is also Caerdig's daughter Corwenna, but an alliance with him would be of little benefit.'

Geoffrey was surprised. 'I thought good relations with the Welsh were important.'

'They are, but Caerdig is too poor to risk open warfare. He would be delighted were you to accept Corwenna, but you can do better. Besides, she has no love for our family.'

'Why?' asked Geoffrey.

'Because Henry killed her husband, Rhys,' said Olivier. 'Henry fired some cottages, and Rhys was trapped inside.'

'Christ's blood!' muttered Geoffrey.

'Caerdig knows grudges are detrimental to his people's welfare, but his daughter is young,' said Joan. 'You could be the most charming man in Christendom, and she would not have you.'

'So, she might have slipped a dagger into Henry, too?' asked Geoffrey.

Joan nodded. 'It would have been easy for her to enter our stables after dark.'

'I will make *you* my heir,' said Geoffrey, suddenly inspired. 'Special dispensation can be granted for women to inherit. I have read about such cases. Then I can remain single, and the problem of an heir will be yours.'

'Baderon would never permit it,' said Joan. 'You would need his permission, and he will not give it when he stands to lose. You have no choice: you must marry, and you must do it soon, so these issues can be resolved.'

'But I do not like the sound of any of these women,' protested Geoffrey. 'Perhaps Roger will know a suitable lady from Durham—'

'That will do no good,' said Joan firmly. 'You must choose someone from here. And you will not be safe until you do.'

Two

When Joan and Olivier retired to their chamber, Geoffrey was not tired. He supposed it was not surprising, given that he had slept late that morning and then lain in a drunken slumber for most of the afternoon. He went to his room, but he could not settle. If there had been a tavern nearby, he would have gone, but the nearest was across the river.

He sat at the table, struggling to read a scroll he had brought from the Holy Land. But he was not in the mood for philosophy, and his mind kept returning to Henry's murder. Perhaps Joan was right: he would never discover the killer's identity. But he knew that he would remain uneasy if he didn't at least try, and he resolved to press on as diplomatically as he could. He was about to make a list of suspects – which included all six suitors and their fathers – when a scratching sound caused him to jump up and draw his dagger. He moved quickly to the door and ripped

38

it open, causing the man outside almost to tumble in. The fellow recovered himself quickly, and his face went from alarm to an impassive mask.

'Torva,' said Geoffrey, recognizing Goodrich's steward. Torva was thin-lipped, with greasy hair that parted in the middle and dangled limply around his shoulders. Joan swore that he was honest, but Geoffrey did not like the way the man looked at him.

'Sir Geoffrey,' replied Torva flatly.

'Well?' asked Geoffrey, when Torva said no more. 'What do you want?'

'I saw a light under your door,' said Torva expressionlessly. 'We are always worried about fires, so I came to investigate.'

'I was reading,' explained Geoffrey, indicating the scroll on the table.

'I see,' said Torva, in a voice he might have used had Geoffrey confessed to chanting spells to summon the Devil. 'Remember to blow out the candle before you sleep.'

'Of course I will remember,' said Geoffrey, wondering if the man thought him an idiot. He glanced down and saw that Torva carried a hefty dagger. Was it something he always wore, or just when he slunk around at night? Geoffrey could not recall seeing it before, but had not paid close attention. Then it occurred to him that Henry had bullied Torva, and the steward was yet another murder suspect. 'What happened the night Henry died?'

'I did not kill him,' Torva said in alarm. He turned to leave, but Geoffrey caught his arm.

'I did not say you had, but I would like an answer to my question.'

'You already know what happened.' Torva tried to free himself, but Geoffrey was strong and he soon abandoned the attempt. 'Henry started to drink. He kicked Peter and Jervil, and he punched me.' He pointed to the side of his jaw, and Geoffrey saw a small scar where Henry's ring had cut it.

'I am sorry,' he said, releasing Torva when he realized that he was bullying the man, too. 'My brother was too ready with his fists.'

'Like you, he did not like being in the hall with us servants, so he went to the stables. Sir Olivier found him dead the next morning.'

'Do you know who killed him?' asked Geoffrey. He had actually left the hall for the servants' benefit – so they could sleep without being disturbed – but doubted Torva would believe him.

'I have a number of suspects,' replied Torva. 'FitzNorman, Isabel and Margaret; Baderon and Hilde; Wulfric and his children Ralph, Eleanor and Douce; and Corwenna and half of Wales. Henry was unkind to every servant, poor villein and free man from here to Monmouth; he maltreated peddlers; and he hanged three "poachers" he caught in our woods. Then there are Baderon's knights – Seguin and Lambert. Would you like me to continue? It might be easier to list those who did *not* want to kill your brother.'

'Then do so,' said Geoffrey mildly, refusing to be drawn by the man's hostility.

Torva thought for a long time. 'Father Adrian,'

he said eventually. 'Because he does not own a dagger with a double-edged blade.'

'What happened to the weapon?' asked Geoffrey. 'I know the killer left it in Henry.'

'Well, he would. You do not keep a Black Knife after it has done its work, do you?'

'A *black knife*?' asked Geoffrey, confused.

'A Black Knife is a weapon strengthened with curses by a witch,' said Torva, adding as if it were obvious: 'You do not keep one after it has killed. It is too dangerous.'

'And whose dagger underwent this particular transformation?' asked Geoffrey, thinking it nonsense.

'No one knows. But it may strike another Mappestone, if it chooses.'

'Are you threatening me?' asked Geoffrey coolly. 'Or Joan?'

'No, sir,' said Torva with a false smile. 'Not Joan.' And then he was gone.

The next day was wet and cold, but warhorses needed to be exercised daily, so Geoffrey rode towards the hills that overlooked the river, taking the opportunity to familiarize himself with territory that he might have to defend one day. He hoped relations with Goodrich's neighbours would not degenerate to the point where he might have to put his local knowledge to the test, but there was no harm in being cautious.

The land was an odd combination of familiar and alien after his long absence. Trees had grown or been cut down, and there were more settlements and houses, from which people emerged to watch him ride past. Few spoke to him, and none smiled.

In the middle of a wood, not far from the path, he heard a sharp rustle. His hand went to the hilt of his sword. Then he saw a deer staggering among the dead leaves that comprised the forest floor. He dismounted and approached slowly, angry to see its hind leg caught in a trap. It was too badly injured to set free, so reluctantly – he disliked killing anything not in a position to defend itself – he drew his sword. The deer gazed at him in mute terror and tried to squirm away. Knowing he would only prolong its misery by hesitating, he chopped at its skull, forcing himself not to close his eyes in his distaste for the task, lest he missed and hurt it further.

It died instantly. He wiped his weapon in the grass, then smashed the trap to ensure it would never be used again. Determined that whoever had set it would not enjoy venison for dinner, and since the animal had died on his land, he slung the corpse behind his saddle. Blood dripped down his horse's flanks, and belatedly he wondered what people would make of him returning besmeared with gore.

In the afternoon he turned towards the castle. The sun was behind him, which meant he was near the Welsh border, and he hoped that he had not inadvertently strayed into hostile territory. The thought had no sooner crossed his mind than there was a snap behind him, as someone trod on a stick. His dog started to bark, and he spun around, hoisting his shield with one hand and drawing his sword with the other.

'There is no need for that,' came a man's voice, although Geoffrey could see no one. 'I once said there would always be a place for you at my hearth, but although you have been home for almost two weeks now, you have not deigned to visit.'

'Caerdig?' asked Geoffrey, smiling as the Welshman stepped from the undergrowth. 'I was not sure I would still be welcome, given what I have heard about Henry.'

'Speak Welsh,' ordered Caerdig. 'Or have you forgotten how?'

Geoffrey answered in the same tongue, ashamed that his grasp of it was not what it had been; although talented with languages, he struggled if he did not practise. 'I trust you are well?'

'Well enough, now Henry is dead,' replied Caerdig bluntly. 'He killed my son-in-law, you know.'

'Joan told me,' replied Geoffrey. 'I am sorry.'

'You are not your brother,' replied the Welshman with a shrug. 'My daughter may not agree, though, so do not be surprised if she is hostile when you see her. She still mourns Rhys.' Caerdig's attention quickly turned elsewhere. 'I see you still have that fine dog. Will you sell him to me? I could do with a pack of savage beasts like him.'

'You will have some anyway, if you leave your bitches unattended,' laughed Geoffrey.

Caerdig laughed in turn. 'We are not far from

Llan Martin. Come and warm yourself at my fire.'

Geoffrey did not want to oblige, especially after hearing that the man's daughter harboured ill feelings, but could think of no way to decline without causing offence. So he dismounted and fell in next to the Welshman.

'Have you prospered?' he asked conversationally.

Caerdig sighed. 'No. We are all poorer than the meanest of your peasants. Joan sent us grain *again* last year – we would have starved without it. We repaid her, of course, with extra to express our gratitude.' His expression was grim. 'But we should not have put pride before practical considerations, because now we are short again.'

'We can provide more,' said Geoffrey, looking around as they entered Llan Martin. The houses looked as though they had barely survived the winter, and the faces of the people who came out to greet them were pinched and cold, although the welcome they gave was warm enough.

'We might have to accept,' said Caerdig resentfully. 'Although it is not wise to rely on a neighbour's charity every year. I suppose Joan has been after you to marry?'

Surprised, Geoffrey nodded.

'You should listen to her. Goodrich is vulnerable when only you stand between it and the wolves that surround it. They may decide another murder is the best course of action.'

'You think so?' asked Geoffrey uneasily.

'Listen to the advice of a man who means you well,' said Caerdig. 'Marry quickly – any heiress will do, because they are all of a muchness – make her with child and return to Jerusalem with all haste. Then come back at appropriate intervals to repeat the process. Only when you have at least three strong sons should you entertain living here.'

Geoffrey was amused at the notion of skulking in exile, returning only for lightning strikes on his hapless wife. 'You think Goodrich is that dangerous?'

Caerdig did not smile back. 'For you, yes.'

The Welshman pushed open the door to his home. It was dark inside and, even though the afternoon was cool and promised a frigid night, no fires were lit. The floor was of beaten earth, but scrupulously clean, and the few benches and stools were old and lovingly polished. There were bowls of spring flowers on the window-sills, adding touches of colour and a pleasant scent.

The room was large and surprisingly full. Geoffrey recognized Caerdig's wife, and bowed to her. She inclined her head in return, and then asked how Goodrich's grain stores were holding out. She seemed very interested in his answers, as did a number of folk who came to listen. There was an atmosphere of unease, and Geoffrey did not feel safe, although he resisted the urge to stand with his back to the wall, suspecting Caerdig would know what he was doing and be offended. He wished he had not dispensed with his armour.

'Bring logs and tinder,' ordered Caerdig, rubbing his hands as he strode towards the hearth. 'No guest of Llan Martin sits before an empty fireplace.'

'Then what are we?' asked a man in Norman-French as Caerdig approached. He had been listening to a red-haired woman who muttered at his side, evidently translating what the others were saying. 'I am a guest, but you did not order the fire lit for me.'

Geoffrey studied the man with interest. He had a dark complexion, and stood at least a head above the villagers. The cloak thrown carelessly across his shoulders was lined with fur, and his boots were of excellent quality. His bearing indicated that he was a man of some standing, used to having his orders obeyed. He had two companions, who also stood as Caerdig escorted Geoffrey to the hearth; both wore swords in their belts and mail tunics.

The man to the left was shorter, with long, wispy yellow hair and a sardonic smile. Geoffrey immediately saw they were kin. The man to the right was older. He had a thick, grey mane and a white beard that was carefully curled. His clothes were well cut, and his sword was a good one, with a sharp blade and a functional hilt. None were the kind of men Geoffrey would have expected to see in the home of poor Welshmen.

Caerdig forced a smile. 'This is Sir Seguin de Rheims,' he said to Geoffrey, speaking Norman-French with an accent that was almost impossible to decipher. Seguin apparently knew no Welsh.

'I am his brother, Lambert,' said the fair-

46

headed knight. He indicated the older man. 'And this is our friend.'

Geoffrey knew he was being misled: the last man was obviously the most important. He recalled Torva saying that two knights in Baderon's service were called Seguin and Lambert. Unless Geoffrey was mistaken, the older man was a good deal more than their friend.

'Lord Baderon,' he said with a bow.

'*Baderon*?' asked Caerdig in alarm. He reverted to Welsh as he addressed Geoffrey. 'Are you sure? The man himself has come to visit me?'

Baderon seemed amused that his ruse had been exposed. He smiled at Geoffrey. 'How did you guess? We have not met before, because I would have remembered.'

'Who are you?' demanded Seguin.

'He is Geoffrey Mappestone,' supplied the red-haired woman, coming to inspect Geoffrey. 'We played together as children, although he has grown since then. Do you remember me?'

Geoffrey was immediately on his guard, as he could see there was a good deal of animosity bubbling in Caerdig's only daughter. The gangly child had grown into a beauty, with smooth skin and a poised elegance. However, what he remembered about playing with Corwenna was not what she had looked like, but the fact that she had devoted considerable effort in finding ways to ambush him in order to pull his hair.

'I remember,' he replied pleasantly. 'You have grown, too.'

'Are you calling me fat?' she demanded, and he saw that he would have to be more careful with his words if he did not want an argument.

'You are no longer a child,' he replied gently. 'That is all I meant.'

Before she could say anything else, Seguin stepped forward. '*I* am here to pay court to her,' he declared. 'So if you hope to secure her for Goodrich, you are wasting your time. She is promised to *me*.'

Geoffrey felt an instinctive dislike for the man. He saw Baderon wince at Seguin's lack of manners, while Lambert stepped closer to his brother, as if expressing solidarity.

'My marriage to Sir Seguin will improve Llan Martin's fortunes – but, more importantly, it will weaken Goodrich,' Corwenna explained nastily.

Geoffrey doubted it. Llan Martin was too poor to be a serious threat, although Caerdig's word carried weight among other Welsh leaders. The previous night, Joan had mentioned Baderon's penchant for marrying his knights to Welsh ladies, and he supposed that he was witnessing such a match.

'Corwenna cannot remain a widow forever, so it is time we found her a profitable marriage,' said Caerdig to Geoffrey, reverting to Welsh. 'Sir Seguin is wealthy and, although not a Welshman, we are not in a position to be fussy.'

'He is acceptable,' said Corwenna in Norman-French, confident in the knowledge that Seguin would not know what she was talking about. She glowered at Geoffrey. 'Of course, I would not be in this position, were it not for you.'

'Me?' asked Geoffrey, startled.

'Take no notice,' said Caerdig quickly. 'She

means no harm.'

'Do I not?' snarled Corwenna, turning on Geoffrey with such vehemence that he took an involuntary step back. He trod on his dog, which yelped and bit Lambert. Pandemonium erupted, although Corwenna seemed oblivious to the yells that ensued as Lambert tried to stab the dog and Caerdig tried to stop him. 'You killed my Rhys.'

'I did not,' replied Geoffrey. 'I never met him.'

'Henry was your brother,' she hissed. 'Our customs say the blame is now yours to bear.'

'Well, the King's law does not,' replied Geoffrey tartly. 'How could I control what Henry did when I was not here? Besides, he is dead.'

She glared at him, but he saw out of the corner of his eye that Lambert had the dog cornered and was raising his sword to strike. He turned and tore the weapon from the man's hands. Lambert regarded him in astonishment.

'That brute bit me with no provocation.'

'I apologize,' said Geoffrey, handing the sword back. 'He dislikes strangers.'

Lambert fingered the weapon in a way that indicated he was ready to use it. 'What will you do to compensate me? Silver? Or a sister to entertain me for a night when I happen to be passing?'

'I doubt you will want to be entertained by Joan,' said Seguin. 'She is the dragon who keeps Goodrich from hostile invasions. If you interfere with her, it will be the last thing you will do!'

Geoffrey was not prepared to stand by and hear Joan abused by the likes of Seguin. 'Do *you*

49

want to fight me?' he asked coldly. 'Is that why you insult my sister?'

Lambert stood at Seguin's side; weapon ready to join him in any skirmish. Geoffrey regarded them with disdain, thinking the brothers had little honour if they were prepared to pitch two men against one in a private quarrel. He drew his own sword and waited to see who would attack first.

'Put up your weapons!' ordered Caerdig, stepping between them. 'There will be no fighting in my house.'

'What did you expect, father?' demanded Corwenna acidly. 'You invited a Mappestone into our home, which meant it was only a matter of time before someone died.'

Baderon raised his hands to appeal for calm. 'Seguin should not have insulted Joan, but Sir Geoffrey's dog should not have bitten Lambert. So we are even. Let us put an end to this nonsense.'

Lambert complied willingly enough, but Seguin only sheathed his weapon when Lambert muttered something in his ear. Satisfied, Baderon went to the hearth. The feeble blaze did little to warm the house, however, nor did it do much for the atmosphere of frigid resentment that hung over Caerdig's guests. Geoffrey saw that he was a fool to create enemies of Baderon's knights, and knew he should make amends. He sat where Baderon indicated, and tried to be polite.

'Lord Baderon wants to form alliances with

his Welsh neighbours,' said Lambert, addressing Geoffrey with equally forced amiability. 'He has offered my brother a manor if he takes a Celtic bride. We both have lands in Normandy, but they are in an area ruled by Bellême, and he keeps attacking them. It is safer for us to be here.'

'You leave your people to fend off Bellême alone?' asked Geoffrey, startled. Bellême was a cruel and vicious tyrant, and the knights' place should have been with their villagers.

Seguin bristled, but Lambert did not take offence. 'He is less likely to raid if we are away – there is no one to seize and hold to ransom, you see.'

'A marriage here will suit *me* nicely,' said Seguin. 'And Lord Baderon is prepared to be very generous if I take Corwenna.'

'I am,' agreed Baderon. 'The King ordered me to pacify this region, and marriage between my knights and our Welsh neighbours is an excellent way to achieve a lasting truce.'

Geoffrey nodded, although it occurred to him that such marriages might unite the Welsh *against* the English. He wondered how quickly he could leave without offending anyone – he did not want to be near Baderon's fiery knights, or Corwenna.

Caerdig beamed at his guests, relieved that they appeared to have put the spat behind them. 'We must celebrate the upcoming match between Corwenna and Sir Seguin.'

A man afflicted by a serious squint approached Caerdig and whispered in his ear. Geoffrey recalled his name was Hywel, and that he was

51

Caerdig's steward. 'Celebrate with what? We have no ale, and we can hardly offer them water.'

'I have some French claret in my saddlebag,' said Geoffrey to Baderon, hoping the man was not a good judge of such things – it was a miserable brew from the south of England that he kept for medicinal purposes. 'Shall we share a cup?'

Hywel went to look for it, while Seguin talked about how the marriage would benefit him, although Geoffrey could not see what Caerdig would get out of the arrangement.

'Seguin comes with a small herd of cows,' replied Caerdig when Geoffrey asked him. He reverted automatically to Welsh. 'Personally, I wanted a Mappestone to take her, but you are the only one left, and I suspect Joan has her eyes set on a bigger prize than Llan Martin.'

'I would not wed *him* anyway,' said Corwenna icily, also speaking Welsh. 'I will not share my bed with a man who slaughtered his way to the Holy Land. I heard what those Crusaders did on their way to "liberate" Jerusalem.'

'You played together as children,' said Caerdig, trying to silence his daughter by gripping her knee in a painful pinch.

'Stop babbling in that infernal tongue,' ordered Seguin testily. 'I will have no Welsh spoken in *my* home once we are married.'

'Geoffrey speaks it badly anyway,' said Corwenna venomously. 'It hurts the ears when it comes from the mouth of a Norman. There should be a law against it.'

'Corwenna!' exclaimed Caerdig, aghast. 'That is no way to speak to an honoured guest!'

'He is *not* an honoured guest,' retorted Corwenna hotly. 'He is Henry's brother – the man who slaughtered our cattle, burnt our granaries and murdered Rhys.'

Seguin roared with laughter, while his brother grinned. Both evidently considered Corwenna's bold temper a fine thing. Geoffrey wondered how amusing Seguin would find Corwenna's sour moods when they were directed against him, and suspected it would only be a matter of time before they fell out.

The tension eased when Hywel returned with the wine, and measured it into wooden cups. Maliciously, Geoffrey hoped it was acidic enough to make the Normans and Corwenna sick, although he bore Caerdig no ill will. When everyone held a goblet, Caerdig spoke.

'To future liaisons,' he said ambiguously, and everyone other than Geoffrey upended their cups, only to spit the contents out again.

'God in Heaven!' exclaimed Baderon, gagging. 'Is this what you drink in the Holy Land?'

'No,' replied Geoffrey. 'That is saddle oil. Hywel used the wrong flask.'

Corwenna rubbed her lips with a cloth. 'Why did you wait until we had swallowed it? Are you trying to poison us?'

'It was a mistake,' said Caerdig, although he had noticed that Geoffrey had not touched his own cup.

Seguin spat into the fire and then stood. 'It is time to go home. It will be dark soon, and not even knights are immune from outlaws in Wales.'

Caerdig followed his guests outside. 'It will not be pleasant having such a man in the family,' he whispered to Geoffrey, 'but Corwenna likes him, and the cattle he brings will be useful.'

'He is a bag of air,' declared Geoffrey, also in Welsh. He refrained from adding that Seguin and Corwenna deserved each other.

'He is, but everyone seems happy about the union. It is only I who has reservations. I wish she was marrying you instead.'

Geoffrey did not, much as he liked Caerdig. He did not care whether marriage brought him riches, and did not even mind if his wife was plain – he would settle for one capable of intelligent conversation. However, he certainly did not want one who hated him.

'God's blood!' exclaimed Seguin, stalking towards Geoffrey's horse. 'That is a deer! And you killed it with a sword.'

'It was caught in a trap,' explained Geoffrey.

'Where?' demanded Baderon, suddenly angry. 'Where *precisely*?'

'In a clearing about three miles from here,' said Geoffrey, wondering what was upsetting them. 'It was on my land.'

'How do you *know*?' demanded Baderon hotly. 'You have been away for two decades. How can you know your boundaries when they twist and turn so tortuously?'

Seguin took a step towards Geoffrey. 'Fitz-Norman enforces forest law vigorously on the lands under his control, and we do the same for

Lord Baderon. No one kills *his* venison. It is a hanging offence.'

'It is as well the venison is mine, then,' said Geoffrey mildly. 'I found the trap on a hill just south of the river, and even someone who has been away for twenty years cannot be mistaken about which side of the river he is on. It was Goodrich land.'

'Then I shall believe you,' said Baderon. 'But I will not suffer thieves on my land, no matter who they are.'

Geoffrey would have preferred to travel alone, but Baderon offered to accompany him part way, and he did not want to appear churlish by declining.

'What do you think?" asked Caerdig in a whisper, holding the reins of Geoffrey's horse while he mounted. 'Will Baderon be a trustworthy ally?'

'God knows,' replied Geoffrey. 'He is certainly determined to have you on his side, since he is prepared to give away a manor and cattle to make sure Seguin marries Corwenna.'

Caerdig was thoughtful. 'I sense he is a better man than his two knights.'

'He barely controls them – they act more as equals than vassals. Do you want this deer? It will compensate you for the embarrassment of having served saddle oil to your guests.'

Caerdig chuckled as he tugged the corpse from Geoffrey's horse. 'You can embarrass me any time, if you bribe me so handsomely. Stay here tonight and share it with us.'

'Corwenna would have a knife in me,' said Geoffrey. 'The others are waiting, so I should go.'

He followed Baderon, Lambert and Seguin, knowing they would take the same road for about half a mile before their paths diverged. Daylight was fading, and his horse skittered as old leaves blew in the wind. At first, Seguin and Baderon talked about poachers, while Lambert told Geoffrey about his own marriage prospects, naming women from three villages Geoffrey had never heard of. Then the path narrowed, so they were obliged to ride in single file. Conversation waned.

Geoffrey allowed his mind to wander, wondering whether Corwenna had killed Henry. It took little strength to push a blade into a drunken man. His thoughts were interrupted when Baderon spoke.

'Seguin's union with Corwenna is an integral part of my plans for peace – to enhance the stability of the region,' he said. 'Caerdig is poor but respected, and the Welsh lords listen to him. Obviously, you appreciate that a good marriage is vital for good relations, because you are looking for a wife yourself. My daughter Hilde is—'

'I do not want to marry,' replied Geoffrey, with more heat than intended.

'Marriage is a good thing: it saves you having to look for a whore,' declared Seguin. 'I am looking forward to having a ready wench in my bedchamber whenever I feel like her.'

Geoffrey thought Seguin was deluded if he imagined Corwenna would be there whenever he 'felt like her'.

'I offered Hilde to your brother,' Baderon went on. 'He refused her rather cruelly. Still, it did not matter, because Hilde said she would not have Henry if he was the last man on Earth, and I could never force her to do what she does not want. No man could.'

'I see,' said Geoffrey, filing the information away: Hilde was fierce and ungovernable, which would not make for a peaceful domestic environment.

'There are other ways, though,' said Baderon enigmatically. Geoffrey had no idea what he meant. 'But this is where our pathways part. Goodnight, Sir Geoffrey. Beware of outlaws.'

Geoffrey nodded, then touched his heels to his horse's flanks and rode away. He had not gone far before he spotted someone else. When the man saw him, he gave a yelp and turned to flee. It was Goodrich land, and the grim fate of the deer was still fresh in Geoffrey's mind. With his dog barking furiously, he galloped after the shadow and quickly had the fellow by the scruff of the neck.

'What do you want?' the felon cried with rather more indignation than was warranted. 'I have no money to give you.'

The voice was instantly familiar – high and irritable. It sounded exactly like his old squire, Durand, although Geoffrey did not see how that was possible: Durand was currently enjoying a successful career as a royal clerk, revelling in the luxuries of courtly life. Geoffrey peered down at him, and was astonished to see flowing golden locks. There was only one person he knew who sported such glorious tresses.

'Durand?' he asked in disbelief. 'It *is* you!'

Relief broke over Durand's face. 'Sir Geoffrey? Thank God! I thought you were an outlaw!'

'This is a Godforsaken part of the country,' said Durand, while Geoffrey dismounted. His old squire had changed little, and was still small and slender, although regal dining had added a layer of lard around his middle. The beautiful yellow curls tumbled around his shoulders, and his clothes were exquisite, as befitted a man from the King's court. They were grubby, however, and there were leaves in his hair.

'It is my land,' said Geoffrey, rather coolly. 'What are you doing here?'

Durand did not care that he might have offended; he never had. He grinned. 'I heard you lived near here, and intended to pay you a visit. However, I did not anticipate enjoying our reunion in the depths of a wilderness at dusk.'

Geoffrey was surprised that Durand should think to favour him with a visit. They had seldom seen eye to eye in the past: Durand had deplored Geoffrey's military lifestyle and Geoffrey had despised Durand's cowardice and brazen self-interest. But, for all their differences, Durand had a keen mind that Geoffrey missed, and he smiled at seeing the man again.

'You have not answered my question. Why are you *here* – it is unlike you to be alone in a place that might be dangerous.'

'*Dangerous*?' squeaked Durand in alarm. 'Abbot Serlo said all the outlaws around here had been driven off, and that it is safe. I would not have accompanied him otherwise.'

'There are wild animals,' said Geoffrey wickedly. 'And this part of the woods is haunted.'

'Then what are *you* doing here? No, do not tell me. It will be something to do with whores and strong drink. I remember what it was like to be in your service.'

It was an unfair accusation, given that Geoffrey was generally well behaved for a knight. He felt his pleasure at meeting an old acquaintance diminish somewhat. Durand had once wanted a career in the Church, and his monkish ways had remained with him long after his expulsion from a monastery for dallying with a butcher's son.

'My predicament is Abbot Serlo's fault,' Durand went on when Geoffrey did not reply. 'I told him it was impossible to ride from Gloucester to Dene in one day, but he insisted it could be done. Then a horse went lame, we were delayed, and now here we are, lost in a dangerous forest with brutal Crusader knights riding us down from dark places.'

'Abbot Serlo?'

'The principal of the abbey at Gloucester,' replied Durand impatiently. 'I thought you would know that: you told me you were a novice there for six months.'

Geoffrey had forgotten the name of the man who had ruled Gloucester Abbey for the past thirty years, because his mercifully brief noviciate had been a long time before. 'But why are

59

you with him? Have you annoyed the King?'

'That is an unpleasant thing to say,' said Durand. 'And if you had bothered to read my letters, you would know that I have become indispensable.'

'I did read your letters, but...' Geoffrey was about to say that Durand was not always honest, but did not want to offend him further '...but nothing you wrote led me to expect to see you here.'

'The King left me with Serlo for a while, since he is in the area, and—'

'The King is nearby?' interrupted Geoffrey uneasily. Geoffrey held His Majesty partly responsible for his dismissal by Tancred, and did not want to meet him, lest he was unable to stop himself from saying so.

'He has business at Hereford – to do with consecrating its bishop. He brought me with him to investigate various taxation issues. Serlo offered to accompany me to Dene, but I would have been better off hiring soldiers. He insists on travelling like a peasant – on mules and with no guards.'

'Where is he?' asked Geoffrey. He knew Serlo was not in the woods, because his dog would have barked or growled. An uneasy thought occurred to him. 'You have not strangled him, have you, like you did that monk near Westminster last year?'

Durand glared. 'I did that to save our lives – yours as well as mine – as you know perfectly well. I am not in the habit of killing people. I leave that to the likes of you.' He stared at the small arsenal Geoffrey carried, even in civilian clothes.

'Serlo?' prompted Geoffrey.

Durand waved a hand behind him, and Geoffrey saw the outline of a shepherd's shelter. It was poor and dirty, but Geoffrey recalled that its roof was sound, its walls strong, and it had straw pallets to sleep on. It was not the most comfortable accommodation, but he had used far worse.

'He is already asleep,' said Durand resentfully. 'He declared we would be safe, then lay down and started snoring as though he had not a care in the world. He did not even wait until I had finished my supper, and then I had to ... you know.'

Geoffrey did not. 'What?'

'Slip outside to water the trees,' whispered Durand primly, although there was no one to overhear. 'He might have stayed awake to ensure I got back in once piece.'

Geoffrey shrugged. 'Serlo has nothing to fear in these woods.'

'It is not Serlo I am worried about,' said Durand fervently. '*He* wears a Benedictine habit. *I* am the one who will be slaughtered if we meet robbers.'

Geoffrey took pity on him. 'Do you want to come to Goodrich tonight?'

'There is nothing I would like more, but Serlo does not like being woken once he is sleeping. I would rather let the old bear rest than have him grumbling.'

'Then visit me tomorrow,' suggested Geoffrey.

'But how did you escape the charge of theft levelled against you in Winchester? Your letters outlined your rise in fortunes, but they did not mention that.'

Durand gave one of his superior smiles. 'I was accused of stealing equipment from a mint and trying to sell it. However, I proved myself innocent. The man who reported me identified me by my hair. So, I bundled it inside a cap and challenged him to pick me out of a crowd. He could not, and I was exonerated. Then I heard about a series of thefts from the royal kitchens, so I decided to look into them. I watched you enough to know how to go about it, and had the riddle solved in a week.'

'I have never investigated thefts.'

'You have looked into murders, and one crime is much like another. The King was delighted when I presented him with the culprits. He was so pleased that he agreed to employ me as an agent. He is trusting me with more and more important matters.'

'Do you like the work?'

Durand grimaced. 'It is good to own the favour of the King, but I am obliged to deal with some very unsavoury characters – mainly powerful nobles who try to cheat him. I am often in danger. At least when I was with you, I knew you would protect me. These days I have no one.'

'You can always hire guards.'

Durand raised his eyebrows hopefully. 'Will you oblige? I do not want *any* unmannerly lout at my heels when I interview these barons – I would sooner have one I know.'

Geoffrey laughed at the man's audacity. 'You expect *me* to work for *you*?'

Durand's face was earnest. 'I was thinking more of a partnership – I would do the thinking, while you manage the dangerous parts. Between us, we would be a formidable team.'

'It is a tempting offer,' said Geoffrey, still laughing. 'But I must decline.'

'Why?' demanded Durand. 'Because you do not want to be in the King's service? You are deluding yourself if you think you will resist him forever. Tancred no longer wants you, and you will turn to King Henry sooner or later, simply out of desperation.'

Was that true? It was possible, given that Geoffrey was already restless. Like Durand, he had developed a talent for investigating crimes and, although the cases he explored had been perilous, there had been something exhilarating about them.

'Well?' demanded Durand. 'Come work with me. We will make a fortune.'

Geoffrey mounted his horse. Neither withering away at Goodrich nor working for the King held any appeal, but combining forces with the devious Durand was an appalling prospect, and not one he would consider in a hundred years. 'It is a generous offer, but I must refuse.'

'You are leaving?' asked Durand in horror.

'What do you expect me to do?' asked Geoffrey. 'Stand guard outside your hut while you sleep?'

'That is an excellent idea,' said Durand gratefully. 'No one will dare attack when there is a ruffian like you lurking outside.'

'Good night, Durand,' said Geoffrey, laughing.

'Please!' cried Durand, agitated. 'Will you abandon an old friend in the middle of a hostile forest? I am no longer a servant; I am an important man. I own several manors in Suffolk – the King gave them to me as a mark of his esteem.'

Geoffrey raised his eyebrows in surprise. 'The King gave you land?'

Durand nodded. 'My estates are almost as large as Goodrich. I am your equal now.'

Geoffrey was impressed that his old squire had made his fortune so quickly, and saw that he should not have been sceptical of Durand's letters. He had indeed risen rapidly, and, if he was trusted to explore issues pertaining to taxation, it meant the King liked him. It would not be long before Durand was a force to be reckoned with.

'Then I wish you well of it,' he said. 'But Serlo is right: there are no outlaws in this part of the forest. You are perfectly safe.'

Durand did not look convinced, but Geoffrey had no intention of spending the night away from the fire and warm bed at Goodrich. He raised his hand in salute and rode away. When he glanced behind him, he saw Durand standing alone and unhappy, and suspected he would sleep poorly. But Durand would survive. He always did.

Three

Geoffrey spent another restless day at Goodrich, as Olivier pored over accounts and Joan issued orders. He offered to help Olivier – he was good with figures – but his brother-in-law pointedly suggested that Geoffrey might like to exercise his horse. With nothing else to do, Geoffrey tried to gain information about Henry from the servants, but they were wary and uncommunicative, and his attempts failed miserably. He had been a popular leader in Tancred's service, and his amiable, easy temper meant people usually liked him. But at Goodrich, only Joan and Olivier seemed pleased he was there. He wondered why. Was it because the servants thought he might be like Henry? Or because they were afraid he might find his brother's killer among them?

In the afternoon he splashed across the Wye ford, his dog at his side, and rode through the woods until he saw Bicanofre in the distance. Its little church huddled into the hillside, and its motte and bailey dominated the cluster of houses around it. Two women whom Joan had identified as potential wives lived there – Eleanor and Douce – and since he did not want to seem to be paying them court, he turned back, following the way he had come.

When he reached the ford again, a man with long, curly hair and a thin face was swearing furiously at some men for miring his cart in the shallows. Geoffrey could see from their resentful eyes that his fury was not helping. He supposed the foul-mouthed fellow was one of his new neighbours.

'May I help?' he offered politely.

The cart's back wheels were fast in sticky mud, and the only way to extract them would involve some hard pushing. It would mean standing waist-deep in water, and Geoffrey was not enthusiastic about the idea, but in the interests of good relations...

'Mind your own business,' snapped the man.

Geoffrey touched his heels to his horse's sides and continued on. When he reached a bend in the path, he glanced back and saw them still struggling, the thin man lashing the nags with a stick. The fellow could have been of more use by helping his men push, and Geoffrey felt sorry for the bewildered horses. But it was not his place to interfere. He cantered back to Goodrich, stopping on the way to visit Helbye. He drank some ale – although he was careful not to over-indulge this time – and interrupted Helbye's eulogy about his prize sow to tell him about meeting Durand.

'So, Durand is reviewing taxes for the King,' mused Helbye. 'Well, he always was better at clerking than fighting.'

'He asked me to work with him, to undertake the dangerous parts of his investigations.'

66

Helbye grimaced. 'Doing the King's dirty work involves meeting some very evil men, and he is right to want someone trustworthy. But not you: you must stay here and provide us with an heir.'

'Just like your pig.'

Helbye nodded. 'You and Henrietta are in much the same position. She will go in the pot as soon as *she* fails to produce a litter, and you ... well...'

He left the rest of the sentence hanging. When Geoffrey arrived at the castle, Jervil – the most sullen of Goodrich's servants – took his horse.

'Have you worked here long?' Geoffrey asked, attempting to be friendly.

'Yes,' replied Jervil, turning his back so brusquely, it verged on insolent. He led the horse inside the stable, and began unbuckling the saddle.

'You have some fine horses in your care,' Geoffrey said, struggling to remain patient. 'Does Olivier inspect them every day?'

'He does not visit the stables. A man was murdered here, in case you did not know.'

Geoffrey decided he had had enough disrespect. He would never have permitted such an attitude from his soldiers, nor should he be expected to tolerate it from his retainers.

'Show me where Henry died,' he ordered curtly.

Jervil regarded him uneasily, but walked to a stall about halfway down the building. It was occupied by a fierce, grey-brown stallion. Before Geoffrey could ask anything else, he saw

67

stains that were instantly identifiable as blood. He glanced at Jervil and saw defiance combined with triumph, and supposed they had been kept as some kind of ghoulish trophy marking a victory over a hated man. He wondered why Joan had not ordered them scrubbed away.

He squeezed past the horse, and bent down to inspect them. In one place it appeared that blood had pooled on the ground, and there were several smears along the wall, giving the impression that Henry had lived for some time after he had been wounded, perhaps trying to climb to his feet. Geoffrey moved the straw and saw trails that looked like footprints: the killer had trodden in the gore. Or were they the prints of the people who had carried the body to the church?

Geoffrey was not superstitious, but the stables had an eerie feel, and he felt the hairs on the back of his neck begin to prickle. As he glanced up, he saw a number of dead birds hanging in the rafters – black ones with sharp black beaks and their eyes eaten away.

'God's teeth!' he exclaimed. Dead crows were peculiar things to keep in a stable – the horses might react to the smell of blood, or simply to the sight of such strange things perched above them.

Suddenly, the stallion began to buck. Geoffrey threw himself to one side and avoided the hoofs that would have split his skull had they hit it, but in doing so tumbled to the floor. Heavy feet flailed above him, then started to descend.

* * *

68

Geoffrey rolled to one side, and the stallion's hoofs thumped hard to the ground, again narrowly missing him. Then it began an awkward, prancing dance towards him, as though someone was encouraging it to move in a direction it did not want to take. He scrambled to his feet and shoved with both hands as its body crushed him against the wall. It was a heavy animal, and he was hard pressed to force it back. When it finally yielded, he squeezed out of the stall and glared at Jervil.

'Sorry,' said Jervil, sounding more disappointed than apologetic. 'He needs more exercise, so he is difficult to control.'

'Especially when you hold the bridle tight enough to draw blood,' snapped Geoffrey, snatching the strap and calming the agitated animal by rubbing its nose.

Its eyes rolled in pain, and it was some time before it settled.

'*You* should be doing this,' he said, trying to keep the anger from his voice, lest it disturbed the horse. 'And if he needs exercise, *you* should make sure he has it.'

When he received no response, Geoffrey fetched some oats and fed the animal, inspecting the cut on its lip as he did so. The injury had been caused by twisting the bridle to an agonizing tightness, and he was not surprised the beast had objected.

'Why did you do this?' he asked. 'If you do not like horses, Joan will find you another post.'

For the first time emotion sparked into Jervil's voice. 'I do like them! Dun was bucking, so I had to hold the bridle tight. He did not like you behind him.'

Was it possible the cut had been caused by Jervil trying to control the animal? Somehow, Geoffrey did not think so.

'Why did you not wash away Henry's blood?' he asked, changing the subject abruptly. 'And why are there dead birds in the rafters?' He glanced along the building; there were no decomposing crows above any other stalls.

'The crows keep evil spirits away. And the blood tells the Devil to keep his distance.'

'Does Joan know about this?' asked Geoffrey.

'She never comes here,' replied Jervil, evasively. 'Nor Sir Olivier.'

'What happened that night?' demanded Geoffrey. Jervil started to edge away, but Geoffrey grabbed him, finally exasperated into using force. 'Tell me or you *will* be removed from this post.'

Jervil was angry. 'There is nothing to say. It was harvest, and we were all tired after a hard day in the fields. I was woken the next morning by Sir Olivier shouting that Henry was dead.'

'You sleep here?'

'The horses rest easier when I am close,' said Jervil, pointing to where a ladder led to a loft. 'But we wondered how long it would be before you started getting rid of us and bringing in Normans.' He spat in rank distaste.

'Jervil!' came a sharp voice from the door. It was Torva. 'That is enough. Your insolence will see us all homeless.'

It was a hypocritical statement, when Torva

70

had been insolent himself. Geoffrey noted that the dagger had been replaced by a small knife. Had Torva intended him harm two nights before?

'There is no reason for anyone to lose his post – *yet*,' Geoffrey said. Torva and Jervil regarded him with unfriendly eyes, and he sensed that they wanted him gone from Goodrich. The knowledge made him determined to linger. 'Tell me what you saw and heard the night Henry was stabbed, Jervil. Do not say nothing, because it will be a lie. Henry did not die quickly, because the bloodstains suggest he tried to gain his feet. He probably called for help.'

'I did not hear anything,' Jervil said sullenly. 'Not until morning, when Olivier started to yell.'

'You heard Olivier, but not Henry? But Henry was drunk – there would have been a commotion.'

'Perhaps there was,' said Jervil. 'But I sleep heavily.'

Geoffrey studied the groom. Jervil was rude, untruthful and impertinent, and may well have harmed Henry. Or was it fear of someone else that kept him silent? Then Geoffrey looked at Torva, who also refused to meet his eyes. Geoffrey found him impossible to read, but was certain of one thing: Torva and Jervil definitely knew something about Henry's murder.

The following day was Sunday, and the members of Goodrich's household attended mass in the chapel of St Giles – a pretty place, with a thatched roof and walls of wattle and daub.

71

Standing in the nave and listening to Father Adrian's precise Latin, Geoffrey looked around him.

Joan and Olivier were at the front, wearing their best clothes, although Olivier was by far the more elegant. They were talking in low voices. Behind them was Torva, and next to him was the cook, Peter, fat and smiling. Geoffrey had tried several times to draw Peter into conversation, but had been treated to blank stares. Jervil was with them, biting his nails. Joan claimed they were hardworking, sober men, but Geoffrey was unconvinced. All three had already reacted oddly to Geoffrey's attempts to uncover the truth about Henry. Did their curious attitudes imply guilty consciences?

The mass ended, and Geoffrey walked outside, collecting his dagger as he went – Father Adrian had refused to let him inside until he had divested himself of weapons. Bale, his new squire, had offered to guard it, and during the interim had honed the blade to a vicious edge. It sliced through the sheath as Geoffrey slid it away.

'God's teeth!' he exclaimed. 'There is no need to make it quite so sharp, man.'

'You never know when you might need to slit a throat,' hissed Bale. 'And a sharp knife is better than a blunt one.'

'I do not envisage—' began Geoffrey uneasily.

'Slitting a throat is the best way to dispatch an enemy,' interrupted Bale in a confidential whisper. 'It is quiet and quick. I can show you.'

'No,' said Geoffrey, moving away in distaste.

Bale followed.

'A man can never have too many sharp knives,' he went on, a manic light gleaming in his brown eyes. 'I always carry at least three.'

Geoffrey regarded him warily, wondering whether he was entirely in control of his faculties. He was a massive man, standing half a head above Geoffrey, and his arms and shoulders were unusually powerful. His head was bald, kept free of hairs by constant shaving and application of some sort of shiny grease. He was too old to be a squire – at least five years Geoffrey's senior – but Olivier had insisted Geoffrey take him. Geoffrey had accepted, but was having serious misgivings. Bale was far too interested in slaughter.

'He is the epitome of violence,' said Father Adrian, as he stood with Geoffrey and watched Bale pulling the heads off spring flowers. 'It is only a matter of time before he commits other murders, and the sooner you take him away, the better.'

Geoffrey stared at the priest. *'Other murders?'* Here was something Olivier had not mentioned.

Father Adrian was annoyed with himself. 'I should not have said that – there was no proof, so I might be maligning an innocent man.'

'Whom did he kill?' demanded Geoffrey.

'His parents,' said Father Adrian, glancing around to make sure that Joan could not hear. 'They were found butchered, although Bale claims he was in a tavern at the time. That was about two years ago. Then there was a brawl that ended in death, but witnesses say Bale was goaded.'

Bale's company was sounding distinctly unappealing, and Geoffrey saw he had gone from one extreme to the other: Durand fainted if he saw blood, while Bale revelled in it.

'Tell me about more about Henry,' said Geoffrey, looking away as Bale went after a blackbird with his sword. 'We were interrupted when we talked before, and you were beginning to tell me about his affair with Isabel fitzNorman.'

Father Adrian backed away. 'Joan says it is a matter best left alone.'

Geoffrey followed him into the church. 'Was Henry's affection for Isabel reciprocated?'

'She says not,' said the priest. He changed the subject. 'When will *you* marry?'

'When I feel like it,' replied Geoffrey tartly.

'It will not be long. Joan will not let you leave until you have impregnated a wife.'

'I am not a breeding bull,' said Geoffrey, not liking the notion that an entire estate was waiting for him to perform his duties in the wedding bed.

'Perhaps you will wed Isabel,' mused Father Adrian. 'If she already carries Henry's child, then it makes sense for fitzNorman to give her to you.'

'How do you know she carries Henry's child?' asked Geoffrey. 'Did she tell you so?'

'I cannot say,' said Father Adrian firmly.

'The seal of confession?'

'Joan said not to, and her wrath is more terrifying than breaking the sacred secrecy of a man's business with God.'

'Then I shall ask Isabel myself,' said Geoffrey.

'No! You will cause all manner of problems.' Father Adrian rubbed a hand over his face. 'Very well. Henry said bedding her was the best way to secure her as a bride.'

'FitzNorman was against the match?'

Father Adrian nodded. 'He wanted an alliance with Goodrich, but he disapproved of Henry taking Isabel before the marriage agreements were drawn up.'

'And what about Isabel? Did he force her to lie with him?'

Father Adrian shrugged. 'She says she thought he was someone else.'

Geoffrey raised his eyebrows. 'Is she short of wits, then? Or fond of her wine?'

'Neither,' replied Father Adrian. 'She is blind.'

The priest could not be persuaded to say more, and Geoffrey began to suspect that the only way to gain answers would be to visit Dene. He was mulling over the prospect when he became aware that someone was behind him. He turned quickly, dagger in hand.

'Do not creep up on me like that, Bale,' he advised irritably. 'Most soldiers do not ask questions before they stab.'

'I know,' said Bale with a grin, giving the impression that he had stabbed a few hapless victims himself. 'But something arrived for you, and Sir Olivier said I should bring it.'

Geoffrey waited. Several moments passed, but Bale merely continued to beam. 'What did Olivier tell you to bring?' he asked, when he saw that they might be there all morning unless he spoke.

'A letter,' said Bale. 'On scraped calfskin.'

'Vellum,' said Geoffrey, wondering who would send him a message on vellum when parchment was cheaper. Could it be Roger, who had appropriated a considerable quantity of silver from Bristol the previous winter, and who liked making extravagant gestures? He waited again. 'Where is it?'

Bale fumbled in his unsavoury clothes and eventually found what he was looking for. He handed the message to Geoffrey and then came to loom over his shoulder.

'I thought you said you could not read,' said Geoffrey, moving away.

'I cannot,' replied Bale, following him.

Geoffrey edged away again, wanting to read the message in peace, but Bale moved with him, standing uncomfortably close. Geoffrey began to lose patience. 'What are you doing?'

Bale was surprised. 'Waiting for orders, Sir. Anything written on vellum is likely to be sinister, and you will not want to speak loudly. So I am standing close.' He reconsidered. 'Although, if anyone overhears, I can slit his throat to ensure his silence.' He looked around hopefully.

Shaking his head, Geoffrey turned his attention to the letter. It carried a seal that he recognized immediately: William Giffard, the Bishop of Winchester. He was assailed by an immediate sense of unease. Giffard was a good man, but was entrusted with a lot of the King's business. Geoffrey considered tossing the missive away, to remain oblivious to whatever Giffard wanted, but he supposed there was no point when Olivier, Bale and probably others knew it had been delivered. Reluctantly, he broke the seal.

The message was brief. It told him Giffard was currently at the nearby estate of Dene, and asked Geoffrey to visit. It was badly written, as if penned in a hurry, and its brevity lent it an urgency that the knight found worrisome.

'I am going to Dene,' he said. Despite the voice inside his head warning him that it might be wise to decline the summons, he liked Giffard, and did not want to fail him.

Bale fell into step beside him as he strode towards the castle, and began to chat. 'The forest around Dene belongs to the King, and Constable fitzNorman looks after it and its animals – so the King can slaughter them whenever he likes.'

Geoffrey could think of no reply to such a remark, so he walked to the stable, where Jervil and Torva were talking. They stopped when they saw him.

'We are off to Dene,' Bale announced, shoving past them. 'Move. I must saddle the horses.'

Groom and steward exchanged a glance. 'Why Dene?' asked Torva.

Geoffrey was inclined to tell them it was none of their affair, but said instead, 'An old friend invited me.'

Jervil turned to Torva in agitation. 'He is going to talk to Lord Baderon about Henry. And the Constable and his daughter and God knows who else. Will there be no end to this business?'

'Seguin is a violent man,' said Torva. 'You

would do well to stay well clear of him and his brother Lambert. And Baderon, for that matter.'

'They are not at Dene,' said Geoffrey. 'I met them yesterday in Llan Martin. They—'

'Baderon and his henchmen *are* at Dene,' insisted Jervil. 'For a week's hunting. So do not try to mislead us.'

'Here!' snapped Bale, emerging from the stables with Geoffrey's horse. 'Watch your mouth. No one talks to him like that when *I* am here.'

'I am not trying to mislead anyone,' replied Geoffrey, stepping forward to prevent Bale from making good his threat. 'However, I *will* find out what happened to Henry, no matter what it takes – and if that means talking to Baderon, Seguin and Lambert if I happen across them, then so be it.'

Torva indicated with a jerk of his head that Jervil and Bale were to leave them alone. Bale went to saddle his own horse, while Jervil, scowling, walked Geoffrey's stallion a short distance away.

'I am sorry if we seem rude,' Torva began in a conciliatory voice. 'But it really is better if you let Henry's death lie.'

'Better for whom?' asked Geoffrey archly. 'The killer?'

'For all of us, including your sister. Henry was always vicious, but in the months before his death, he grew beyond control. He broke Sir Olivier's arm, and beat a shepherd so badly that he died. He prowled the countryside picking fights, and it was only because Lady Joan is so

78

respected that Goodrich was not razed to the ground.'

Geoffrey was not sure whether to believe him. 'What precipitated Henry's sudden wildness?'

'Lady Joan made some wise investments, and Goodrich's fortunes soared. It meant there was money for luxuries like wine. Henry could not keep from drinking. He started the moment he woke, and he continued until he slept.'

'Did no one stop him? For his own good?'

'Olivier tried – and had his arm snapped for his troubles. Joan locked Henry in the cellar for a week, hoping that forcing him to become sober would make him see the error of his ways. But he threatened to get a message to the King, and Joan did not want to attract royal attention. She was afraid the King might demand some favour from you, as payment for overlooking an un-lawful imprisonment. From what I have heard, it was not an unreasonable fear.'

Geoffrey supposed it was not. 'Then what happened?'

'Henry was worse than ever. Ask anyone – they will all tell you the same.'

'And that is why you want me to forget his murder? Because you think I will learn that someone here killed him? Jervil, for example.'

'Jervil did not kill him,' said Torva with abso-lute certainty. 'He heard the scuffle, although he will never admit it to you. But he *saw* nothing.'

'How do you know Jervil is not the killer?'

'Because of the Black Knife that killed Henry,' replied Torva. 'It had a ruby in its hilt. Jervil could never afford such a valuable thing – and if he had, he would not have left it in a murdered corpse for everyone to identify. Jervil has light fingers where valuables are concerned, and nothing would have induced him to leave such a fine dagger in Henry.'

'Whose was it, then?'

'We do not know. But it belonged to a wealthy man, not a groom.'

'FitzNorman?' asked Geoffrey. 'Or Baderon?'

'Not Baderon,' replied Torva, again sounding certain. 'But Seguin and Lambert are a dangerous pair. Baderon does not have them under his control, as he should vassal knights. I am not saying they are the killers, but they were the first ones who came into our minds when *we* saw the dagger.'

'Where is this dagger now?'

'Joan took it,' replied Torva. 'She has it locked away.'

Geoffrey donned full armour before he went to Dene: a mail tunic that reached his knees, his stained Crusader's surcoat with its distinctive cross, a mail hood and his conical helmet. It was far in excess of what was required for a normal ride, but he did not want to meet Baderon or his knights unprotected.

He packed a bag with a few items he thought he might need for a day or two – a scroll to pass the time if Giffard could not see him immediately, a spare dagger and the needle and thread he used to repair damage to his armour. At the last moment, he included a tunic Joan had given him, which she said was the kind of thing worn

80

when dining in polite company. It was green, and therefore a little bright for his liking, but it was smarter than the brown one he wore at Goodrich. He jammed it in and then buckled the sack closed. Slinging it over his shoulder, he walked down the stairs and into the bailey. Bale and Jervil were waiting with the horses, and even from a distance, Geoffrey could hear that they were arguing.

'It is *not* wrong,' Jervil was saying. 'I am offering you a couple of pennies for doing nothing. I do not see why you are making such a fuss. It will be the easiest money you ever earn.'

'No,' said Bale, and Geoffrey could hear the stubbornness in his voice. 'He is my master and I will not spy on him.'

'You will *not* be spying,' Jervil insisted, trying to press coins into the big man's hand. 'I only want to know if he meets Lord Baderon. Surely you can do that for two silver pennies?'

'No,' said Bale, pushing him away with considerable force.

Jervil replaced the coins in his purse. 'Very well. It is your loss.'

He turned and walked away. Geoffrey rubbed his chin thoughtfully. Torva believed that Jervil had not murdered Henry, and had given reasons Geoffrey was prepared to accept. So, why was Jervil interested in whether Geoffrey met Baderon? Had Jervil left gates open and turned a blind eye while Henry was stabbed by someone from Baderon's retinue? It made sense: Jervil should not have slept through the murder, no matter what he claimed, and was obviously protecting someone.

And what of Bale's reaction to Jervil's bribe? Was he really loyal to a man he had served for so short a time? Loyalty was earned, not bought overnight. So was Bale simply eager to serve his new master well, or was he already in someone else's pay – someone more powerful than Jervil?

Geoffrey took the reins and set off with his squire behind him. He looked for his dog, but it was not to be seen, and he supposed it was just as well. It had bitten Lambert the last time, and he did not want another altercation. He was riding across the drawbridge when he met Joan.

'Where are you going so heavily armed?' she demanded.

Geoffrey smiled reassuringly. 'Bishop Giffard is in Dene, and has asked me to visit. And it is a fine day for a ride.'

'It is going to rain,' countered Joan. 'And Dene is not worth the journey – it is only a few miles distant, but the tracks are poor. You will not be able to travel there and back today.'

Geoffrey shrugged. It would not be the first time he had slept by the roadside.

'Do not go,' pleaded Joan. 'Wait until Roger arrives. He will watch your back, and I will feel happier knowing he is with you.'

Geoffrey was surprised. 'You think someone at Dene might try to harm me?'

'FitzNorman might if you accuse him of killing Henry.'

'Then I will not do it,' promised Geoffrey, wondering why she had so little faith in him when his diplomatic skills had impressed kings and princes.

Joan sighed. 'If you must go, then at least look at Margaret, Isabel and Hilde while you are there, and see if any meet your expectations. If they do, I can have you wed this week. And take this.'

'I have knives,' said Geoffrey, declining to accept the minuscule blade she proffered. It was no longer than his finger, and he wondered what she thought he could do with such a thing.

She tucked it into the cuff of his tunic, securing it there with a series of folds. 'Your daggers are large and flagrant, but this is discreet.'

'Speaking of daggers, I am told you have the one that killed Henry. Where is it?'

She gazed at him coolly. 'Jervil wanted it, but I did not think it right that the blade that killed my brother should be used to remove stones from horses' hoofs – although others thought it a suitable epitaph. I kept it in my bedchamber for a month, wrapped in cloth that had been soaked in holy water, but its presence disturbed me, so I gave it to Father Adrian. There was a ruby in its hilt, and I thought he could prise it out and sell it to buy bread for the poor. You must ask *him* what he did with it.'

'It might help me identify his killer.'

'How? None of us had seen it before and, if we do not know it, then how can you? You could look at it all day and it would tell you nothing.'

Without further ado, she reached up to touch his cheek, wished him God's speed and returned to her business.

With Bale behind him, Geoffrey followed the

path of the Wye as it meandered through the forest. The roots of trees snaked across the path, and in places Geoffrey was obliged to dismount, to make sure his horse did not stumble. Bale watched his every move and did the same, showing he was prepared to learn, which Durand had never been.

It was a cool day, with clouds slung low across a dark sky, and it was not long before it started to rain. Bale tugged his cloak over his bald head, and they rode in silence. Geoffrey was alert for any unusual sounds or movements. Forests were good places for ambushes, and he had not lived to the ripe old age of thirty-three by being careless. But no one else seemed to be out, and the only sound was the patter of rain.

They left the river and passed through Rwirdin, which Geoffrey's mother had bequeathed him. He studied it with interest – he had only been there twice before – and saw a neat place with a sturdy manor house and well-tended houses. He stopped to pay his respects to the steward, and stayed longer than he should have.

It was mid-afternoon before he set out on the final leg of the journey, and he hoped Giffard would find him a corner that night, because a wind was picking up, carrying with it a drenching drizzle. It was no weather to be sleeping in the open. Geoffrey urged his horse to greater speed.

Suddenly from the shadows a woman stepped out on to the track in front of him and raised her hand imperiously.

* * *

Her appearance was so abrupt that it startled Geoffrey's horse, and he was hard pressed to prevent it from riding her down. Warhorses were strong animals, capable of carrying a knight in full armour into battle, and were not always easily controlled. That evening, it was skittish, and only at the very last moment was Geoffrey able to pull away from the woman.

'Keep still,' she ordered. 'I want to talk to you, and I cannot while you are prancing around like a maiden who has set eyes on a spider.'

Geoffrey was tempted to ignore her and give his horse free rein to thunder along the track to Dene, but the woman was well dressed and spoke Norman-French with an accent that suggested she had learnt it in the home of a high-ranking noble. He suspected that she was from fitzNorman's entourage, so decided to be courteous. He dismounted.

'He is a fine beast,' she remarked, inspecting the stallion with expert eyes. She wore a green kirtle that fitted rather too snugly over her ample hips, and a wimple that cut severely under her chin. Her face was square and determined, and it was clear that she was not a woman to be crossed. 'You have ridden him too far today, and he is restless for oat mash and a bed of clean straw.'

'Yes,' agreed Geoffrey. 'And you are keeping him from it. What are you doing out here on your own? It will be dark soon.'

'I am not afraid of the dark,' declared the woman. Geoffrey was sure she was not, and

85

imagined there was very little that would disturb her. 'I am Hilde, daughter of Lord Baderon.'

'Even more reason why you should not be here alone,' remarked Geoffrey. He was shocked to think that Joan considered her a suitable match for him – her plain face and powerful shoulders rendered her rather manly. 'The kin of wealthy barons risk seizure by outlaws—'

Hilde gave a gusty sigh. 'No outlaw would be so foolish – I would kill him where he stood. But I am not alone. My brother Hugh is with me, and so is Eleanor de Bicanofre.'

Two more people stepped from the shadows. Hugh was smaller than his sister, and his slack jaw and vacant expression indicated that he was not right in his wits. Although his clothes were fine, he wore them untidily, and he carried no sword or dagger, suggesting that he was not trusted with sharp implements.

Geoffrey looked with considerably more interest at Eleanor – another of Joan's suggested brides. She wore a kirtle that was tight enough to reveal every curve of her sensuous body and a bright red cloak with matching gloves. Oddly, for someone happy to flaunt herself, her lower face was concealed by a scarf-like veil. All he could see was a pair of very bright blue eyes.

'You are Geoffrey Mappestone,' she said. 'Brother of dear Henry.'

Geoffrey could not tell whether she was being facetious. Her voice was soft, his horse was breathing in his ear and he could not see enough of her face to judge her expression.

'How do you know?' he asked.

'Your surcoat,' said Hilde. 'There are not many *Jerosolimitani* in these parts. You would not be our first choice to help us, but you will have to do. As you said, it will soon be dark.'

Geoffrey noticed Hugh was leaning heavily on Eleanor, and supposed there had been an accident. 'Do you need to borrow my horse?'

'Hugh does not ride,' said Hilde. 'And certainly not a horse of that size. You must go to Dene and send someone back with a cart.'

Geoffrey mounted, thinking he should hurry. Dusk would not be long in coming.

'Tell them we are near the Angel Springs,' said Eleanor. 'Hugh followed me there, then slipped on wet stones and hurt his foot. He was lucky Hilde was close.'

'I knew you intended to visit the springs this afternoon,' said Hilde coolly. 'And I know Hugh follows you. So, when I realized that he was missing, it seemed the obvious place to look. You are fortunate I used my wits, or you would both have been here all night.'

Eleanor's eyebrows went up, and Geoffrey had the impression that Hugh's damaged foot would not have stopped *her* from returning to the castle.

'I am going with Geoffrey,' Eleanor said. 'I do not want to wait until he returns.'

Geoffrey offered her his hand, happy to have her company – and her directions – as he rode the last stage of the journey, but Hilde was having none of it. She stepped forward as Eleanor put her foot in the stirrup.

'Hugh will be calmer with you here.'

Eleanor's eyes were furious, but Hilde clearly meant business, so she said no more. She went to sit on a tree stump, and Geoffrey could see she was in a poor mood, even without benefit of a face to assess. He raised his hand in a salute, and rode away in the direction that Hilde indicated.

'I do not like *them*!' exclaimed Bale, when they were out of earshot. 'It is an odd business: Eleanor slipping off to visit the Angel Springs, and that lunatic Hugh going after her. And then Hilde following him. You should not marry either of *them*, Sir.'

'Not Hilde, for sure,' agreed Geoffrey. 'But Eleanor looked all right – what I could see of her.'

'It is the bits you *cannot* see that you should worry about,' replied Bale enigmatically. 'Just ask yourself what she was doing at the Angel Springs in the first place.' He pronounced the name in a way that made it sound sinister.

'Is it a holy place?' asked Geoffrey. 'A well or some such thing?'

Bale regarded him through narrowed eyes. 'The Angel Springs are not holy – at least, not to our God.'

Geoffrey supposed he should have guessed as much from Bale's pronunciation. 'What, then? A pagan temple?'

Bale's eyes gleamed. 'Witches linger there. I do not know what they do, but a knife left overnight will have a keen edge in the morning – especially if you leave a coin.'

'Someone whets them during the night?' Geoffrey supposed he should not be surprised that Bale had turned the conversation to the thing that seemed to interest him most: sharp knives.

'They whet themselves,' asserted Bale firmly. 'And it is famous for other things, too.'

'Enlighten me,' encouraged Geoffrey.

'Spells,' elaborated Bale. 'If you want a man to die, then you leave a lock of his hair and a coin at the Angel Springs and your enemy will be in his grave before the next moon appears.'

Geoffrey did not believe a word of it.

'So, if anyone offers you a haircut, refuse,' Bale went on. 'I would not like to lose you yet. Not before you have paid my first month's wages.'

It was farther to Dene than he had anticipated, but after a while, a sound caught Geoffrey's attention, and he reined in, raising one hand to silence Bale.

'Horses.' Bale could also hear hoofs and the clink of metal.

'Several of them,' said Geoffrey. 'Men riding together. It must be one of fitzNorman's patrols.'

'Or outlaws,' said Bale, alarmed. 'We should take cover, so we can ambush them before they attack us. I will cut their throats, while you claim their horses.'

Geoffrey laughed. 'Outlaws will not be riding along a well-travelled path so close to fitz-Norman's stronghold, so these must be his men. We are on legitimate business; we have no reason to hide.'

The group that rounded the corner was astonished to see him. It comprised a knight, a monk and several soldiers, and all reached for their weapons. Geoffrey raised his hands to show he did not mean to fight, but that did not prevent them from spurring their way towards him with drawn swords. A pair of archers fumbled for bows and soon had arrows pointing in his direction.

'I told you we should hide,' whispered Bale accusingly. 'Now it will be *us* with slit throats.'

'Hold!' shouted Geoffrey, wondering whether Bale had been right to be cautious. He had assumed that a lone traveller and his squire would present no threat, but saw he had been wrong. 'I am here to see Bishop Giffard.'

'You are poaching,' said the knight. Short grey hair poked from under his helmet, and his cloak was blue with an ermine trim. There was embroidery around the hem, sewn to accentuate the presence of several semi-precious stones. His eyes were small and black, and he did not look friendly. 'There are laws against poaching.'

'We are not poaching,' said Geoffrey. 'I have come to—'

'There is blood on your saddle,' snapped the knight, riding forward to inspect it. 'I can tell when a man has slaughtered an animal and carried it on his horse.'

Geoffrey tried to be patient. 'I am here because Bishop Giffard summoned me.'

'I know nothing about it,' said the knight in a voice that suggested Geoffrey was lying.

'I have a letter,' said Geoffrey. 'I can show you.'

The knight gave a curt nod, so Geoffrey retrieved Giffard's letter and handed it to the monk. The Benedictine was a small, wiry man in his sixties, and his habit was made from good wool. He was vaguely familiar, although Geoffrey was more concerned with the knight.

'It is true, fitzNorman,' said the monk. 'This *is* a message from Giffard asking him to come to Dene as a matter of urgency.'

FitzNorman laughed in an unpleasant manner, while Geoffrey regarded him with renewed interest. Here was the man who controlled the forest and was father to Isabel. He was large and fit, and his advanced age had apparently not reduced his readiness to fight. He also looked like the kind of man who would stop at nothing to have his own way – including murdering drunken neighbours.

'I suppose Giffard summoned him over the Duke and his harlot,' he said.

Geoffrey regarded him uneasily. He did not like the sound of it, and hoped Giffard did not intend to drag him into intrigues involving nobles and their lovers.

'I met Hilde Baderon near the Angel Springs,' Geoffrey said, remembering his mission. 'With Hugh and Eleanor de Bicanofre. Hugh has hurt his foot and they need a cart to—'

FitzNorman spat. 'A likely story! Hilde would not seek out Eleanor's company, while Eleanor would have climbed on the back of your horse and insisted on riding with you. You lie!'

The monk spoke before Geoffrey could reply. 'The letter is addressed to Sir Geoffrey Mappestone.'

FitzNorman's eyes settled on Geoffrey. 'The man whose brother despoiled my daughter?'

Geoffrey was not sure how to reply. 'Henry is dead these last six months, my Lord.'

FitzNorman continued to stare. 'He wanted to force my hand, so I would let him have Isabel. She loves Ralph de Bicanofre, and wanted *him*. So, Henry came one night, pretending to be Ralph. She is blind, and could not tell the difference. Now Henry is dead, but Ralph will not have her. Between them they have broken her heart.'

Geoffrey had met other blind people, and they had developed other senses to make up for their lack of vision. He did not see why Isabel should be any different, and if she loved Ralph, she would recognize his smell, his voice and the feel of his body. Isabel mistaking Henry for Ralph seemed an odd tale, and not one he was ready to believe. But he could hardly say so to a doting father.

'I am sorry he used such tactics,' he said, seeing fitzNorman expected a reply and feeling uncomfortable with the men-at-arms clustering around him.

FitzNorman seemed lost in thought. Then he suddenly hissed, 'I swore no Mappestone would ever set foot on my lands again,' and swung his sword at Geoffrey's head.

Four

Geoffrey had sensed fitzNorman's pent-up rage, so had been on guard. He raised his shield to fend off a blow so hard that splinters flew.

'I have no quarrel with you!' he cried.

'I have a quarrel with *you*!' yelled fitzNorman. 'Your brother ruined my daughter's reputation.'

Seeing the futility of trying to reason, Geoffrey went on the offensive. It was not long before he had the older man backing away, although the archers stood ready, should Geoffrey pursue his advantage. Bale rode quickly to Geoffrey's side, awaiting orders.

'All right!' fitzNorman finally shouted. 'You have proved your point.'

Geoffrey lowered his weapon, keeping a wary eye on the man and his companions.

'You should be ashamed of yourself, attacking a man without provocation,' said the monk to fitzNorman. He turned to Geoffrey. 'I am Serlo, Abbot of Gloucester.'

Serlo's face clicked into place in Geoffrey's mind. They *had* met before, although he hoped the monk would not remember. His mother had taken him to Gloucester Abbey when he was eleven, intending him to remain there. It took six months for Geoffrey to convince Serlo that he was unsuitable. Serlo had aged, and his brown hair had turned white, although his eyes were still filled with humour.

'I hear your new church was consecrated two years ago,' said Geoffrey politely.

A wry gleam showed in Serlo's eye. 'Many things have changed since you were last there.'

Meanwhile, fitzNorman gazed with hostility at Geoffrey. 'Have you come to take up where your brother left off, to secure Isabel?' he asked. 'She will not have you, but I have a sister—'

'No,' interrupted Geoffrey. 'I have come to see Giffard.'

'And see him, you shall, for we should return to Dene for Vespers,' said Serlo. His voice was commanding, and the soldiers immediately obeyed. He indicated Geoffrey was to come, too, but the knight hesitated, loath to travel with fitzNorman. Serlo sighed. 'Come on!'

FitzNorman led the way along a winding valley, and it was not long before the castle at Dene came into sight. It stood at the heart of the royal forest, with steep slopes on three sides and a gentler one on the fourth. It was a large complex, with a tower-topped motte and fenced bailey, but it was primarily an administrative and residential structure, not a military one.

The largest building was the manor house, comprising a hall on the ground floor with five chambers above. To its left was a handsome stone edifice – newer, cleaner and containing real glass in its windows. Serlo told Geoffrey it was used when the King came to hunt in the forest, which he owned. Other buildings included a kitchen range, placed at the far end of the bailey to avoid fires, and stables, pantries, store-rooms and a brewery.

'I do not like it here,' whispered Bale. He glared at fitzNorman's back. 'And I do not trust *him*.'

Geoffrey agreed. 'We will see Giffard, then be on our way. Will you make sure someone sends a cart for Hugh? I do not want Hilde accusing me of failing to keep my promises.'

'You do not,' agreed Bale. 'Especially if they force you to marry her. I will see to it now.'

Geoffrey caught his arm as he started to leave. 'Thank you for standing with me.' It made a pleasant change: Durand would have fled.

Bale grinned, and bashfully rubbed a hand over his bald head. 'You are welcome,' he murmured, blushing. 'It is what squires are for, is it not?'

Geoffrey had never had a squire who had thought so. When Bale had gone, Geoffrey followed a servant to the room he was to sleep in that night. It was one of the five chambers on the upper floor of the main house, and the man said he would have to share with Bishop Giffard, because space was limited. Geoffrey was not entirely pleased to learn that the King was expected at Dene within the next few weeks, and local dignitaries were beginning to gather. Determined to meet Giffard and leave before His Majesty arrived, Geoffrey started to ask the servant where the Bishop might be, only to find him gone.

'They are not well trained,' came a familiar

95

voice from the corridor. It was Durand, resplendent in an outfit that shimmered orange and red as he moved. Geoffrey supposed it was silk, another example of his old squire's expanding fortunes. 'FitzNorman has low standards where servants are concerned. He is a low-standards sort of man.'

Geoffrey smiled at him. 'I see you survived your night in the forest.'

'Abbot Serlo led us halfway to Shropshire before we found someone to bring us here,' grumbled Durand. 'Now we are waiting for the King. He cannot arrive too soon, as far as I am concerned. I wish to leave this dull place and return to the centre of power.'

Geoffrey felt the Marches held more than enough excitement for him, with his brother murdered and hostile neighbours with marriageable daughters converging at every turn. 'I leave at first light tomorrow. Dene is about to become very crowded, and fitzNorman will not want me here.'

'You want to be away before the King spots you,' surmised Durand astutely.

Geoffrey winced at being so transparent. Durand was the King's man, so he should not let him know he did not want to meet the monarch. 'Have you seen Giffard?' he asked.

'Yes, but *you* will not – not tonight, at least. It is the eve of the Annunciation – and there is a vigil. You will not see Giffard until tomorrow, because he will not break from his devotions. Have you been asked to dine with fitzNorman tonight?'

96

Geoffrey nodded. 'But he did his best to kill me this afternoon, so I think I shall plead tiredness and stay here instead.'

Durand settled on a chest near the window. Bale arrived and closed the door, then began to unpack the meagre contents of Geoffrey's saddlebag.

'If you do not attend willingly, he may drag you there by force,' said Durand. 'His sister will be wanting to inspect you, and so will the paupers from Bicanofre.'

'I am supposed to inspect them, too,' said Geoffrey. 'We will be like wives at a meat market.'

Durand giggled. 'Enjoy it! You will never have the chance to make this sort of decision again.'

'I will if I outlive whichever lucky lady catches my eye.'

'You will not do that,' predicted Durand confidently. 'Not the way you court danger. But I understand there are six women to choose from – I have been bored, so I have amused myself by assessing them for you. Do you want to hear my conclusions?'

Geoffrey did not, but Durand intended to tell him anyway.

'Isabel is the prettiest, but she is in love with someone else. Her aunt Margaret is old enough to be your mother, but is a pleasant woman. You will like her, and she *may* still be young enough to give you the son you need.'

'She gave her last husband two,' added Bale. 'Fine, strong gentlemen.'

'And who,' asked Durand, giving him a cool

stare, 'are you? Why do you interrupt me?'

Bale nodded at Geoffrey. 'His squire.'

Durand pursed his lips. 'My successor! A great, stupid, ugly ape! You have gone down in the world, Geoffrey.'

'Actually, women find me very handsome,' protested Bale.

'Well, *I* do not,'said Durand. He turned his back on Bale and continued his analysis. Geoffrey braced himself for trouble, but Bale only made an obscene gesture as repayment for the insult.

'Then there are the Bicanofre women – Eleanor and Douce,' Durand went on. 'Eleanor is too clever, Douce not clever enough, and there is something odd about both. They are poor and a marriage with either is a waste. The same is true of Corwenna of Llan Martin, although her father would be willing.'

'She is being courted by someone else,' said Geoffrey.

'Sir Seguin de Rheims,' said Durand, nodding. 'A shallow man who will not be able to control her. His brother Lambert is the same – they think they will take Welsh wives and continue their wild bachelor habits. Fools! And finally, there is Baderon's Hilde. He is sure to foist her on you, but you should resist. I know you like a challenge, but she will prove too much.'

Geoffrey was amused. 'So, which would *you* choose?'

Durand considered carefully. 'I would leave immediately, and not have any of them – unless you like your women old, stupid, cunning, mannish or insane.'

Geoffrey rubbed his chin. He had come to much the same conclusion, but it was disconcerting to hear it so succinctly summarized. His future looked bleak, and he was overwhelmed by the desire to grab his horse and ride hard for the Holy Land. He would sooner take his chances with Tancred's anger than live out his days with a local wife.

'You cannot go to Tancred,' said Durand, reading his thoughts. 'You showed me the last letter he wrote, and to say it was hostile is an understatement. Do you want to be slaughtered in his next battle, because he orders you to a futile skirmish? You would do better joining forces with me. It will allow you to escape from Goodrich *and* use your wits.'

Durand's offer was beginning to sound more attractive, but he thought about Joan and knew he could not shirk his responsibilities. 'I cannot.'

Durand shrugged. 'Then you have my deepest sympathy. Your future looks dismally grim, and I would not be in your position for a kingdom. Where are you going?'

Geoffrey had stood when a bell rang to announce the evening meal. 'To the hall. You said I should go willingly or risk being dragged.'

Durand was aghast. 'You cannot go dressed like that! FitzNorman would be insulted. Your full armour tells him you do not feel safe in his house.'

'I do not,' said Geoffrey, surprised anyone should think otherwise.

'Perhaps so, but you cannot announce it by

dining in mail! Besides, he will not attack you tonight. There will be too many witnesses.'

'That did not stop him earlier,' grumbled Geoffrey, although he suspected Durand was right. Reluctantly, he divested himself of his armour, while Bale tried to clean his boots. He inspected his equipment and saw with annoyance that fitzNorman's attack had damaged his shield, which had, in turn, left several splinters in his arm.

'You should get those out before they fester,' advised Bale. 'My knife is sharp—'

'You do not use a knife for splinters,' said Durand disdainfully. 'It would be like using a bucket to serve fine wine.' He glanced at Bale in a way that suggested he thought the squire probably did just that. 'You must prise them out with your teeth. I will do it.'

'No, thank you,' said Geoffrey hastily, not liking the sound of either option. 'Joan will do it tomorrow – without recourse to knives or teeth.'

'Suit yourself,' said Durand with a shrug. 'But they will itch furiously tonight.' Geoffrey took the green tunic from his saddlebag, and Durand's jaw dropped in horror. 'What is *that*?'

'My best tunic,' replied Geoffrey, mystified by his reaction.

Durand glared at Bale. 'You packed it as though it were a rag, and now it looks like one. Do you *want* him to appear shabby among the suitors? What kind of squire are you?'

Bale snatched the offending garment and shook it so hard that one of the hems began to unravel. 'The other creases will fall out by the

100

end of the evening.'

'But by then, everyone will be drunk, and it will not matter,' said Durand. 'Give it to me.'

With the help of water and a lot of judicious flattening, Durand eventually had the garment looking reasonably wrinkle-free, and Geoffrey pulled it over his head. The hem Bale had ruined began to drop, so Geoffrey pinned it in place with the tiny dagger Joan had given him. It pulled the skirt at an odd angle, and bumped against his leg when he moved, but it could not be helped. Durand pursed his lips in disapproval when he saw the result, and circled for some time, patting and tugging, before pronouncing himself satisfied.

'It will have to do. At least these hapless women will know in advance what an untidy ruffian you are.'

Feeling self-conscious after Durand's fuss, Geoffrey walked to the hall. Bale disappeared to eat with the other squires, but Durand accompanied Geoffrey to the tables near the dais, where those of significance dined. He assumed Durand knew what he was doing – he was in the King's household, after all, and had a strong sense of his social standing.

The first people he met were Baderon and his knights. All three wore finery, and Geoffrey was grateful Durand had insisted that he change.

'You have come to visit fitzNorman,' said Baderon coolly. 'Might I ask why?'

Geoffrey's immediate reaction was to tell him he might not, but chose not to antagonize him. 'I am here to see Bishop Giffard,' he replied instead.

Baderon seemed relieved. 'I thought fitz-Norman might have summoned you to inspect Margaret and Isabel. But you must meet my daughter Hilde later. She has expressed an interest in you, and such an alliance would be most beneficial.'

'She did not look very interested when I encountered her in the woods.'

Baderon pursed his lips, while his knights exchanged knowing smirks. 'You met her. Damn! I wanted to be there, to make sure...' He trailed off, waving a hand expansively.

'To make sure she did not bite you,' Seguin chortled.

'To make sure each knew who the other was,' said Baderon, glaring at him. He forced a smile at Geoffrey. 'You must visit us in Monmouth. I am told you are a favourite of the King, and the King's friends are always welcome.'

'It is always wise to be gracious to friends of the King,' said Durand. 'I—'

'*You* are not a friend of His Majesty,' said Baderon in surprise. 'You are a clerk. Abbot Serlo told me. Why are you here, anyway? You should be dining with the servants at *that* table.' He pointed to the corner.

Durand's small, sharp face grew dark with anger. 'I am a trusted agent, not a clerk. And I am a landowner, too.'

'You are not,' said Seguin in distaste, grabbing Durand by the scruff of the neck and propelling him away. 'You sit at the lower end of the hall.'

Durand's eyes flashed dangerously. 'I resent you manhandling me.'

Seguin made as if to grab him again, and Geoffrey was about to intervene when others entered the hall. Seguin's eyes lit up when he saw Corwenna among them, and Durand was forgotten. Magnificent in a violet kirtle, Corwenna smiled smugly as she took his arm and allowed him to lead her to her place. When she passed Geoffrey, she looked him up and down disdainfully.

'FitzNorman allows *anyone* to dine here, I see,' she remarked.

'Take no notice,' whispered Baderon. 'She has a sharp tongue, but Seguin will blunt it once they are married.'

Geoffrey sincerely doubted it. He watched Seguin fuss, determined to impress her, and it occurred to him that Seguin might do anything to secure her favour. Would he stoop to murder, to rid her of the man she claimed had killed Rhys?

'I wish she would blunt it on *him*!' muttered Durand venomously. 'Insolent bastard!'

'Ignore him,' said Geoffrey, seeing humiliation burn on Durand's face. 'Seguin is a lout.'

'Not Seguin. He is nothing – a brainless bag of wind. I was talking about Baderon. How dare he tell me where I may sit! Does he not know who I am?'

Geoffrey was saved from a further tirade when fitzNorman arrived. On his arm was an older woman, with kind grey eyes and a surprisingly trim figure. She wore a kirtle with plain sleeves and a long, decorative girdle made of silk. As befitting a lady of rank, a veil covered her hair, although the chestnut curls showing at her temples indicated they were not yet touched by grey. FitzNorman nodded greetings to various guests, including Durand, then approached Geoffrey.

'This is my sister Margaret,' he said. 'I would like you to sit with her this evening.'

'Where is Isabel?' asked Durand, of a mind to make trouble. 'Is she too busy to dine with us?'

FitzNorman glared at him. 'She is indisposed.'

'She refuses to see you while she pines for Ralph de Bicanofre,' muttered Durand, going to take a seat, not quite at the level of Baderon and his men, but not far away. Geoffrey saw he had indeed risen in society.

'I hear your first meeting with my brother was eventful,' said Margaret, leading Geoffrey to the dais. Uncomfortably, Geoffrey was aware of Corwenna and Seguin glaring at him from one side, and fitzNorman watching with hawk-like eyes on the other; Geoffrey wished that he had not dispensed with his armour. 'Do not take him amiss. He wants an alliance with you.'

'You mean by marrying you?' asked Geoffrey bluntly.

Margaret was not embarrassed. 'I do not want another husband, but I may have no choice, and neither may you. However, I will not try to beguile you with false words, if you do me the same courtesy.'

Geoffrey smiled. 'But we can be friends?'

She looked as relieved as he felt. 'I would like that very much.'

104

'Tell me about your husband,' said Geoffrey, as the meal wore on.

'He went on the Crusade, although he did not live to enjoy his glory. He died at Antioch.'

As Margaret talked, her spouse's face appeared in Geoffrey's mind. He recalled a gentle knight with calm, brown eyes, who had spoken fondly of his wife. She was moved when he told her so, and asked many questions about Antioch and its towering walls. She believed her Robert had died in battle, although Geoffrey knew that he, like so many others, had died of the bowel disease that struck at those weakened by hunger and exhaustion. He did not tell her the truth.

'Who is that?' he asked, nodding towards the fellow he had offered to help when his cart had stuck in the Wye. With him was an older man and a young woman wearing a white wimple. Geoffrey had a fleeting impression of dark eyes and clear skin before someone stepped into his line of sight.

'Wulfric de Bicanofre and his son Ralph. It is Ralph for whom Isabel pines, poor thing. The woman is Wulfric's youngest daughter, Douce.'

But Ralph was being hustled from the hall by his father, and Douce followed. Ralph shouted something, and Geoffrey thought he heard, 'Henry'. When he saw Ralph scowl in his direction, he was sure it was his presence that had caused the father to remove the son so hastily.

Margaret chuckled. 'Ralph is a silly boy, all puffed-up pride. His father knows he will quarrel with you, and is afraid it will spoil Douce's

105

chances. If you were to take Douce – or Eleanor – it would improve Wulfric's standing in the area, and he is keen to make a good impression.'

'I had no idea Goodrich was so important,' said Geoffrey.

'It is strategically located, as you know. But you may as well enjoy being fawned over. It will not last.'

'That is what my old squire, Durand, told me,' said Geoffrey.

'Poor Durand. Baderon should not have addressed him so rudely, and Seguin should not have shoved him. He is a favourite at Court, and is likely to remember insults. The King likes men who are resourceful, clever and devious.'

'I hear the King will be here soon. Do you know when?'

'So you can leave before he arrives?' Margaret laughed when he looked alarmed. 'It is obvious that you are not a man to hang around in the hope of securing some regal crumb. But His Majesty is not expected for days. You have plenty of time to see your bishop and escape.'

'Tomorrow,' vowed Geoffrey. 'When Giffard has finished his vigil.'

'He is a devout man, but deeply troubled. I hope you can ease his burden.'

'What burden?' asked Geoffrey.

'I suspect it is something to do with his kinsmen and the Duke ... What do *you* want?' Her voice was suddenly cool, and Geoffrey glanced up to see Corwenna behind him, a knife in her hand.

'I want some of Geoffrey's hair,' she said,

reaching out. 'It is part of an experiment, to see whether Norman or Celtic hair is stronger.'

Geoffrey was not particularly superstitious, but he recalled Bale's warnings about hair, and leant away from her. Undaunted, she grabbed at him.

'No,' said Margaret, catching her wrist. 'Choose another Norman. And go away.'

She met Corwenna's angry gaze, until the Welsh woman gave a stiff bow and moved away. She did not approach anyone else, and Geoffrey doubted there was any such experiment.

'Thank you,' he said.

'She would have taken it to the Angel Springs and had it cursed,' said Margaret. 'Personally, I do not believe such nonsense, but you cannot be too careful. Now, tell me more about the Fall of Jerusalem.'

She asked more questions about the Holy Land and then talked a good deal about her Robert. It was an easy, relaxed discussion, and Geoffrey was grateful for her company. He saw fitz-Norman nod with satisfaction, as if drawing up wedding contracts in his mind, and was aware that Baderon watched with irritation. Eventually, Abbot Serlo stood and intoned grace: the meal was at an end.

Margaret patted Geoffrey's hand in a motherly fashion as she bade him goodnight, and when she had gone, he went outside for air. He sat on some steps, but did not enjoy his solitude for long. A youth of fifteen or sixteen, whose clothes copied those favoured by the most fashion-conscious members of the King's court, came to stand nearby. Despite his finery, he was unprepossessing, with a bad complexion, poor teeth and a large nose.

'It is a beautiful morning,' he said in heavily accented Italian. 'And the cows are in the river.'

Geoffrey gazed at the boy in bemusement. 'It is a cold night,' he replied in Norman-French. 'And I imagine the cows are in the byre.'

It was the youth's turn to look surprised. 'You know Italian?'

'My liege lord comes from Italy,' replied Geoffrey in Italian. 'Have you been there?'

'You are speaking too fast,' snapped the boy in Norman-French. 'And how do you know Italian? There cannot be any call for it in these Godforsaken parts.'

'I like learning languages,' replied Geoffrey, reverting to French. 'And you?'

'I love the sound of Italian.' The boy closed his eyes, gesturing with his hands. 'The bells chime in pigs. Dogs eat cabbages and the trees swear red.'

'Very poetic.'

'It impresses women,' said the boy with a leering grin. 'They think it is romantic, and invite you to kiss them.'

'I shall remember that.'

The boy looked around. 'I will demonstrate. You see that woman over there with the white veil? She is called Douce, and is the daughter of some upstart peasant. Watch me.'

He sauntered to where Douce stood with her brother and father. Both men gaped when the youth doffed his hat, accompanying the gesture

with a stream of meaningless words about par-
snips fighting inkwells and directions to the
latrines.

Douce released a squawk of outrage. 'Rude!'
she cried, cuffing him around the ears. 'Rude!'

The boy regarded her with astonishment. 'I
was praising your beautiful eyes in the moonlight,' he objected. 'What did you clout me for?'

'It sounded obscene,' said Ralph angrily. 'Push
off.'

The boy sensed a lost cause and slunk away,
pausing only to mutter to Geoffrey, 'She is a
peasant. It works better on ladies of the court.'

'What are you staring at?' demanded Ralph,
suddenly recognizing Geoffrey.

Geoffrey was not in the mood to quarrel. He
raised his hands to indicate he was sorry, and
started to leave. Ralph followed, drawing his
dagger, and Geoffrey was about to do likewise
when Ralph suddenly beat a hasty retreat.
Geoffrey watched in surprise, then jumped when
a shadow loomed behind him. It was Bale.

'He was going to fight you, sir,' said Bale, who
held Geoffrey's broadsword in his meaty hands.
'But he backed away when he saw he would
have to contend with me, too.'

Geoffrey might have backed away from Bale,
too. The squire looked especially intimidating in
the dark, with his massive bulk and dome-
shaped head. He thanked Bale for his watch-
fulness, although the squire's attention was now
on a commotion as the gates were hauled open.

Three people were ushered inside: Hilde,
Hugh and Eleanor. Hilde carried her brother on

her back, and when she set him on the ground, people converged to fuss over his injured foot. He was sobbing, and had evidently not enjoyed the trek. Geoffrey glanced at Bale, who stood with his hand over his mouth and his eyes wide with horror, indicating that he had forgotten to dispatch the cart. Hilde was furious, and Geoffrey tried to escape before she saw him. He was far too slow.

'What happened to you?' she demanded. 'I had to carry Hugh, and Eleanor was all but useless.'

'The cart did not arrive?' Geoffrey asked feebly. 'I am sorry. I—'

But, after shooting him a withering look, Hilde strode away, not waiting to hear excuses.

It was hot in the chamber that Geoffrey shared with Bale, and he was plagued by an itch from the splinters in his arm – as Durand had predicted. He finally abandoned his attempts to sleep, and went to see if there was wine left for guests in the kitchens. The night was pitch-black and he sensed dawn was a long way off. He moved stealthily, not wanting to disturb those sleeping.

His room was at the far end of a long corridor that had another four doors opening off it. Most were open, to allow air to circulate, and he could see people inside as he crept past. In the first were Seguin, Lambert and their servants; Baderon had been housed in the more sumptuous guesthouse. In the middle room were Hilde, Douce and various other women, while the next was occupied by the spotty boy who had spoken

110

Italian and his retinue. In the last room fitz-Norman snored, with his female kin around him.

Geoffrey was relieved when he reached the yard, breathing in deeply of the heady scent of wet trees and cold earth. He was waiting for his eyes to become accustomed to the darkness when he saw that he was not alone.

'Do not worry,' said Eleanor, immediately recognizable by her veil and red cloak. 'I am not as cross about the cart as Hilde.'

'I should have seen it on its way. I was remiss to trust others to do it, and I apologize.'

She inclined her head. 'Apology accepted. I do not mind the forest, although I prefer my own company. Hugh follows me everywhere, and nothing I say deters him. He is attracted by my veil. Most men are unnerved by it, but Hugh is not like other men.'

'He seems simple-minded.'

'Yes. He is Baderon's only son, which is why Baderon uses his knights to establish peace – Hugh will not be capable of maintaining it once Baderon dies. He would like you for Hilde, but I doubt she will have you. Normally, a strong lord like Baderon would not care about the likes and dislikes of daughters, but Hilde has refused more suitors than you can imagine. Meanwhile, my father wants you for Douce. Or for me. But I expect your sights are set higher?'

'They are not set at all. What are you doing out at this time of night?'

'The same as you, I imagine. I want something to drink.'

They walked to the kitchens, where she lit a

111

candle, then poured wine into a cup. When the heavy jug slipped in her grasp, she removed her scarlet gloves to hold it more securely, and Geoffrey saw that her hands were marred by a rash. Something had aggravated her skin, which perhaps explained why she covered everything except her eyes. He indicated she was to drink first, curious how she would do it without removing the veil. Her eyes crinkled in a smile, as if she knew what he was doing, and she turned away as she set the cup to her lips.

'You keep scratching your arm,' she said, as he sat near the dead hearth. 'Let me see.'

She moved next to him, but he edged away. There was something unnerving about being inspected by a woman when only her eyes were showing, and he had a flashback to an unfortunate incident in the Holy Land, when he had inadvertently burst into a gathering of Muslim ladies. Covered from head to foot, he could only see their eyes, but there was no question that they were furious. Eleanor, however, was laughing at him.

'You are afraid of me,' she said.

'I am not!'

'Then let me see what is making you scratch like a dog with fleas.'

'Splinters. I do not need help.'

The humour in her eyes faded. 'We all need help, Sir Geoffrey, and only a fool refuses an offer of kindness. Let me see.'

With considerable reluctance, he pulled up his sleeve. She removed her gloves again and began to press with her fingernails, hauling his arm this

112

way and that to see in the dim light of the candle. When he objected to her ministrations, she sighed in irritation.

'The only person in Dene with decent healing skills is Isabel – and you will not want *her* doing this. She is blind.'

'My sister will do it,' said Geoffrey, trying to pull away.

'It might fester by then. Sit still. I have almost finished.'

He did as he was told, and it was not long before she was done. Then she scattered powder into the wine they had been sharing, and indicated he should drink.

'What did you put in it?' he asked suspiciously.

'Why? Do you think I might poison you? I am unlikely to kill a man after I have put myself through the annoyance of removing splinters. Drink the draught, and I will send Isabel to you. She has more patience with soothing poultices than I.'

'I do not need poultices or Isabel. But you have been kind.'

'You will return the favour at some point,' she said, as though he had no choice. 'If you drink my potion, you will sleep soundly tonight. Or, if you prefer, give me a lock of your hair, and I shall say a charm that will work just as well.'

'That is not necessary,' he said hurriedly.

Her eyes crinkled in another smile and she shrugged. When she left, he poured the doctored wine down the slop drain and refilled his cup from the jug. It was not long before he was joined by another sleepless guest: Durand, complaining about Abbot Serlos's snoring.

'You can hear him from here, and he is in the room above the buttery! He was put there, rather than the guest hall, because he is such a noisy sleeper. But *I* am obliged to share with him.'

Geoffrey could indeed hear someone breathing hard and strong. Durand drank two cups of wine in quick succession, claiming they would make him drowsy.

'I saw Eleanor leaving just now,' he said, pouring a third. 'I waited until she had gone, because I did not want to meet *her* in the dark.'

'Why not?'

'She is more comfortable during the night than is appropriate for a young woman,' said Durand primly, although Geoffrey was not sure what he meant. 'She still wore her veil. I thought she might not bother in the dark, when her face cannot be seen. I hear she is dreadfully scarred.'

'Is that so,' said Geoffrey without interest.

Durand sensed his reluctance to gossip, so changed the subject. 'Corwenna hates you. What have you done to her?'

'My brother killed her husband.'

'But then your brother was killed in his turn. Did Corwenna do it? Or Seguin or Lambert?'

'Why would Lambert—'

'He loves his brother – you can see his devotion a mile away. He might have killed Henry at Seguin's request. Or perhaps they did it together.'

Without waiting for a response, Durand reeled away, across the yard towards the buttery. Geoffrey settled into the chair again, swearing under his breath when, no matter how hard he scratched, he could not stop his arm from itching.

'That is not polite language,' came a soft voice from behind him.

Geoffrey came to his feet and studied the woman who had glided into the room so softly that he had not heard. Everything about her was pale. Her hair, coiled into circles over her ears – a fashion adopted by women in the privacy of their quarters, but never in public – was so fair it was almost silver. Her skin had a delicate translucency, and he had never seen eyes such a light shade of blue. He saw the way she looked past his shoulder.

'Isabel?'

She inclined her head. 'Eleanor told me your arm itches. Is that why you are swearing?'

She indicated he was to sit, then knelt beside him, groping for his hand. He started to object, but she began to rub a white paste on his arm that almost instantly relieved the itching.

'Now you should be able to sleep, especially if you drink Eleanor's poppy juice – although I hope you did not give her your hair. She does odd things at the Angel Springs, I am told.'

'I hope she did not wake you for this.'

'I was awake anyway.' There was a catch in her voice. 'I seldom sleep these days.'

'I am sorry,' he said gently. 'Is there anything I can do?'

'You can agree not to marry me. I sense you are a good man, but I do not want you. My heart lies elsewhere.'

'With Ralph.' He could not imagine what she saw in such a surly fellow.

The mention of Ralph's name drew a smile. 'I have loved him since we were children. But your brother...' She took a shuddering breath. 'Now Ralph will not have me. He says I am tainted, even though...' She did not finish, and tears spilt down her cheeks.

'He is young,' he said, thinking about what Margaret had said. 'When he sees your devotion, he may recant.'

She wiped her eyes with her sleeve. 'Do you think so? Then perhaps everything will work out. But you should sleep now.'

And she was gone.

When Geoffrey awoke, his first thought was whether to don armour or the green tunic. He was still undecided when he climbed out of bed, and, to his amazement, Isabel glided in. He wondered whether she would have entered so blithely had she known he was clad only in undergarments. Aware that it would not look good if anyone found them, he hauled his tunic over his head and tugged on his boots, eluding her outstretched hands until he was properly dressed.

'Stand still,' she ordered. 'I want to assess if you need more of my ointment.'

'I do not,' he said. 'But thank you for asking.'

'You are nothing like your brother. I paid a priest to say a mass for him when he died, although it will not be enough to free him from purgatory. He was not a good man.'

Isabel had been kind to Geoffrey, but that was no reason to duck from the truth. Her unfinished statements from the previous night had allowed him to deduce exactly what had happened the night Henry invaded her bedchamber – and it was not what most people believed.

'You risked a great deal to protect Ralph, did you not?' he said, watching her intently.

He saw alarm flit across her face. 'What do you mean?'

'You lay with Ralph and then discovered you carried his child. Not wanting your father to kill him for despoiling you, you allowed Henry into your chamber – or perhaps you invaded his, as you have just done to mine. It would not matter if your father killed Henry, because no one liked him.'

She was appalled. 'What a horrible thing to say! You question my virtue and Ralph's honour.'

'You slept with Henry to protect Ralph. I know from personal experience that your father strikes first and hears explanations second. You did not want him to hurt Ralph.'

'I was wrong,' said Isabel coldly. 'You *are* like your brother.'

'You are not with child,' said Geoffrey, noting her body's slender lines. 'Were you mistaken?'

Isabel gave a choking sob, and he thought she might flee. Instead she groped for the bed and sat heavily, shoulders heaving with silent weeping.

'The baby came too soon, so I buried her in the churchyard.' She took a deep breath as more tears spilt down her cheeks. 'Why am I telling you this, when I have even kept it from my confessor? Only my aunt Margaret knows the truth. And Ralph, although he...'

'But the child was not Henry's?'

'Ralph's. We must have made her the first or second time we...'

'You took a risk,' said Geoffrey, thinking he had never come across a more flawed plan. 'What would you have done if your father had ordered you to marry Henry – or if Henry had insisted on marrying the mother of his heir?'

'Henry *did* insist,' said Isabel unhappily. 'I thought he would not – I made no effort to please him. But he did not have very high standards – or perhaps the quality of love did not matter to him.'

Geoffrey refrained from pointing out that physical satisfaction seemed irrelevant when advantageous matches were being made. 'Surely, there was another way?' he asked instead.

She raised a tear-stained face. 'I could not think of one. Ralph was in Normandy, so I could not ask him, and I dared tell no one else. But my plot had three flaws: it pleased Henry, it soured relations with the Mappestones and, worst of all, it drove Ralph away.'

Geoffrey felt sorry for her. She had been desperate, and her plan had misfired horribly. The only way it could have been worse was if Henry had not been stabbed, and she had been obliged to marry him. 'I am sorry,' he said softly.

She wiped away more tears. 'Bishop Giffard told me you are a skilled investigator, and he

118

was right – you have coaxed secrets from me. It is a pity we were not friends when I discovered my predicament – you would have devised a better idea.'

Geoffrey thought that even Bale could have done that. 'I only wanted the truth about Henry. I would like to know who killed him.'

'Sir Olivier thinks he took his own life.'

'Henry was too convinced of his own importance to harm himself. He was murdered without question, but there are too many suspects.'

'I am sure my father is on your list,' she said. 'But he is not that kind of man.'

Geoffrey was not so sure. 'Ralph is on my list, too: not only was he deprived of the woman he loved, he lost a prosperous marriage in the bargain.'

Her face grew even more pale. 'Not Ralph! He would never harm anyone.'

Geoffrey thought otherwise. Ralph had been ready to fight him the previous night, and only left when he thought he might have to do battle with Bale, too. And Geoffrey had not forgotten the man's brutality at the ford. Isabel was wrong about his character. He listed his other suspects.

'All Goodrich's servants hated Henry, while Corwenna knows how to bear a grudge. Seguin wants to please her, and might have presented her with a trophy – with the help of his brother.'

She nodded, eager to lead the discussion away from Ralph. 'Baderon had much to gain from Henry's death, too – he wants manors to give to knights like Seguin and Lambert, and Goodrich can be divided into neat parcels that will suit his needs.'

'*You* are on my list, too,' said Geoffrey. 'Your plan misfired and Henry was clamouring to marry you. You have as good a motive for killing him as anyone.'

Isabel grimaced. 'But I did not! And please do not tell anyone about Ralph and me. My father will be come enraged, and I do not want Ralph driven even further away.'

'I do not understand what drove him away in the first place. Surely, you explained what you had done? He should have been grateful you were ready to risk your reputation to save him.'

Tears sprouted again. 'He says that when a woman loves a man, he is the only one she should lie with. He is a man of principle. I wish with all my heart that I could undo what I did.'

Geoffrey changed the subject, hoping to distract her from her misery. 'Have you heard when the King is due?'

'Not for some days, although people are beginning to arrive in anticipation. Baderon would never normally stay with us, but he wants to be here when the King hunts. Indeed, we are so well endowed with powerful guests at the moment that we are obliged to provide a feast tonight with music, so I must leave you and ensure something suitable is performed. I cannot trust my father to do it: the kind of songs he favours will not be appropriate.'

Having met the belligerent Constable, Geoffrey was sure her concerns were justified.

Five

By mid-morning, Geoffrey thought Giffard should have completed his devotions, so he went in search of him. When the Bishop saw Geoffrey, he broke into a rare smile and jumped to his feet, grasping the knight by the shoulders.

Giffard was tall and lean, with a face made for the sober business of religion. Geoffrey had never heard him laugh, although he was occasionally ecstatic when he prayed. He wore a hair shirt under his habit, and was noted for his abstemiousness. He seldom drank, never overate and was reputed to have been celibate since joining the Church. But his unsmiling, dour demeanour hid a gentle heart, and Geoffrey respected his honesty and integrity.

'Why did you ask me to come?' Geoffrey asked.

Giffard was about to reply, but was interrupted by a discordant jangling. 'There is the bell for the next meal. I have not eaten since yesterday, because of my vigil. Come with me, and I shall tell you all.'

Geoffrey thought about taking a sword with him – Giffard was worse than hopeless in a fight – but something bumped against his leg, and he recalled Joan's little dagger. He pulled it from his hem and secreted it in his sleeve.

He followed Giffard into the hall. There were too many folk to be seated, and, with the exception of an honoured few at the dais, most ate standing, taking what they wanted from tables laden with meat and bread. The first person they met was Abbot Serlo, who watched in disbelief as Giffard took only a sliver of bread and a cup of water. While the Bishop nibbled, Serlo and Geoffrey shared a greasy chicken.

'Lord!' muttered Serlo suddenly, as people pushed into the hall. 'Here comes Baderon's fiery daughter and she looks peeved. I shall leave you.'

Before Geoffrey could reply, the abbot fled, taking the chicken with him. The knight braced himself for a dressing down when he saw Hilde stalking purposefully towards him, holding a limping Hugh by the hand. He decided to take the wind out of her sails before she could get started.

'I am sorry about the cart,' he said sincerely. 'I really did think it would be sent, but I should not have delegated the matter to others. I apologize. It was my fault.'

The angry lines around her face softened. 'You admit your error? You do not offer excuses?'

'There are none to give.'

She nodded. 'You are right, although I did not expect you to confess so honourably. Very well, I forgive you. I was obliged to carry my brother, but I am no weakling. I shall have to make sure he does not follow Eleanor again, if she will not look after him properly.'

122

'Why were you following her?' Geoffrey asked Hugh.

'Pretty lady,' said Hugh, with a vacant grin.

Geoffrey wondered how he knew, when all that could be seen of Eleanor were her eyes.

Hilde lowered her voice, so Hugh could not hear. 'She wears a veil because she is disfigured, so she is not pretty at all, but Hugh has always liked her. I used to wonder whether she had put him under a spell – a marriage to him would be very lucrative – but she gives the impression she would rather be left alone. I suppose the veil attracts him, although it unnerves others.'

'What was she doing at the Angel Springs?' asked Geoffrey.

'She would not say,' replied Hilde. 'But it is no place for Christian folk. The forest is not safe for Hugh – slow in the wits, but heir to a fortune – and I need to be mindful of him, since he cannot do it himself.'

Hugh began pulling at her hand, indicating he wanted something to eat, so Hilde gave Geoffrey a rather mannish bow and left. Then Serlo reappeared, dropping gnawed chicken bones into the rushes that covered the floor. He had managed to devour the bird in a remarkably short period of time, and Geoffrey made a mental note not to 'share' with him again.

Geoffrey was on his way to fetch more bread for Giffard, when a commotion erupted, as someone shouldered his way into the room. Geoffrey's heart sank when he recognized the stocky body and thick black hair. He glanced at Giffard, but the Bishop was already down on one knee, and was not looking to see how Geoffrey would react to this particular presence.

It was the King.

Geoffrey glanced towards the door, and wondered if he could leave before being spotted. He did not want King Henry to repeat his offer of employment, because it was becoming increasingly difficult to refuse. He was angry with himself for obeying Giffard's summons, and felt he should have guessed that the King would be involved, given the close relationship between bishop and monarch.

'God,' he groaned, as the King, having greeted the most important people, started to move in his direction with fitzNorman and Isabel at his heels. He saw Giffard's agonized glance, and supposed he had spoken louder than intended.

'Is Sir Geoffrey unwell?' Henry asked fitz-Norman. 'He seems to think I am God.'

'An understandable mistake, Sire,' said fitz-Norman with a sickly smile.

Henry regarded him coolly. 'Most folk imagine God to be taller,' he said, while fitz-Norman looked bemused, not sure whether the King was making a joke and he should laugh.

'I have never seen God,' fitzNorman managed eventually.

The King turned his attention to Geoffrey. 'So, why are you here? Have you come to offer me your services at last?'

Geoffrey raised a hand to rub his chin, trying to think of an answer without landing himself in trouble. To say yes would mean doing the King's dirty work, while to say no would smack of rebellion. Henry reached forward and grabbed his wrist, revealing the knife tucked into his sleeve. He showed it to fitzNorman.

'Your guest does not feel safe in your home.'

'His brother was murdered, Sire,' said Isabel reasonably. 'He probably feels unsafe everywhere.'

'Perhaps,' said the King, gazing at the assembly. 'However, no one will harm Sir Geoffrey. I have plans for him, so he is under my protection. If he is harmed, you will answer to me. Am I clear?'

There was a muted murmur of assent, and Geoffrey supposed that he was now safe from open attack, although still at risk from covert ones. He wondered what Henry's 'plans' entailed, and glared at Giffard – the Bishop knew he would avoid an invitation to meet the King, but would respond to a summons from a friend. It was a low trick, and Geoffrey was disappointed in him. Giffard, however, seemed as surprised by the King's early arrival as everyone else.

'We were not expecting you until next week, Sire,' he said.

'My business at Hereford was concluded sooner than anticipated,' said Henry. He clapped his hands, making his courtiers jump. 'But you must all leave us. I want a word with Sir Geoffrey, and now is as good a time as any. Sit.'

Geoffrey had no choice but to obey, so he perched in a window seat. The King watched the courtiers flow away, and only spoke when they had left.

'Why are you here?' he asked, pacing restlessly. 'Did you want to see me?'

'No, Sire,' said Geoffrey, wincing when it sounded a little too fervent. His tone did not escape Henry, whose dark brows drew together in a frown.

'What, then? Have you come to see which of the region's heiresses you will have? Is there one you like in particular? I can help you. A word from me goes a long way.'

'No, Sire,' said Geoffrey again. He rubbed his head. It was the wrong answer. 'Yes, Sire.'

Henry regarded him thoughtfully. 'You are not in your right wits today. But which of these women do you want? Isabel is pretty, and a match with fitzNorman is good. Margaret is too old, so do not take her. Hilde will be lucrative, because her brother is a half-wit and Baderon will leave his estates in her care. Do not bother with the Welsh. And do not bother with Bicanofre, either. They may be keen for the match, but I am not.'

'Why?' asked Geoffrey, surprised Henry should be so well informed about such petty affairs.

'Because they are poor,' said Henry impatiently. 'Why do you think, man? You can do better, and marriage is important. Your only real choices are Isabel or Hilde. So, make your decision, and I shall ensure you have the one you want.'

'Very well, then,' said Geoffrey with a sigh.

Henry frowned, although there was humour in his eyes. 'The proper response is to thank me with appropriate gratitude, not assume a long-suffering expression. Most men would be honoured to have their monarch's friendship.'

'Yes, Sire.'

'Now, since I have just offered to help *you*, there is something you can do for me. It concerns your old squire, Durand – the one you so obligingly released from your service so he could work for me, and whom you so strongly recommended.'

Geoffrey regarded Henry in astonishment. He had not recommended Durand – Durand had been dismissed under a cloud, and had not dared ask for a testimonial. And although Geoffrey did not bear grudges, and had allowed Durand to repair the rift with friendly letters, he would never encourage anyone to hire him – Durand was too ambitious and selfish, and the concept of loyalty was anathema to him.

'I did not...' He hesitated. He did not want to be responsible for Durand's downfall by saying the man had probably written the recommendation himself. 'Durand has remarkable abilities,' he said instead. Henry waited, obviously expecting more, but since Geoffrey was not sure what the King was about to say of Durand's recent activities – and would not be surprised to learn they were self-serving or dishonourable – it seemed wise to say as little as possible.

'He does have remarkable abilities,' agreed Henry, sitting next to Geoffrey. 'His rise has been meteoric, and I am impressed by his talents. He will be invaluable in the future.'

'Good,' said Geoffrey.

'But there is a problem,' Henry went on, standing and pacing again. 'Others resent his success, and I do not want to lose him to a dagger in the back.'

'Is that why you sent him to Abbot Serlo?' asked Geoffrey. 'For safety? I thought it was because he was investigating taxes.'

'There *are* tax irregularities in this region, which he is cleverly unravelling. But it was also a way to keep him out of harm's way until I could find other posts for these rivals – which I must do carefully. An angry agent is a dangerous thing, and I need time to organize matters properly. It is a pity Durand is not more agreeable. He has a sharp tongue and does not care who he wounds.'

'He *can* be testy,' agreed Geoffrey.

'He can be downright rude,' countered Henry. 'But here is my problem: I do not want him at Westminster until I have relocated his rivals, but I do not want to leave him with Serlo, lest he decides to become a monk. I need somewhere he will be safe, with someone who is patient with his abrasive character.'

'I have a new squire,' said Geoffrey quickly, sensing what was coming next.

'Yes, I have seen him. Your taste in servants continues to astound me, Geoffrey. But this is a nuisance. I cannot leave Durand with fitz-Norman, because they would argue and someone would die. And I cannot leave him with Baderon, because he is ineffectual and a poor protector.'

'He would be safe with Giffard, Sire,' suggested Geoffrey. 'He has loyal bodyguards, and his hair shirt, poor diet and life of chastity will do more to persuade Durand against a monastic career than anything else would.'

Henry rubbed his hands together, pleased. 'I should have thought of this myself. It is an excellent solution. I will inform them of the good news at once – I am sure they will be delighted.'

Geoffrey was sure they would not. Giffard would be appalled to have such a flagrant libertine in his household, while Durand would be horrified to be trapped with the dour, ascetic bishop. He sincerely hoped Henry would not tell them whose idea it had been.

'But I want Durand to complete his work here first,' said Henry. 'You can watch him for a week or two, then escort him to Giffard when he has finished.' He stood, business completed. 'It is time I went hunting. You are dismissed – unless you would like to accompany me?'

'My horse is lame, Sire,' lied Geoffrey.

Geoffrey went to his bedchamber the moment Henry released him, and began to don his armour, intending to leave immediately. There was no need to linger and risk being asked for further favours. Giffard followed him from the hall, and watched him struggle into mail and surcoat.

'The reason I summoned you had nothing to do with the King,' he said. 'He came here to hunt, and your meeting was pure chance. Do not think he engineered this encounter – he did not.'

'*He* probably did not,' said Geoffrey, letting the unspoken accusation hang in the air.

Giffard winced. 'I did not expect him until next week, which is why I thought it would be safe to ask you to meet me. I know you prefer to be away from court and its machinations.'

'The King,' corrected Geoffrey, not caring that he was speaking imprudently. 'I prefer to be away from the *King* and *his* machinations.'

'There is no need to blare your treasonous feelings for all to hear – and I already know what you think. But hear me out. I accompanied the King when he came this way because I need your help.'

Geoffrey was sceptical. 'Henry told you to say that.'

Giffard sighed irritably. 'He did *not*. He likes you, even though you verge on insulting him every time you meet. Could you not at least have pretended to be pleased to see him?'

'He took me by surprise.'

Giffard went to stare out of the window. 'I need your help, Geoffrey, and I swear, by all that is holy, the King has nothing to do with it. It is personal ... I am at the edge of an abyss...'

Geoffrey did not like the sound of that at all. 'What is wrong?'

Giffard beckoned him to the window, throwing wide the shutters. 'You see that lady there?'

He pointed down to the yard below, to a dark-eyed woman, whose laugh revealed a mouth full of small white teeth. She was exquisitely beautiful, with an athletically curved body. She fluttered her eyelashes at fitzNorman, and the old warrior preened. She was confident of her beauty, and her laughter and the way she flirted said she was a woman who liked fun.

'Her name is Agnes Giffard,' said the Bishop softly.

'*Giffard*?' asked Geoffrey, startled. 'She is your wife?'

Giffard shot him a withering glance. 'That is a remarkably stupid question! How can I be married? I am in holy orders.'

Holy orders meant little where powerful prelates were concerned, as Giffard knew perfectly well, and the question was far from stupid. Sensing the Bishop's temper derived from anxiety, Geoffrey forced himself to be patient. 'Is she your sister? She does not look like you; she is attractive.'

Giffard raised his eyebrows. 'Are you insulting *me*, now the King is not here to be a receptacle for your barbed tongue?'

'She smiles more than you do,' hedged Geoffrey, who had not meant to offend.

Giffard's face was glum. 'I find little to amuse me in this world. It is brutal, cunning and greedy. I wish I were not Bishop of Winchester. I am not even consecrated, did you know that? I am, in fact, only a deacon.' His voice was uncharacteristically bitter.

Geoffrey was confused. 'But you were invested with your pastoral staff and ring by the Archbishop of Canterbury himself. You said it was the most satisfying day of your life.'

'Being invested is not the same as being consecrated,' snapped Giffard. 'I am able to

131

perform my episcopal duties, but have not been properly blessed in my office by *God*.'

Geoffrey shrugged. 'Ask Henry to arrange it.'

'The problem is Archbishop Anselm, who is in a dispute with the King over who should pay homage to whom. Anselm will not consecrate anyone until the issue is resolved. Henry has asked the Archbishop of York to do it, but York is inferior to Canterbury.'

Geoffrey thought it sounded like a lot of fuss. Giffard was a powerful man and had the King's favour, so consecration was a formality. 'I am sure you will be consecrated soon,' he said. 'Archbishops and kings are always fighting over something, but these rows do not go on forever.'

Giffard took a deep breath, and Geoffrey saw that his hands were shaking.

'Tell me about your sister,' Geoffrey suggested, in order to take his mind off the problem. It did not work. Giffard's frown became deeper; he had never seen the man so unhappy.

'Agnes is not my sister. She is – was – my brother's wife. Walter was the Earl of Buckingham, and he died last summer, when you and I were chasing rebels in the north. You see that boy standing near her? That is their son, also called Walter.'

'The one with the yellow hat?' asked Geoffrey, recognizing the would-be Italian speaker.

'He is a cockerel and, as the new Earl of Buckingham, he has funds to indulge himself. I have tried to teach him restraint, but with a mother like Agnes, it was inevitable that he should transpire to be all fluff and no substance.'

'You do not like him, then?'

'I think *he* may have encouraged Agnes to ... do what she did.'

'And what was that?' asked Geoffrey patiently.

Giffard took a shuddering breath. 'I summoned them from Normandy as soon as I heard about Sibylla. But it will not be long before people realize that Agnes' husband died last July and Sibylla died less than a month ago.'

Geoffrey had no idea what he was talking about. 'Who is Sibylla?'

'Sibylla de Conversano. The Duchess.' Giffard turned an anguished face to Geoffrey. 'I fear she was poisoned.'

Geoffrey was bemused by Giffard's confidences. 'The Duke of Normandy's wife? But I heard she died from complications following childbirth.'

'I have tried to crush the gossip,' said Giffard. 'But it is common knowledge that Agnes dallied with the Duke during Sibylla's confinement.'

'You think Agnes murdered Sibylla?' asked Geoffrey, trying to follow what Giffard was saying. 'So she could continue to frolic with the Duke?'

'Worse. I think she killed Sibylla – and perhaps my brother, her husband, too – so she could *marry* the Duke, and rule Normandy with him.'

'Then you thwarted her,' said Geoffrey. 'Agnes is here, and the Duke is in Normandy.'

'That is not the point,' snapped Giffard. 'I fear evil deeds, and Sibylla was a beautiful and intelligent lady. Normandy is a poorer place without

133

her careful hand on the Duke's shoulder and, if someone did kill her, then a great wrong has been perpetrated.'

'Perhaps,' said Geoffrey. 'But it is only a matter of time before our King – whom *you* serve – invades Normandy. He will be delighted that the Duke no longer has Sibylla at his side.'

'But it is *murder*!' whispered Giffard, turning haunted eyes on Geoffrey. 'I knew Sibylla, and she was remarkable. I see her in my dreams, and hear her calling to me for vengeance. I need to know the truth: did Agnes and her brat poison Sibylla, or was her death due to tragic illness?'

'You may not like what you find,' warned Geoffrey. 'And what if they *did* kill her? Will you tell Henry? He admires initiative, and might employ them to do it again.'

Giffard was aghast. 'How can you say such things?'

'I am being practical. You want to be told that Agnes and Walter are innocent. But you must accept the possibility that you will learn otherwise. And you should consider what you would do with such knowledge. If you think your dreams are haunted by Sibylla's cries for vengeance now, imagine what they will be like if you discover your family *is* responsible.'

'So, what should I do?' Giffard's face was anguished.

'Marry Agnes to a man who will keep her in a remote manor. Or place her in a convent. You must know some trustworthy abbesses. But we are assuming she is guilty. What evidence is there?'

'None,' admitted Giffard. 'Just the fact that she dallied with the Duke when Sibylla was in confinement, and that Sibylla was conveniently dead a few days before that confinement was due to end. And my brother's death was very timely, too. He died the very week that this lustful liaison between the Duke and Agnes began.'

'That is nothing but a set of coincidences – and there is certainly nothing to implicate Walter.'

'You think I should ignore that my brother might have been murdered by his wife and son?' cried Giffard. 'Ignore that, buoyed by their success, they then struck at Sibylla? And ignore that their selfish actions have caused immeasurable damage to Normandy, because its one sane voice is stilled forever?'

Geoffrey accepted his point, but did not think much could be done to rectify such wrongs. 'I do not see what else you can do.'

Giffard turned on Geoffrey, and the knight saw anger in his eyes. He had never seen the prelate so disturbed. '*Your* brother was killed. Will *you* look the other way and pretend it did not happen?'

'No,' admitted Geoffrey.

'Nor I. I want the truth, Geoffrey, and I want *you* to find it.'

Geoffrey did not see how he could oblige, and attempted to convey this to Giffard. Duchess Sibylla had died in Normandy, and he could hardly travel there and start asking questions in the Duke's household.

'Then you must make do with who is here,'

argued Giffard. 'Agnes and Walter did not travel alone – a number of people were in Normandy when Sibylla died, and many of them have come to meet the King. That is how I was able to order Agnes and Walter home without arousing suspicion.'

'Who?'

'Eleanor de Bicanofre, for one. She went to be inspected by a Normandy knight as a possible bride, but she is back, so the man obviously did not take her. Her brother Ralph accompanied her. Then there was Abbot Serlo, who had business in Rouen. Also Baderon and his children: Hilde and Hugh. And fitzNorman and his sister Margaret.'

Geoffrey's head was spinning. 'All these people went to Normandy?'

'Will you help me?' asked Giffard desperately. 'If you do not, I shall have to do it myself, but I do not know how.'

'I cannot – I have no authority to interrogate these people. Besides, I must investigate my own brother's death, and I cannot ask too many questions. Some of the people you mentioned are on my list of suspects for *his* death, too.'

'All I want to know is whether *Walter* had a hand in Sibylla's death,' said Giffard. 'I believe Agnes is guilty, but I need to know about *him*. He will come of age soon and, although Earl of Buckingham is not the richest title, he may use it to become powerful. I do not want him to be another Bellême.'

'He will not,' said Geoffrey, not believing Walter to have the strength of personality to become a despot.

'I *must* know,' insisted Giffard, almost tearful. 'How can I be consecrated when my conscience is troubled by such dark family affairs?'

The two men stared at the throng in the yard below. Agnes moved away from fitzNorman and smiled at Baderon, who bowed. Walter followed her closely, watching with a face Geoffrey found difficult to read. *Had* he encouraged Agnes to poison the Duchess? Geoffrey thought about the boy's clumsy Italian and confident swagger. He was certainly imbued with a sense of his own importance, and might well believe himself a cunning manipulator.

'I did not sleep last night,' said Giffard eventually. 'I should rest, or I might doze off during an audience with the King. We shall talk again this evening.'

While Giffard slept, Geoffrey paced. He longed to be out riding, but was loath to quit the room, as he was almost certain to meet someone who wanted to fight him, marry him or demand a favour. He sent Bale for ale, and the squire returned with Isabel in tow. She sat in the window and talked about her father in terms that did not coincide with Geoffrey's impressions.

'You do not believe me.' She was whispering, so as not to disturb the dozing Bishop. 'I can tell.'

'I do not know him well enough to say,' he replied honestly. 'I am sure he has his virtues.'

'He has not forced me into a marriage that would make me unhappy. Nor Margaret. She is a wealthy widow, and it would be advantageous to use her, but he stays his hand. *You* should consider her, though – she is better than the others on offer. Hilde would bully you, Douce is stupid, Corwenna would flay you with her tongue and Eleanor ... well, you know about Eleanor.'

'She is poor,' said Geoffrey.

'Well, there is that, but I was thinking about her other drawbacks.' Isabel gave a deep, sad sigh. 'If Ralph continues to refuse me, I shall ask Abbot Serlo to make me a nun.'

'Give yourself time before you take such a drastic step,' advised Geoffrey, thinking Ralph was a fool to be put off such a dignified and generous bride. 'Convents are not pleasant for those there for the wrong reasons.'

They both looked up as Margaret tapped on the door. 'Your father wants you, Isabel,' she murmured. 'Do not linger or he will jump to the wrong conclusion.'

Geoffrey wondered what conclusion that might be. That Isabel had made her choice regarding husbands, and it was not Ralph? That Geoffrey had taken over where Henry had left off, and was having another go at impregnating a fitzNorman? Obediently, Isabel slipped away, leaving Geoffrey with Margaret.

'I am sorry I did not warn you that the King had arrived,' Margaret whispered. 'My first thought when I saw him was that you would want to escape, but there was no time. He was not expected so soon, and his arrival threw everyone into confusion. He asked who was here, and your name was mentioned before I could tell my brother to leave it out.'

'You would have misled the King on my account?'

She smiled. 'You are transpiring to be a good friend – you are gentle with Isabel, for a start. I understand she told you about her misguided attempt to save Ralph.'

'It is a pity you were not here to stop her,' remarked Geoffrey.

Margaret agreed. 'I was appalled when she told me. The pity is that it was all for nothing: she lost the child anyway.'

They were silent for a while, with only Giffard's deep breathing accompanying their thoughts.

'Your bishop sleeps well,' remarked Margaret.

'He has a clear conscience. He spent last night in prayer.'

'If only his family were like him. His nephew is a stupid peacock who thinks only of fine clothes, while his sister-in-law seems determined to bed every man she meets.'

'You speak very bluntly.' Geoffrey was interested in Margaret's astute insights. 'I understand she is a recent widow.'

'Last July. Then she set her sights on the Duke, and she was not pleased to be dragged away by Bishop Giffard's summons.'

'I thought the Duke was in love with Sibylla. Why would he be interested in Agnes?'

'Agnes has a way that makes men helpless. She smiles and they flock to carry out her every whim. I am fond of the Duke, but he is like wet clay in her hands.'

'I imagine she is looking for another husband, now that her first is dead,' probed Geoffrey. 'Would the Duke be interested?'

Margaret gave a mirthless laugh. 'He will never marry *her*, no matter how able she is in the adulterer's bed. He does not have the time, for a start, what with all his wars and troubles.'

'You may know that,' said Geoffrey. 'But does she?'

Margaret regarded him with surprise. 'I did not think you were the kind of man to gossip.'

'I am not,' said Geoffrey. He glanced at Giffard, resenting being obliged to be. 'Not usually.'

'I suppose Agnes *might* make you a suitable wife,' said Margaret, misunderstanding him. 'She is beautiful, although you would be hard-pressed to keep a clean marriage bed. Perhaps she *is* looking for a husband. She is not stupid, and perhaps she *has* realized the Duke will never have her. There is, after all, a tale that says he suspects Agnes of sending Sibylla to an early grave.'

Geoffrey looked out the window. 'Do you think Sibylla was poisoned? And Agnes is the culprit?'

'There have been whispers to that effect. However, while I am unfamiliar with poisons, there was no retching or violent sickness during her demise. Sibylla slipped quietly away, in view of a roomful of people.'

'Did Agnes give the Duchess anything to eat or drink?'

'Just one thing,' said Margaret. 'A dish of dried yellow plums – about a week before she died.'

Geoffrey wandered into the yard, eventually leaning over a gate to stare at the pigs, while thinking about the Duchess and wondering how Giffard expected him to assess whether Agnes and Walter were responsible when the crime – if there was a crime – had happened so far away. He looked up as someone came towards him. It was Baderon.

'This is hardly a conducive spot for repose,' said the Lord of Monmouth, eyeing the pigs in distaste. 'Most men would be watching horses – or, if they want to attract female company, new-born lambs. But perhaps that is why you chose pigs: you want solitude?'

'I did not think about it,' replied Geoffrey.

'I will come to the point,' said Baderon, standing closer and lowering his voice. 'Goodrich and its estates are small, but they command the ford over the Wye. You do not need me to tell you that the alliance your family will forge when you marry is important to the security of the area.'

'No,' replied Geoffrey. 'I do not need you to tell me that.'

Baderon pursed his lips. 'The King wants peace. Therefore, I must want it, too, and I am willing to offer Hilde and a large dowry to secure it. She is a fine woman and will bear strong sons. I find haggling distasteful – as must you – but we have no choice. Your brother was prepared to listen.'

'Was he?' asked Geoffrey. 'I thought he wanted Isabel.'

Baderon nodded. 'But he and I had other irons in the fire.'

Geoffrey was intrigued. 'What irons?'

But Baderon was not to be drawn. 'They are irrelevant now. Will you consider my offer?'

'Will Hilde?'

'She is a practical woman.'

'Do you have land in Normandy?' asked Geoffrey, wanting to bring the subject around to Giffard's problem, and to ask Baderon what he knew about Agnes and the Duchess.

Baderon scratched his head. 'Well, there is a manor near Rouen you could have, I suppose, but I am not sure it would be worth your trouble. Normandy is unsettled, and you would find yourself obliged to be there more than it warrants.'

Geoffrey laughed, amused that his attempt to change the subject had led Baderon to think he was angling for a better bargain. 'I was not asking for land – I barely know how to manage what I have. I wondered whether you were in Normandy when the Duchess died.'

Baderon was transparently relieved that Geoffrey's enquiry was only about distant politics. 'It was a dreadful day when Sibylla passed away. She was sensible and courageous.'

'How did she die?' asked Geoffrey. 'I heard it was a sickness following the birth of her son.'

'Her physicians say so, but there is a rumour she was poisoned. Yet such tales always circulate when a good person dies young.'

'I have heard the Duke had a mistress,' said Geoffrey, heartily cursing Giffard for making him assume the role of gossip. 'Could *she* have harmed Sibylla?'

'Agnes?' asked Baderon, startled. 'I would not think so. She was all care and concern when the Duchess took a turn for the worse. She even ordered dried plums, at great expense, to tempt Sibylla's appetite and make her stronger. I doubt Agnes would have harmed Sibylla. But we are moving away from my original question: will you consider my offer of Hilde?'

'I will mention it to Joan,' hedged Geoffrey.

Baderon smiled and patted his shoulder. 'That is all I ask.'

He moved away, leaving Geoffrey contemplating, while absently staring at the pigs. Margaret thought the dried plums were sinister, while Baderon proffered an innocent interpretation. When he glanced away from his porcine companions, he saw Eleanor emerging from the kitchen, her veil and gloves in place. She carried a pot.

'How are you?' she asked. 'Did you manage to sleep after I removed those splinters?'

He nodded. 'And you?'

'I rest during the day, when I have the room to myself. Can I test this ointment on you? I need to know whether you can detect a warming sensation, or whether it needs to be stronger. As I said last night, I am not good with medicines. My talents lie in other directions.'

'What is it?' he asked suspiciously.

'Nothing that will do you any harm. Hold out

143

your arm.'

Geoffrey tucked both hands in his surcoat. 'My mother told me never to accept potions from strange women.'

'You think I am strange, do you?' Eleanor laughed. 'Well, perhaps you are right: everyone else seems to think so, too. However, I devised this salve for the pigs. There is something wrong with them, and I do not like seeing animals suffer.'

'Then test it on them.'

'Yes,' she said caustically. 'But they will not tell me whether they feel a tingling sensation that means it is working, will they?'

'Try it on yourself. Surely, you are the best one to judge its potency?'

'I have an aversion to mandrake root. It makes my skin blister.'

He regarded her uneasily. *'Mandrake root?* I thought that was poisonous.'

'Only when applied improperly. That is why I use so little, and why I need a *person* to tell me if there is warmth. I may have been too careful, and the pigs will not have any benefit.'

'A simple wash would do them more good than potions. Or a clean sty.'

He left Eleanor looking for another victim, and was crossing the crowded hall when he met Durand. The clerk was wearing yet another outfit, this one a glorious deep red, cut so closely that it looked to be part of his skin. Geoffrey would never have worn such a revealing costume, especially if he had Durand's paunch.

'The King is here,' said Durand, dancing a jig

that had Seguin and Lambert gaping in astonishment. 'My rescue is at hand. You cannot imagine how I yearn to be back in Westminster.'

Geoffrey was grateful he would not be the one to break the news of the sojourn with Giffard, and sincerely hoped Henry would not disclose the idea's origin. 'Have you considered Normandy? Its turbulence gives it much potential for a man who enjoys intrigue.'

Durand nodded. 'I have, but it is safer here.' He leant close to Geoffrey, who resisted the urge to move away when he was treated to a waft of flower water. 'I hear tales of terrible happenings. And some of them include women you have been talking to.'

'Isabel?' asked Geoffrey. 'Or do you mean Margaret?'

'Neither,' said Durand dismissively. 'I was referring to *Eleanor*. She has a way with poisons, and there is a suggestion that the Duchess died by foul means. What do you conclude from that?'

'That you should ask yourself why Eleanor would want to murder Sibylla before spreading nasty stories about her,' said Geoffrey tartly. 'She has no reason to—'

'She is friends with Walter Giffard,' interrupted Durand. 'And Walter's mother was the Duke's mistress. Of course, Eleanor helped him with a potion or two.'

He gave a smirk and minced away, leaving Geoffrey staring. *Had* Eleanor supplied poison to Walter, who had encouraged his mother to use it? Or was it Agnes who had asked Walter to

145

procure the poison?

'You were in the right place earlier,' came an unpleasant voice at his side. Geoffrey jumped; so deep in his thoughts, he had not heard Corwenna approach. Seguin and Lambert were behind her. 'Were you attracted to kindred spirits?'

'Pigs,' said Seguin, in case Geoffrey had not understood. 'You were looking at the pigs.'

'Enjoy them while you can,' said Corwenna. The tone of her voice implied it was a threat.

It was not one Geoffrey understood. 'Why? Are you planning to steal them when you go home?'

She glowered at him, and answered in Welsh. 'Because your days are numbered. Soon my people will pit themselves against England.'

Geoffrey answered in the same tongue. 'Baderon is trying to promote peace. That is what the King wants – and what his knights should want, too.'

She shrugged. 'What the King wants is unimportant. We are interested in our own welfare. You will soon be crushed by a great enemy – we have not forgotten last summer.'

'*Last summer*?' asked Geoffrey, bewildered. 'You mean when my brother was killed?'

'Your brother is nothing,' spat Corwenna. 'Last summer we were ready to fight for Bellême, but Prince Iorwerth changed sides and we went home empty-handed. Since then, the English have chipped away at our lands, taking a manor here, a church there. Well, we have had enough, and will rise against you. Your grain and cattle will be ours, and your lands will burn.'

Geoffrey was appalled at the prospect of a war along the Marches, and hoped Corwenna was exaggerating. But he had the feeling she was not. 'Fighting will damage all our peoples, and—'

'What is he saying?' demanded Seguin, struggling to understand.

'She is telling me that Baderon's alliances will not work in the way he hopes,' said Geoffrey. He knew Corwenna had spoken Welsh because she did not want her future husband to know she was plotting insurrection. 'She claims his new "friends" will unite to attack England.'

'I did not,' said Corwenna sharply in Norman-French, and Geoffrey could see that they believed her. 'I said he should leave the region before someone runs him through.'

'Like someone did his brother,' said Lambert.

'Geoffrey did that himself,' sneered Seguin. 'To get his hands on Goodrich. I hear the stable where Henry died is full of dead birds, put there by his servants to make sure he does not murder them, too.'

'When will this invasion take place?' Geoffrey asked Corwenna. 'And what will Baderon get out of it? I am sure *he* does not want to raid Goodrich for grain and cattle.'

'We will never join Wales to attack England,' said Seguin, laughing at the notion. 'Baderon may be foolish, but he is not entirely stupid.'

They walked away, although not before Geoffrey saw the frown that crossed Lambert's face. The discussion had sparked something in his mind, and he was not ready to laugh it off like his brother. Geoffrey watched them go uneasily. Would the Welsh princes use the alliances Baderon had forged for their own ends? Until now, everyone had assumed the alliance would work in England's favour, but there was nothing to say that the Welsh would not capitalize on the situation.

Six

The next morning Geoffrey woke early following a restless night. He attended matins in the church of Dene, but found it difficult to concentrate. He was not the only one whose mind was elsewhere.

'You are not listening to me,' Giffard hissed, uncharacteristically speaking during the sacred office. 'I *asked* whether you have thought any more about Agnes and Sibylla.'

'I cannot help you.' Geoffrey saw hope fade from the Bishop's eyes. 'Not because I do not want to, but because I do not see how it can be done. If we were in Normandy, it might be different, but we are talking about something that happened far away. For all you know, the Duchess might have had many enemies – perhaps even the Duke himself.'

'No,' said Giffard firmly. 'He loved Sibylla.

The only person who wanted her gone was Agnes. I accept *her* guilt. All I want to know is whether Walter helped.'

'Ask him,' suggested Geoffrey. 'You are his uncle.'

Giffard grimaced. 'I tried, but he told me to ... well, let us say he was not polite. I need someone with your skills to find the truth.'

The Bishop continued his appeal at breakfast in the hall. The King was there, and all was fuss and flurry as he and his courtiers prepared for a day of hunting. He wanted Giffard and Geoffrey to come, but the Bishop was alarmed by the prospect of slaughter, so Henry asked him to look at some documents from the Archbishop of Canterbury instead.

As a knight, Geoffrey could hardly plead an aversion to killing, and had no choice but to accompany the royal party. He was about to mount up when he heard screams from a nearby storeroom. It was Hugh. When Geoffrey arrived, he found several others already there, including Seguin and Lambert.

'It is nothing,' said one of the King's retinue as he pushed his way out. 'Baderon's half-wit son has himself in a bother over a rat.'

Geoffrey entered the room to see Hugh on a table, while an equally terrified rodent quivered in a corner. The rat could not escape without passing Hugh, and Hugh was going nowhere as long as the rat was there. Cruelly, Seguin feinted towards the animal, which scurried in alarm and caused Hugh to begin another bout of anguished shrieks. Several onlookers laughed uproariously.

Pleased by their response, Seguin made as if to do it again, but Geoffrey grabbed his arm.

'Stop,' he said quietly. 'This is not kind.'

'To the imbecile or the rat?' quipped Seguin, shaking him off and making Lambert guffaw.

Seguin took another step towards the rat, which bared its teeth, and Geoffrey saw tears of terror on Hugh's face. Geoffrey shoved Seguin roughly towards the door.

'Enough,' he said sharply.

Seguin gaped in astonishment and his hand went to his sword. 'Do you dare tell me—'

'Don't,' said Lambert, stepping between them. 'Brawling will incur the displeasure of the King.'

'You will certainly incur his displeasure if you follow Corwenna,' said Geoffrey. 'He will not be pleased if Baderon and his Welsh allies invade England.'

'We will not invade *England*,' said Lambert. 'But we may attack Goodrich. We will tell His Majesty it was full of traitors. As long as the "invasion" goes no further, he will not risk a war just because *your* estates have been sacked.'

He dragged his brother away, leaving Geoffrey with Hugh and the rat.

'Take my hand, Hugh,' Geoffrey said. 'We are going outside.'

'No!' wept Hugh, putting his fingers over his eyes. 'It will bite.'

'It will not,' said Geoffrey. 'Look, I have my sword. Take my hand, and then we will find your sister.'

Hugh shoved plump fingers towards Geoffrey,

who helped him off the table. As soon as he moved, the rat aimed for the slop drain and its freedom. Hugh became calmer when it had gone.

'That was kindly done,' said Hilde from the door. 'Hugh is frightened of rats. I am none too keen on them myself, and was wondering how I was going to extricate him.'

Surprised there was something that could unsettle her, Geoffrey handed Hugh into her care and started towards his horse. Hilde caught his sleeve.

'Seguin and Lambert are strong, aggressive and determined to make their fortunes. I do not like them, but they are the kind of men we need on our side if we are to have peace. Do not make enemies of them, Geoffrey. Look what happened to your brother when *he* did so.'

Geoffrey regarded her uncertainly. 'What are you saying? That *they* killed him?'

She met his eyes. 'I have heard rumours to that effect, although I have no proof. Nor have I heard them talking about it, as I might, had they been responsible – Seguin is boastful and revels in such tales. But your brother was murdered, and I would not like to see you go the same way.'

'Your father would. Then he could take Goodrich for himself, which would be far better than an alliance by marriage.'

'My father is not a murderer. He wants peace.'

'Does he?' asked Geoffrey.

'I heard Margaret's comments when you thought

I was sleeping yesterday,' Giffard said that evening, as he sat with Geoffrey in their chamber. The Bishop drained his goblet and held it out for Bale to fill. Bale raised his eyebrows, but said nothing as he obliged the thirsty prelate for the fifth or sixth time in a short period. 'She *also* believes Agnes killed Sibylla. I am not alone in my suspicions.'

Giffard's face was flushed as he emptied his cup and thrust it out for yet more, and Geoffrey hoped that he was not one of those drunks who talked gloomily all night, because he wanted to sleep. Meanwhile, he drank some honeyed milk that Isabel had provided. She said it was her own concoction, and he did not want to offend her by tipping it out of the window. He usually avoided milk, on the grounds that it was for children, but Giffard's wine had a strong, salty flavour, underlain with something unpleasant. The milk tasted much better.

'Margaret was not a regular figure at the Duke's court,' Giffard went on. 'So, if *she* suspects Agnes, others will do likewise.'

'Probably,' agreed Geoffrey, recalling that Durand had done just that.

Giffard gagged slightly. 'Wine really is a nasty substance. I do not know why people like it.'

'You will be ill tomorrow, if you drink it like water,' warned Geoffrey, wondering what was making the normally abstemious bishop guzzle the stuff.

Giffard ignored him and took a healthy gulp. 'It will not be long before *everyone* knows my family killed the most beloved woman in

Christendom. I had already asked Margaret about Agnes, and she told me *nothing*. You had more from her in a few moments than I managed to prise from her in a week. Where is that damned squire? I want more wine.'

'Have some milk,' suggested Geoffrey, indicating with a nod that Bale was to remain in the shadows. Giffard had had enough for one night. 'It tastes like sweet vomit.'

'Why would I imbibe sweet vomit?'

'As penance,' said Geoffrey, 'for forcing a poor knight to do your dirty work.'

Giffard gave a startled smile. 'You will do it? You will help me?'

'I will try,' said Geoffrey unhappily. 'You would probably do the same for me.'

'I would not,' declared Giffard drunkenly. 'I am not qualified, and would render matters worse. But I shall not forget your kindness.' Tears formed in his eyes.

'Tell me about Agnes and Walter,' Geoffrey said hastily, knowing Giffard would be mortified the next morning if he lost control of his emotions. 'She does not look old enough to be his mother.'

'A combination of marrying young and potions,' said Giffard, pronouncing the last word with considerable disapproval. 'She looks better from a distance than close up, which is why she likes to come out at night, I suppose. It is dark and men are full of ale – less inclined to be critical.'

'You sound like some old abbess, jealous of her younger nuns,' said Geoffrey, watching Giffard lurch to his feet and fetch the wine himself. He was thoughtful. 'Her knowledge of substances that keep her young may also extend to less benign purposes.'

'What do you mean?' asked Giffard, flopping into his chair so hard that the contents of the cup spilt down his habit. When he tried to drink, he was puzzled to find the cup empty.

'I mean that she may know enough about poisons on her own, so had no need to recruit Eleanor,' elaborated Geoffrey, wondering whether he should postpone the talk until Giffard was not so inebriated. 'What else can you tell me?'

'Her marriage to my brother was not happy.' Geoffrey leant forward, obliged to concentrate on the Bishop's slurred words in order to decipher them. 'They fought constantly, and I am sure her affair with the Duke was by no means her first. She is greedy and very ambitious. You will see that the moment you speak to her – if she does not drag you into her bed first. Damned whore!'

'Easy,' said Geoffrey, seeing a drunkard's rage in Giffard's eyes. 'And what about Walter?'

'Ambitious and avaricious, like his mother. He was delighted when his father died, because he became Earl of Buckingham.'

'It is odd that so many people in Normandy when Sibylla died are now in Dene.'

Giffard hiccuped, and for a moment he looked as if he might be sick. Geoffrey prepared to dive out of the way.

'Not really. Many barons with English manors

own land in Normandy, and they travel together for safety. The roads in Normandy are very dangerous, with Bellême on the rampage. He is an evil bastard, burning villages, destroying crops, killing men who look at him the wrong way. Now Sibylla is not there, his power will increase. Our King is delighted, of course. A weak Normandy works in his favour: its barons will welcome him when he finally invades.'

Geoffrey was shocked at Giffard's bluntness. He knew it would not be long before King Henry turned greedy eyes on Normandy, but he had not expected to hear it from his loyal Bishop. 'You are drunk. You will be sorry for saying these things tomorrow.'

Giffard tried to stand, but fell back in his chair. 'You are right. I should let you sleep, before I say anything else – although I trust you not to repeat my ramblings to the King. I shall pull my chair across the door, so any nocturnal invaders will have to pass me before they reach you.'

'You will protect me, will you?' Geoffrey was amused.

Giffard nodded. 'A drunk is a terrible object to surmount. He flops in your way, is heavy and almost impossible to steer where you want him to go, and when you think you have him under control, he is sick over you.'

Geoffrey laughed. He had only previously seen Giffard drink water or weak ale, but supposed the Bishop might partake of powerful wines when unhappy. 'Are you speaking from experience?'

'From observation. My brother had a liking for

wine. I cannot imagine why. Thank God my vocation gives me an excuse to decline it.'

'Except for this evening. You have finished an entire jug on your own.'

'Nonsense,' slurred Giffard. 'You had most of it. I had but a sip, and only because I am thirsty. Go to sleep, or you will have a thick head tomorrow.'

The snores began before Geoffrey could reply. The knight moved a chair to the door himself, which Bale offered to occupy. When Geoffrey lay on the bed, confused thoughts washed inside his head. He was not sure that he could help Giffard – the only people who knew whether Agnes and Walter were guilty were Agnes and Walter themselves, and he did not expect them to confess. Others could only repeat rumours and speculation.

Eventually, Geoffrey slept, but his dreams teemed with disjointed images. He spoke to people he did not know and walked through unfamiliar villages. Then he was in the tunnel under a castle Tancred had been besieging before it collapsed. Geoffrey had been trapped for days in the dark, with water rising around him. Even years later, his dreams sometimes took him back to the pitch-blackness and the prospect of slow, lonely suffocation. He knew it was only a nightmare, but he still could not breathe. Then Bale was shaking him. His squire's hands clawed at his chest and throat, and, for a moment, he thought he was being strangled. He wrenched himself into wakefulness, but still could not catch his breath.

'There is a fire!' Bale was shouting. 'Smoke is coming under the door!'

Bale hauled Geoffrey to his feet. It was still the middle of the night, but people were screaming and there was a steady thump of footsteps on wooden floors. Terrified horses were whinnying in the stables, and dogs were barking furiously. Giffard was still slumped in the chair, so Geoffrey lurched across to him. The Bishop was either drunk or comatose from the smoke, and barely moved when Geoffrey shook him.

'Look!' Bale shrieked.

Geoffrey followed the outline of his pointing finger and saw orange flickering under the door. The fire was close. He heard a dull roar and the light flared. The blaze would not be easy to control, and the house might already be lost. He crossed the room and touched the metal latch. It was searingly hot, and he jerked his hand away.

'If we open that, flames will rush in, and the room will ignite like a haystack. We must escape through the window.'

'It is too far down!' cried Bale. 'We will break our necks.'

'There is a rope in my saddlebag. Tie it to the mullion.'

With shaking hands, Bale rushed to do as he was told, then helped Geoffrey haul Giffard from his chair. The knight grimaced. Giffard had not been exaggerating when he described the difficulty of moving a drunk, and Geoffrey was sweating heavily by the time they had the Bishop lowered to the ground. He glanced at the

157

door and knew that they did not have much time. The fire was hungry for air, and it would only be moments before the frail barrier disintegrated and flames tore into the room.

Even as he turned, there was a crackle and the door was suddenly alive with fire. In the sudden brightness Bale grabbed him and almost hurled him through the window. He snatched at the rope and slid down it. Bale was directly above him, feet kicking wildly as he gripped the windowsill. Then a wave of heat washed over them, accompanied by a tongue of flames. Geoffrey jumped the last few feet; Bale quickly joined him.

Geoffrey seized Giffard's arm and tried to shake him awake. More flames shot out of the window and showers of sparks rained down on them, causing Bale to curse like a demon. He pushed Geoffrey aside, tossed the insensible Bishop over his shoulder and raced away. Geoffrey hurried after him, joining members of the household who were gathering in the yard.

In the leaping flames it was difficult to recognize people, but he glimpsed Eleanor's red cloak. Someone followed her closely, and Geoffrey saw the pair hand in hand, stopping only for a quick embrace. Then flames lit her companion's face, revealing the pretty features of a woman. The wearer of the red cloak was not Eleanor at all, but a man with an identical garment – or perhaps he had borrowed it from her.

A bell was clanging, and Geoffrey heard fitz-Norman yelling to his servants. Orange flames shot high into the sky, and the soldiers who had been ordered to douse the blaze could not get close enough to do any good – the heat drove them back before their water could touch the flames. It was hopeless.

Bale dumped Giffard, then raced towards the stables to save their horses. Geoffrey marvelled at his dedication to duty; Durand would not have thought of the animals. Geoffrey hauled Giffard to his feet and half-carried, half-dragged him to a hedge outside the main gate, where he would be safe and untrampled if the fire spread. He leant close and heard a snore that suggested Giffard was still drunk rather than overcome with fumes, so he rolled him on to his stomach, tucked his cloak around him and trotted back to the yard.

He tried to locate Isabel and Margaret – he did not want them roasted for lack of a guiding hand – but he could not see them, so pushed his way into a confused throng. The first people he recognized were Seguin, Corwenna and Lambert. All three had smoke-blackened faces.

'Have you see Isabel?' he asked urgently. 'Or Margaret?'

Seguin barely looked at him as he hurried away. 'I am more interested in my horse.'

'Heroics will not win you Isabel,' said Lambert. 'She loves only Ralph. I paid her court myself – I am by far the richest of Baderon's knights – but she was not interested. If she will not have me, she certainly will not have you.'

Geoffrey broke away from Lambert and moved through the survivors, peering into smoke-streaked faces. But Isabel was not there.

159

He wondered if she had fallen, or been knocked down in the panic, and was disorientated and unable to find a way out. He recalled his own experience in the collapsed tunnel – especially vivid because of his dream – and thought it would be an awful way to die. He redoubled his efforts to find her.

'Is Isabel safe?' he shouted when he saw fitz-Norman. The Constable was bellowing orders, clearly under the impression that he could still save his home.

'I saw Margaret, and I assumed they were together,' fitzNorman replied. He looked numb with shock. 'What have I done to deserve this? And when the King is visiting, too!'

'Where *is* the King?' asked Geoffrey. If Henry had not escaped, fitzNorman would have to contend with far more serious issues than the loss of his manor – some people would conclude that the blaze was deliberately set to deprive England of her monarch.

FitzNorman's face grew whiter still. 'I do not know.'

'We should find him,' said Geoffrey. 'You go that way; I will look near the stable.'

FitzNorman lumbered away, leaving Geoffrey to scan the faces of those still flooding from the buildings. Smoke swirled thick across the yard, and he raised an arm to protect his eyes, then collided heavily with someone doing the same. It was Serlo, holding Hugh by the hand. Baderon's heir was sobbing helplessly.

The Abbot responded to Geoffrey's question about the King by gesturing vaguely towards the

guest hall. Geoffrey moved on again, as ano
familiar figure approached, hacking
staggering.

'I have been burnt!' cried Durand, cradling a
bloodied hand to his chest. 'And my hair caught
fire!' His golden locks had been singed and,
combined with the dirty water he had used to
extinguish them, were a sorry mess.

'Have you seen Isabel or the King?' Geoffrey
asked urgently.

'I saw nothing,' said Durand, coughing hard.
'But I *heard* yells coming from the guest house.
It sounded like Henry's voice, but I think his
servants are seeing to him.'

'You *think*?' asked Geoffrey uneasily. 'You do
not *know*?'

'Several men ran in that direction, but the
flames were fierce and the smoke too thick to
see. I did not want to be in the way, so I left them
to it.'

He staggered and almost fell, so Geoffrey took
his arm and bundled him along until he was sure
that he could make his own way. When they
parted, Durand shoved something at him. It was
a pair of gloves, which he said would protect his
hands, should he need to touch anything. Geoffrey tugged them on. He rounded a corner and
saw Agnes and Walter together, hurrying along
under a wet cloak. They were loaded down with
bags that were inadequately buckled and Walter
was struggling to keep their contents from spilling out.

'I hope he is dead,' Agnes muttered venomously.

161

'Mother,' said Walter sharply; he had seen Geoffrey. He smiled affably. 'Have you seen my uncle? We are anxious for his safety.'

Geoffrey sent them in the wrong direction. Walter carried a knife, and Geoffrey did not like what Agnes had said. He dashed on, trying to orientate himself in the smoke.

Suddenly, someone grabbed him by the shoulder and spun him around. It was Ralph, and Geoffrey only just evaded the dagger that was thrust at him.

Ralph's face was twisted into a grimace. 'It is time you paid for your brother's deeds.'

Geoffrey gazed at Ralph in astonishment, scarcely believing he would choose such a time for a brawl. Ralph lunged again, and Geoffrey knocked his blow out of the way. The man fought with no skill, and his attack was more a nuisance than a threat.

'I do not want to fight you,' snapped Geoffrey, sidestepping Ralph's next move.

'I do not want to *fight* you, either,' hissed Ralph. 'I want to *kill* you.'

He launched himself at Geoffrey, but suddenly halted mid-move. Geoffrey's mouth dropped as he saw Hilde holding his assailant in her burly arms. Ralph screamed his fury and frustration as he tried in vain to struggle free.

'Have you seen Hugh?' she asked, pinioning Ralph with effortless ease.

'I hope he is with the Devil!' shrieked Ralph, rather unwisely given his situation. But Hilde kept her eyes on Geoffrey as she waited for an answer.

'He is safe,' said Geoffrey.

Hilde closed her eyes in relief, but opened them as Geoffrey moved away. 'You are going the wrong way. The flames are fiercer in that direction.'

'Isabel is missing, and so is the King.'

'It would serve Isabel right,' said Ralph spitefully. 'She is a whore, who—'

The diatribe stopped when Hilde tossed him away as though he were made of rags. Whether by accident or design, he landed in a slippery pile of compost.

'I will help you look,' she said. 'But we will not waste time with vermin.'

Curses and threats followed them both. Smoke swirled, stinging Geoffrey's eyes to the point where he could barely open them – not that it mattered, because he could not see anyway. Nor could he breathe easily, and his armour and surcoat were not garments he could pull over his face, as Hilde was doing. He buried his nose in his sleeve and staggered on, following the line of a wall.

As he reached a corner, the smoke thinned, and he felt a waft of clean air. The wind was blowing from the north, and they were finally upwind of the choking fumes. Geoffrey opened his smarting eyes and saw others had gathered there, gazing at the devastation. He headed towards them, and dropped to one knee beside Margaret, who sat weeping.

'Where is Isabel?'

'She was behind me one moment, and gone the

next,' cried Margaret. 'I think she has gone to the guest house to find Ralph.'

'Stay here,' ordered Hilde. 'Sir Geoffrey and I will find her.'

Geoffrey followed Hilde towards the thickest pall of smoke, not sure anyone would still be alive within. He saw Baderon and some courtiers standing with a tiny mound of salvaged possessions.

'What caused this?' demanded Baderon hoarsely. 'How could it have taken hold so fast?'

'It started in the manor house,' replied a servant. 'I assumed it was the kitchens – that is where fires usually begin – but they are still intact. It is very suspicious.'

Geoffrey's thoughts whirled. Was the fire started deliberately? If so, was it directed against the King? Or did Agnes and her son want to make sure that gossip about the two of them and Sibylla did not spread? Or was it aimed at fitzNorman, to shame him before the King? Or Baderon, because his knights were too strong for him and he was forming alliances that were uniting the Welsh against the English?

Geoffrey tripped over a bucket of water, abandoned by someone who had fled. He grabbed Hilde's arm and brought her to an abrupt stop, indicating she was to dip her cloak in it and put it over her head. She did not need to be told twice. Muscles bulging, she ripped the garment in two, jammed it in the bucket and then handed half to Geoffrey. With the material wrapped turban-like around their faces, they hurried on. When they reached the guest hall, Geoffrey stopped, chest heaving from exertion and lack of clean air.

He heard a voice. He listened harder, moving towards it. It was a man calling for help. He staggered on, using the voice to guide him, Hilde at his heels. He could see nothing but grey-whiteness, and could barely make out his own feet. He was dizzy, and considered escaping while he was still able, but then heard the voice again, louder and closer. It was the King.

'Where are you?' Geoffrey yelled.

'Here!' It was Isabel who answered. 'We cannot go back because of the flames, and we cannot open the door.'

Geoffrey moved forward, feeling his way. The air was burning hot, and the water in the cloak was beginning to evaporate. Then his outstretched hands encountered wood. He moved his fingers down it, and located a beam lodged across the bottom of a door. Someone hammered furiously.

'Open the damned door!' bellowed the King. 'Or we shall be roasted alive.'

The beam was not big, but it was jammed tight against the wall and was hot. Geoffrey and Hilde tugged with all their might – he grateful for the gloves Durand had lent him, and she using her sleeves to protect her hands – but it did not budge. Inside, Henry was growing angry with his would-be rescuers.

'Open the door!' he shouted furiously. 'Now! The fire is getting closer while you play around. Do you want your King to die?'

'No, Sire,' gasped Geoffrey, scrabbling for something to use as a lever. The first piece of wood snapped like a reed, and he groped for something thicker. The piece he found was so heavy, he could barely lift it, and it took all his strength to manoeuvre it into place. Hilde helped him, but she was growing weaker as she ran out of air. Then she flopped to the ground, and he was on his own.

'Geoffrey?' shouted the King. 'Is that you? Hurry, man!'

Geoffrey had no breath for talking and knew it would not be long before he collapsed like Hilde. There was a shriek from inside, followed by a low roar that suggested the flames were taking a firmer hold. Voices pleaded for him to hurry. He leant hard on his lever, but it slipped out of position and he crashed to his knees. He staggered up and was trying again when he saw that a leather strap was preventing the timber from moving. He needed to saw through it. But when he fumbled for his dagger, it was not there. He clawed at the leather with his hands, but it was hopeless – Isabel and the King would die because he could not break a strap. Then his cuff caught on a splinter and something jangled to the ground. It was the little knife that Joan had given him, since honed to a vicious edge by Bale.

For once he was grateful for his squire's fetish, because the tiny blade cut through the tough leather like warm butter. Now only dimly aware of the cacophony of shrieks emanating from within, he summoned every last ounce of strength to lean on the lever as hard as he could. Blood pounded in his ears, and he felt the tendons in his arms and shoulders protest. Suddenly, the lever splintered, sending him sprawling backwards. But the beam also moved. It was not much, but it was enough for the trapped people to batter their way out. They spilt out of the building and staggered into the smoke-filled yard.

'God's blood!' gasped Henry. 'I can still barely breathe!'

Geoffrey climbed to his feet, legs wobbling. He saw a man grab Hilde and hoist her to her feet, urging her to walk.

'I cannot see!' yelled Henry. 'Which way did you come?'

Isabel took the King's hand. 'The wind is blowing from the north, so we must go this way.'

'How do you know?' demanded Henry. 'I cannot see my own feet.'

Isabel did not reply, but pulled both the King and Geoffrey in that direction. The courtiers followed, moving quickly, as Isabel went without hesitation. Then, suddenly, they were in clean air.

Geoffrey sank to the ground in relief, hearing the babble of voices as Henry was recognized, and people hurried forward to assist him. Fitz-Norman bounded up to Isabel, and there was a catch in his voice when he told her how worried he had been. Baderon went to Hilde, wiping her smoke-stained face with his sleeve. Bale arrived, and rested a shy hand on Geoffrey's shoulder.

'The horses are safe,' he said. 'But a number of

people are missing. If they are still inside the hall or the guest house, they are dead for certain.'

Watching the flames, Geoffrey could only agree. He wanted to make sure that Agnes and Walter had not used the diversion to harm Giffard, but he did not have the energy. He was racked by coughing, and could not seem to suck enough air into his lungs.

'Drink this,' Margaret said, kneeling beside him. 'It will make you feel better.'

It did, but it tasted foul, and he did not like to imagine what was in it. He looked up to see Isabel nearby, standing forlorn.

'Margaret said you went to look for Ralph,' he said, coughing again.

'He was gone when I reached the guest house. He must have been looking for me, and we missed each other in the confusion. My father has gone to tell him I am safe. Can you see him?'

Geoffrey spotted Ralph some distance away, clearly uninterested in his former lover.

'Do you know where the fire started?' Geoffrey asked to avoid answering.

'Not in the kitchens, or the guest house would have burnt before the manor, and it was the other way around,' replied Margaret, grateful for the change of subject, for her niece's sake. 'The hall is relatively undamaged, but the rooms above it are burnt out. That means the fire must have started in one of them. I assume it was not yours?'

Geoffrey recalled the flames at the door. 'No,

but it was not far away. I supposed it was a carelessly tended hearth – fires spread quickly in wooden houses with thatched roofs.'

'Our servants are careful,' countered Margaret firmly. 'None would have left a badly banked fire. This blaze was started deliberately.'

Geoffrey tried to think clearly. 'If it started where you say, then it was not an attack on the King – he was in the guest house.'

Margaret grimaced. 'No one will harm the King – not when so many of us have just arrived from Normandy. If Henry dies, then England will go to the Duke, and no one wants *him*, when Bellême is sure to follow, bringing violence and bloodshed. No, Geoffrey, this fire was set for another reason.'

Geoffrey rubbed his head and tried to remember who had been sleeping where. 'You, Isabel and fitzNorman were in the room at the far end of the corridor – the farthest chamber from mine.'

Margaret made a dismissive gesture. 'We have no reason to destroy our own home. And you and Giffard did not do it, either – neither of you would burn innocent people alive. That leaves the three rooms in the middle. One was occupied by Agnes Giffard and her son.'

Geoffrey recalled what he had overheard Agnes say, and wondered whether she and Walter had set the blaze to be rid of a meddlesome kinsman. 'They may be the guilty party,' he conceded.

Margaret nodded. 'Giffard thinks they are killers, and anyone with a brain can see why:

169

Agnes' husband and her lover's wife both dead at convenient times. Walter probably helped her. He is a stupid, malleable boy.'

Isabel's head was cocked to one side as she scanned the babbling voices for the one that was most important to her, but she was paying attention to the discussion nonetheless. 'Then perhaps Giffard *did* set the fire, to dispense some divine justice.'

'Giffard was drunk,' said Geoffrey. 'Besides, I was with him. I would have seen him.'

'Not necessarily – I put a sleeping draught in your milk,' said Isabel. She sensed Geoffrey's shock and turned defensive. 'Only a light one, just enough to make sure you rested properly.'

'Why?' demanded Geoffrey. He recalled how heavily he had been asleep when Bale had woken him. He was lucky his squire had not shared the milk, or all three of them would have perished.

Isabel flinched at the anger in his voice. 'Because you slept so poorly the night before. I wanted to help.'

'One of those three middle rooms was occupied by Baderon's knights,' said Margaret, to bring the subject back to the fire and save Isabel from further recrimination. 'Baderon himself was in the guest house, but Seguin and Lambert may have followed his orders.'

'Why?' asked Geoffrey tiredly. 'Who would *he* want to harm?'

'My brother?' suggested Margaret. 'Baderon would gain, no matter what the outcome. Either my brother dies, which means Baderon is the only powerful lord in the region, or my brother survives – to be in trouble for almost incinerating the King. Baderon may also have wanted *you* dead, so he could take Goodrich.'

'The last of those three rooms was occupied by Hilde and the women from Bicanofre,' said Geoffrey, thinking Baderon was not the kind of man to set a house alight just to inherit a small manor. He was not stupid.

'I doubt Hilde set the fire, considering she risked her life to save others,' said Margaret. 'But I have not seen Eleanor or Douce since the fuss began.'

Geoffrey recalled the figure in the red cloak, but then remembered that it had stopped for an embrace with a woman. He glanced around, but could not see Eleanor, although that meant nothing. People had scattered into small groups and she could have been anywhere.

'Eleanor may have started the fire to rid herself of Hugh,' Margaret went on. 'He follows her everywhere, and must be tiresome.'

'He loves her,' said Isabel. 'But why would she bother with a fire, when she has other skills at her disposal? She *is* a witch, after all.'

'A *witch*?' asked Geoffrey uncertainly.

Isabel nodded. 'She could be a great healer, but she dislikes helping people. You were lucky she did not poison you when she removed those splinters. Why do you think I came so quickly after she told me what she had done? I wanted to counter any evil she might have managed.'

'Why would Eleanor want to harm me?'

'You forgot to send the cart – and witches can

171

be vindictive. But more importantly, her father would like her to marry you, and she does not want to.'

'Few women do,' said Geoffrey, thinking that Isabel, Margaret and Corwenna had already refused him, while Hilde was not keen, either.

'Eleanor communes with the Devil,' Isabel went on. 'Why do you think toads and bats seek out her company, and ravens do her bidding?'

'Oh, really, Isabel!' Geoffrey said, his weariness making his tone a bit sharp. 'That is nonsense!'

She gripped his hand. 'It is not, and you would be a fool to ignore it.'

Geoffrey sat for some time, trying to summon the energy to move. Next to him, Isabel and Margaret fell silent, and soon Hilde came to join them, her brother at her side. Hugh curled into a ball and promptly went to sleep.

'Have you seen Ralph?' Isabel asked her.

'Just moments ago, cursing the grooms in the stables,' Hilde responded.

Isabel jumped to her feet, but did not get far before fitzNorman intercepted her. They exchanged words and, reluctantly, he turned to walk with her towards the horses.

'Ralph is a mean-spirited bastard,' said Geoffrey, watching them go.

Margaret nodded. 'He is a pompous, arrogant fool, and does not deserve Isabel. She is usually astute where men are concerned, but he has blinded her. So to speak.'

'I fell in love with a duchess once,' admitted

Geoffrey, immediately wondering why he had said it. 'It was wrong, but there was nothing I could do to stop it. Love is difficult to control and impossible to predict.'

'What happened to her?' asked Margaret curiously.

Geoffrey shrugged. 'She still lives with her husband.'

Margaret did not push him. She nodded towards Hugh. 'He has the right idea. There is no more we can do, and it is sensible to rest. Everything will look better in the morning.'

'I doubt it. Your home will be reduced to hot rubble; Isabel will still love Ralph; Agnes will still be suspected of killing Sibylla; and Giffard will still be stricken by sorrow.'

'But we may *feel* better about it,' argued Margaret. She left him and went to where Isabel was calling for Ralph. FitzNorman was standing helplessly, at a loss for what to do.

Geoffrey stood unsteadily, and walked to the hedge where Giffard still snored, oblivious to the chaos. Geoffrey flopped down beside him, bone-weary, and closed his eyes. His peace did not last.

'Well, Geoffrey,' said the King, outlined by the flames that still leapt into the air. 'What do you make of this? FitzNorman claims someone set the blaze deliberately, while Baderon thinks it was careless servants.'

'At first I thought it was set to harm you, but it was not,' said Geoffrey, scrambling to his feet.

'Why?' asked Henry. 'Do not look as though you wished you had not spoken, man. I asked a

173

question, and I want an answer. You are one of the few people here who does not tell me what they think I should hear.'

'If the fire *had* been aimed at you, it would have started in the guest house. But it almost certainly began above the hall – the room I shared with Giffard was there, and the fire raged very close to it.'

'You think someone wants Goodrich without an heir?'

Geoffrey shook his head. 'But the adjoining rooms contained fitzNorman, the Bicanofre women and Hilde, Agnes and Walter, and Baderon's knights. The fire could have been directed at any of them.'

'It could have been *started* by any of them, too,' mused Henry. 'Or by someone from the guest house. I heard Baderon slipping out to the latrines, while his son is apt to wander, too – I caught him watching me in my bedchamber last night, which was disconcerting.'

'It could even be a disgruntled servant.'

'Well, whoever it is, I shall not forget what you did tonight,' said Henry, reaching out and grasping Geoffrey's shoulder. 'You saved my life while others ran to save their own skins.'

They both looked down when Giffard groaned and began to stir. Geoffrey helped him sit, but the Bishop's eyes were bleary, and his breath carried the sweet scent of wine.

'Lord!' he muttered. 'You should not have given me so much to drink, Geoff. My head is swimming, and there is a smell of burning in my nostrils that I cannot dispel.'

'Giffard?' asked Henry. 'Thank God! I was worried about you.'

'Why would you be worried?' slurred Giffard, resting his head in his hands, evidently unaware that he was speaking to his King. 'I *am* a Bishop.'

Henry glanced sharply at him. 'I am saying that I do not want to lose you – there are few who can administer an important see as well as you.'

'Bugger the see,' spat Giffard truculently. 'I am going home to Rouen, where a man can buy a decent sausage.'

Henry looked at Geoffrey in alarm. 'What is the matter with him?'

'Smoke, Sire,' said Geoffrey diplomatically. 'It can do strange things to a man's wits.'

Seven

It was the early hours before the flames were under control. The main house still smouldered and crackled, and the thatches of surrounding buildings dripped with water. FitzNorman had abandoned his attempts at directing his men: he sat with his head drooped, while Margaret tried to comfort him. Isabel wandered hopelessly, while everyone prepared to make the best of a night outside. Durand flopped down next to Geoffrey.

'You survived,' he said hoarsely. 'I hoped you would, because you may yet agree to work with me.'

It was typical of Durand that he should see Geoffrey's escape in terms of his own interests, but Geoffrey was too tired to care. He handed back the gloves, which were wet and burnt through in places. 'I am sorry; I am afraid they are ruined.'

'They are,' agreed Durand. 'And they were virtually new, too. I should have known better than to trust *you* – you always were careless. Can I assume that they were of use?'

Geoffrey nodded: he could not have touched the hot beam without them, so they had made the difference between the King rescued and in-cinerated. 'And you? You said you were burnt.'

'Gashed.' Durand showed him a cut on his hand. 'But Isabel gave me a salve. It is a pity she has set her heart on Ralph, because he does not deserve her. He was standing next to her when she was calling for him, but he only slunk away. Indeed, there has been a lot of slinking tonight.'

'What do you mean?'

'The King is safe, but I did not notice many folk rushing to his aid. I was weak from breathing smoke, but others were not – Baderon and his knights just stood and watched the blaze.'

'What else could they have done? It was obvious the house was lost.'

'You rushed into the flames without thought for your safety. I do not condemn Baderon for not doing so, but he could have directed people with water or organized shelter for the survivors.

176

FitzNorman is numb with shock and Baderon should have stepped up. But he is probably chary of ordering his knights to do anything: he allows them to influence his decisions, when he should go with his instincts. That is something I learnt from you. You listen to ideas and suggestions, but you do not let them sway you from what you think is right.'

'I taught you something, then?' asked Geoffrey, who had assumed his old squire had gained nothing from the year in his service.

'A great deal, although most of it is useless. Clerks of *my* status are seldom required to break locks with daggers or produce meals from grass and leaves. But Baderon is not the only one who acted shabbily. I do not like the way Agnes gloats over Giffard's absence – she hopes he is dead.'

Geoffrey glanced to where the Bishop was sleeping again. 'He is alive, but unwell.'

'Smoke,' said Durand, coughing raspingly himself. 'Incidentally, everyone suspects Agnes of making an end of Sibylla, but the more I think about it, the more I am certain that the whole thing was Walter's idea.'

'Why?' asked Geoffrey, trying to pay attention through his weariness. Durand was astute and might well have deduced something that would help solve the mystery.

'Walter saved his belongings from the fire, but did not have time to pack them properly. He dropped a couple of items as he ran to safety – and this was one of them.' Durand rummaged in the embroidered purse he carried on his belt and presented the knight with a tiny phial.

Geoffrey also recalled Walter's inadequately buckled bags. 'Do you know what is in it?'

Durand shook his head. 'But it is the kind of ampoule that normally contains powerful medicines – Abbot Serlo keeps some in his abbey's infirmary, for the very sick.'

Geoffrey suspected he was right. Strong potions tended to be stored in small quantities, and the phial that he held – which, despite being tiny, was made of hard-baked clay and possessed a sturdy stopper to prevent leakage – certainly looked as though it might contain something potent.

'I wager a shilling that it contains something Walter should not have,' said Durand. 'There is writing on one side, but the language is not Latin or French. I cannot read it.'

'Italian,' said Geoffrey, struggling to make out the tiny letters in the remaining light of the fire. 'Some of the inscription is eroded – this is a very old bottle – but I think it says "mandrake juice".'

'So, I *was* right,' said Durand, pleased. 'Mandrake is deadly. However, Walter will not be killing anyone now, because it is empty.'

Geoffrey pulled off the lid and saw that Durand was right. In fact, he imagined the pot had been empty for some time, because it was dry and dusty, and the scent of whatever had been inside was so faint as to be almost undetectable. He doubted the contents had been used to dispatch the Duchess, because her death was too recent. But it proved that Walter had a familiarity with poisons.

'Before the fire, the King told me I am to spend a few months with Bishop Giffard,' said Durand after a while.

'You must be disappointed,' said Geoffrey. 'I know you wanted to return to court.'

Durand grinned. 'Henry said *you* suggested I stay with Giffard until the jealous wretches at Westminster have dispersed. You really should consider my offer, Geoffrey, because we understand each other so well that we would make an excellent team. I am delighted and grateful for your kindly word in Henry's ear.'

'You are?' asked Geoffrey warily.

'Giffard is Bishop of Winchester. And if there is a place in England that suits me more than Westminster, it is Winchester – where the royal treasury is, and where important decisions are made. But you know this: it is what prompted you to suggest it in the first place. However, before I go, Henry wants me to review what Baderon is doing.'

'You mean his taxes?' asked Geoffrey.

'Ostensibly. But what I will *really* be doing is gathering other information. Henry thinks he may be forging too many Welsh alliances.'

'He is probably right.'

Durand was thoughtful. 'I despise Baderon. He treats me like a servant, whereas I am a landowner, worthy of respect. However, he is mannerly enough towards you. I want you to join with me to find out what he is doing. If he is uniting the Welsh against England, he should be exposed as a traitor.'

'No,' said Geoffrey firmly. 'I cannot spy on

179

my neighbours.'

'Then help me by taking me back into your service. Baderon will not harm me if he knows I am under your protection. I will be your squire again, and will reside at Goodrich until I have completed my report. Then I shall go to Winchester.'

'Hey, you!' came a voice from behind them. It was Seguin, and he was snapping his fingers at Durand. 'Clerk! Come here. I want you to write something.'

'You see?' said Durand. 'That is the kind of treatment I can expect from Baderon's household.'

'I said *come here*!' shouted Seguin, advancing angrily. 'Do not pretend to be deaf.'

Durand squealed as he was yanked upright. 'Geoffrey, tell him to stop!'

'Well?' sneered Seguin, addressing Geoffrey. 'Will you tell me to stop?'

Seguin had tugged Durand away before Geoffrey could respond. Durand shot Geoffrey a foul look, but crouched on the damp grass next to Lambert and Corwenna and began to write an inventory of the belongings they had managed to salvage. Geoffrey thought he was a fool to let himself be bullied so, but it was none of his affair if Durand was too lily-livered to stand up for himself.

He looked at the phial that he held, then pushed it inside his surcoat before turning his attention to what possessing an ancient pot of mandrake might mean.

* * *

As the long night continued, fitzNorman progressed from shock to anger, and began looking for someone to blame. Geoffrey wanted no part of it, so he collected his horses and set out towards Goodrich, intending to find a glade where he could rest until dawn. With Giffard swaying in his saddle, and Bale behind, they reached the spot where Hilde had hailed Geoffrey, then passed along a narrow valley. Eventually, they found a small mud hut with a sheet of leather for a door. It was not much, but it sufficed. Bale tethered the horses, while Geoffrey made a fire and settled Giffard in a litter of dead leaves, covering him with a blanket from his saddlebag.

'I do not like this place,' said Bale with a shudder. 'It feels evil, as if spirits linger.'

'It is just a shepherd's hut,' retorted Geoffrey. 'And you are safer here than you would be at Dene. I will stay awake to make certain we are not attacked.'

Bale shook his head. 'You need rest more than me. I will wake you in an hour. In the meantime I will stand in the doorway, so that I do not doze off. I do not want woodland spirits coming to slit my throat as I lie dreaming.'

'Doubtless you would prefer to slit theirs,' said Geoffrey. He had not meant it to be a joke and did not like the manic grin Bale shot in his direction.

Geoffrey lay down, but was not sure he could trust Bale to be sufficiently watchful. The squire was still an unknown, and Geoffrey was not in the habit of putting his safety in the hands of men he did not know. He resolved not to sleep.

'I did not do it, sir,' whispered Bale, coming to crouch next to him.

Geoffrey edged away. 'Do what?'

'Kill my mother and father.' Bale's voice was little more than a hiss and it made the hairs stand up on the back of Geoffrey's neck. He sat up as Bale continued. 'Everyone assumed it was me, but I swear before God it was not.' He crossed himself in the darkness.

'There is no need to whisper,' said Geoffrey, not liking the sibilantly sinister quality of the man's voice. 'I doubt you will disturb Giffard.'

'All right.' Bale's normal speaking tones made Geoffrey feel a little more comfortable. But only a little. 'My father had a liking for ale, and when he was drunk, he was free with his fists. He was not like the Bishop, who just sleeps. He was nasty in *his* cups.'

'You mean he had enemies?' surmised Geoffrey. 'And one of them killed him?'

Bale nodded. 'He had enemies, all right, but only one killer: your brother Henry.'

Geoffrey shot to his feet, dagger in hand. It sounded like a confession made just before vengeance was taken, but Bale only continued to stare into the darkness.

'How do you know?' Geoffrey asked, when it became clear that Bale was not going to move.

'Because I saw him,' replied Bale. 'I saw him enter my house, and I know my father was alive, because I heard them shouting at each other. I saw Henry leave, but there was no shouting. I went inside, but my mother and father were

182

dead. Stabbed.'

Geoffrey took a deep breath. 'I am sorry, Bale.'

Bale shrugged. 'I caught up with Henry and saw fresh blood on his dagger. But my father may have attacked him, so perhaps he was only defending himself.'

'Why did you not tell anyone?'

Bale shrugged again. 'What good would it have done? When they failed to prove I was the culprit, the whole thing died down. Henry saw to that, by forbidding people to talk about it.'

'Did you kill Henry?' asked Geoffrey.

'I wish I had,' said Bale. 'But the truth is that I have not killed anyone, not even the man in that tavern brawl. *He* fell backwards and cracked his skull on a table.'

'I see,' said Geoffrey, not sure whether to believe him. 'Why are you telling me all this?'

'So you will know,' said Bale simply. 'You are uneasy with me, but there is no need.'

'My brother killed your parents,' said Geoffrey. 'You may think I—'

'You are not Henry, sir,' interrupted Bale. 'I like you; I did not like him. But it is late and you are tired. Sleep, and I will take the first watch.'

Geoffrey sat again, but kept his dagger in his hand, even more resolved not to sleep. Could Bale be believed when he said that he had not killed Henry? The bloody murder of his parents was certainly a good motive. Geoffrey closed his eyes to mull over the matter more carefully, and the next thing he knew was Bale's hot breath against his cheek. He jumped into wakefulness,

183

his hand moving instinctively to his sword.

'Steady,' said Bale. 'It will be light soon, and I am too tired to stay awake any longer. It has been much longer than an hour, but I did not have the heart to wake you.'

Geoffrey staggered to his feet, stiff but refreshed. He was astonished that he had slept when he had been determined not to, and supposed Isabel's milk must have been stronger than she had led him to believe. He stretched, and watched his squire curl up next to Giffard.

'Thank you, Bale,' he whispered.

'You are welcome, sir,' replied Bale drowsily. 'I told you I would keep you safe.'

It was still twilight when Geoffrey stepped outside. In the distance he heard someone coming. He ducked into the shadows, but the figure strode briskly past the hut – not even glancing at it – and continued down the hillside.

The previous night had been too dark to see much, but Geoffrey could now make out the outlines of trees and rocks. The valley descended into a steep gorge, and he watched the figure move stealthily to the bottom. He was sure that the person was alone, but listened for some time, just to be certain. Then, cautiously, he followed.

At the bottom of the gorge, the figure bent to touch the ground, then began to sing. Immediately Geoffrey heard that it was a woman. Her song was deep and eerie, and it sent shivers down his spine. A sudden rustle in the trees set his heart pounding. When her singing grew stronger, so did the wind, and he ducked farther

184

back into the undergrowth. He grasped his sword firmly, and told himself that the wind could do him no harm, but, even so, his hand was slippery with sweat.

Eventually, she stopped singing and began to walk back the way she had come. When she reached the undergrowth where Geoffrey hid, she hesitated, and he had the sense that she knew he was there. Then she was gone, apparently keen to be away now that she had finished her business.

Geoffrey took a deep breath and waited for his heart to stop pounding. He was disgusted with himself for being unsettled by a song and a gust of wind. But even though the rational part of his mind told him there was nothing to worry about, it took considerable willpower to look at what she had been doing. On a flat rock, which stood near a bubbling spring, were a variety of objects.

The first things to catch his eye were locks of hair, tied with twine and stuck to the stone with some sort of paste. A dark, sticky substance lay over them, which, in the grey light of dawn, he thought was blood. There were chalk drawings, too. In the centre was a crude depiction of a house with blood fashioned into flames: he could only assume that someone had wanted the manor to burn, and had appealed to sinister forces to make it happen. Then he heard rustling from the trees again and glanced upwards.

With horror, he saw the head of a goat hanging there, its horns splayed to either side and its teeth bared and yellow in the rictus of death. Flies had found its eyes, and, even as he watched, a maggot dropped from it on to his shoulder. He turned and clambered up the hill as fast as he could. He found it hard to catch his breath, and when he arrived at the hut his heart was thumping hard.

'What is wrong?' asked Giffard as he exploded inside. 'You look as though you have seen a goat.'

'*A goat?*' echoed Geoffrey in alarm, wondering how the Bishop could have known.

'I said *ghost*,' said Giffard, enunciating carefully. 'Have you never heard the expression? It is quite common. Is there anything to eat? I need something to settle my stomach or I shall be sick.'

Geoffrey felt a little sick himself. He rubbed his head. 'My ears are ringing.'

Giffard's expression softened. 'That is the bells of Dene. Come and sit down, and let your man prepare breakfast. We will both need our strength today.'

'Why?' asked Geoffrey warily.

Giffard frowned. 'What is wrong with you? I am the one who drank too much – so much that I do not recall how I come to be here. I simply meant that we must discover whether Walter had a hand in murdering the Duchess, God rest her soul.'

'You do not remember the fire?'

'What fire?'

Geoffrey sat next to him, accepting the dry, hard bread that Bale handed him, with a cup of water to dip it in. He felt better when he had eaten it, and pondered what he had just seen, while Bale gave Giffard an account of the manor house blaze.

'There are locks of hair and a dead goat down there,' interrupted Geoffrey.

'Well, there would be,' said Giffard. 'I was saying to Bale, before you burst in, that I am surprised you brought me here. It is obviously a place frequented by heathens.'

'It is not obvious to me,' said Geoffrey.

Giffard gazed at him in astonishment. 'This place reeks of evil, and there are pagan symbols everywhere. Just look at the ceiling, and the trees over there.'

Geoffrey glanced at the rafters and saw several dead birds hanging by their wings, while there was another goat in an oak outside. He was unable to repress a shudder.

'I told you, sir,' said Bale, reproachfully. 'I said it felt wicked.'

Giffard stood. 'It is not a place Christian men should linger. It is more for the likes of Eleanor of Bicanofre, whom I hear comes to recite spells and incantations.'

Unhappily, Geoffrey wondered how to tell Giffard that it had not been Eleanor who had sung to make the trees rustle, but Agnes.

As soon as Giffard had completed his morning prayers, Geoffrey led the way back to Dene and the devastation that a few hours had wrought. FitzNorman's once fine home was a blackened shell, although most of the outbuildings had survived. Smoke still curled from the ruins, and when rain started to fall, it hissed as it hit the

187

smouldering timbers.

The King had ordered his scribes to make an inventory of what and who had escaped, as fitzNorman was incapable of doing so. Several servants had died, and Eleanor was missing. Looking at the charred ruins, Geoffrey doubted they would be able to identify her body if it was found. He thought about the red-cloaked man from the previous night and supposed that the garment had been taken from her corpse in the chaos. Hugh was also missing, and some gossips were insisting that he and Eleanor were enjoying each other's company elsewhere.

Geoffrey decided to leave for Goodrich immediately, desperate to be away from the grief-stricken servants. They reminded him of people in villages he had seen put to the torch after battles. He was on his way to tell Giffard when there was a howl from the stables.

'What has happened?' he asked, as Lambert emerged from the building.

'Margaret,' replied Lambert, ashen-faced. 'She must have staggered from the fire and died – the grooms just found her when they came to saddle the King's horses. His Majesty rides to Gloucester today.'

'*Margaret*?' asked Geoffrey, aghast. 'But I saw her after the fire. She was fit and well.'

Lambert touched his shoulder in a rough gesture of sympathy. 'We all liked Margaret, motherly soul that she was, and I understand you were considering her as a wife. She was old, but she would have made a kindly and affable partner.'

Geoffrey eased his way through the onlookers, and saw the King standing with fitzNorman, while Isabel knelt next to a prostrate form, crying. Henry was talking, and Geoffrey noticed the Constable was not too shocked to nod and bow obsequiously to whatever suggestions the monarch was making. Isabel was far more distressed than the hard-hearted old warrior.

'This is a sorry way to begin the day,' said Durand to Geoffrey. 'Poor Margaret.'

'Take her to the church and say a mass for her soul,' Henry ordered Durand. 'Make sure it is done properly; she was a good woman.'

'She was, Sire,' agreed Durand. 'She will be in Heaven soon.'

Henry nodded, but everyone could see that he was chafing at the delay. He patted the stunned fitzNorman on the arm, muttered a few more words of sympathy and left. Most people were more interested in helping him mount up than in Margaret's death, including fitzNorman. Geoffrey heard him apologizing for the blaze and assuring him that the castle would be rebuilt by the time His Royal Highness next visited. It was not long before the stable emptied, leaving only Geoffrey, Isabel, Bale and Durand.

'Cover her face if it is not,' said Isabel. 'I do not want people staring. Does she look frightened or in pain?'

'Neither,' said Geoffrey. He had nothing appropriate to cover her, but Margaret had worn a veil that comprised a large square of clean linen. He started to unwrap it, intending to wind it around her head. When it fell from her neck, he

189

gazed in shock. Dark bruises lay in an even line down both sides of her throat, and he saw that she had not died from smoke. Someone had strangled her, and the evidence was in eight fingers and two thumbs that had pressed into her pale skin.

'She looks as though she is sleeping,' said Durand, for Isabel's benefit. He, too, had seen the marks and his face expressed horror. 'She is peaceful.'

'God help us, Sir!' breathed Bale from the adjoining stall. 'Margaret is not the only corpse here. So is Jervil, our groom!'

Shocked, Geoffrey saw that Bale was right. Why was Jervil in the Dene stables? Had he come to check on Geoffrey? Or had he carried a message from Joan and died in the smoke while looking for someone to give it to? Geoffrey searched Jervil's clothes but could find no letter.

'Jervil?' asked Isabel, confused. 'Goodrich's stable-hand? Why would he be here?'

It was a good question, but she was more concerned with her aunt than the answer, and began to cry afresh. Durand took her hands in his, crooning gentle words to calm her.

Uncertain what prompted him to do so, Geoffrey moved the tunic around Jervil's throat, where he saw that Margaret was not the only one to have been strangled: marks indicated that strong fingers had gripped Jervil's neck, too. Geoffrey sat back on his heels, perplexed. How had Goodrich's groom come to be killed in the same place and manner as fitzNorman's sister? Had Jervil seen Margaret slain, and been mur-

190

dered to ensure that he did not tell? Or was it the other way around? Or had Jervil killed Margaret, and then been dispatched in turn?

'There is a knife in Jervil's hand,' said Durand.

Geoffrey moved straw away from the body and saw that Durand was right.

'Was he attacking, or protecting himself?' asked Bale.

Geoffrey frowned. 'It is unusual to see a man wielding a knife in his left hand. Did he fight left-handed?'

Bale closed his eyes and went through an elaborate mime of some previous fight he had enjoyed with the groom. He jigged for so long that Geoffrey began to wonder whether the proximity of violent death had finally turned his mind.

'No,' he said eventually, opening his eyes. 'He fought right-handed, like me.'

In the yard the King was issuing orders. Some people were instructed to remain at Dene, while others were to travel to Gloucester. Since a large area of virgin forest lay between Dene and Gloucester, Henry intended to hunt along the way, and a few courtiers were invited to accompany him in search of a large stag that had recently been seen. People hurried to collect their horses; among them were Baderon, his knights and fitzNorman.

'Good God!' exclaimed Lambert, peering over Geoffrey's shoulder. 'Is that Goodrich's groom? What is he doing here?'

'He must have been carrying a message from Lady Joan,' said Bale, before Geoffrey could reply. 'He died of smoke, just like poor Margaret.'

'Dangerous stuff, smoke,' said Baderon, in a way that made Geoffrey glance at him sharply. Evidently, the Lord of Monmouth suspected something odd, too, and Geoffrey wondered why.

'That makes six dead,' said fitzNorman, standing behind him and staring sadly at his sister's remains. 'Five servants and one noblewoman.'

'And my son and Eleanor are missing,' added Baderon. Geoffrey studied him closely and saw lines of worry etched into his face.

'Eleanor will look after Hugh,' said Seguin, exchanging a lewd grin with his brother.

Baderon frowned. 'I hope you are right. Hilde is looking for him, but he might be anywhere.'

'Will someone fetch Ralph?' asked Isabel tearfully. 'I need his comfort.'

Ralph was standing near the door with an unreadable expression on his face. He heard his former lover's pathetic appeal, but turned and strode away.

'I think he is looking for Eleanor,' lied Durand.

'Why would he do that?' cried Isabel. '*I* need him and Eleanor is able to fend for herself.'

'He thinks you have Margaret,' said fitz-Norman gruffly. 'If only he knew.'

It was an odd thing to say, and Geoffrey wondered what he meant. He glanced at the Constable's impassive features, and thought there was a good deal strange about the previous night's events. However, sad though he was about the kindly woman who had wanted to be his friend, it was not his business to investigate her murder. He left the stable and walked towards Giffard. He stopped abruptly when he saw the King regarding him thoughtfully.

Baderon was burbling about the stag and Abbot Serlo talked simultaneously about a writ that required approval, but Henry raised a royal hand and they both faltered into silence.

'We shall look for the stag as we ride, and I shall ratify the advowson at Gloucester,' the King said, indicating that he was capable of listening to two monologues at the same time. But now he ignored both, as he edged his horse towards Geoffrey and Giffard.

'There is something very wrong here,' he said, after looking around to make sure that no one else could hear. 'There was a lot of confusion during the fire, and I find myself puzzled as to what actually happened. Do you have any ideas, Giffard?'

'None, Sire. I was overcome by smoke and recall nothing at all.'

Geoffrey regarded him with surprise. It was the first time he had ever heard Giffard lie. Unfortunately, the prelate immediately grasped the cross around his neck in a gesture that bespoke wretched guilt at the falsehood. Henry saw it and smothered a smile.

'I have been told smoke can do strange things to a man's wits. What about you, Geoffrey? We discussed the matter briefly last night. You told me it was not aimed at me. Well, then, who?'

Geoffrey shook his head slowly. 'There is a lot

I do not understand about the men who own these lands, and I cannot begin to imagine a solution, Sire.'

'Do try,' invited Henry drily. 'I am sure you have been pondering the matter.'

Geoffrey looked at the people milling in the yard. 'Baderon and fitzNorman are rivals. It is possible Baderon or one of his knights started the fire to make fitzNorman look careless in your eyes. Corwenna is a spiteful woman who does not care whom she harms. Eleanor de Bicanofre, who is said to be a witch, has disappeared, along with Hugh. The list is endless.'

Henry regarded him with his clear grey eyes. 'Did you inspect Margaret's body? I saw you kneel next to it. She did not die in the fire, did she?'

'No, Sire.'

Henry sighed impatiently. 'You are being remarkably obtuse this morning. Must I drag the information from you piece by piece? How did she die, man?'

'She was strangled,' replied Geoffrey. 'One of Goodrich's servants lies next to her, dead the same way.'

Henry was thoughtful. 'Margaret was a good lady, and deserves to be avenged. And you must be concerned about the loss of a servant – for whatever reason he was killed. Would you like to find out why? Or shall I ask Giffard to do it?'

'I will,' said Geoffrey, not wanting anyone – even Giffard – prying into Goodrich's affairs. And he had liked Margaret. He had talked to her about the only woman he had ever truly loved,

194

and he did not tell just anyone about his duchess.

'Good,' said Henry. 'But you cannot ask your questions here. We shall invite everyone to Goodrich for a few days, and you can do it there.'

'No!' exclaimed Geoffrey, not wanting possible killers near Joan.

'*No?*' queried Henry mildly. 'One does not say "no" to one's monarch quite so bluntly.'

'I did not fight on the Welsh borders all summer only to invite murderers to Joan's home.'

'Joan can look after herself,' said Henry wryly. 'And she liked Margaret, too, so I am sure she will be supportive. I insist you do as I suggest. Durand will help. He has some spare time before he joins Giffard in Winchester.'

'What?' exclaimed Giffard, who had not been told about the new plans. 'I cannot take Durand, Sire. He is far too venal, and I am a Bishop.'

'It will do you good,' Henry said firmly. 'He may even bring a smile to those sombre features. But he will not be with you for a while yet. I am worried about the situation that is brewing with Baderon and his Welsh friends.'

'Baderon wants peace on the Marches, but it is equally possible the Welsh will unite in war,' said Geoffrey, relieved to share his concerns with a man in a position to do something about them.

Henry nodded. 'I shall pass through Goodrich in a week or so, and Durand can report his findings then. Meanwhile, you can look into these three murders.'

'*Three murders?*' asked Geoffrey, startled.

'Margaret, Jervil and...'

'And Henry – your brother. My agents visited Goodrich after he died, and they told me that a man called Jervil was in the stables when Henry was killed. They took Jervil to a tavern and prised information from him while he was drunk. He did not see the killer, but he *heard* him.'

Geoffrey nodded. He had already established as much, although he doubted whether *he* could have persuaded Jervil to go to an inn and allow his wits to be pickled and rummaged for information. Perhaps that was why Jervil had been reluctant to answer further questions.

'I saw Jervil arrive yesterday evening,' Henry went on. 'I happened to be looking out of my window when he rode into the yard, and I sent a squire to find out his business. I assumed he was carrying messages for me – strangers arriving at odd hours usually are. But Jervil said his business was with Baderon, which intrigued me, given that he was from Goodrich.'

Geoffrey gazed at him. It intrigued him, too. What business could a groom from his own manor have with the lord of a rival one?

Henry continued. 'I saw Baderon speak to Jervil and pay him – handsomely.'

Geoffrey continued to stare. Jervil had asked whether Geoffrey was going to see Baderon, and had asked Bale to spy to find out. So why had he then come to Dene to meet Baderon himself? Geoffrey recalled Jervil and Torva's belief that Henry had been killed by Baderon's knights. Was the clandestine meeting about that? Geoffrey's thoughts whirled.

'There was no purse of money on Jervil's body, Sire,' he said eventually.

'Perhaps he was killed for his earnings,' suggested the King. 'Of course, what happened to Margaret is obvious: clearly she was killed because she was in the wrong place at the wrong time – she happened to enter the stables when Jervil was murdered and was strangled to prevent her from telling anyone what she had seen.'

'She was probably looking for Isabel,' suggested Giffard.

'There was something else about Jervil's meeting with Baderon that was odd,' said Henry. 'I saw Baderon pass him a purse, but before that, I saw Jervil give Baderon a dagger.'

'*A dagger*?' asked Geoffrey.

'Yes, a large one with a ruby in its hilt. I saw it quite clearly. Why would Jervil give an expensive thing like that to Baderon?'

'I do not know,' said Geoffrey, his thoughts tumbling inside his head. 'But your description sounds very like the weapon that killed my brother.'

The King's announcement that he wanted some of his subjects to meet him at Goodrich after his visit to Gloucester met a mixed response. Fitz-Norman was relieved, because he took the summons to mean that he had been forgiven for the fire. Baderon was bemused and his knights resentful, while Geoffrey heard Corwenna bluntly informing Seguin that she would not go. Her interpretation was that Geoffrey had persuaded the King to order it so that he could kill her.

Abbot Serlo, astride a fat donkey, came to speak to Geoffrey while he waited for the cumbersome train of horses and carts to begin their journey to Gloucester. 'Has Giffard asked you to find out whether Walter and Agnes poisoned the Duchess?' he asked without preamble. 'I know he is concerned, and Durand tells me you have rare investigative skills.'

'Durand is exaggerating.'

'They had a lot to gain from Sibylla's death, and Agnes has not capitalized on it only because Giffard dragged her away before she could push her claws further into the Duke. I have been watching them carefully, but now *you* must be vigilant for Giffard's safety. I do not want him poisoned, too. He is a friend.'

Geoffrey recalled that Serlo had been in Normandy when Sibylla had died. 'Can you tell me anything to help? I know Walter owned a mandrake pot, but it has been empty too long to have been used on Sibylla.'

'*Mandrake*,' mused Serlo. 'Its roots are its most dangerous part – they shriek when they are pulled from the ground. Any man hearing it will die, so the Italians use dogs to harvest them.'

'So they grow in Italy?' asked Geoffrey, re-calling the Italian words carved on the pot and Walter's use of the language.

'Among other places. The leaves are also poisonous, and there is a red-yellow fruit like an apple. It is used in medicine, but only externally, because it is so strong. Witches use it in charms – to bring love.'

Geoffrey thought about the charms that he had seen at the Angel Springs, and wondered whether Eleanor employed mandrake. Then he thought about the dead birds at the shepherd's hut and above the place where Henry had died. Had a witch put them there, or just superstitious peasants?

'To bring love?' he asked, dragging his thoughts back to Serlo.

'It is supposed to produce strong and rampant lovers,' explained Serlo. 'With such a powerful plant, the line is a fine one: too little will not have the desired effect, while too much will kill.'

'You seem to know a good deal about it,' said Geoffrey warily.

Serlo smiled. 'We have a fine library at Gloucester, as you know – you spent enough time there during your noviciate.' He sketched a benediction, exhorted him again to look after Giffard, and took his place in the cavalcade.

'So,' announced the King in a ringing voice. 'Baderon, fitzNorman, Bicanofre, Giffard and their households will travel to Goodrich today or tomorrow. The rest of you shall come with me.'

'Good morning and give me some bread,' said Walter in Italian, bowing deep and low to the King. 'My horses are lame and I own seven children.'

'My son is learning Italian,' Agnes explained, poking him hard to stop him from showing off. 'Someone told him it was the language of love.'

'Actually, French is the language of love,' said Henry, leaving no room for debate. 'Italian is the

199

language of poisoners.' He gazed coolly at mother and son.

'Then I shall make sure he abandons the project,' said Agnes smoothly. She smiled at Henry with eyes full of promise, and Geoffrey saw that she was preparing to practise her wiles on him, too. The King returned the smile, and Geoffrey had the distinct feeling that when they next met, they would not be discussing Italian.

'I will arrive at Goodrich in about a week,' Henry went on, addressing his subjects again. 'And then I shall continue to Monmouth, where I shall inspect my borders.'

Baderon stepped forward. 'It will be an honour, Sire, to explain how I have gone about creating a land that is secure and peaceful.'

Henry gathered his reins and touched a spur to his horse's flanks. 'I hope I am not disappointed.'

Henry glanced at Durand as he rode past, and Geoffrey saw their eyes meet. Durand gave a slight nod, as if reassuring the monarch. Geoffrey was more than willing to help Durand on that score: it was in Goodrich's interests to see Corwenna's plans exposed. He watched the royal cavalcade ride away and then turned his thoughts to his own investigations.

The first thing he wanted to know was why Jervil had given Baderon a dagger that sounded remarkably like the one that had killed Henry. The opportunity to initiate a conversation about it came sooner than expected, because Baderon came to stand next to him. Hilde was with him, tired and dishevelled from her hunt for Hugh.

Seguin and Lambert hovered, but were too far away to hear what was said.

'It is good of you to offer us the use of Goodrich, now Dene is gone,' said Baderon amiably. 'It will be pleasant to spend a day or two hunting and hawking while we wait for the King. Sir Olivier and Lady Joan are excellent hosts, and it is a pity the relationship between our estates is not sealed with a marriage.'

Hilde spoke sharply, embarrassed by his candour. 'You could at least wait until I have gone. You are obsessed with alliances these days, and think of little else.'

'I am growing old, and need to consider what I leave behind,' replied Baderon. 'If Hugh were strong, I would be content. But he is not, and I worry about what will happen when I die.'

'You have two daughters wed, and a host of knights who owe us allegiance,' said Hilde. 'Hugh is immaterial. Have you seen him, Geoffrey? He is still missing, and I have been looking all night.'

'Seguin says he is with Eleanor,' said Baderon, before Geoffrey could reply. 'You know how he follows her.'

'Seguin is guessing,' snapped Hilde. 'Besides, just because he says something does not make it true. You listen to him far too readily.'

'Hold your tongue, woman!' cried Baderon, although Geoffrey thought he would be wise to listen to her.

'When I was looking through my brother's possessions, I found something missing,' said Geoffrey in the awkward silence that followed.

'He owned a large dagger with a ruby in the hilt, but it is nowhere to be found.'

'Did he?' asked Hilde, raising her eyebrows. 'He was a man who liked show, but I never saw him wearing such a weapon.'

Geoffrey looked hard at Baderon, who refused to meet his eyes.

'Such baubles come and go,' mumbled the Marcher lord. 'They are given as gifts and stolen by servants. I have learnt not to grow overly attached to them.'

'Are you saying Henry's dagger was stolen?' asked Geoffrey. 'By Jervil, for example?'

'I would not know,' replied Baderon, clearly flustered. 'But your manor is no different from anyone else's, and retainers have light fingers.'

'Jervil,' mused Hilde. 'He *was* a thief, was he not? I recall a fuss over thefts at Goodrich. Joan kept him because he was good with horses, but he was not allowed to sleep in the hall, because he plundered his friends while they slept.'

'Do *you* know Jervil?' asked Geoffrey of Baderon, wondering whether the man would admit to buying stolen property from him.

'I had met him,' replied Baderon. His face became crafty. 'I saw him arrive last night and went to greet him. I was afraid he might have brought bad news about dear Joan, but he was just on his way to visit his brother. He stopped here to break his journey. It is a pity, because if he had slept in the forest, instead of at Dene, he would still be alive.'

He took his daughter's arm and escorted her away. Baderon had guessed that there was a witness to his meeting, and had taken steps to make it sound innocent. Geoffrey rubbed his chin. Baderon was not easy with lies, and there was clearly something amiss.

'You would be wise to mind your own business,' said Seguin, advancing on Geoffrey from one side while Lambert approached from the other. 'No one likes a man who asks too many questions.'

'I am sure you are right,' replied Geoffrey. 'But it is odd that a Goodrich servant should come here to speak to Baderon, but not to me. And it is odder still when money changes hands – money that is now missing.'

'Henry asked questions, and look what happened to him,' said Seguin, leaning close in an attempt to intimidate. 'Go back to Goodrich and tend your sheep. You have quite enough enemies already.'

'Baderon likes you,' said Lambert, countering his brother's bluster with reason. 'I understand he has offered you Hilde. But he will not continue to like you if you ask dangerous questions.'

Geoffrey studied them carefully. They showed signs of having been in the fire, and Lambert had a gash across his forearm. He thought about the knife in Jervil's dead hand. If he had used it to protect himself, it was possible he had injured his assailant. However, it being in Jervil's left hand, and not his dominant right, indicated that it had been placed there *after* he was dead – either to claim self-defence should the killer be caught, or to confuse whoever looked into the murder.

'What are you doing?' asked Lambert uncomfortably. 'Why are you staring at us like that?'

Geoffrey shrugged. 'It is possible to tell a good deal from a man's clothes after a murder.'

Seguin was angry. 'I *will* commit a murder if you do not leave us alone. You are treading on thin ice, and I advise you to stop while you can.'

Eight

It was no easy matter to transport several households and their travelling possessions from one manor to another, and Geoffrey, despite having seen entire armies on the move in the Holy Land, marvelled at the arrangements required. They took all morning, before being interrupted by the requiem mass for Margaret.

'I know the King has charged you to look into Margaret's death,' said fitzNorman as they emerged from the chapel. 'But *I* forbid it.'

'Do you?' asked Geoffrey mildly. 'And why do you think I should obey you, and not the King?'

'Because I will kill you if you start asking personal questions,' replied fitzNorman. 'You will *not* pry into my family's affairs.'

'Your sister was murdered. Surely you want to know the culprit?'

'Look,' said fitzNorman, leading him to one

side so they would not be overheard. 'Margaret was a friendly woman, and liked a dalliance, if you take my meaning. She may have loitered in the stables with this Jervil, and I do not want her name sullied by such a rumour.'

Without waiting for a reply, he was gone. Geoffrey doubted that Margaret had 'liked a dalliance', given her devotion to her husband's memory, and thought fitzNorman cruel to suggest it. Had he killed her himself, because she would not take a new husband? He had a temper, and Geoffrey had seen nothing to imply that he would not turn it on a woman.

After the midday meal, Geoffrey decided to leave, whether his guests were ready or not. He did not want to spend a second night in the hut near the Angel Springs, and space in the ravaged manor house was severely limited. He saddled his horse, sent Bale ahead to Goodrich and prepared to set off himself. His actions prompted the others to shift themselves, and the yard quickly became a hive of activity, with horses readied and the last few travelling chests tossed into carts.

Agnes had intended to flout the King's orders and follow him to Gloucester, believing Henry would not object once she presented herself. Geoffrey remembered the looks that had passed between them and was sure she was right, but Giffard insisted that she and Walter go to Goodrich. Mother and son were angry, but Giffard was immovable.

Baderon and his knights were also ready, although Hilde resolutely refused to abandon the

205

hunt for Hugh. Corwenna grudgingly accompanied Seguin, and Geoffrey felt like telling her that since she did not want to come, and he did not want her to, she should return to Wales. But he did not want a row, so he held his tongue.

'Must *he* come, too?' muttered Lambert. Geoffrey glanced behind him and saw Durand, mounted on a small pony.

'The King wants him to audit my accounts,' muttered Baderon. 'I cannot imagine why.'

'If you are concerned about the grain you "forgot" to tax, do not worry,' said Seguin. 'I imagine Durand will overlook anything, for a price.'

'Is that true, Durand?' asked Baderon. 'Are you amenable to bribes?'

Geoffrey started to laugh, amused that Baderon should phrase his question quite so bluntly.

'Why?' Durand asked frostily. 'Are you thinking of offering me one when I discover you have not been paying the King's taxes?'

'What makes you think you will find evidence of dishonesty?' asked Baderon, offended. 'You may uncover mistakes, but you will find no deliberate wrongdoing.'

'I shall make up my own mind about that,' sniffed Durand, and Geoffrey was sure that he would find something to embarrass Baderon, whether true or not.

On the way they stopped in Rwirdin, where the villagers brought wine for Geoffrey's companions. Seguin and Lambert were soon bored, and wandered off to play dice. While they waited for the horses to be watered, Baderon talked to

Geoffrey about his ambitions to make the region prosperous and safe, and Geoffrey realized that the man had a genuine, deeply held conviction that he was acting in the best interests of his people. There was a lot to like about him, and Geoffrey thought it a pity that he had surrounded himself with louts like Seguin and Lambert – and that he had purchased a murder weapon from Jervil.

It was even more of a pity that Corwenna had attached herself to Baderon's party, and Geoffrey jumped when he straightened up from inspecting his horse's leg to find her nearby with a knife.

'I do not want to go to Goodrich,' she said coldly. 'I made a vow never to set foot in it again, unless it was to kill every last Mappestone.'

'Then go home,' said Geoffrey, walking away from her. He sensed her moving behind him and ducked as the knife sailed towards him. It fell harmlessly in the grass, and he picked it up and added it to his personal arsenal.

'I saw what she did,' said Durand, coming to hold Geoffrey's stirrup while he mounted, as he had done as a squire. 'You should not let her inside Goodrich.'

Geoffrey watched her stalk towards her horse. 'I cannot believe she tried to kill me when so many people are watching. Does she want to be hanged?'

'She is a woman,' replied Durand with a shrug. 'They are not the same as you and me, and there is no point trying to understand them. Why do you think I prefer men?'

Geoffrey smiled, but declined to follow up on the discussion. When they left Rwirdin, he contrived to ride with Giffard. He would not have minded hearing more about Baderon's plans for the region, but to talk to the Lord of Monmouth meant he would have to be near Corwenna. However, the journey was doing nothing for the Bishop's fragile health, and he was a poor travelling companion, morose and irritable.

'I shall *never* touch wine again,' he vowed miserably. 'I feel sick.'

'I am not surprised. I thought you rarely touched wine, and it was hardly a brew that warranted unrestrained guzzling.'

'I had a burning thirst,' said Giffard, 'which the wine did nothing to quench. It was poor quality, was it? I am no judge of such matters.'

'I am sure someone put salt in it, and that it was intended for something other than drinking. Cleaning the silver, perhaps. Joan uses salty cloths soaked in wine to polish spoons.'

'Agnes gave it to me. I might have known *she* would resort to a low trick. I thought it was a peace offering, but—'

'Did you hear anything about Eleanor and Hugh before we left?' asked Geoffrey, changing the subject before Giffard launched into a diatribe. 'Are they still missing?'

Giffard nodded. 'But they did not perish in the flames. No more bodies have been found. Glance behind you, and tell me whether Agnes and Walter are still glaring at me. Walter is sulking, because he resents being told what to do, and Agnes is peeved because she hoped to seduce the King today. But neither can afford to be too cross, because they want me to make Walter my heir.'

'Walter is scowling like a spoilt brat,' said Geoffrey. 'You should leave everything to the Church. He does not deserve anything.'

'I fully intend to,' said Giffard with a humourless smile. 'My will is already drawn up to that effect – although he does not know it.' He then became uncommunicative, so Geoffrey dropped behind to ride with Agnes. She smiled prettily, her eyes full of mischievous promise.

'Sir Geoffrey,' she crooned. 'What can I do for you?'

'Have you spoken to Eleanor since the fire?' he asked.

She shook her head. 'We do not like each other.'

'Why not?' Margaret had told Geoffrey that the two women had spent time together in Normandy, so he suspected that she was lying.

'We had a disagreement.'

'It was not about the Duchess and poison, was it?' Geoffrey watched her intently.

She gaped at him. 'What makes you think I know anything about that sort of thing?'

'I found a phial of mandrake recently. It is good for killing – strong and fast.'

'The Duchess did not die quickly. She was ill for weeks.'

'Then perhaps it was administered in small doses,' suggested Geoffrey.

'Perhaps, but not by me. I know very little about mandrake – only that it shrieks when pulled from the ground and its root, leaves and fruit are poisonous. Tell me about Goodrich's palace instead. Will I like it?'

'Probably not – and it is no palace.'

Agnes showed her small teeth in a tinkling laugh that had Giffard glancing back admonishingly. She poked her tongue out at him.

'Gloomy old fool! He hates the notion of anyone being happy. He thinks we should all be miserable, cheerless and thinking only of our eternal souls.'

'He is a good man,' said Geoffrey, a little coldly.

'That is what makes him a bore. I warrant *you* are not so saintly. What do you say we slip away and get to know each other better? We can tell the Bishop we are looking for firewood.'

'I doubt he will believe that,' said Geoffrey, trying not to show astonishment at her suggestion. 'He is not totally naïve.'

'He most certainly is! Moreover, he needs to open his eyes to the world instead of keeping them fixed on a Heaven that does not exist. Do not look shocked! We all know the Bible is a lot of nonsense.'

'What do you believe in, then?' Geoffrey asked, declining to voice an opinion on such a dangerous issue.

'In having a damned good time before I die,' Agnes replied fervently.

He thought about her visit to the Angel Springs. 'Do you believe in frequenting stone altars at dawn?'

'I suppose Giffard told you I went there? I thought I heard him snoring in that shepherd's hut. If you must know, I was looking for Eleanor.'

'Whom you dislike?'

She scowled. 'You are too quick with your questions! But let us talk of nicer things. You have a fine, strong body and a handsome face. Would you like to—'

'I would like to know why you were looking for Eleanor,' interrupted Geoffrey, rather repelled by her salaciousness.

She pouted. 'You prefer Eleanor to me? I am prettier.'

'I could not say: I have never seen Eleanor's face.'

'She has no lower jaw,' confided Agnes. 'One of her magic potions blew it off.'

Geoffrey laughed, thinking it an outrageous claim. 'What were you really doing at the spring? Was it you who did the drawing of the manor?'

'That was probably Eleanor. I went to *cancel* the spell, so the fire would not break out again. My actions were noble.'

'You know about cancelling spells, do you?'

His questions were making her angry, and her answer was sharp. 'I learned from my mother, who was a very wise woman.'

'Did she teach you about poisons, too?'

'As I told you before, I know nothing about those.'

* * *

211

Geoffrey was relieved when Goodrich's sturdy walls appeared. He was tired of Giffard's misery, Agnes' attempts to make him behave indiscreetly and her son's resentful looks.

'My mother is recently widowed,' Walter said tightly. 'And she loves the Duke, so leave her alone. I did not teach you how to seduce women in Italian so you could have *her*.'

'Where did you learn Italian?' Geoffrey asked, before he felt compelled to box the boy's ears for his impudence.

'I spent much of my life in Italy,' replied Walter loftily.

'How much of your life?' asked Geoffrey, wondering why he had not, then, learnt the language properly.

'A whole week. There is much that is admirable about Italy.'

'Including its poisons?' asked Geoffrey.

'You must ask Eleanor the witch about that,' replied Walter.

'I would, but she seems to be missing. Have you seen her since the fire?'

'I saw her before the blaze, playing some game with Hugh that made him squeal like a pig,' replied Walter. 'But not after. I hope they are dead.'

'Why?'

'Because Hugh is an imbecile, and I want Baderon to leave his property to Hilde – if he does, then I might marry her: she will be sufficiently wealthy. And because Eleanor is a witch.'

'I thought you and Eleanor were friends.'

'We were – but she turned against me when I tried to bed her. I cannot imagine why, because I spoke Italian. I do not like women who are friendly one moment and hostile the next.'

'There are rumours the Duchess was poisoned,' said Geoffrey. 'Do you think Eleanor provided the toxin?'

'It would be the kind of thing she would do,' agreed Walter spitefully.

When the travellers arrived at Goodrich, smartly dressed servants hurried out to tend the horses. Joan and Olivier appeared almost as quickly with wine. Olivier served Baderon and his knights, while Joan offered it to Giffard – who refused with a shudder – Agnes and then Geoffrey, who was touched by the courtesy. Durand was given a sip of ale by Torva.

'Why is *he* here?' whispered Joan. A plain-speaking woman herself, she did not like Durand's slippery, unscrupulous ways, or that he had earlier been disloyal to Geoffrey.

'To spy on Baderon. Henry thinks the alliances with the Welsh might not be good for England.'

Joan was thoughtful. 'Henry is right. It is always better to have hostile nations divided into factions. Baderon is knitting them together too efficiently. They have been restless for war ever since Prince Iorwerth promised them one last summer. And many are starving. It is only a matter of time before they encourage each other to raid English granaries, and ours will be one of the first.'

'It will, if Corwenna has any say in the matter,'

said Geoffrey, looking to where she sat astride her horse, frostily refusing the wine that Olivier proffered.

Joan grimaced. 'She made a vow to see us in our graves. I have tried to win her round, but she is implacable. Still, as long as she is here, she is not encouraging the Welsh to unite against us.'

'Do they listen to her?'

'She is Caerdig's daughter, and he is highly respected. Also, she likes to orate about honour and glory, and knows the kind of talk to get men's blood up. Still, if the King is aware of the problem, I imagine it will soon be resolved.'

'I hope so,' said Geoffrey. 'Have you heard about Jervil?'

She nodded. 'Bale told us when you sent him ahead with the news that we were to expect guests. It is a pity; he was not nice, but he had a way with horses. But what was he doing at Dene?'

'I wish I knew.' Geoffrey lowered his voice. 'The King saw him talking to Baderon, and says money changed hands.'

Joan's eyes narrowed. She did not like the King, either. 'Do you believe him, or was he making up tales so you would agree to conduct another of his investigations?'

Geoffrey thought about it. 'He had no reason to lie.'

'None you know about,' corrected Joan. 'He is crafty, with many plans and agendas. But assuming he *was* being honest for once, why did Baderon pay Jervil?'

'In exchange for a dagger – one with a ruby in

its hilt.'

Joan stared at him. 'That sounds like ... like the blade that killed our brother. I suppose Father Adrian finally sold it. Did I tell you I wrapped it in holy cloth once I removed it from Henry's corpse? Nevertheless, it felt tainted, and I could not even bring myself to look at it when I gave it to Father Adrian.'

'So, how did it go from Father Adrian to Jervil. Did Jervil steal it?'

Joan shook her head. 'Even Jervil would not steal from a church.'

'Father Adrian kept a murder weapon in his church?' asked Geoffrey, startled.

'It was a Black Knife, and needed to be somewhere holy – to cleanse it. Father Adrian put it under the altar and said it must remain there until Easter. By then, it would have lost its evil.'

'None of this answers why Jervil sold it to Baderon. Was it Baderon's in the first place? If it was valuable, then it probably did belong to a nobleman. But, if it was Baderon's, then it means he or one of his men killed Henry.'

Joan sighed. 'Baderon is low on *my* list of suspects. I like him: he is weak, but essentially decent. Top are fitzNorman and Ralph.' She faltered into silence, watching the arrival of the wagons full of their guests' possessions.

'I hope you do not mind half of the county descending on you,' said Geoffrey apologetically. 'The King gave me no choice.'

'I like visitors,' said Joan. 'Now we have the funds to entertain them, they are a pleasure. But I should see to your friend the Bishop. He looks unwell.'

'Geoff!' came a bellowing voice from the door of the hall. It was loud enough to still the buzz of conversation in the yard, and everyone turned to look. Geoffrey felt his spirits rise when he saw Goodrich had another visitor.

'I almost forgot,' said Joan, not entirely pleased. 'Sir Roger of Durham arrived yesterday.'

Geoffrey smiled as the massive, familiar figure of his fellow *Jerosolimitanus* strode towards him. Roger was resplendent in a fur-lined cloak, fine boots and new surcoat, although the latter was already stained. The Crusader's cross was bright and sharp, and proclaimed to all that here was one of those who had wrested Jerusalem from the infidel. His black hair was long, and he sported a fashionable beard: he was adapting to civilian life far better than Geoffrey.

'I am glad to see you,' Geoffrey said, as the friends embraced. 'Life here is dull.'

'That is not what I hear,' said Roger, laughing. 'You are looking into your brother's death; Giffard wants you to find out if his nephew poisoned the Duchess of Normandy; the Welsh are girding their loins for war; and a groom and a noblewoman have been strangled. If you call *that* dull, we had better find a battle somewhere. And fast.'

Father Adrian was reciting mass when Geoffrey entered Goodrich's little church the following morning. Joan had been directing a lively and erudite conversation around a blazing fire for

216

those who preferred to be indoors, while Olivier had taken the others hawking. Even Geoffrey, who had never taken to the sport, could see that his brother-in-law was very good. With no social obligations, Geoffrey had decided to find out about the Black Knife.

Roger had accompanied him part way, but they had met Helbye, and a cup of ale with an old comrade held more appeal for Roger than seeing a priest. They agreed to meet later, although Geoffrey suspected it would be a good deal later. He stood at the back of the chapel, listening to Father Adrian and finding peace in the familiar words and cadences. Unlike many parish priests, Father Adrian's Latin was good. Durand, who liked churches, nodded approvingly.

'He is excellent,' he whispered. 'I could listen to him all day.'

Geoffrey soon saw they might have to: Father Adrian went on and on. Geoffrey left to roam in the graveyard, breathing in the spring-scented air. Eventually, he reached the area that held the Mappestones. Henry's cross was down again, and it occurred to Geoffrey that it had not simply fallen – someone had forced it over. He began to pull it upright, but abandoned his labours when someone approached.

'What happened to Jervil?' demanded Torva. 'Did you kill him?'

'No,' said Geoffrey firmly. 'However, I do know he took a dagger with a ruby in its hilt and sold it to Baderon before he died. Why did he do that, Torva?'

'I do not know,' said Torva furtively.

217

'I overheard Jervil trying to bribe Bale to spy on me,' said Geoffrey, watching the steward's reactions carefully. 'Why?'

'Why do you think?' snapped Torva. 'Because we need to know what you are up to. Now I have work to do.'

He hurried away, and Geoffrey could see that he was deeply worried. He decided to further question Torva later. After a while, Father Adrian emerged with those who had endured his mass. The parishioners nodded to Geoffrey as they passed, although few were familiar. To his surprise, Geoffrey saw that Ralph de Bicanofre had attended the service, too, with Douce and their father Wulfric. Geoffrey ducked behind the porch, not wanting Ralph to start another quarrel.

'You are right to make yourself scarce,' said Helbye's wife – Geoffrey had no idea of her name, because Helbye never used it. She was one of Father Adrian's most dedicated attendees and had seen Geoffrey move into hiding; uninvited, she joined him. 'Ralph has a nasty temper.'

'I am here, too,' came a hot voice at Geoffrey's ear, making him jump. It was Bale, and the three of them were uncomfortably cramped in the narrow space between porch and buttress. 'Your sister told me where you were, so I thought I should make sure the priest does not do anything rash.'

'Father Adrian?' asked Geoffrey. 'He is not violent.'

'He keeps a knife under his altar,' confided

Bale. 'A sharp one. I have seen it myself.'

'It is the Black Knife that killed your brother,' said Helbye's wife. 'Joan gave it to him, to sell for the poor. But it has lain in the church for months, and he has done nothing with it.'

'It is not there now,' said Geoffrey. 'Jervil sold it to Baderon.'

'Did he?' asked Bale. He sounded sorry. 'It was a fine thing, with a good, sharp blade. But Jervil was a fool if what you say is true. He risked his immortal soul if he stole from God.'

Geoffrey was bemused by Bale. He was brave and seemed honest, which made him a refreshing change from Durand. However, his fascination with pointed implements was sinister. He wondered if he ever would feel comfortable with the man, and tried to move away – but to no avail, as Mistress Helbye was wedged too firmly on his other side. He hoped no one could see them.

Bale, meanwhile, was gazing at Douce, who was dressed in a blue kirtle that fell in tidy folds to the ground. 'You see her?' he asked in a hoarse whisper. 'Mistress Helbye says *she* is the woman you will wed.'

Geoffrey raised his eyebrows, but Helbye's wife did not seem at all disconcerted that her confidences had been so baldly betrayed. 'Wulfric brought her here today, so she can get a good look at you,' she said. 'I heard them talking earlier. She was due to meet you at Dene, but the fire started before you could be introduced.'

'Ralph would never allow his sister to marry me.'

219

'Ralph is not lord of Bicanofre,' said Helbye's wife dismissively. 'Wulfric is, and he wants you for Douce, so he is here to point you out to her. She is slow in the wits, you see, and will need to be told which man to allure, or she may go after the wrong one.'

'She will do,' said Bale, assessing Douce critically. 'She has fine hips for breeding and strong bones. A little long in the face, perhaps, but good teeth.'

'The poor woman is not a horse,' said Geoffrey, indignant on her behalf. Realizing that he could not hide forever, he struggled into the open and the family immediately sailed towards him.

'Now is your chance to size her up,' whispered Helbye's wife helpfully. 'Before Joan and Wulfric settle matters without you.'

The man who stepped forward to bow to Geoffrey wore clothes that were well cut, but too small, giving the impression that they had been hauled from storage especially for the occasion. Next to him, Ralph scowled. When Geoffrey studied Douce properly, he saw that Bale's equine terminology was not misplaced. She had a long face with widely spaced eyes, large teeth and heavy lips.

'I am Wulfric de Bicanofre, and this is my son, Ralph,' Wulfric said gushingly.

'Ralph and I have already met,' replied Geoffrey.

Ralph looked away. Wulfric ignored the hostility between them, and his smile became simpering. 'And *this* is my daughter Douce. She is

220

twenty years old, has a dowry *and* is a virgin.'

Geoffrey glanced at Douce, to see whether she was chagrined by her father's outrageous words, but she merely continued to beam in a way that made him wonder whether she was an idiot.

'We are looking for a good match,' said Ralph, lest his father's words had been too subtle. '*He* thinks one will be found in Goodrich.' The expression on his face made it clear that he did not concur.

'A union between Bicanofre and Goodrich would be excellent for both manors,' enthused Wulfric. 'We hope you will look favourably on us. You are said to be more pleasant than your brothers, and a *Jerosolimitanus*, too. Douce would be honoured to accept you.'

'What do you say, Douce?' asked Geoffrey. 'Are you as keen to secure a husband as your family is?'

'Of course she is,' said Wulfric, while Douce continued to smile and nod. 'A more demure soul you will never meet. She will make any man happy with her gentle manners. Nor is she the kind to object to you seeking pleasure elsewhere on occasion, if you take my meaning.'

'But I would kill any man who used her badly, *Jerosolimitanus* or not,' snarled Ralph.

'We brought her here today, rather than attending our own church, so you could have a look at her,' said Wulfric, stamping on his son's foot to shut him up. 'Then, if Joan mentions Douce, you will know who she is talking about.'

'We are to have singers with balls tonight,' announced Douce loudly.

'Musicians and jugglers,' explained Wulfric hastily, seeing Geoffrey's confusion. 'Bicanofre is a small manor compared to Goodrich, but we have offered your guests an evening of entertainment. I hope you will come. Douce will be there.'

'What about Eleanor?' Geoffrey asked. 'Have you seen her since—'

'You are interested in Eleanor?' pounced Wulfric. 'I had no idea anyone would take her! But, if you are willing, then of course we can reach an agreement.'

'That is not what I meant,' objected Geoffrey. He glanced at Douce, to see if she was offended, but she wore the same stupid smile, and he suspected that she was not following the conversation at all. 'I was going to ask whether you had you seen her since the fire.'

'She is missing.' Wulfric sounded more annoyed than concerned. 'But she likes to wander in the forest, and I am told her red cloak was seen flitting in the trees after the fire was out.'

'Enough of this,' blurted Ralph unpleasantly. 'My father wants to know your decision about Douce. Will you consider her? I do not want to waste time if you have already decided against us.'

Geoffrey felt sorry for Douce. He ignored Ralph and offered to escort her to where a servant was waiting with their horses, bringing about a triumphant beam on her father's face.

'Is it far to Bicanofre?' Geoffrey asked, flailing around for polite conversation.

'Bicanofre,' she said brightly. 'It is a village.'

'I know,' said Geoffrey. 'I asked how far it is from Goodrich.'

'My brother Ralph has a green cloak with silver thread,' burbled Douce happily. 'And our cat had fifty kittens last week. Or was it five? I can never remember numbers.'

'I see,' said Geoffrey. He was relieved when they reached the horses and a servant stepped forward to help her into her saddle.

'She is a good lass,' said Wulfric, winking at Geoffrey. 'You will never have any trouble from her – not like some of the others you could choose. Hilde is manly, Margaret is dead and Corwenna would kill you on your wedding night.' He took the reins of his daughter's horse and led her away.

'I did as you asked, Father,' Geoffrey heard her say. 'I did not answer any questions I did not understand and I kept the discussion to pleasant, normal things.'

'And Isabel?' asked Geoffrey of Ralph, aware that Wulfric's list had not included the fair, grieving figure. 'What about her?'

'She needs to do penance for her sin with your brother,' said Ralph contemptuously.

'She needs you,' said Geoffrey, fighting the impulse to say he could not imagine why. 'She grieves for Margaret, and has been asking for you.'

'I no longer know her,' said Ralph coldly. 'And we will not speak of this matter again.'

'God's teeth!' swore Geoffrey, as Bale and Helbye's wife came to stand next to him to watch

223

the Bicanofre contingent ride away. 'That man is asking for my sword in his unfeeling heart.'

'Isabel is better off without him,' said Helbye's wife. 'Love is double-edged; it brings misery as well as happiness. People should try to avoid it, because it is such a gamble.'

'I was in love once,' said Bale. 'But she said she would only marry me if I agreed never to bring a blade into the house. So I turned her down.'

'What did you think of Douce?' asked Helbye's wife in the silence that followed.

'She is half out of her wits.'

'More than half,' agreed Bale. 'But that will not matter if she begets you children – and she will.'

'What makes you so sure?'

'She has already produced a couple, which is why her father wants her settled,' replied Bale. 'He will not want her worn out before she can produce legitimate ones.'

'He said she was a virgin,' objected Geoffrey.

'Perhaps he thinks you will not know the difference. Well? What did you think of her? Helbye's wife says she is the best of the batch. Now Margaret is dead and Isabel wants to take the veil, there is only Hilde, Corwenna and Douce left.'

'Well, there is Eleanor,' said Helbye's wife. 'I doubt *she* is dead. But you must not accept her, not if she was the last woman on God's Earth.' She folded her arms.

'Why?' said Geoffrey, understanding that he was expected to ask.

'Her suitability,' said Helbye's wife, while Geoffrey thought that if insanity and pre-marital pregnancies did not make a woman unsuitable, then he could not imagine what Eleanor had done. But Helbye's wife had had enough gossip, and moved away. Meanwhile, Geoffrey remembered why he had gone to the church in the first place.

'Father Adrian!' he called. 'I want to talk to you.'

'No,' said Father Adrian in alarm. 'Not about your brother, and not about any of those women Mistress Helbye has been telling you about, either. Joan will have her own views, and I will not interfere.'

'It is about the dagger Joan gave you.'

'She said I could sell it, to provide alms for the poor. So I took it to Rosse two days ago. A silversmith gave me three shillings for it. Why? Did you want it back?'

'Three shillings is a good price,' said Bale. 'Did you tell this silversmith it was a Black Knife?'

Father Adrian looked furtive. 'He did not ask. Besides, it had lain under my altar for months, so it was clean. The merchant would not have given me three shillings if I had told him its history. People can be superstitious.'

'Including you,' said Geoffrey, 'if you felt it needed three months in a church before it was fit for sale.'

'That is different,' replied Father Adrian primly. 'That is *religion*.'

Geoffrey was not sure where the line lay, but

he wanted answers, not a debate. 'How many people knew the dagger was there?'

'The whole village,' replied Father Adrian. 'I asked people to pray for its purification, so it would raise money for the poor.' He looked smug. 'It worked: three shillings *is* a fine sum.'

'Have you done business with this silversmith before?' asked Geoffrey, wondering how it had gone from the Rosse craftsman to Jervil. Perhaps the groom had been uncomfortable stealing from a church but was not squeamish about robbing a merchant.

Father Adrian shook his head. 'It is not every day I have valuable knives to sell. I thought I might have to break it up – sell him the silver hilt and prise the emerald out to sell to a jeweller. But he agreed to take the whole thing.'

'*An emerald*?' asked Geoffrey. 'But they are green.'

Father Adrian nodded patiently. 'It was a green stone.'

'Joan said it was red.' And the King had mentioned a ruby in the knife Jervil had given to Baderon – and Geoffrey was sure that *he* knew his precious jewels.

'It was green,' said Father Adrian firmly. 'She cannot have looked properly.'

But Geoffrey knew Joan would have been familiar with what she possessed.

'It was covered in blood,' said Bale keenly. 'There was a great wound in Henry's stomach. Right here.' He indicated a point just below his ribs. 'And it was deep. I shoved my finger in it to see.'

226

'Bale!' exclaimed Father Adrian, aghast. He glanced nervously at Geoffrey, who was not in a position to be squeamish, since he had poked fingers in wounds to assess their depths himself. Father Adrian hurriedly changed the subject. 'It *was* an emerald, Geoffrey. And there was not enough blood to make a green stone red. I will give you the three shillings, if you want to buy it back, although the poor will suffer...'

'I do not want it back,' said Geoffrey absently, reviewing the facts. Joan had pulled a red-jewelled knife from their brother, and it was a red-jewelled knife that had been sold to Baderon. Yet Joan had given the knife to Father Adrian, whereupon the jewel had become an emerald. There was only one conclusion: someone had swapped it in her bedchamber. She said she could not look at it, so she had probably given it to Father Adrian without making sure that it was the same one. But who had access to Joan's room?

He considered the servants. But an emerald was a valuable jewel, and no servant would casually provide one to swap for a ruby. The only sensible answer was that someone outside Goodrich had asked a servant to make the exchange, and had no doubt been delighted when the deception had gone so long undetected. Baderon came immediately to mind. But then why had Jervil waited to give it to him?

'Henry's grave,' he said to Father Adrian, changing the subject when no answers were forthcoming. 'I straightened his cross twice last week, but it was back on the ground again today.'

'People come to spit and trample on it,' said Father Adrian, more matter-of-fact than Geoffrey felt was warranted for such desecration. 'But I have seen no one attacking it recently.'

'It must stop,' said Geoffrey firmly. 'Henry is dead, and his sins are between him and God.'

'I will try to dissuade them,' said Father Adrian. 'But it will not be easy.'

Geoffrey hovered in the churchyard while the priest closed the church door – then opened it again when he realized that he had shut someone inside. There emerged an ancient crone, devoid of teeth and with skin so brown and wrinkled, it looked more vegetable than human.

'Mother Elgiva,' said Father Adrian suspiciously. 'What have you been doing?'

'Listening,' replied Elgiva with a predatory smile. 'Folk seek my advice, so eavesdropping is helpful. It is astonishing what you can learn. For example, I know Sir Geoffrey has asked several people about the fate of his brother, but no one has told him anything useful. And I know most folk think he should marry Douce, despite her lack of wits and loose morals.'

'Why do they favour her?' asked Geoffrey. Personally, he was disturbed by Douce not knowing the difference between five and fifty. It did not auger well for household finances.

Elgiva began to list reasons on her gnarled fingers. 'Hilde is too manly. Corwenna is comely, but she will not rest until your family lies dead.'

'Not a good idea to marry her, then,' said Geoffrey flippantly.

'No.' Elgiva frowned. 'She was just another vengeful woman when she was Rhys' widow, but her betrothal to Seguin has made her feel powerful. I fear her.'

'There is no need,' said Father Adrian gently. 'Llan Martin is not in a position to harm us. Besides, Caerdig would never let it happen.'

Elgiva's rheumy eyes flashed angrily. 'That *was* true, but things have changed. Baderon listens too much to Seguin and Lambert. *They* are not interested in peace, but in expanding their wealth.'

'You think they might bring us to war?' asked Geoffrey.

'I think Corwenna will try to use them so. And Baderon will not be able to stop her. We stand at the edge of a precipice, and I hope we do not all go clattering down it.'

Father Adrian shook the old woman's arm. 'Enough, Mother! You are unnerving me.'

'Good,' said Elgiva, before turning back to Geoffrey. 'But we were talking about marriages. We have discounted Corwenna and Hilde, but there are others. Isabel, for example.'

Father Adrian tried to escort her from the churchyard. 'No good will come from gossip-ing—'

Elgiva pulled away from him. 'He needs to know. All these folk are staying at Goodrich, and it would be unfortunate if he was run through for saying something in ignorance.'

Geoffrey entirely agreed, finding her attitude

229

refreshing. 'Who killed Henry?' he asked, aiming to make the most of someone willing to talk.

'Most people say fitzNorman. Others think Ralph, because Isabel was a good match, and by coupling with Henry, she became untenable. No man wants his wife deflowered by another man.'

'Yes and no,' said Geoffrey. 'First, Ralph did the deflowering himself; Henry came later. And second, people here seem to set great store by wealth. Isabel was no poorer after her night with Henry. Besides, Douce is no innocent, with her illegitimate children, but I am still expected to consider her.'

'But Ralph has principles,' said Father Adrian.

'Not ones he applies to his sister,' said Geoffrey. 'Besides, I have principles, too. I am not marrying Douce.'

Elgiva took Father Adrian's arm and walked towards the gate. Geoffrey trailed after them, his mind flitting between his brother's death and the complex politics of acquiring a wife.

'Do not speculate with Sir Geoffrey, Mother Elgiva,' Father Adrian said. 'Henry was an evil man, and I doubt many angels wept when he died. But some may weep if Sir Geoffrey discovers the killer, and a good man ends up kicking empty air under a gibbet – or if Geoffrey runs him through, as *Jerosolimitani* are wont to do.'

'Good men do not murder those too drunk to defend themselves,' retorted Geoffrey, resenting the implication that he enjoyed random slaughter.

Elgiva abandoned the priest and took Geoffrey's arm instead. 'My house is behind that barn. Come with me, and I will answer any questions you want.'

'Do not demean yourself by listening to gossip,' pleaded Father Adrian.

'Why not?' demanded Geoffrey. 'No one else will tell me anything – including you.'

He followed the old woman to her home. It was a round shack, with a thatched roof and walls of hazel twigs packed with mud. Smoke billowed from the hearth, and Geoffrey started to cough as soon as he ducked around the leather sheet that served as a door. His throat was still raw from the blaze at Dene, and he was loath to spend more time hacking in confined spaces, but he supposed it was all in a good cause. Father Adrian hovered outside, and Geoffrey wondered why: did the priest think to prevent Elgiva giving information that would expose the killer?

Geoffrey continued to cough as he glanced around the hut. Unidentifiable objects hung from the rafters, and there were pots and jugs everywhere. Lurking beneath the odour of burning wood was an aroma of spices and potions that was vaguely pleasant. Elgiva pushed a three-legged stool in his direction, and he lowered himself on to it, watching her sit cross-legged on the floor.

'This will cure your cough,' she said, proffering something in a wooden cup. It looked like water, and he had taken a large gulp before a burning sensation gripped his chest. He gagged, feeling the potion sear into his stomach. Suddenly, he understood why the hut was so well endowed with pots and smells: Elgiva was a witch. And he had just swallowed a brew that seemed to be dissolving his innards.

Nine

'Do not drink anything,' advised Father Adrian from outside, although it was already too late. Geoffrey felt as though his insides were on fire, and it was difficult to breathe. He could not see, his eyes blinded by tears. Then the terrible burning eased and he found he could draw breath again.

'God's teeth!' he spluttered. His lips were numb and there was a foul taste in his mouth that made him want to be sick. 'Have you poisoned me?'

'You are not supposed to gulp it like ale,' said Elgiva with a disapproving frown. 'It is to be sipped and savoured. What a waste!'

Geoffrey set the cup on the hearth, feeling an odd weakness in his legs, while the liquid continued to scald his stomach.

'You do not remember me, do you?' said Elgiva through the gloom. 'I gave you salves when you were injured in childish play.'

After the Devil's brew he had just downed, Geoffrey's mind was a blank about her salves. 'It was a long time ago. Are you a witch?' he asked.

'I prefer "wise woman". "Witch" conveys the wrong impression. I know the plants of the forest and people come to me for advice. They go to Father Adrian, too, but they prefer me because I do not force them into penance for honest mistakes.'

'I also do not know how to make women unpregnant, or how to render a man potent in the marriage bed!' called Adrian caustically. 'However, when they are in distress, it is God's comfort they crave, not a mouthful of that stuff I use for cleaning my pigsty.'

'I imagine there is room for both,' said Geoffrey, before they could argue. 'I do not suppose Isabel came to *you* with her problem, did she? For the child that might have been Henry's?'

'I could not say,' replied Elgiva, but she looked away. Geoffrey heard voices outside, followed by a laugh. Father Adrian had met some parishioners, and was no longer listening.

'When did she come?' he asked.

She regarded him coolly. 'Perhaps I should not have invited you here. You are too quick. Poor Isabel. By the time she summoned me, it was already too late and the girl-child she carried was lost.' She tipped her head to one side. 'If I gave you a potion to bring Ralph back to her, would you make sure he drank it?'

'Only if you assure me it will kill him in the process.'

Elgiva cackled her amusement. 'He is a headstrong man, so my elixir of mandrake will have to be a powerful one, or it will not work.'

'*Mandrake*?' asked Geoffrey. 'I thought that

233

was poisonous.'

'Only in the wrong hands. It can cause vomiting and purging.'

'Do you know Eleanor de Bicanofre? She is a wise woman, too.'

'No, *she* is a witch,' corrected Elgiva. 'I hear she is missing, which is a bad thing. With women like Eleanor, it is always best to know where they are.'

Geoffrey recalled the laughing eyes when Eleanor had removed the splinters from his arm. She had done him no harm, and he did not like the way people maligned her. 'She is all right.'

Elgiva pursed her lips. 'You and Hugh are the only ones who think so. He is smitten, and it is to her credit that she has not pushed him over a cliff. I wonder what she is planning with him this time. The last time they went missing was September.'

'That is when Henry died.'

'Yes,' agreed Elgiva, meeting his eyes. 'I saw them in the woods about a week before his murder. It is rumoured that she put a curse on Henry.'

'Why would she do that?'

'He pulled off her veil in a drunken rage. He claimed it was accidental; she says otherwise. But she was angry, because it showed her jaw had been blown off during a demonic experiment.'

'So, you consider her a suspect for Henry's murder?' asked Geoffrey. 'Because even if she did not wield the dagger herself, she chanted evil charms?'

Elgiva took a sip from her cup. 'I do not know who dispatched your brother – his killer made sure there were no witnesses, although Jervil heard them talking. Later, Jervil told me Henry cursed everyone with his dying breath, including Joan. Henry predicted *you* would come and expel her, and subdue Goodrich with a mailed fist.'

'Is that why people are suspicious of me? Henry's deranged ramblings?'

'They do not know what to expect!' called Father Adrian, listening once again. 'Perhaps it is my fault. I preached hard against the Crusade, and my descriptions of *Jerosolimitani* as blood-drenched, lust-craven thieves were powerful.'

'Jervil is dead,' said Geoffrey to Elgiva, not deigning to address the priest's prejudices. 'He was strangled after selling a dagger to Baderon. He was paid in silver, but that had disappeared when I saw his body.'

'You had a rummage, did you?' asked Elgiva wryly. 'Perhaps you are not so different from Henry, after all. But tell me about this dagger. What did it look like?'

'There was a ruby in its hilt.'

'*A ruby*?' asked Elgiva. 'The Black Knife Joan gave Father Adrian contained an emerald.'

'It did,' agreed Father Adrian. 'In that case the dagger Jervil sold Baderon was not the one I had in my church. It was not the one that killed Henry, either – so Jervil's transaction with Baderon can have nothing to do with your brother's death.'

'I think it was exchanged in Joan's bed-

235

chamber,' explained Geoffrey. 'Jervil had the real one; you did not.' He turned his attention to Elgiva. 'How well did Jervil know Baderon?'

Elgiva grinned, pleased to show off her knowledge. 'Joan used Jervil as a messenger, because he was a good rider. He often visited Monmouth when she needed to communicate with Baderon.'

Geoffrey rubbed his chin. It seemed obvious that Baderon or one of his knights had killed Jervil, either so he could never tell anyone that Baderon had the murder weapon, or to retrieve the silver Baderon had paid for it. And Margaret was murdered because she had witnessed the killing. Or was that too simple an explanation?

'Can you tell me any more about Henry?' he asked.

'I cannot list all the folk who bore him a grudge,' said Elgiva. 'We would be here all day. There was not a man, woman or child on Goodrich's estates who did not hate him.'

'But none of these owned a jewelled dagger,' Geoffrey pointed out. 'And if they had, they would not have left it behind.'

'True,' admitted Elgiva. 'That narrows your list. But you still have Caerdig, Corwenna, Ralph, fitzNorman and Isabel. Margaret also disliked Henry, because of what happened to her niece. Then there are Baderon's knights. Not Baderon himself, though.'

'Why not?' asked Geoffrey.

'Too indecisive,' replied Elgiva. Geoffrey dismissed her opinion; Baderon's indecision was not a good enough reason to strike him from

236

the list.

'I do not think it was Baderon, either,' said Father Adrian. 'He and Henry treated each other with respect, and were on better terms than one would have imagined – especially given Henry's callous rejection of Hilde.'

'You say no one from Goodrich killed Henry, because the dagger was such a fine weapon,' said Elgiva. 'However, Joan and Olivier like to entertain, and many of their visitors are wealthy. Some are so rich that they might not miss a jewelled dagger, if it were "borrowed" by a servant.'

'You think a servant stole the blade and used it to kill my brother?'

Elgiva shrugged. 'Why not? Jervil detested Henry, and so did others. Many would have willingly stabbed him. And do not forget Joan and Olivier, either. They struggled to protect Goodrich from Henry's depredations. So ask yourself why *they* are so determined to let his murder lie?'

It rained that afternoon, bringing those who had gone hawking home earlier than expected. Joan lit additional fires, and the whole castle became hot, stuffy and uncomfortable. The conversation was mostly about the upcoming entertainment at Bicanofre. Walter and Agnes were delighted at the prospect, while Baderon intimated that they were likely to be disappointed. Maliciously, Seguin and Lambert exaggerated Bicanofre's charms to the point where the Bishop's family could not help but be disappointed. Geoffrey

237

grew tired of the lot of them, and climbed the spiral stairs until he reached the battlements.

It was peaceful away from the hubbub, and he did not mind the drizzle that blew in from the west. He leant his elbows on the wall, and for some reason Margaret's husband came to mind. He recalled a skirmish in which they had fought near each other, and Robert had screamed her name several times. It was a pity, Geoffrey thought, that *he* would never enjoy such a marriage, but would be obliged to take a woman who would rather have someone else – or no one at all.

He heard footsteps and turned to see Durand, wrapped in a thick, well-oiled cloak and wearing a hood to protect his golden mane. He looked angry.

'Baderon has the manners of a peasant,' he snapped. 'He has just informed me that manors in Suffolk are inferior to those in Gloucestershire.'

'Did you goad him?'

Durand glared. 'I said Suffolk is fertile, and my land is worth three times his.'

'Then it is not surprising. No man likes to be told his estates are worthless.'

'But it is true,' said Durand sulkily.

'Perhaps,' said Geoffrey, not wanting to argue with Durand, either.

'You seem preoccupied,' said Durand after a while.

Geoffrey nodded. 'Did I tell you I met Margaret's husband on the Crusade?'

Durand shook his head, and his spiteful face

softened. 'I know people do not respect me – I am different from other men – but Margaret was always kind. If I can help you to catch whoever snuffed out her life, ask. I promise I will not use it as a lever to persuade you to help me with other investigations.'

Geoffrey stared at him in surprise. It was not often his old squire was sincere, and even more rare that he liked someone enough to be touched by a death. 'I think she saw Jervil killed, and was murdered in her turn, so she could not tell anyone what she had witnessed.'

'Perhaps she saw the villain placing the knife in Jervil's dead hand – his non-dominant hand, as you so quickly established. That must have been what happened. She would have run to raise the alarm, had she seen the culprit actually strangling Jervil.'

'So, to find out who strangled her, I need to know who killed Jervil. But he was wary and suspicious – and would have been even more so after receiving a purse of coins. Why did he relax his guard? I looked at his hands, and there were no marks on them. Why did he not fight back?'

'Perhaps he was hit on the head and stunned first.'

'I saw no bumps, but it is possible.' Geoffrey smiled: it was good to have someone of Durand's intelligence and insightfulness to talk to, because it helped clarify his own thoughts. 'We *are* right to assume Jervil was killed first, are we not? It is not possible that Margaret was strangled, and then Jervil dispatched to ensure *his* silence?'

Durand shook his head. 'She was worried about Isabel. I imagine she went to the stables looking for her and surprised the culprit while he was covering his tracks.'

Geoffrey supposed he was right. He told Durand all he knew about the deaths, and then outlined his thoughts about Henry. Unfortunately, however he presented the facts, it was difficult to see how Baderon could be innocent. It was a pity, because Geoffrey liked him more than the other suspects.

'I do not see Baderon strangling his victims in a dark stable,' he said, somewhat lamely.

'I am not so sure.' Durand was thoughtful. 'He is smug, opinionated, vacillating and weak – *exactly* the kind of character who kills in the dark. And ask yourself *why* he was prepared to pay Jervil for this ruby dagger. There is only one conclusion: Baderon stabbed Henry, and left the knife behind in his panic. That is the *only* reason he would have been prepared to buy it.'

Geoffrey was forced to concede that Durand's deductions made sense.

The clerk continued. 'Then, not trusting a thief to keep his silence, Baderon followed Jervil to the stables and strangled him. It was a good opportunity to retrieve his money, too. Then, as he was placing the knife in Jervil's hand – to make the murder look like self-defence – Margaret came in.'

'Damn!' muttered Geoffrey, although he had reasoned much the same himself. 'This scenario fits the facts. It is a shame: Baderon cares about his people and is not a bad man.'

'Not all killers are cold-hearted,' said Durand. 'I have met enough – mostly through dealings with you – to know they can be charming. And if Baderon had stopped with your brother, I would have advised you to look the other way – no one seems to have liked him and it is generally agreed that Goodrich is better off without him. But he has struck three times now.'

'I cannot accuse Baderon with the "evidence" we have. It is mere speculation.'

'You may never get it,' warned Durand. 'He is clever, and has Seguin and Lambert to help him. You must be careful, or you may find you are next in line for a death without witnesses.'

'I am under the King's protection. His agents will investigate if I am murdered.'

'But that will not do *you* any good. You must not be complacent. I am glad Roger is here: you need your friends around you when you do not know your enemies.'

'Can I count you among my friends?' asked Geoffrey.

Durand smiled. 'We have not always seen eye to eye – you consider me a coward because I abhor violence, while I think you are a lout. Yet there *is* a bond between us, and you *can* rely on me. But I must go. We are invited to hear the "singers with balls" at Bicanofre, and I must fetch a clean tunic and scarlet ... what does *he* want?'

It was Bale. The squire saw Durand and Geoffrey standing together, and his heavy features creased into a scowl. 'What are *you* doing here?'

241

he demanded jealously.

'Talking,' replied Durand stiffly. 'Not that it is your affair.'

Bale took a threatening step forward. 'I am his squire now, and he does not need you wriggling around. Clear off. If I catch you near him again, I will slit your throat.'

Durand turned to Geoffrey, outraged. 'Will you let him talk to me like that?'

'What is the matter, Bale?' asked Geoffrey, declining to take sides.

'Lady Joan says to tell you that people are getting ready for Bicanofre. She wants you to go, too, so you can have a good look at Douce.'

'I had better go, or they will leave without me,' said Durand, pushing past Bale more vigorously than necessary. Geoffrey reached out to stop Bale from retaliating, feeling the raw strength in the man's arm as he did so.

'Do not listen to anything he tells you, sir,' said Bale venomously. 'He is a snake, and you can never trust a snake. Would you like me to slip into his room tonight and slit—'

'No,' said Geoffrey firmly. 'Not tonight and not ever. I do not want a squire who murders people while they sleep.'

Bale looked suitably chastised. 'Very well,' he said stiffly. 'But if you change your mind...'

'Mother Elgiva thinks you may have murdered Henry,' said Geoffrey to Joan, as they sat with Olivier in the hall that evening. He wore the green tunic she had given him, and was translating an Arabic text, afraid that he would forget

242

the language unless he practised – as he had forgotten much of his Welsh. He supposed it would not matter unless he returned to the Holy Land, but he had nothing better to do: Roger had disappeared with Helbye, and the other guests were at Bicanofre. Geoffrey had declined the invitation.

'Many people do,' said Joan, unperturbed. 'I even received messages saying I had done the right thing.'

'But Henry was *not* murdered,' said Olivier wearily. *'He killed himself.* Men do odd things when they are soaked in drink.'

Geoffrey watched his diminutive brother-in-law. 'Did I tell you about the dagger?' He saw the reaction he had expected and felt a twinge of satisfaction tempered with unease.

'What dagger?' asked Joan, concentrating on her sewing.

'I hardly think daggers are a subject to discuss before we retire,' said Olivier primly.

'The dagger that killed Henry,' said Geoffrey to Joan. His discussion with Durand had helped him clarify more than Baderon's involvement in Henry's death, and he felt it was time to put some of his suppositions to the test. Olivier regarded him with wary eyes.

'What about it?' asked Joan, squinting at her work.

'It had a ruby,' said Geoffrey, still looking at Olivier. 'The one Father Adrian sold in Rosse – that had been under his altar these last three months – had an emerald.'

Joan was puzzled. 'But the dagger we found in

Henry had a *red* stone.' Suddenly, her hands flew to her mouth, and she gazed at her husband in horror. 'Oh, no! Once I had made up my mind to get rid of it, I wanted it gone as soon as possible. I opened the chest and took out the cloth without looking inside. Oh, Olivier! I gave Father Adrian the dagger you inherited from your father. That had an emerald in the hilt.'

She looked stricken, but Geoffrey did not think she should be. 'It was not a mistake. You took the right cloth to Adrian.'

She looked at him, then turned back to Olivier, who would not meet her eyes. 'I do not understand.'

'I exchanged them,' said Olivier in a low voice. 'I did not think you would notice. I tore Adrian's holy cloth in half, and put the ruby dagger in one part and my emerald knife in the other. I left the green knife behind and removed the red one.'

'But why?' asked Joan, bewildered.

'You kept a suicide weapon in our bed-chamber,' said Olivier with a shudder. 'It was evil, tainted, and I hated having it near us. I did not want the servants accused of stealing if I removed it, nor did I want you to think me a weakling for itching for it to be gone. So I substituted my father's for the real one.'

'And, a few weeks later, Joan donated the false one to Father Adrian,' concluded Geoffrey. 'By then, it was too late to exchange them, or you would have done so. So what did you do with the red one?'

'It was cursed,' said Olivier in a whisper. 'I did

244

not want it near my wife.'

'I understand that,' said Geoffrey impatiently. 'But where—'

'You do *not* understand!' cried Olivier, uncharacteristically irate. Geoffrey was startled: Olivier had never shouted at him before. 'I mean it was *cursed*. Literally. By a witch.'

'Eleanor?'

Olivier nodded. 'I heard her. My horse threw me when I was out riding one day, and I was looking for it when I stumbled across her. Because I was embarrassed about losing my mount, I decided to hide until she had gone. She knelt at the Angel Springs and uttered incantations.'

'Over the ruby-hilted dagger?' asked Geoffrey.

Olivier nodded again. 'She dripped blood over it while she spoke some diabolical language.'

'A Black Knife,' said Geoffrey, recalling what Torva and Jervil had told him.

Olivier took a hearty gulp of wine and continued in a shaky voice. 'Quite so: a Black Knife. I was curious, so when she had gone I crept forward and had a look. There was a dead frog with it, and blood everywhere. I ran for my life.'

'You were afraid of a dead frog?' asked Geoffrey incredulously.

'It was more than that!' cried Olivier. 'You have not been to the Angel Springs, or you would not say such things. While she was muttering, there was a wind...' He faltered, and Joan hugged him.

'Olivier and I have few dealings with witchcraft,' she said quietly. 'It is to his credit that he was frightened by what he saw.'

'Not frightened,' objected Olivier with as much dignity as he could muster. 'Unsettled. And that is why I did not want that ruby knife in our bedchamber. I sensed it was dangerous – especially after Henry killed himself with it.'

'Did you know there are dead birds hanging in our stables?' asked Geoffrey. 'In the stall where Henry died. There is blood, too – his, I suspect.'

Both seemed surprised. 'I ordered the place cleaned,' Joan said. 'But I never checked to see if it was done.'

'The stables unnerve me, too,' acknowledged Olivier. 'Ever since Henry. But I will order it all removed tomorrow. I expect the servants bought counter-spells to ward off Henry's restless spirit.'

'Who collected the Black Knife from the Angel Springs?' Geoffrey asked, noting the way Olivier would still not meet his eyes – the little knight had known about the dead birds and condoned their presence, although he would not admit it in front of Joan.

Olivier shrugged. 'The next time I saw it, it was in Henry's corpse.'

'So, *that* is why you were so shocked at finding the body!' said Joan. 'You had seen the dagger before and knew it was cursed. I wondered why you were so horrified. Why did you not tell me?'

'It did not show me in a good light,' said Olivier stiffly. 'I had abandoned an evil thing in the forest, and it killed your brother.'

'What happened after you took it from your

246

bedchamber?' asked Geoffrey.

'I did what I should have done the first time. I destroyed it – not long after Henry's death, we rode to Bicanofre, and on the way I dropped it in the ford.'

'You did dally by the river,' recalled Joan. 'I assumed you were nervous about going to confront a possible murderer.'

'Did you think it might be Ralph, then?' asked Geoffrey.

Joan shrugged. 'He and Henry had argued the day Henry died. But speaking to him was a formality at the time, because I believed Henry had been killed by Bristol merchants. When I finally learnt he had not, there seemed no point in stirring up the matter.'

'Henry was a vile man,' said Olivier vehemently. 'Not worth the trouble.'

'He broke Olivier's arm,' elaborated Joan. 'I was not there when it happened, or a Black Knife would not have been necessary.'

'He did not break it,' argued Olivier. 'It was bruised. And I *could* have bested him, but he was drunk and imbued with a diabolical strength.'

Geoffrey sincerely doubted Olivier could have done anything of the sort. Henry was strong and had been trained to fight, while Olivier was better with military theory than its practice.

'So, you see?' said Joan. 'It is better to let the matter lie. Henry did so much harm that I cannot find it in my heart to condemn his killer. That is between the culprit and God.'

'It was premeditated,' pressed Geoffrey.

'Someone was so determined to have Henry dead that he asked Eleanor to provide a charmed knife.'

'You still do not see!' cried Olivier, agitated. 'There *was* no murder: the Black Knife found its way to Henry, because that is what such things do. Then he used it to kill himself. Eleanor is guilty of issuing the curse, but that is all. *Henry killed himself!*'

'Jervil heard someone talking to him,' insisted Geoffrey.

'Jervil heard Henry, and *assumed* someone was with him,' corrected Olivier. 'Henry was drunk – talking to himself. He was doubtless stricken by his sins, and was trying to make a confession.'

'I was told he was cursing,' said Geoffrey.

Olivier smiled without humour. 'That was a tale Jervil invented when pressed for details. Any sensible person will tell you his story became more elaborate each time. Unfortunately, now he is dead, you cannot demand the truth.'

Later that night, not ready for sleep, Geoffrey prowled the hall, drawing uneasy glances from the servants. The torchlight was too poor for reading, and he could not concentrate anyway. He was tempted to seek out Roger and Helbye, but suspected they would be intoxicated, and there was nothing more tedious than being sober with drunkards. Meanwhile, Olivier and Joan had retired early, so were unavailable for conversation.

Geoffrey saw Torva playing dice with the cook

and his assistant. They scrambled to their feet when he approached, but he smiled to reassure them and gestured for them to sit. They did so reluctantly, and he became aware that the hall was very quiet. Everyone was pretending to be absorbed in some task, but all were paying attention.

Geoffrey studied the dice players carefully. Peter the cook was large, fat and oily and wore an apron thick with grease, while Torva's pinched features reminded Geoffrey of a rat. Peter's assistant, Ynys, was thick set and fair-headed. The eyes of all three were wary, and Geoffrey recalled how Father Adrian had described *Jerosolimitani*. He also remembered that Henry had assaulted Torva, Peter and Jervil on the night he died. He dropped to one knee and indicated he wanted to join their game, hoping to put them at their ease.

'What will you bet?' asked Peter, alarmed. 'We do not have silver.'

Geoffrey revealed a handful of raisins, part of a gift he had brought Joan from his travels. She adored them, although he thought there was little nastier than a raisin.

'And there are plenty more where these came from,' he said confidently, intending it as a joke.

No one smiled, and he was startled to see they had taken him seriously.

'High stakes, then,' murmured Torva, regarding the raisins with some trepidation.

Peter took a deep breath and looked Geoffrey straight in the eye – the first time he had done so. 'In that case I wager fifty dried peas against ten of your raisins.'

He bent his head to concentrate, and they played in silence, except for the statements necessary for the game. Geoffrey soon had a pile of peas and a horseshoe to add to his fruit, and Torva was becoming exasperated by a run of bad luck. It was difficult to cheat with their dice, so Geoffrey could not even lose to win their trust. As his winnings mounted, he realized that he was giving them even more cause to resent him.

'Six raisins for these peas,' said Torva, with such a serious expression that Geoffrey was tempted to laugh. He suspected it would be a mistake. The entire hall was now watching, and the atmosphere was tense. People stood close behind, hemming him in, and it occurred to him that his brother might have been caught in a similar situation – surrounded by hostile minions who wanted him dead.

Ynys leant forward as Geoffrey tossed the dice, and his sheathed dagger pressed into the knight's shoulder. Someone else took a step closer, too, pushing Geoffrey off balance, so he was obliged to use his hands to steady himself. He wished he had not dispensed with his armour. He had a knife, but so did virtually everyone else, and he could not hope to fight them all. He began to think that he had made a foolish mistake. Ynys moved forward again, and the pressure of the weapon against Geoffrey's shoulder became painful. Was this what had happened to Henry? Stabbed in the hall, then carried to the stable? He rested his right hand on his thigh, ready to draw his knife if he detected a hostile move.

'Move back!' shouted Torva, when he saw Geoffrey shoved again. 'You are putting him off.'

There was an instant relief in the press around Geoffrey's back, and he felt a little easier.

'But I cannot see,' objected Ynys. He stepped forward again, and this time the dagger jabbed hard enough to hurt. Geoffrey was unable to suppress a wince.

'Ynys!' snapped Peter. 'Watch what you are doing! If you damage his new tunic, Lady Joan will be vexed.' Ynys stepped back smartly, and Peter addressed Geoffrey in a softer voice. 'What will you wager?'

'Twenty raisins.' There was an appreciative murmur around the hall at Geoffrey's boldness.

'*Twenty*!' breathed Peter. 'That would be quite a win for me.'

'Raise, him, Peter!' called one of the shepherds. 'Tell him you want twenty-five.'

There was a growl of encouragement and a small cheer when Geoffrey added another five fruits. First Peter, then Geoffrey, rolled the dice, and there was a groan of disappointment when Geoffrey won. Peter handed Geoffrey three nails and an awl, and declared he could afford to lose no more. His game was over, although the onlookers begged him to continue.

'*I* will wager against him,' declared Torva, chin jutting forward with determination and a good deal of hostility. 'Who will lend me something?'

Several items were dropped in front of him,

including a buckle from Ynys' shoe, a bundle of feathers that might have been a charm and several wads of dried meat. The crowd pressed forward again, and Geoffrey began to perspire. Making it look casual, he rested his hand on his dagger.

'All this,' said Torva, gesturing to his haul, 'for *thirty* raisins.'

Geoffrey nodded without bothering to argue. He wanted the game to be over, so people would either leave or launch the attack he sensed was imminent. The waiting was unbearable, and his head was beginning to pound. It was impossible to look at everyone at once, and he had no idea who would be the first to strike.

He rolled first, but his score was low. He was surprised to hear one or two sighs of sympathy; a few people were on his side. Torva threw, but his score was lower still, evoking a loud moan of disappointment. The atmosphere crackled, and all Geoffrey wanted to do was lose, sensing it was the only way to escape alive. But for the time being, there was nothing to do but continue playing.

The game seemed to go on forever, and the tension made Geoffrey's neck tight. His legs ached from crouching, but he did not dare move, afraid that coming to his feet would be considered hostile. Slowly, he wiped sweat from his forehead with his sleeve.

'All this against your last two peas,' he said, indicating his pile of trinkets. There was a collective gasp of astonishment, and then absolute

252

silence while Torva gazed at him open-mouthed.

'You would risk all that for two peas?' he asked in disbelief. '*All* of it?'

If he had not felt so fraught, Geoffrey would have laughed. But he simply nodded.

'Are you sure?' asked Peter worriedly. 'There are a lot of raisins here, along with Ynys' charm, the promise of three chickens and a good deal more. It is a lot to lose.'

Geoffrey nodded again, and drew an appreciative murmur from the crowd.

Torva shrugged, and then grinned. 'Well, *I* have nothing to lose,' he said, throwing the dice. It was a high score, but no one cheered.

With a prayer that his tally would be lower and the ordeal would end, Geoffrey threw the dice, then gaped in horror when he scored the highest amount possible. There was a brief silence, then Ynys gave a whoop of delight and pounded him on the back. Others joined in, and Geoffrey scrambled to his feet. But the hands that thumped him, although vigorous, were not hostile, and he could see glee in the faces around him. Torva elbowed people out of the way and grabbed his hand.

'You are a brave man,' he said with a grin. 'What nerve! Anyone would think you wanted to lose. You have entertained us royally this evening.'

Geoffrey forced himself to smile back, feeling relief wash over him. He eased backwards until he was against a wall, feeling safer with no one behind him. He glanced at the people who clamoured around, pressing winnings into his hands, and wondered what they knew about Henry's death. Torva was still laughing at Geoffrey's last gamble, but there was a hard core in him that was unsettling. Fat Peter was grinning, too, but his eyes were watchful. And there were others, too – men who worked in the stables, sculleries and storerooms – strong, sober fellows who had tasted his brother's fists.

'I cannot take these,' said Geoffrey, who did not want rusty nails, charms and promises of livestock. However, he did not want to offend anyone by refusing their treasures, so he added, 'I will win them all back from you next time, anyway.'

There was more laughter, and people stepped forward to reclaim what they had lost. He was particularly pleased when the feathered charm was one of the first things to be retrieved.

'Henry would have kept the lot,' confided Ynys. 'He did not play by our rules.'

'It is the game that is important,' explained Peter, when Geoffrey looked blank. 'We never keep our winnings, because that would be gambling, which Father Adrian tells us is a sin.'

Geoffrey supposed he had had a lucky escape with his 'generosity'.

'Here are your raisins,' said Ynys, pressing them into Geoffrey's hand. 'They are all there.'

Geoffrey pushed them in his purse, thinking he would throw them in the river the following day. They had been through numerous grubby hands, and he did not imagine that Joan would eat them now. Peter exchanged a glance with Torva, then indicated that Geoffrey was to sit with them near the embers of the fire, while the rest of the servants, still chattering and laughing, went about the business of hauling straw mattresses from the pile in the corner and distributing blankets.

'You trust us,' stated Peter.

Geoffrey was a little startled, because he did not.

Torva nodded. 'You did not count the raisins, like Henry would have done. You believed us when we said they were all there.'

'My mother always told me never to speak ill of the dead,' began Peter in the kind of voice that suggested he was about to do just that. 'But your brother was a nasty man.'

Geoffrey nodded, but said nothing, hoping his silence would encourage them to say more.

'No one here killed him,' added Torva. 'I know you think otherwise, but you are wrong. This is a small manor, and we would have known by now.'

'Olivier believes Henry committed suicide,' Geoffrey said, to encourage speculation.

Torva shook his head. 'The wound *could* have been self-inflicted, but it is unlikely. It was driven in with considerable force, by someone strong.'

'Or someone angry.' Geoffrey knew from experience that it did not take powerful arms to stab a man in the stomach.

'Lots of people were angry with Henry,' said Torva.

'I am sorry Jervil is dead,' said Geoffrey. He was tired of beating around the bush, so spoke bluntly. 'But he went to Dene to sell Baderon a dagger with a ruby in its hilt. It was the weapon that killed my brother, the one Olivier threw in the river.'

They gazed at him. 'How do you know that?' asked Peter uneasily.

'It does not matter,' said Geoffrey. 'Why did Baderon want this weapon?'

Torva and Peter exchanged another glance and then Torva gave a heavy sigh. 'The ruby knife was Baderon's. He wanted it back.'

Geoffrey finally felt he was getting some- where. 'But why now? It is months since Henry died.'

'Because of you,' said Peter, as if the answer were obvious. 'Henry's death was all but for- gotten, but then *you* started asking questions. Baderon knew it was only a matter of time before you learnt Henry was killed with a ruby dagger, and that *he* had owned such a thing. By buying the weapon, he could deny it.'

Geoffrey had so many questions, he barely knew where to begin. 'How did Jervil get the knife when Olivier had thrown it in the river?'

'Because the Black Knife did not stay in the water,' explained Torva. 'We do not know how – perhaps Olivier did not hurl it as far as he thought – but it came back again, like the cursed thing it was. It appeared one day in the stables – where it had killed its victim.'

Geoffrey was sceptical. 'It does not have legs to walk or wings to fly. So, how—'

'It was a Black Knife,' insisted Torva force- fully. 'They *always* return. It brought *itself* back to the stables, where Jervil found it. It is what these things do, unless they are properly de-cursed.'

'How do you "de-curse" one?' asked Geoffrey.

Torva pursed his lips, as if Geoffrey were remiss for not knowing. 'The man who com-missions a Black Knife must destroy it – as soon as his victim is dead. If he fails to do so, it increases in power and starts to look for other victims.'

Peter nodded. 'It is six months since Henry's death, so the Black Knife is very strong – Bad-eron will not want it to do more damage. Since it was not with Jervil's body, we must assume Baderon has it and will have to de-curse it. Of course, it is much easier to lay a curse than to break one.'

'How did Jervil become involved?'

'He told Baderon the dagger had reappeared and offered to sell it to him,' explained Torva. 'Baderon agreed, but insisted the exchange be in secret. But then you decided to ride for Dene, and Jervil was afraid you had guessed his plan. You almost overheard him telling me about it.'

'Baderon said it was imperative that no one from Goodrich should witness the exchange,' added Peter, 'on the grounds that it would look bad.'

'He was right,' said Geoffrey grimly. 'It does. And they did not manage the transaction very discreetly. The King saw them.'

'Jervil may have been careless,' acknowledged Peter. 'He wanted the Black Knife passed to Baderon and the silver in his purse as quickly as possible.'

'So it was Baderon who killed Henry,' concluded Geoffrey, sorry Baderon had stooped so low as to stab a man deep in his cups.

'No,' said Peter, with certainty. 'He did not, although I cannot speak for his knights.'

Torva agreed. 'I do not trust Seguin and Lambert. It is only a matter of time before Corwenna encourages them to do us serious harm. But Baderon did not hurt Henry.'

'You sound very sure,' said Geoffrey. 'Why?'

'Baderon had too much to lose if Henry died,' replied Torva. 'They had an arrangement.'

'What kind of arrangement? Henry marrying Hilde?'

'Hilde would never have taken Henry,' said Peter. 'All I can tell you is that Baderon and Henry signed a document to their mutual advantage. I saw them doing it, and made my mark as a witness.'

'What did this document say?' asked Geoffrey. Father Adrian had also mentioned an agreement, while Baderon himself had said that there were 'other ways' to secure truces, and that he and Henry had 'irons in the fire'.

'I could not read it,' said Peter. 'I am a cook, not a scribe. They were both very pleased, though, and made many toasts to each other and the futures of both estates.'

Geoffrey wracked his brain for a solution, but none came. 'When was this?'

'Early September,' replied Peter. 'Three weeks before Henry's death. I know you are sceptical – so are we, because we do not know the whole story, either. But Baderon was the last man who would kill Henry, because he needed him alive.'

The following morning Geoffrey woke early and considered what he knew. He had been informed that Baderon could not be Henry's murderer, because of some secret arrangement. It was not a marriage, because Henry had hoped for Isabel. Or was that the problem – Henry had offered himself to Hilde, but had reneged for Isabel? Of course, the servants did not think so, and try as he might, Geoffrey could not imagine what Henry and Baderon might have devised. The Lord of Monmouth was still at Bicanofre, but would be back soon; Geoffrey resolved to ask him.

However, just because Baderon wanted peace did not mean Seguin and Lambert – fuelled by ambition and Corwenna's hatred of Goodrich – felt the same. Geoffrey believed Torva and Peter were right when they said it was only a matter of time before they harmed the whole region.

He shifted into a more comfortable position, aware that people were moving in the hall below, and that he was likely to earn a reputation as a lie-abed if he lingered there much longer. But there were still many questions in need of answers – the most pressing, who had killed Jervil, and why was Baderon so determined to retrieve the dagger if he was not Henry's killer?

Geoffrey's thoughts turned to Duchess Sybilla. Walter had owned a pot of mandrake, although Geoffrey doubted its contents had killed Sibylla. Geoffrey had also discovered that Agnes knew about mandrake, and that she had courted the friendship of Eleanor. Eleanor was now missing. Could she be dead? And was Agnes telling the truth about her and Eleanor's disagreement?

Knowing that he would solve nothing by lounging around, Geoffrey rose and went to the garderobe. He stared at the shelves that concealed the passage to the woods. He still had not asked Joan whether it was intact, and knew he was being remiss. If Goodrich came under attack, it might be a vital part of a plan to protect it. He took a deep breath and pushed the hidden door before his courage failed. It swung open, revealing a black, sinister slit with dusty steps. It was draped with cobwebs, and just looking at it made the bile rise in his throat.

'Where does that go?' whispered Bale from behind him, making him spin around in alarm.

Geoffrey pressed a hand over his thudding heart. 'You must stop creeping up on me like that, Bale, or one of us is likely to die. It leads to the woods. I cannot remember where exactly.'

Bale's eyes gleamed. 'I might have known cunning old Godric Mappestone would have installed something like this when he raised Goodrich. Shall we explore it?'

'I am not going down there,' said Geoffrey firmly. He saw Bale's surprise, but did not want to confess his weakness about such places. 'Another time – I have work to do today.'

He pushed past the squire, and headed for the hall, to see if there was any breakfast. Bale followed, chatting about Olivier's hawks, and Geoffrey saw that he was not in the least bit puzzled by his master's disinclination to investigate the tunnel. Durand would have smelt a rat in an instant and set himself to learn why Geoffrey had bolted. Geoffrey smiled. Perhaps there was an advantage in having a servant who was not quite so sharp after all.

Torva nodded affably when they met near the stairs, while Peter, hauling a vat of pottage from the kitchens, gave Geoffrey a grin. Several others acknowledged him with waves, and he began to hope the game had been worth the aggravation – at least *some* servants no longer seemed to think that he was Henry's more violent brother.

Tables bearing food were ready, although there were not many takers – most guests had either returned to Goodrich late, or had slept at Bicanofre. Joan and Olivier were on hand to make pleasant conversation, although the only person to arrive so far was Giffard. The prelate had declined to waste an evening on 'singers with balls'.

'You kept us awake last night with your noisy revelry,' said Joan, when Geoffrey sat beside her. 'What in God's name were you doing to cause all that cheering and groaning?'

'Nothing *in God's name*,' muttered Giffard. 'I imagine he was gaming.' He pronounced the last word as though it was a sin tantamount to sodomy.

'He would not do that,' said Joan. 'He knows I do not allow it.'

Peter gave Geoffrey an enormous wink behind her back and tapped the side of his nose. But

Geoffrey did not like the notion that he was part of a conspiracy.

'Actually,' he said, 'we did play a game of chance, but Father Adrian says it was not gambling because no one kept his winnings.'

Joan glared at him, unconvinced. 'If you do it again, I shall not be pleased.'

Geoffrey felt like telling her he would do what he liked in his own house, but did not want to quarrel. He seldom gambled anyway, so it was not something he would miss. He nodded acquiescence, and she turned to make sure that Giffard had enough food.

'You should not have confessed,' muttered Peter, ladling pottage into his bowl. 'We would not have told on you, not like we would have done Henry.'

Geoffrey supposed this represented an improvement in relations, and hoped they would not degenerate again if he were to discover that one of the servants had killed his brother. There was a clatter of hoofs outside, heralding the return of more guests from Bicanofre, so Joan and Olivier hurried to greet them, leaving Geoffrey and the Bishop alone.

'What have you learnt?' Giffard asked. 'Has anyone confided in you yet? You do not have much time. Agnes fluttered her eyelashes at the King, and he is certain to take her to Westminster. Then she and Walter will be beyond my control.'

'It is not looking good,' Geoffrey admitted. 'I am uneasy that she has gone to Bicanofre, where Eleanor lives. Eleanor knows a lot about poisons, although Agnes claims they are no longer friends. However, I am not sure I believe her.'

'But Eleanor is missing,' Giffard pointed out. 'Probably dead in the fire. She is not at Bicanofre.'

Geoffrey thought about the charms at the Angel Springs, and was certain that Eleanor would not have been killed in a fire that had been planned there. Moreover, since Eleanor kept her face veiled, she could be walking around openly and no one would know. He wondered whether to tell Giffard that his nephew had owned mandrake, but decided it would serve no purpose.

'Joan told me a messenger came to you yesterday,' he said instead. 'Did he bring good news?'

Giffard smiled at last. 'There is one silver streak in the dark clouds around me. The King asked the Archbishop of York to consecrate me, and York agreed. I shall have God's blessing for my work.'

'That *is* good news,' said Geoffrey, knowing it meant a great deal to his dour friend.

'I would like you to come. The ceremony will be in St Paul's Cathedral in London, and two other bishops – Salisbury and Hereford – will be blessed at the same time.'

Geoffrey was torn. The cathedral was said to be a fabulous building, and he longed to visit it, but he did not want to see the King. He promised to think about it and headed outside, so the servants could clear the hall. Giffard followed, yawning.

'You should sleep more,' Geoffrey advised. 'And pray less.'

'I will,' said Giffard, a little irritably, 'if you cease staying up with the servants and making so much noise.'

Ten

Geoffrey left the hall and ran down the wooden stairs to the bailey. It was a fine day, and he felt his spirits soar. He rubbed his hands, trying to decide whether to go riding or to see if Roger fancied some swordplay.

'You will be busy this morning,' said Durand by way of greeting. 'As your guests trickle back from Bicanofre, I assume you will be on hand to greet them.'

'Do you think I should?' asked Geoffrey, feeling his ebullience slip. 'Joan and Olivier are here.'

'You cannot delegate everything,' said Durand. 'It is unfair to them – and insulting to your visitors. I am always available when guests honour *me* with their presence.'

Geoffrey reluctantly resigned himself to a morning of duty. Only then did he notice that Durand was pale and his eyes heavy from a lack of sleep.

'Did you enjoy yourself last night?' he asked,

assuming Bicanofre was the cause of the man's shabby appearance.

Durand winced. 'I was grossly misled. The singers were toneless and *I* can toss and catch balls better than those so-called jugglers. If that is the level of "entertainment" I am to expect here, then I must increase the pace of my investigation.' He closed his eyes and fanned his face with his hand, looking like an elderly nun.

'Do not expect nights of wild debauchery when you are with me,' warned Giffard sternly, as he joined them. 'My household retires to bed with the sun, and rises early for religious devotions. There is no levity.'

Durand looked alarmed that his sojourn in Winchester might not be as much fun as anticipated, and he swallowed hard. 'Really?' he asked in a small voice.

'Did Geoffrey keep you awake, too?' asked Giffard pointedly. 'People returned very late from Bicanofre, but they did not make nearly as much noise as *he* did. I am used to the quiet of the cloister, where the only sounds are men breathing and bells announcing holy offices. I find it hard to sleep through illicit games of dice.'

'I agree,' said Durand ingratiatingly. 'I saw a good many such games when I was in his service – especially with Roger – but last night *was* particularly jubilant.'

'Here come more of your guests, Geoffrey,' said Giffard, turning at the sound of hoofs. 'Baderon, his knights and Corwenna.'

'I am surprised *she* is here,' said Durand. 'She

265

ranted long and hard about how the Mappe-stones should be destroyed. Baderon tried to silence her, but it needed a stronger voice than his.'

'Baderon is a God-fearing man, but he should take a stand against his knights – and Corwenna, too,' said Giffard. 'Their outspokenness will only lead to trouble.'

Geoffrey only hoped that Goodrich would not bear the brunt of it. He went to greet his guests, staying away from Corwenna.

'Do not worry,' whispered Olivier in his ear. 'I will not allow Corwenna anywhere near Joan.'

Geoffrey gave a tight smile, thinking that if Corwenna decided to do harm, the likes of Olivier would not be able to stop her. Olivier read the thought, and his expression soured.

'I will not attempt to fight her, so you have no cause to look dubious. My skills lie in other areas: Corwenna is unlikely to strike when Joan is surrounded by people, so *that* is how I shall protect her – how I have protected her all the years you were away fighting wars. Joan will not be alone for an instant while Corwenna is here.'

Geoffrey saw that he had underestimated his brother-in-law. 'I am sorry, Olivier. I did not mean to doubt you. I am sure Joan is safe in your care.'

'She is,' replied Olivier coolly. 'So *I* will look after her, and you can look after yourself. Cor-wenna is more keen to kill you, because it will mean the end of Goodrich's hopes for an heir. It is a good thing Sir Roger is here, because you might need him.'

The hall was busy all morning, as guests returned. Geoffrey was amused by their different reactions to Bicanofre's amusements. Baderon was polite, claiming them to have been an 'interesting diversion', but his knights were brutal, describing the performers as 'lumbering peasants with rough voices'. Corwenna had enjoyed herself, although she thought that next time Wulfric should consider including a rendition from a Welsh bard. She recited a passage from a particularly bloody epic to demonstrate what they had been missing.

'She is a fine woman,' Seguin said, standing with his hands on his hips. 'She rides better than most men and handles her weapons like a knight. You should see her with a battleaxe!'

'She has an axe?' asked Geoffrey warily.

'Your mother was fabulously skilled with an axe, so do not look disapproving,' snapped Seguin. 'And your sister is said to be no mean fighter, too – especially compared to that husband of hers.'

'Are you insulting my sister?' demanded Geoffrey.

Seguin shook his head impatiently. 'I am *praising* her, man. I like a woman who can hold her own, and Joan and my Corwenna can do just that: they are hard, strong and uncompromising. When we are married, I shall be able to leave Corwenna in charge of my estates, and they will be in one piece when I return – just as Joan does for you.'

Geoffrey supposed he was right, although he

did not relish the prospect of meeting Corwenna if she were armed with as formidable a weapon as an axe.

When Geoffrey helped Isabel from her horse, she was silent and sad, going straight to the room allocated to her and her father. She barely acknowledged his greeting, and he could tell from the redness around her eyes that she had been crying.

'Ralph?' he asked of fitzNorman, as they watched her flee to solitude.

The old warrior grimaced. 'He barely spoke to her last night and refused to sit near us.' He looked hard at Geoffrey and cleared his throat. 'I see you have taken my advice.'

'I have?' asked Geoffrey.

'I told you to forget Margaret's murder, lest her penchant for men become common knowledge, and you have complied. I am obliged. I loved my sister, and do not want her good name soiled.'

'*I* would never soil her name,' said Geoffrey pointedly, thinking it was a good deal more than her brother was currently doing.

'Good,' said fitzNorman. 'I do not like folk going against my wishes.'

Geoffrey did not want to make polite conversation with people he did not like, so he remained outside, enjoying the feel of the sun on his face. To keep himself busy, he went to the stables and removed the dead birds. Then he took a broom and scrubbed away the bloodstains, not caring that it was menial work. When he finished, he sat next to Durand on a wall near the kitchens.

'Where are Agnes and Walter?' Geoffrey asked.

'Agnes captured Ralph's attention last night, so boy and mother are doubtless still with him, enjoying his "witty" company. The fellow is a beast – and not just for his treatment of Isabel. I am not keen on women, but I do like *her*.'

Geoffrey eyed him askance. 'Do I take it Ralph upset you in some way?'

'He is rough with his servants, unkind to his dogs and he hogs the latrines when his guests are waiting. He also humiliated his priest when the poor man said grace last night – almost reduced him to tears with his criticism. I am no lover of bastard Latin, but when one is in remote areas full of sheep, one should expect no better. I was obliged to intervene and say the prayer myself.'

It was a damning statement coming from Durand, who was neither kind nor patient. He was always mocking parish priests for their low education, and if *he* had defended one, then Ralph's behaviour must have been particularly cruel.

The clerk's eyes gleamed with sudden malice. 'I think I might ask Ralph to read us some poetry this evening, since he claims he is good at it. I shall let him embarrass himself with what is sure to be a paltry rendition, then step forward and demonstrate how it should really be done.'

'Yes, do that,' said Geoffrey. 'Do you want some books? I have several in my chamber.'

Face shining with the prospect of mischief, Durand hurried away, obviously intending to select a particularly difficult text. He stopped when Corwenna said something to him, and Geoffrey saw him shake his head. She grabbed his arm, but he pulled away with a gesture of impatience and continued his journey towards the hall. Geoffrey frowned, wondering what she had wanted. Whatever it was, he was certain she had not been successful.

'There is a face to curdle milk,' said Hilde, coming to stand next to him. 'But then, what can you expect from a woman who thinks watching six oafs tossing old apples is fun?'

'I understand she was the only one who enjoyed herself last night,' said Geoffrey.

Hilde chuckled. 'Certainly Ralph should not have boasted about the quality of his minstrels when we were in Normandy. I suspect he was appalled when Wulfric invited us to hear them, thus exposing him as a liar. It is always better to be honest, even when the truth is painful.'

Geoffrey fully agreed. 'The King ordered me to investigate the murders of Jervil and Margaret, but I am not sure where to begin,' he said. 'I do not suppose you have any ideas?'

Hilde sat next to him, shooting him a sympathetic glance. 'I heard about that – and I heard fitzNorman advise you against it. Do not go against him, Geoffrey. It would be rash.'

'Who? The King or fitzNorman?'

'FitzNorman,' said Hilde impatiently. 'I am hardly likely to recommend you flaunt the King's orders, am I? I do not want him to seize Goodrich. *He* would not be an easy neighbour.'

'FitzNorman thinks Margaret was in the

stables with Jervil for...' Geoffrey trailed off, not liking to state the case too bluntly, out of his respect for Margaret.

'For *what*?' asked Hilde. He watched her expression turn from puzzled to incredulous. 'He told you they were there *together*? That his own sister would seduce an uncouth servant?'

'He did not *say seduce* exactly...'

'What is wrong with the men in these parts? First there was Henry, a stupid brute. Then there is Ralph, an unmannerly pig. And now fitz-Norman spreads that sort of tale about a good woman.'

'I think I was right with my first assumption: Margaret was killed because she witnessed what happened to Jervil. If I learn who murdered Jervil, then I will have Margaret's attacker, too. Do you know anything that might help?'

'Nothing I have not already told you – and I was fond of Margaret, so I would like to be of assistance. Jervil was a thief, but Joan was patient with him, hoping kindness would cure his sticky fingers. I have no idea why he should have been in Dene. Did Joan send him with a message?'

'He went to sell a dagger to your father,' said Geoffrey, deciding to be honest. 'They were seen.'

Hilde stared at him. 'Then your witness is wrong. Jervil knew my father, certainly, because he delivered messages to us from Joan. But they did not have the kind of relationship where my father would *buy* anything from him. Jervil was a thief, and anything *he* brought to sell would

271

almost certainly be stolen.'

She sounded very certain, and Geoffrey saw that there was no point in pressing her further. Either she knew about the ruby knife and was not going to admit it, or she was ignorant of the affair. Regardless, pursuing the matter would be a waste of time. Geoffrey abandoned the discussion, although he was determined to ask the same questions of Baderon as soon as he could.

'Have you found Hugh?' he asked instead.

She fiddled with a ring on her finger. 'No. He has disappeared before and turned up safe, but I will only be easy when he is home. People think I am foolish to fuss, but he is my brother.'

'It is not foolish at all,' said Geoffrey gently. 'And if I can help, please ask.'

Hilde smiled and he saw that she had pretty eyes – pale honey-brown, just a little darker than the curls that escaped from the scarf-like veil covering her head and neck. Suddenly there was a flurry of activity heralding the arrival of two servants from Dene. Hilde was after them in a trice, Geoffrey forgotten, as she demanded news of Hugh. Geoffrey hoped the man would be found soon, and that there would not be yet another death.

Geoffrey decided to speak to Baderon as soon as possible. He hovered in the yard, waiting for an opportunity, but Seguin and Lambert were with their master, and showed no sign of leaving. Since he did not want to interrogate Baderon while his knights listened, Geoffrey had no choice but to wait. He did so reluctantly.

While he kicked his heels, he heard someone shout his name. He looked up to see Roger striding towards him. The big knight looked pale, and his eyes were watery.

'Had a good time, did you?' asked Geoffrey wryly. Roger always gauged good times by how dreadful he felt the following day – the worse he felt, the better the occasion.

Roger grinned. 'Helbye knows how to entertain – more than the Lord of Bicanofre, judging by the comments I have heard this morning. Did you go?'

'I stayed here and won a pile of dried peas from the servants.'

'Exciting!' remarked Roger caustically. 'I do not like it here, Geoff. That Welsh woman keeps scowling at me; Baderon's louts insult me in low voices – just soft enough so I cannot hear and challenge them; fitzNorman threatened to wring my neck if I helped with your investigation; and Joan thinks I am a bad influence on her husband.'

Geoffrey regarded him in alarm. 'You are not leaving, are you?'

'I have business in Rosse.'

Geoffrey nodded, although he was disturbed. If ever he needed the comforting presence of Roger, it was now, and he was sorry that his friend felt compelled to leave. He doubted Roger had anything to do in Rosse – unless it was finding a tavern with willing wenches – and Geoffrey knew that he was just uncomfortable and wanted to be away.

Roger slapped his shoulder and set off to

where his squire waited with his horse. 'Just a few days, Geoff, I promise. And then I will be back.'

'You are going *now*?' asked Geoffrey, startled by the haste. 'At least have something to eat first.'

But Roger shook his head. 'The sooner I go, the sooner I will return.'

And then he was gone, leaving Geoffrey staring after him in dismay. He turned to the activity in the bailey, where his guests were gathering for a day of hawking, and considered saddling his own horse and following Roger. But to abandon his investigation would deliberately flout the King's orders, and Henry was not a forgiving man.

The prospect of continuing to play host depressed him, and he could foresee days filled with unpleasantness. Suddenly, it no longer seemed important to talk to Baderon, and he felt an urgent need for solitude. He started towards the stables, thinking to take a lone ride.

'Where are you going?' asked Giffard, following. 'Hunting with Roger?'

'Roger is not going hunting,' said Geoffrey, unable to keep the bitterness from his voice. He took a deep breath and pulled himself together. He was behaving like Ralph – petulant, because something had happened that he did not like. He grabbed his saddle and strapped it on, aware of the animal's pleasure at the prospect of a gallop. 'I am going to exercise my horse.'

'You are not going hawking? I hear Olivier has some excellent birds – not that I would know about such things – and virtually everyone is going with him.'

'Good,' said Geoffrey, grateful that Olivier was prepared to be hospitable.

'I shall join you, but I do not feel like mounting an overpowered beast,' said Giffard, strolling the length of the stables to inspect what was present. 'But here is a donkey. I shall ride that.'

Before Geoffrey could point out that ambling by the side of a plodding mule was not what he had in mind for his warhorse, Giffard had taken possession of the hapless beast. His long legs touched the ground on either side, and it snickered malevolently at the weight. But it was a feisty little animal and shot across the bailey towards the gate as soon as it was out of the stables, Giffard hauling for all he was worth on the reins. Geoffrey followed quickly, fearing an accident.

The donkey kept up gamely when Geoffrey cantered, then outstripped him when he reined in to pass through a muddy stretch. It reached the top of a mound not far from the castle, then did an immediate about-turn and raced home as though the hounds of Hell were after it, Geoffrey in anxious pursuit. They arrived breathless and a good deal sooner than Geoffrey had anticipated – he had wanted to be out all day, not just a few moments.

'It is good it was not *this* thing that carried Our Lord into Jerusalem,' Giffard muttered, straightening his legs and allowing the donkey to walk out from under them. 'The triumphal Palm Sunday procession would have happened so fast that

275

most people would have missed it.'

Geoffrey dared not laugh, lest Giffard had not meant to be amusing; the grim bishop was not a man to jest about religion. He was about to change the subject when there was a sudden yell, and people arrived in the bailey. It was Agnes and Walter, and even from a distance he could see that something was wrong. Agnes held herself stiffly, while Walter was frightened. Geoffrey was not entirely pleased to see Ralph with them, then felt the first stirrings of unease as Agnes flung herself from her horse and came tearing towards the Bishop.

She hurled herself at Giffard's feet and began to cry, grasping the hem of his habit. Walter stood behind her, biting his lip, looking as though he might cry himself. Ralph joined them.

'You must help me, my Lord Bishop!' Agnes howled. 'You must, or I am undone.'

'My child!' exclaimed Giffard, moved by her distress. 'What is the matter?'

'It is Hugh,' said Agnes, raising a tear-streaked face towards Giffard. 'Baderon's son.'

'What about him?' demanded Geoffrey.

'He is dead,' wept Agnes, keeping her eyes on Giffard. 'And his father is sure to blame me.'

'Or me,' added Walter. 'And that would be worse, because I have my whole life in front of me, while you are already old.'

Agnes scowled at him, then resumed her appeal to Giffard. 'You have always been a friend, so be one now. Tell Baderon it was not *me* who stabbed Hugh and left him dead at the Wye ford.'

* * *

Agnes' words created quite a stir among the guests who had gathered to go hawking, although Baderon and his knights were not among them, and neither was Hilde. Joan told Geoffrey that they had gone into the forest at Hilde's insistence, to again look for their missing kinsman.

'Why would Baderon think you killed Hugh?' asked Geoffrey. His first instinct upon hearing the news and witnessing Agnes' reaction was to assume that she had. Why else would she be so alarmed?

'Because I was *there*!' Agnes cried, refusing to look at anyone except Giffard. The prelate laid a calming hand on her head. 'There are those who accuse me of killing Duchess Sibylla, just because I happened to be in her chamber the night she died.'

Giffard's hand dropped away. 'Were you? Then did you?'

'Of course not! There are others you must ask about that.' Agnes' eyes slid towards Walter, but then returned to Giffard. 'You *must* believe I had nothing to do with Hugh's death!'

'How do you know he is dead?' asked Durand. His practical question calmed the buzz of speculation that had broken out among the crowd.

'His body was at the river,' replied Walter. 'It is all bloody and wet.'

'Was Eleanor there, too?' asked Geoffrey, wondering whether there was a second nearby.

'Eleanor!' exclaimed Walter, grasping a ready-made solution with relief. '*She* killed Hugh!

277

They went missing together, so it must have been her. She tired of him and stuck a dagger in his heart.'

Geoffrey watched Agnes consider the possibility, her small, delicate features hard and calculating. 'Eleanor might be the culprit,' she said slowly. 'However, it was not us, and you must protect me if Baderon and his knights try to say it was. All we did was find the body.'

'That is what happens when you have a reputation for murder,' said Durand unfeelingly. 'It comes back to haunt you at inconvenient times.'

It was obvious that a fear of comments like Durand's was exactly what had thrown Agnes into such paroxysms of alarm. She grabbed Giffard's hand, kissing his ecclesiastical ring.

'Please, my Lord Bishop,' she sobbed. 'You must believe I am innocent of bringing about *any* death. Pray over me, then you will see I have God's favour. He will strike me down if I am guilty. But when He does not, you will see I am telling the truth.'

'Be careful, Mother,' said Walter in alarm. 'Think about what you are saying.'

Agnes shot him a look that might have killed him, too, if eyes had been weapons. 'Join us,' she ordered. 'Come and prove your innocence.'

Walter swallowed hard and looked away, a reaction that did not escape Giffard. The Bishop's hands shook when he rested them on Agnes' head and began to pray. Geoffrey saw the look of triumph that flickered across her face, and, recalling the views she had expressed about religion, suspected that Giffard's God held no terrors for her. Walter kicked at a stone, uncertain of what to do, and Durand backed away, pulling Geoffrey with him.

'What are you doing?' Geoffrey demanded.

'She is committing a grievous sin,' hissed Durand. 'Surely you saw the looks that passed between her and Walter? Neither is innocent, and they are challenging God. I do not want to be close when divine lightning forks from the sky and strikes them.'

He spoke with such conviction that Geoffrey took another step away.

'She is lying,' Joan remarked as she passed Geoffrey on her way to the hall, disgusted with the entire spectacle. 'She may have convinced Giffard that she had nothing to do with Sibylla's death, but she does not fool me.'

'Nor me,' said Durand. 'I do not like the fact that she flew here so quickly, protesting her innocence about Hugh, either. It smacks of a felon committing a crime then dashing to claim sanctuary.'

Geoffrey remembered his manners, aware that he ought to make some hospitable gesture, even to guests like Agnes, Walter and Ralph. He offered them wine and indicated that they should precede him into the hall.

'That is a good idea,' said Walter, pushing past him. 'I have had a nasty shock and need something to calm my nerves. It is not every day I see a murdered man.' He crossed himself, adding in Italian, 'The fruits fall from the bushes like thunder.'

'*Murdered*?' queried Durand, following the party inside. 'You said he was stabbed.'

Ralph took the best seat at the hearth and then waved a peremptory hand to indicate that he wanted a drink. Torva obliged in his own time, making sure he received the dregs. The others came to stand around him.

'Stabbing generally means murder,' Ralph said in surprising support of Walter. 'It is not an outrageous conclusion to draw.'

'My brother was stabbed,' Joan pointed out. 'But Olivier believes he did it himself. Being stabbed does not necessarily imply someone else struck the blow.'

'It does in this case,' said Ralph tartly. 'The wound was in his back.'

'Tell us from the beginning,' ordered Geoffrey, 'How did you come to find him?'

'What authority do *you* have to question us?' demanded Ralph.

Geoffrey hesitated. Ralph was right: he had no authority. But Durand stepped in.

'You can tell Sir Geoffrey now, or you can tell the King when he arrives,' he said coldly. 'His Majesty dislikes vassals who allow murders to go unremarked, and if you interfere with Sir Geoffrey's attempts to identify the culprit, *I* shall make sure he knows about it.'

'My mother and I found Hugh when we were on our way from Bicanofre,' said Walter sullenly, while Ralph fumed silently. 'We left later than everyone else, because my mother had been enjoying Ralph's company.'

'He was showing me his collection of silk hats,' elaborated Agnes smoothly, as more than one person shot her speculative looks.

'*Silk hats*?' asked Geoffrey in disbelief.

Agnes glared at him, and Ralph was on his feet. 'You dishonour a good lady's name with your suspicious tone!' he snapped. 'What do you infer?'

'He was inferring nothing,' said Joan, also standing. Ralph sank down again when she took a step towards him. 'It is *your* hostile manner that makes us not want to believe her.'

Ralph became piqued, but continued the tale. 'Agnes and I were longer than we intended with the hats, and only became aware of the time when Douce disturbed us.'

'They did not appear at breakfast,' added Walter. Geoffrey saw that he was jealous of the time his mother had spent with Ralph and was determined to make them suffer. 'And this examination of headwear began the previous night, so Ralph must have a lot of hats.'

'Where were you all that time?' asked Geoffrey, supposing Ralph and Agnes had lingered under the blankets while the other guests had returned to Goodrich. Or had they? It was equally possible that one had slipped out and stuck a knife in the hapless Hugh, although he could not imagine why. Unless, of course, Hugh had witnessed something sensitive during the fire at Dene, and someone had decided to silence him for it.

'*I* slept in Bicanofre's hall,' replied Walter sullenly. 'But I kept myself to myself and spoke

281

to no one. I was not in the mood for idle chatter.'

Geoffrey was sure he was not, while his mother frolicked in bed with Ralph. But his lack of an alibi was unfortunate nonetheless.

'Why did *you* not accompany them?' Giffard demanded of Ralph. 'It sounds as though it was your fault they were delayed.'

'Because Douce was fretting about Eleanor,' said Ralph curtly. 'And I was obliged to calm her. I followed as soon as I could.'

'When we reached the ford, we spotted someone lying face-down in the shallows,' continued Walter. 'I thought it was a peasant at first, who had fallen in a drunken stupor and drowned. I dismounted to look and recognized Hugh. There was a great bloody wound between his shoulder blades. We started back for Bicanofre for help.'

'We met on the road,' finished Ralph. 'I begged a cart from Walecford and arranged to have the body taken to the village church.'

Geoffrey was thoughtful. Others had returned earlier than Agnes and Walter, and if the body had been at the ford then, they would have seen it first. He concluded that Hugh had been killed not during the night, but some time that morning.

'Who do you think is responsible for Hugh's death?' he asked.

Ralph's expression was spiteful. 'That is for *you* to find out, King's man. All I can say is it was not me.'

'It must have been Eleanor,' said Agnes, 'as Walter suggested. She is missing, too, and we all know the kind of thing *she* does when alone in the forest.'

There was a general murmur of agreement. 'I am afraid it is true,' said Ralph. 'My sister *is* in the habit of disappearing into the woods on occasion, and she *does* have a penchant for un-Christian activities.'

Geoffrey gazed at him with dislike. He felt sorry for Eleanor, having a brother who thought nothing of tossing her to the wolves on the whim of his latest lover. It was clear that he was besotted with Agnes, who no doubt intended to keep him that way until she no longer needed a protector.

'But you can see why we are worried,' Agnes was saying to Giffard. 'I have been accused of murder ever since I arrived, so I am the obvious scapegoat here.'

'Baderon will want someone hanged,' agreed Ralph.

'Baderon does not hang innocent people,' declared Joan, casting an icy glance towards fitzNorman, to indicate the same could not be said of him. 'If you have done nothing wrong, you have nothing to worry about.'

'Hugh was his only son,' said Ralph. 'He will lash out at anyone available. And do not think you are immune from his wrath, Geoffrey. *I* shall point out that it is easy to kill a man on Goodrich land, then dump the body elsewhere.'

Geoffrey met his gaze evenly. 'But it would not be true.'

Ralph shrugged. 'Perhaps not, but it will make him think twice about accusing Agnes. Or me.'

'So,' Geoffrey surmised, treating Ralph with

the contempt he deserved by ignoring him. 'Hugh disappeared after the fire, only to appear stabbed at the ford. Eleanor is still missing, which may mean she is the culprit, but which may equally mean she is dead, too. We should look for her, if for no other reason than she might need help.'

'I will go,' offered Giffard. 'I will ride that donkey to the forest and try to find her.'

'I do not suppose the killer left his knife in Hugh, did he?' asked Geoffrey hopefully. Knives were distinctive, and finding the murder weapon might result in an early solution.

'Yes,' came the unexpected reply from Walter. 'It was still in his back when we found him – before we rushed back towards Bicanofre for help.'

'It was a horrible thing,' said Agnes with a shudder. 'A long dagger with a ruby in its hilt.'

'But someone stole it,' finished Walter. 'By the time we returned, it was gone. A greedy peasant must have grabbed it.'

Geoffrey was unconvinced by Walter's claim – local people would recognize Hugh and would appreciate the danger of stealing a murder weapon. Even the greediest would think twice, since it would be distinctive and difficult to sell. It occurred to Geoffrey that the killer might have been nearby when Walter and Agnes had stumbled on the body, and had retrieved his dagger after they had gone. Or were they lying? It was no secret that Henry had been killed with a similar blade, so perhaps they had described it to create confusion, and thus divert suspicion from themselves.

Geoffrey travelled the short distance to Walecford to inspect the body himself. He took Durand with him, because Bale was helping Peter in the kitchens, using his sharp knives to slice onions. He tensed when he saw Corwenna and Seguin behind them, wondering if they intended to ambush him, but they turned left at the first fork in the road, while he went right.

'She is going back to Llan Martin,' explained Durand. 'She has been telling everyone she will not wait at Goodrich to be stabbed by Mappestones. The King ordered her to stay here, but clearly she considers herself exempt from the commands of a king.'

Geoffrey was thoughtful. 'I heard her tell Seguin that Henry will not reign for much longer.'

'I heard her, too,' said Durand. 'The woman is mad to make such statements in the earshot of loyal subjects.'

Hugh was no more attractive in death than he had been in life, his jaw hanging open and his eyes glazed slits. Geoffrey asked Durand to stand guard at the church door, to tell him if anyone was coming, then began his examination. He quickly learnt that Hugh had been killed by a single stab wound to the back. The weapon had made an oval injury, with sharp V-shaped incisions at the top and bottom. It told Geoffrey that its blade was double-edged, a killing weapon rather than an everyday knife.

He inspected Hugh's hands and arms, looking

for marks to indicate that he had fought his attacker, but there was nothing. Then he examined Hugh's head, to check whether he had first been subdued, and came across a lump. Finally, he assessed his neck, and was startled to see the clear imprint of fingers. Geoffrey sat back on his heels. It seemed to him that someone had hit Hugh on the head, hard enough to stun him, and then strangled him. The knife wound had merely been for show.

He frowned as he considered further. According to the King, the ruby-hilted dagger should be in Baderon's possession. Did that mean Baderon had killed his own son? Or had someone in his household murdered Hugh, using the weapon Baderon had been to such pains to acquire? But who? One of his knights, on the grounds that their master would have more property to give away with the lawful heir dead? Or Hilde, so she would inherit all?

'What are you doing?'

The appalled voice behind him made him jump violently. Unsure of how to reply, he said nothing. He glanced angrily at Durand for letting Hilde past in the first place, but Durand only shrugged, to convey that he had been unable to stop her. Geoffrey's spirits plummeted further still when he saw that Hilde was not alone: Baderon and Lambert were with her.

'No!' groaned Baderon, dropping to his knees. 'Not Hugh!'

'Who did this?' Hilde demanded coldly. 'And what are you doing here? Joan sent word to tell us Hugh was found, but she did not warn us that

286

ghouls would be poring over his poor corpse.'

'Hugh is wet,' said Baderon in a strangled whisper. 'Why is he wet?'

'Because he was found in the ford,' explained Durand.

'Stabbed,' said Hilde. 'Or so we were told. Where is the knife?'

'Actually, he was strangled,' said Geoffrey, pointing at the bruises. 'He was probably subdued with a blow to the head and then had the life choked out of him. The stabbing seems to have been an afterthought.'

Hilde stared at him. 'How do you know?'

Geoffrey took a deep breath. 'Agnes and Walter claim they saw a ruby-hilted knife embedded in Hugh. It was stolen by the time they fetched help.'

Horror flickered briefly in Baderon's eyes. *'Ruby hilted?'*

'Like the one used to kill my brother,' said Geoffrey, watching him. Alarm replaced the shock on Baderon's face. Geoffrey glanced at Hilde, but could read only grief, while Lambert was impassive and watchful.

Baderon swallowed hard. 'I did own such a weapon, but it was stolen months ago. I doubt *that* killed Henry *or* Hugh.'

Geoffrey pressed on. 'You were seen buying one from Jervil on the eve of the fire.'

Baderon's eyes narrowed. 'Who told you these lies?'

'I thought you were becoming our friend,' said Hilde, hurt plain in her voice. 'I told you before that your witness was mistaken. What are you

287

trying to infer from his lies? That *we* killed Henry – and now have murdered my own dear brother?'

'He just wants someone to blame for Henry's death,' said Lambert to Baderon. 'Now he will tell the King *you* did it – and that you killed Hugh, too.'

'You bastard!' exclaimed Baderon, and there was a ringing sound as he drew his sword, and Lambert did likewise. 'I will kill you!'

Baderon lunged towards Geoffrey, but the younger, quicker knight had no trouble jumping out of the way. He drew his own weapon, and put a pillar between himself and Baderon and Lambert, to gain a moment to speak.

'We can fight if we must, but before we do, be aware that the King saw you buy the dagger from Jervil, and I am investigating at his request. I now know a similar weapon killed Hugh, and I would like your explanation.'

Baderon froze. 'The King saw me with Jervil?'

Geoffrey nodded. 'And several of Goodrich's servants say you were buying what was originally yours – that Jervil had retrieved it for you.'

Baderon's sword clattered from his hand, and his shoulders sank. Hilde ran to him, putting her arm around him. Lambert remained armed, however, and Geoffrey stayed behind the pillar.

'This cannot be right,' said Hilde to her father. 'We had nothing to do with Henry's death. He deserved to die, but it was not at our hands. *Tell* him!'

'Henry was murdered with a dagger *I* owned,'

said Baderon, raising a white, anguished face towards Hilde. 'I was uneasy when I first heard the description of the weapon that had killed him – the one Olivier told me Eleanor had cursed – but no one connected it to me, and I saw no need to complicate matters by mentioning it.'

Hilde's protective hug loosened. 'Your blade murdered Henry?' She sounded shocked.

Baderon nodded. 'I knew as soon as I met him that Geoffrey would investigate – and that he would be more thorough than the others. Peace is important to me, and I did not want the dagger to spoil our chance of friendship. So, I asked Jervil to get it back before Geoffrey could identify it as mine. I intended to destroy it, to be free of its evil.'

'Why ask Jervil to help you?' asked Geoffrey. 'Why not Joan or Olivier?'

'What could I say to Joan?' cried Baderon. 'My dagger killed your brother, and I would like it back now, please? That was exactly what I wanted to avoid. I want peace, not a feud.'

'I would have listened to your explanation,' said Geoffrey reasonably.

'Yes, and *then* you would have attacked us,' said Lambert.

Baderon took no notice of his knight and continued to address Geoffrey. 'Perhaps you would, but I had already asked Jervil for help. He was good at getting hold of things. He told me he followed your priest to Rosse and bought it from the silversmith – although I suspect he actually stole it. He sold it to me the night of the fire.'

Geoffrey said nothing, but Jervil had lied to

Baderon – the weapon that Father Adrian had sold in Rosse was Olivier's heirloom, not the blade that had killed Henry.

'And the King saw you,' said Hilde. She regarded her father in dismay. 'Could you not have made this transaction in secret? *I* know you are innocent, but others may not.'

Baderon glanced at Geoffrey with a face that had aged ten years. 'I did not kill Jervil, lest you accuse me of that, too.'

'Was this the dagger Seguin gave you?' asked Lambert. 'The one intended as a sign of his fealty?'

Baderon nodded. 'I appreciated the gesture, but the knife was too garish for my tastes. I did not even notice it was missing until I heard about the blade that killed Henry. Then I looked for it – and found it gone. I thought long and hard, and the only time it could have gone missing was at the Feast of Corpus Christi, last June. We had invited our neighbours to celebrate with us. One of them must have taken it.'

'Whom would you suspect?' asked Geoffrey.

'It could have been anyone,' replied Lambert. 'Wulfric, Ralph, Eleanor or Douce from Bicanofre; Henry, Joan and Olivier; fitzNorman, Isabel and Margaret. A host of servants.'

'Was Jervil there?' asked Geoffrey.

Hilde shook her head. 'Joan would not let him come, because he had sticky fingers.'

'Your brother came, though,' said Baderon. 'He ruined the occasion for everyone with his rude manners and inflammatory comments. If he had been killed then, it would not have surprised me. But the knife was stolen instead by someone who intended to kill him with it later.'

'That means his murder was premeditated,' said Geoffrey. 'For *three months*!'

'Yes, but not by my father,' said Hilde firmly. 'He has not killed Henry, Hugh, Jervil or anyone else. All he did was lose a dagger and try to get it back so *you* would not think badly of him.'

Geoffrey rubbed his chin, trying to gather his scattered thoughts. 'I believe you, but there are still many unanswered questions. For example, if you bought this knife from Jervil, then how did it come to kill Hugh? And where is it now?'

'I do not know,' said Baderon. 'I assumed it was lost in the fire, but I was wrong to think it could be destroyed so easily. Its curse continues. How many more people will it claim before it is sated?'

Eleven

It was with a heavy heart that Geoffrey rode back to Goodrich, Durand at his side. The day was still clear and fine, with sun streaming through branches beginning to show the first greening of spring.

'What do you think of Baderon's story?' Geoffrey asked. 'Do you believe him?'

'No,' said Durand, without a moment's hesitation. 'Seguin gives him a dagger with a ruby in it – a ruby, mark you, not a piece of glass – and he shoves it in a chest and does not realize it has been stolen for months? A likely story!'

'But Goodrich's servants say Baderon wanted Henry alive.'

Durand was dismissive. 'He has a temper – you saw how quickly he attacked you in that church. I imagine he did the same to Henry, only Henry was drunk and unable to defend himself.'

Geoffrey supposed that was a possibility.

Durand continued. 'Then this wretched Black Knife starts to rove all over the place. Joan wraps it in holy cloth, but Olivier removes it from their bedchamber and it disappears for a long time. Then you arrive, and it appears again. The King sees it passed to Baderon, and it is used to murder Baderon's own son. But Baderon is a liar: I do not believe for a moment that he paid good silver to retrieve a dagger that *might* cause a rift between him and Goodrich.'

'You do not like him, do you?'

'No,' declared Durand fervently. 'He would have killed you, had you not ducked out of the way – and then he would have told Joan that he had nothing to do with the death of her youngest brother, either. No, I do not like him.'

Geoffrey imagined the real reason Baderon had earned Durand's dislike was because of what had happened at Dene. Durand did not forgive insults to his dignity, and he was no doubt delighted to see Baderon in such dire straits. But although Durand was spiteful, his reasoning was flawless. Geoffrey saw Baderon was still very much a suspect.

They arrived at Goodrich, where people continued to discuss Hugh's death. Giffard was quiet and withdrawn, so Geoffrey sat with him, hoping he would take comfort from a friend's proximity. He knew exactly why Giffard was upset: the glance Agnes had shot her son had all but confessed Walter's involvement in Sibylla's death.

'I should not have drawn my sword against you,' Baderon said to Geoffrey as the company assembled for the midday meal. He looked old, weary and tearful. 'You offended me, but you had good reason to do so. I hope my poor manners will not damage our friendship?'

Geoffrey accepted the apology with amiable grace and then left the hall, not wanting to discuss the matter further. Outside, Olivier was struggling in a strong wind to saddle his pony, and Geoffrey wondered why he did not do it in the stables. Then he recalled Olivier's admission that he had avoided the stables since Henry's death. It seemed ridiculous that a grown man should be so unnerved – especially since Geoffrey had removed the charms and dried blood – but Olivier tartly reminded him of his own unease in caves.

'Where are you going?' he asked, watching Olivier's inept fumbling.

'Out,' replied Olivier. 'I like visitors, but these guests are taxing.'

Geoffrey knew what he meant. 'May I come with you?'

Olivier smiled. 'I should be glad of the company – and the protection. This Black Knife is at large again, and who knows when the thing will strike next?'

'Never, with luck. May I ride your palfrey? He is not exercised enough.'

'Dun? Yes, but do not expect *me* to take a turn on him. I do not like undisciplined horses.'

Bale came to assist with the saddling, but was more hindrance than help. Eventually, Geoffrey climbed on Dun's back, only to have the horse rear suddenly, as though he had never carried a rider before. Geoffrey was obliged to shorten the reins in order to control him.

'He is a lively beast,' said Olivier. 'Baderon warned he was wild when he sold him to me. I would ask Eleanor for a charm to calm him, but she is gone God knows where and, unless you are prepared to take him, he must be sold, because there is no one else who can manage him.'

Geoffrey quickly discovered what he meant, as Dun shot off like an arrow from a bow, leaving Olivier behind. People scuttled out of the way as he rounded a corner far faster than was safe. He slowed as they passed the church, although Dun still reared and bucked furiously.

'There is something wrong with him,' he said, as Olivier caught up.

'He is itching for exercise,' explained Olivier, spurring his pony forward and heading for the woods. He bounced in his saddle like a sack of grain. 'Give him his head; he will soon tire.'

'Easy for you to say,' muttered Geoffrey, who did not think that Dun's behaviour had anything to do with excess energy. The beast pranced and then bucked hard, forcing Geoffrey to grip tightly with his knees. Another horseman was riding towards him: Seguin, followed by a servant with a cart.

'Having trouble?' Seguin asked, watching Dun's antics with amusement. 'He just needs a decent run. Or are you too frightened to let such an animal have his freedom?'

'Why are you here?' retorted Geoffrey. He glanced at the cart, which carried a wooden box and a blanket. 'Have you come for Hugh? He is at Walecford, not Goodrich.'

Seguin scowled. 'The message I received said he is at Goodrich – where he was murdered.'

'Then it was wrong,' replied Geoffrey coolly. 'Incidentally, Baderon says you gave him a dagger with a ruby hilt. I do not suppose you have seen it recently?'

'It was a fine weapon, but he shoved it in a chest,' glowered Seguin. 'The next thing I knew, it was in Henry. But I have not seen it since. If I do, you will be the first to know.' He made a violent stabbing motion with his hand and rode away.

Gingerly, Geoffrey touched his heels to Dun's sides and eased the pressure on the reins. The horse started to walk in an odd, sideways gait that told Geoffrey he wanted to go faster. He kept the animal tightly under control until they were well past the village, and caught up with Olivier, who was singing to himself. Olivier continued to warble, indicating with a gesture that music calmed horses. It seemed to work, and they reached the edge of the woods without further incident. A long, straight path stretched out in front of them, heading upwards into a twiggy tunnel.

'I think I might trot,' said Olivier, kicking his nag to a slightly quicker pace. The sudden cessation of music and another animal moving ahead were too much for Dun. Ignoring Geoffrey's commands, he began to gallop. Supposing he might as well let him, Geoffrey eased his grip on the reins, as Dun moved like the wind. Then Dun started his curious bucking movements at speed, taking Geoffrey by surprise. He lurched forward roughly, then heard something snap. While he was still trying to regain his balance, Dun bucked again. Geoffrey felt the saddle loose underneath him. And then he was flying head over heels into a patch of brambles.

'Good God!' exclaimed Olivier, trotting up. 'Are you all right?'

Geoffrey did a rough inventory. His head was spinning, but only his pride was damaged. 'Yes.'

'Do not struggle,' instructed Olivier. 'Or you will become more deeply entangled. Let me cut some of these thorns away.'

Geoffrey watched him sawing the thick, spiked branches. 'I have not been thrown by a horse in years. Perhaps you *should* sell him, Olivier. He is too much for me, too.'

Olivier shoved his dagger in its sheath and offered Geoffrey his hand. Geoffrey half-expected them both to end up in the brambles, but Olivier soon had him extricated. Dun stood quietly, head down. Olivier held the bridle and crooned softly, while Geoffrey went to remove the saddle, which clung at an odd angle. He showed it to Olivier.

'The strap is broken.' Geoffrey felt better knowing that the accident resulted from faulty equipment.

'Not broken,' said Olivier, studying it. 'Sawn through. You can see the smooth line of a cut made by a knife, then a jagged part that broke under the strain. Someone deliberately damaged it.'

Geoffrey was angry. 'How could someone have been so stupid? Joan might have been killed!'

'No,' said Olivier. 'This saddle is only ever used for Dun, and Joan does not use him. There was no chance of anyone riding Dun but you.'

Geoffrey gazed at him. 'Someone did this to harm me?'

Olivier nodded. 'Yes, because here is something else – metal shards twisted into the saddle. No wonder Dun bolted! These spikes, along with the damaged strap, were certain to cause an accident.'

'Who would have done this?' asked Geoffrey, bewildered.

'Ralph, perhaps,' mused Olivier. 'Or fitzNorman, Baderon, Seguin or Corwenna. Or Agnes and Walter, who are determined to stop you from learning who killed the Duchess. Or perhaps even a servant who was not won over by your flamboyant gambling techniques.'

Geoffrey sighed. 'A whole host of suspects, as usual.'

They walked back to the castle, leading their horses and discussing suspects. Olivier favoured Ralph, who, he declared, might well use a horse to do his dirty work. Geoffrey was more inclined towards Walter, whose stupidity meant he might not see that such a stunt could hurt the horse as well as his intended victim. They were still debating when they entered the bailey, and Bale came racing up to them grinning from ear to ear.

'You had better come,' he said to Geoffrey. 'Someone has been stabbed in the priest's house – and there is blood *everywhere*.'

Geoffrey followed his squire across the bailey, with Olivier at his side. In the street outside the castle people were spilling out of their homes, looking alarmed. Geoffrey left Olivier to allay their fears and headed for the house next to the church, where Father Adrian lived. The priest was in his garden, being sick on his winter cabbages, while Durand tried to comfort him.

'Aim for the onions,' Geoffrey recommended as he passed. 'Joan says they are more resilient.'

'Do not be flippant,' snapped Durand. 'It is not becoming under these circumstances.'

'What circumstances?' asked Geoffrey. 'Who is dead?'

Father Adrian emptied his stomach again and seemed incapable of speech, and Durand shrugged that he did not know, so Geoffrey entered the house. He had not been inside it for more than a year, but it was much as he remembered. A neat, clean place, with a fire flickering in the hearth, a pot of stew bubbling and an overfed cat sitting on a windowsill.

The room was full of people who had come running when Father Adrian raised the alarm. Agnes and Walter were there, regarding the victim with dispassionate interest, and Geoffrey realized that their horror over Hugh's death had been an act, to convince Giffard that they were not killers. Ralph stood rather closer to Agnes than was necessary, while Giffard knelt by the dead man.

Nearby was fitzNorman, holding Isabel's hand. Her head was tilted to one side, and Geoffrey suspected that she was listening for Ralph. He was glad she could not see him standing so close to Agnes. FitzNorman could, though, and his face was a mask of fury. Joan stood on Isabel's other side; Geoffrey had the feeling that she was ready to step forward and intervene, should Ralph say or do anything unpleasant and fitzNorman react with anger.

Bale was right in that there was a good deal of blood, although it was no worse than many scenes Geoffrey had viewed. The body sat at Father Adrian's table, resting its head on its arm as though it were asleep; the other hand lay in its lap. It looked as though its owner was sleeping – except for the gash in the middle of the back.

'Seguin!' exclaimed Geoffrey. 'How did this happen? He was alive and well when I went riding with Olivier a short while ago.'

'You were the last one to see him alive?' pounced Ralph. Isabel's face softened at the sound of his voice. 'Can anyone verify that *you* did not kill him?'

'Olivier was with me,' said Geoffrey, before realizing that was untrue. Olivier had ridden ahead and had not been party to the discussion.

Father Adrian appeared at the door, white-faced and shaking. 'I am sorry to be feeble,' he said in a whisper. 'I deplore violence.'

'So do we all, Father,' said fitzNorman insincerely. 'Although some of us seem rather more used to it than others.' He shot Geoffrey a nasty glance, then did the same to Agnes.

'I do not know what happened,' said Father Adrian. 'Sir Seguin came to Goodrich because he thought Hugh's body was here. I offered him ale before I set him on the right road, but found I did not have any. I went to beg a jug from Mistress Helbye, and when I came back, I found...' He gazed at the slumped figure, and his hand went to his mouth again.

'Do not look,' advised Geoffrey, standing so that the priest could not see the corpse.

'Do not worry about the blood, Father,' said Bale eagerly. 'I will scrape it up for you.' He made a scooping gesture with his hand, and Father Adrian disappeared outside again.

'Father Adrian came straight to the castle,' said Joan. 'But Seguin was beyond earthly help.'

'Where were you all?' Geoffrey asked, supposing he had better add Seguin's murder to his investigation.

'You accuse *us* of this?' asked Ralph incredulously. '*You* are the one *I* suspect.'

'No, Ralph,' said Isabel. 'Geoffrey would not resort to violence when words could do.'

Ralph burst into mocking laughter. 'He is a

300

Holy Land knight! Resorting to violence is what they do. *He* is the one here who likes slaughter.'

Geoffrey regarded Ralph with dislike, while thinking that Seguin had been stabbed in the back – exactly the kind of cowardly act he would expect from the loathsome heir of Bicanofre.

'Answer my question,' Geoffrey said coolly. 'Where were you?'

'We were walking in the woods,' said Agnes, smiling at Ralph.

'*You* were with Ralph?' Isabel asked unsteadily. 'In the forest?'

'Walter was there,' said Joan. 'And he is always looking out for his mother's virtue. They did nothing amiss, you can be sure of that.'

'My father and I were in the church,' said Isabel in a small voice. 'I was praying for ... for my happiness.' The expression she shot in Ralph's direction made even Agnes flinch.

Voices sounded on the road outside, and Geoffrey heard Olivier speaking. From the tread of spurred feet, Geoffrey knew it was Baderon and Lambert coming. He braced himself for trouble.

'My brother!' whispered Lambert, gazing at the body in horror.

Baderon stepped forward to lay a hand on his shoulder. 'My son and my friend in one day.' His voice choked with emotion. 'How many more will die before we have peace?'

Lambert's eyes were bleak. 'I am going to Llan Martin. Corwenna must be told.'

'No,' said Hilde gently. 'You cannot go to Corwenna yet – not until you know what happened

301

here. If you do, she will claim Seguin was murdered to destroy my father's alliances, and there will be trouble.'

'Yes,' said Lambert coldly. He made as if to pass her, but she blocked his way.

'Listen to her, Lambert,' said Baderon, although he sounded weary and defeated. 'We do not want any more deaths.'

'Your son was murdered!' shouted Lambert. 'And now my brother lies dead. Will you wait for me to die, too? And Hilde? Hugh and Seguin must be avenged, or there will be no end to the slaughter. I am going to Corwenna. At least *she* has the strength to face our enemies.'

He shoved past Hilde, almost knocking her over. Geoffrey darted after him, alarmed by the damage that might ensue if he did as he threatened. Corwenna would be implacable, and Geoffrey doubted Caerdig would be able to prevent her doing something rash.

'Please!' Hilde begged, also hurrying outside to grab Lambert's arm. 'Wait until we have a culprit to show Corwenna, or she will pick one of her own.'

'She will choose Goodrich,' snarled Lambert, glaring at Geoffrey. 'Henry killed her first husband, and now her next one lies dead on Mappestone land. So does your brother.'

'Hugh was not killed at Goodrich,' said Hilde. 'His death and Seguin's are not connected, and you must not make them sound as though they are.'

'You are quibbling over the width of a river!' shouted Lambert. 'Hugh may have been *washed*

302

to the other side. Or his body was dragged over, so blame would fall on someone other than Geoffrey.'

'There are many suspects,' said Hilde with quiet reason, but Lambert was too distraught to listen. He mounted his horse and was gone with a vicious jab of his spurs.

'If he reaches Corwenna, there will be trouble,' said Father Adrian with concern. 'This will provide her with the opportunity she has been waiting for. The Welsh will rally to her call, in the hope that the spoils of war will feed their families. You must stop him.'

Geoffrey leapt on to Baderon's black bay and thundered after the fleeing knight. Lambert glanced behind him and spurred on his mount, ignoring Geoffrey's yells to stop. He began to edge ahead, because Baderon's horse was not as fleet as Lambert's stallion.

Geoffrey's throat became hoarse from shouting, and he saw that they had crossed the brook that marked the territory belonging to Llan Martin. He jabbed his heels hard into the horse's flanks, determined to catch his quarry, then pulled up abruptly when several arrows hit the ground in front of him, like a barrier. He reached for his shield before realizing that he did not have it. Archers emerged from the undergrowth on either side of the track. His horse whinnied in terror as a second volley of arrows hissed around them, and he struggled to control it. A little way ahead, Lambert stopped.

'Come back,' pleaded Geoffrey. 'We can resolve this peacefully.'

'Easy for you to say!' Lambert shouted. 'But my brother is dead, and so is Baderon's son.'

'Hugh is dead?' one of the archers asked. 'Did Goodrich kill him?'

'We do not know yet,' said Geoffrey before Lambert could reply. He tried to ride forward, but arrows thudded at his horse's feet, making it skitter in panic. 'I must speak to Caerdig.'

'You will come no farther,' instructed an archer. 'Corwenna told us to let no Goodrich villains on our land. Go home, or I will put an arrow in your heart.'

Geoffrey saw his options running out as Lambert started to ride towards Llan Martin. 'Let me talk to Caerdig,' he pleaded. 'He said I was always welcome at—'

'No,' said the archer firmly. 'Now go home, or we will send you there dead.'

Lambert had disappeared along the forest track, and Geoffrey saw that there was no more he could do. Defeated, he turned towards Goodrich.

'Damn!' Hilde muttered when Geoffrey dismounted outside the priest's house and shook his head despondently. 'Now there will be trouble. We must leave immediately.'

'You cannot. The archers will shoot you – they are under orders from Corwenna.'

'They will not harm us,' said Hilde. 'But we cannot travel quickly carrying Seguin, so we must leave him here. I trust you will treat him with respect.'

'Of course,' said Joan stiffly, offended she

304

should ask. 'But wait until he is laid out decently, so you can tell Lambert. Then he may change his mind.'

'You really think there will be a war?' asked Isabel in a low voice. 'Over Seguin?'

'Not over Seguin,' replied Hilde. 'Over our Welsh neighbours not having enough to eat, and the alliances my father has forged having brought them together to air their grievances. That and Corwenna's poisonous tongue. We must prepare ourselves for the worst.'

Joan ushered everyone out until only she, Geoffrey, Father Adrian, Baderon and Hilde remained. Geoffrey took a blanket and laid it on the floor so that he could lift Seguin's body into it but, as he bent, he saw something shiny. He reached under the table and picked it up. It was a long dagger with a ruby in its hilt. Baderon sank on to a bench when he saw it.

'Is that what killed Seguin?' he asked weakly. 'The knife he gave me as a sign of his fealty?'

Geoffrey measured the size of the blade against the wound in Seguin's back and nodded.

'What can we do with it?' asked Baderon. 'It claimed the life of my son, and now my friend.'

'We cannot throw it in the river,' said Joan. 'Olivier did that, and it came back.'

'Take it to the blacksmith in Rosse and pay him to melt it,' suggested Hilde. 'Do it today.'

'I cannot,' said Geoffrey. 'Not with a skirmish brewing.'

Baderon closed his eyes. 'Do I stay here, and show my allegiance to England? Or do I ride to Llan Martin and stand with the Welsh, so they know I am in earnest when I offer the hand of friendship? Damn Lambert! He has done immeasurable damage.'

'The security of an entire region is at stake,' said Hilde practically. 'So we have no choice but to side with the Welsh. It is only Goodrich that Corwenna wants to see in flames. When that is done, her fury will abate, and we will be able to prevent her inciting any further attacks.' She glanced at Geoffrey and Joan. 'I do not want to fight you, but I do not see what else we can do.'

'Talk to Caerdig,' urged Geoffrey. 'He will see reason.'

'His hands are tied, too,' said Hilde grimly. 'The other lords are desperate for food and will rally to Corwenna's battle cry – especially if she claims Seguin was murdered by you. Caerdig will not be heard. Besides, he is no longer a power. Corwenna's fiery speeches are more popular than his pleas for peace, and she has a greater following.'

'This is ridiculous,' said Joan. 'I do not want our people to die because Corwenna hated Henry – and that is really what all this is about. You *must* stop this, Baderon. You are in charge of this region, so take control.'

Baderon's face was ashen, and Geoffrey did not think he had ever seen a more broken specimen. No proud Welsh prince would listen to such a man – they would look to Lambert's strong sword and Corwenna's flashing eyes and promises of grain. As Baderon walked towards his horse, Geoffrey could almost see the power draining from him. The Lord of Monmouth climbed slowly into his saddle and rode away without another word.

'You cannot let them leave!' cried Father Adrian, aghast as Baderon and Hilde cantered away. 'They will lead the Welsh against us! You heard Hilde – she plans to sacrifice Goodrich to save the rest of the region.'

'What do you want us to do?' demanded Joan. 'Lock them in our dungeons? That would incite an attack for certain!'

'I told Seguin that Hugh's body was at Walecford, but he did not believe me,' said Geoffrey, watching Hilde and Baderon disappear from sight. 'If he had, none of this would have happened.'

'He did not believe me, either,' said Father Adrian tiredly. 'I had to show him the empty church before he did. Then he said someone had intentionally misled him.'

Geoffrey stared at him. 'It sounds as though he were deliberately lured here. Why?'

Father Adrian had no answer. 'Take it with you,' he ordered, pointing to the knife.

Geoffrey did not want it, either, but wrapped it in a piece of cloth, sprinkled generously with holy water, and set off towards the castle, to see what kind of troops he had at his command. He doubted they would be much, and only hoped they would not run away at the first sight of an enemy.

First he went to Helbye. The old soldier was appalled that his peaceful retirement was being shattered, and his wife gave Geoffrey a piece of her mind, as her man collected his weapons and went to muster those who would fight.

On his way to the castle Geoffrey met Durand, and handed him the cloth containing the dagger. 'You know about holy matters. Will you dispose of this for me?'

'What is it?' asked Durand, unwrapping it. When he saw the stained weapon, he gave a shriek and dropped it. 'It is covered in blood!'

'It was used to kill Seguin,' said Geoffrey. 'Everyone else thinks it is cursed, but I know you are above such superstition. Will you take it to a blacksmith and have it destroyed?'

Durand backed away. 'I am not touching it. It is a Black Knife. You can destroy it yourself.'

'How?' asked Geoffrey. 'I will be organizing our defences. I could drop it down the well...'

'It would put itself in a bucket and come back,' said Durand. 'That is the nature of Black Knives. They must be *destroyed*, not tossed away.'

Geoffrey sighed. 'Then lock it in a chest in my bedchamber, to melt down later.'

'No,' said Durand, backing even farther away. 'I am having nothing to do with it – and no good will come of having it in your castle, either. All I can do is pray for you.'

He turned and strode towards the church, leaving Geoffrey shaking his head, astonished that even Durand was affected by superstition.

Olivier and Joan were already mustering their soldiers, so Geoffrey ran up the stairs to his bedchamber, shoved the Black Knife in the bottom of a chest, hastily donned full armour and set out for the bailey, to test the resources at his disposal.

He was not impressed. The men knew the basics, but were ill equipped for hand-to-hand combat, and their armour and weapons were in poor repair. He saw that he would have to train them hard if he did not want them slaughtered. He did so for the rest of the day, and when the sun set, he took them through night manoeuvres. In the small hours he drew up plans of the estate and considered his natural defences, then woke the garrison before dawn for more drills. By sunset of the second day, they had improved, although he reserved judgement.

That evening, when it was too dark to do more and his body ached from fatigue, Geoffrey went to the hall. Giffard and Walter were there, and he could tell by the sullen expression on the boy's face that Giffard was lecturing him. Not wanting to interrupt, he sat with Joan. She reminded him about the passageway in his bedchamber – which might be used as an escape route, but could also render the castle vulnerable. Geoffrey's first instinct was to block it off, but then what would happen if the invaders gained access to the bailey and the keep was set alight?

Ralph, Douce and Wulfric were also there, evidently considering Goodrich safer than their undefended manor. Douce was with Bale, who was trying, without success, to show her how to use a catapult, while Olivier strummed his harp, mostly for the benefit of the nervous servants.

Isabel sat on her own, head to one side as she listened. At one point Ralph walked past her and whispered something that made her face light up. She gestured that she wanted him to sit next to her, but he murmured some excuse that made her smile slip, and returned to Agnes. It seemed inordinately cruel to Geoffrey.

'You look exhausted,' said Giffard, abandoning his efforts with Walter. The lad immediately went to Olivier and ordered him to play something livelier. When Olivier declined, he snatched the instrument and began to plonk out a melody he claimed was popular in Italy. The servants promptly dispersed.

Geoffrey stared into the flames. 'I should never haver returned to England. Goodrich would be quieter and calmer if I were not here.'

'Not so,' countered Giffard. 'Dene would still have caught fire – only the King, Isabel and I may not have escaped; Eleanor would still be missing; and Hugh and Seguin would still have been stabbed. And your presence means your sister is safer.'

'What do you think of my daughter, Sir Geoffrey?' asked Wulfric, approaching uninvited and nodding towards Douce. 'A beauty, eh? A fine woman?'

'Not tonight,' said Giffard, giving Wulfric a severe look. 'His mind is engaged with the defence of Goodrich.'

'Yours might be,' said Wulfric, looking Giffard up and down disparagingly. 'But Sir Geoffrey is a red-blooded man who is always ready for a lass. Would you like to try her out? Tonight?'

Geoffrey stared at him. 'Are you serious?'

Wulfric nodded. 'Of course. Then we can finalize the details of your betrothal tomorrow. I guarantee you will not be disappointed. There are many men who would give their sword arms to possess a fine, sturdy girl like Douce.'

'Let the poor man rest,' said Gifford sharply. 'He has been working all day and needs sleep, not a romp. Besides, he has competition – his squire has reached Douce first.'

Wulfric shot to where Douce was leading Bale to an upper chamber, her expression full of carnal promise. Geoffrey smiled when Wulfric snatched her away, disappointing both parties. But, to his alarm, Wulfric began to drag Douce back towards him.

'You are right, Giffard,' said Geoffrey, standing hastily. 'I *am* tired. I am going to bed.'

Nodding a curt farewell to Wulfric and Douce, he climbed the stairs. The sounds of the hall were soon below him, but he did not stop at his chamber. He walked to the top of the stairs, then out on to the battlements. A sharp, cold wind gusted, but the soldiers were alert and watchful, swathed in thick cloaks to keep them from freezing. He checked that all was well, then started to descend. He paused at one of the attic rooms, where he heard an odd humming. Curiously, he pushed open the door and was startled to see Mother Elgiva there, busy with what looked to be a corpse.

'Come in, Sir Geoffrey, if you have a mind for company,' said Elgiva, without turning around. He wondered how she knew it was him. 'I am laying out Jervil, who was returned to us today.'

311

'Why is he here and not in the church?' asked Geoffrey.

'It is his right to lie in the castle for a day,' said Elgiva. 'People will be offended if he goes into the ground without the proper respect. Did you not know this tradition?'

Geoffrey saw again there was a lot he did not understand about his manor's customs. He would have sent the body straight to Father Adrian, and was grateful that Joan had known what to do.

'I brought you a gift,' said Elgiva, 'since you asked about certain things last we met. A book.'

'A book?' asked Geoffrey, immediately interested. 'What kind of book?'

'One my mother gave me,' said Elgiva. 'I knew my letters once, but I have not bothered with them for too long, and they are all forgotten now. Joan tells me you are fond of books, so you can have it. It will tell you all about mandrake and the like.'

'It is about poisons?' asked Geoffrey. If so, it was not something a knight should own.

'Poisons *and* healing potions,' replied Elgiva. 'You will find all you need to know about mandrake, and a good deal more.'

Geoffrey accepted a very small volume with minuscule writing. He sat on a chest and leafed through it, admiring its intricate drawings.

'Poor Jervil,' said Elgiva, turning back to the body. 'He did not deserve this. Joan says you have been charged to find out who killed him.'

Geoffrey nodded. 'But I have not been very successful.'

'Then perhaps I can tell you one or two things that might help. For example, Jervil went to Dene to meet Baderon and sell him the Black Knife. He told me himself – he came for a protective charm, but obviously my magic was not strong enough.'

'Did he tell you how this dagger came into his possession? He told Baderon he bought it from the silversmith in Rosse, but it was not the knife Father Adrian sold there.'

'I know,' said Elgiva. 'You mentioned it last time. I probably should have told you what I knew then, but I wanted to find out more about you first.'

'What do you know about the dagger?' Geoffrey asked, struggling to mask his irritation.

'Sir Olivier threw the real one in the river,' said Elgiva. 'I overheard him at confession, although he should have asked *my* advice, not God's. I could have told him the Wye was no place for a Black Knife. Two things conspired to bring it back again. Do you know what they were?'

Geoffrey was far too tired for mental games, but strove to oblige her. 'Jervil's liking for treasure and Olivier's feeble throw?'

Elgiva cackled her appreciation. 'You have a quick mind! Jervil happened to see Sir Olivier toss the Black Knife in the water. It landed in the shallows, so he fished it out.'

Geoffrey tried to make sense of the dagger's travels, starting at the beginning. 'So, Seguin gave a ruby-handled dagger to Baderon as a gift. It was stolen from Baderon during the Feast of

Corpus Christi and taken to Eleanor for cursing. It was used to kill Henry, spent a week or two in Joan's bedchamber wrapped in holy cloth, was hurled in the river...'

'...from where Jervil retrieved it. He brought it to show me, but I frightened him into burying it, for his own safety. There it might have remained, but for you. Baderon did not want a feud when you discovered it was *his* weapon that had killed Henry.'

Geoffrey thought about it. 'Baderon – like everyone except Olivier, Jervil and you – thought the real one was in Father Adrian's church. *That* was the blade he paid Jervil to retrieve.'

'But Baderon would have known Father Adrian's was the wrong one, so Jervil dug up the Black Knife. I advised against it, but Baderon's silver spoke louder than my wisdom.'

'Was it coincidence that Baderon asked Jervil for help, when Jervil happened to be the one who had retrieved it from the river?'

'Well, everyone knew Jervil was a thief. He was the obvious person to approach.'

Geoffrey resumed his analysis of the Black Knife's fortunes. 'Within hours of Baderon buying it, there was a fire at Dene, and he assumed it was destroyed with his other possessions.'

'But he was wrong – Black Knives do not fall foul of accidents. It was probably found in the rubble. Whoever did so was overwhelmed by its power and used it on Hugh and Seguin. Now I understand it is with you. You should be careful.'

314

'Thank you for telling me this,' said Geoffrey, wishing she had done so sooner. He stood to leave, feeling tiredness wash over him in a great wave. But Elgiva had not finished.

'Come here, and smell Jervil's mouth when I push on his chest.'

'No, thank you! I have had a long day, and sniffing corpses would not be a good way to end it.'

'Come,' said Elgiva. 'You are not the kind of man who is unsettled by such a request. It will not take a moment.'

With considerable reluctance, Geoffrey did as she asked, hoping it was not a ghoulish trick. He leant close to Jervil's mouth, and inhaled when she pushed on his chest. A slightly sweet smell came from it.

'Now this,' she said, handing him a tiny phial.

'It is the same,' said Geoffrey, watching her nod in satisfaction. 'What is it?'

'Poppy juice,' said Elgiva. 'It is a strong medicine used to induce sleep or ease pain in the very sick. Jervil must have swallowed a powerful measure, if we can still detect it after four days.'

Geoffrey rubbed his head. It was not the first time he had encountered the slightly sweet smell, and he tried to recall where he had come across it before. He knew it was recent, but the memory remained frustratingly beyond his grasp. He was just too tired to think.

'Jervil was given a sleeping draught before he died?' he asked.

Elgiva nodded. 'The draught made him drowsy and weak – and then he was strangled.'

Twelve

Geoffrey thought about Elgiva's discovery regarding the poppy juice while he lay in bed. It proved that someone had badly wanted Jervil to die and had given him a soporific to ensure he did so. It also indicated that the groom had died before Margaret. But who was the culprit? He supposed Baderon was still his prime suspect, followed by Hilde, Seguin and Lambert, because they had the best reasons for wanting Jervil silenced. And then there was Ralph, whose manor was poor, and so would have coveted the silver Jervil had earned. Or was the villain Eleanor, so conveniently missing – unless she was dead, of course?

Although Geoffrey was bone-weary, sleep would not come, so he lit a candle and picked up the book Elgiva had given him. He found the page on mandrake, struggling to make out the tiny words and swearing when hot wax dripped on his fingers. Eventually, he doused the candle and closed his eyes. He was still dwelling on what he had read when the door opened and someone crept into the room and made himself comfortable on a straw mattress.

'Bale?' he called.

'It is Durand; Bale is bedding Douce in the

stables. Did I wake you? I was trying to be quiet.'

Since Durand did not sound sleepy, Geoffrey relayed everything Elgiva had told him, feeling a need for his former squire's sharp wits.

'The villain is Baderon,' said Durand immediately. 'He had the most to gain from Jervil's death, as we have reasoned before. There is not only the fact that he would get his silver back, but he could be certain of silence. And it has been well worth his while.'

'What do you mean?' asked Geoffrey.

'I mean he has already employed the weapon at least twice since he bought it.'

'But the victims have been his son and his friend. They are not men he wanted dead.'

'How do you know?' asked Durand. 'Hugh was a half-wit, and maybe Baderon did not want an imbecile as his heir. And who can blame him? Meanwhile, Seguin was a brute, and perhaps Baderon regretted giving him so much power by betrothing him to Corwenna – the woman who has brought the region to the brink of war, when he has been striving for peace. Perhaps he killed Seguin in a futile attempt to prevent what has happened anyway.'

Geoffrey leant on one elbow. It was true. Baderon *had* been proud of the alliances he had forged and was convinced they would bring stability. But they had achieved the opposite, and now Baderon was powerless to control the monster he had created.

'And do not forget that Hugh was found where Olivier disposed of the Black Knife,' Durand went on. 'Olivier thought he was destroying the thing, but it escaped from the river via Jervil. Now Jervil is dead, and Baderon's only son is murdered at that exact same ford.'

'That must be coincidence,' said Geoffrey, although he was aware of the uncertainty in his voice. Was it possible? Had Hugh been strangled elsewhere and brought to the ford to make a point about the Black Knife?

'You need me to guide you through these mazes of intrigue,' said Durand smugly. 'I am a much better companion than Bale.'

'Bale saved me from the fire,' said Geoffrey, suspecting that Durand would have let him burn.

'I am not physically brave,' admitted Durand. 'But I have far more valuable assets. But you should sleep if you are to turn a rabble into an army tomorrow.'

Geoffrey tried to reassess the clues that rattled around his head, but he was almost instantly lost to the world. It seemed only moments later that he was woken by an urgent hammering and shaking of his shoulder. His first thought was that Goodrich was under attack, and he staggered to his feet, sword in hand. He found that he was weak and disorientated, and barely able to see.

'Never mind weapons!' shouted Durand. 'Help me with the flames, before we are roasted alive.'

It took a moment for Geoffrey's befuddled mind to grasp what was happening. There was a fire in the mattress next to his bed, which had filled the room with smoke. He saw Durand flapping furiously with a blanket to smother the

318

flames. Then the clerk darted to the window and threw the shutters wide, before pushing Geoffrey towards them. The thumping at the door grew louder.

'We cannot jump,' said Geoffrey. 'It is too far down.'

'Just breathe the clean air,' ordered Durand. 'The blaze is almost out.'

And then it was over. Durand doused the remains of the fire with a bowl of water, and the blaze hissed into nothing. Durand waved the blanket in an attempt to usher the smoke through the window, then the door flew open and Joan stood there, Olivier behind her.

'What happened?' she cried. 'I told the servants not to light a fire in your hearth, because you complain about the stuffiness. How did this come about?'

'The fire was not in the hearth,' said Geoffrey, coughing. 'It was in the bed.'

'We should have bolted the door,' said Durand. 'We assumed we were safe, but the castle is full of people who do not like you. We should have anticipated the attack.'

'You mean it was started deliberately?' asked Joan, aghast.

Durand nodded, pointing at kindling still on the mattress. 'We are lucky I woke when I did, or we would have burnt to cinders – and the whole castle with us.'

Olivier inspected the blackened mess. 'We could not open the door, because someone did something to make it stick. I suspect someone *did* mean you harm, Geoff. Do not forget what happened with Dun's saddle the other day.'

Geoffrey stared at the damage. Who would want him dead? Someone in Baderon's pay – or Corwenna's – to make sure he did not fight against them? Ralph, because he detested him? The same arsonist who had started the blaze at Dene – Eleanor, perhaps? One of the servants? Walter and Agnes, to prevent him learning the truth about the Duchess's murder?

'What woke you?' he asked Durand when no answers came.

'The smoke made me cough myself awake. I saw what was happening and set about dousing the flames. I yelled for your help, but you were dead to the world. Did you drink much wine last night?'

'None,' replied Geoffrey.

'Well, it is over now,' said Durand. He kicked the mattress and then hauled it to the window, where he tipped it out. 'It will be cold, but we should leave the shutters open. I do not want to be suffocated by residual fumes.'

Awkwardly, Joan patted Geoffrey's arm, then she gave Durand a shy smile as she left. 'I would have been without a brother if you had not acted so quickly.'

Durand pursed his lips after she and Olivier had gone. 'You should have listened to me in the first place, and then this would not have happened. You endangered me as well.'

Geoffrey was puzzled. 'Listened to you about what?'

'About the dangers of the Black Knife,' snapped Durand. 'It is here, in your chest, and now an attempt has been made on your life.'

Geoffrey was too tired to begin an argument about the efficacy of curses. He shot Durand a wan smile instead. 'Thank you. I shall not forget what you did tonight.'

'Good,' said Durand. 'Because neither shall I.'

An innate soldierly sense woke Geoffrey about an hour before the first streaks of dawn touched the hills. He rose immediately, hauled his mail tunic over his head, followed by his padded surcoat, a pair of boiled leather leggings with metal links sewn on for additional protection, his newest helmet and a mail hood that protected his neck and throat. It was the heaviest armour he owned, and that morning he was imbued with the sense that he would need it.

The servants were preparing breakfast in the hall, and he begged a goblet of watered ale and a piece of bread before striding into the bailey. His dog stood at his side with its ears pricked. It uttered a low whine, and Geoffrey stood stock-still, listening. He closed his eyes to blot out what he could see: Helbye walking towards him, faint lights on the battlements, the silhouette of walls against the night sky. And then he was certain.

'Sound the alarm!' he yelled. 'Bale! Order the servants to their battle stations, and tell Torva to keep anyone not fighting inside the hall, out of the way.'

Olivier hurried to his side. 'What is wrong? We are not under attack!'

'We will be,' said Geoffrey grimly. 'There are

horses in the woods to the west, and I can smell cooking fires. They are readying themselves. Tell Peter to prepare food as quickly as possible.'

As he sped away to oversee his troops, Geoffrey hoped it would not be their last meal. Soon, all was action. Villagers were issued arrows and staves, and stationed around the wooden palisade, augmenting the soldiers assigned to the fighting platforms. Geoffrey's tiny unit of mounted men mustered in the bailey, looking nervous. He gave Joan and Olivier several more orders and rode out, flanked by Helbye and Bale. He heartily wished that Roger was there.

As first light began to illuminate the black countryside, Geoffrey took a small path that led south. His meticulous survey of the surrounding land told him exactly where the enemy would gather and how they would attack. He would not have chosen the west himself, because the hills were thickly wooded and thus unsuitable for the sort of warfare he was sure Corwenna and her raiders had in mind. However, the river lay to the east, and he supposed she did not relish the prospect of being trapped against it, should her attack fail.

Warning his men to move as quietly as possible, he eased around the foot of the nearest hill, then cut around its southern flank to turn north again. They dismounted and then began scrambling up it, cutting behind the enemy forces. The sound of curses, swords clanking on armour and cascading stones sounded like thunder to him. He increased the pace, hoping to launch an attack before the would-be invaders heard them. He arrived at the top of the hill, sweating and breathless, just as the sun's first rays appeared.

Smoke curled through the tops of the trees, and he heard voices and the snicker of horses. He could smell bread, too, telling him they were still eating – they intended to wait until full light before making their move. His party eased down the hill, and he arranged his cavalry into two lines, then climbed on his horse. He drew his sword and raised it above his head, looking both ways until he was sure that he had the attention of every man. Then, screaming a battle cry learnt from the Saracens, he plunged forward.

The camp erupted in confusion. The men were eating, and their weapons were not readily to hand. Some fled, unwilling to be slaughtered by wheeling swords, but others stayed. Geoffrey killed two who faced him; one of whom released an arrow that soared across his shoulder and narrowly missed Bale. Then the assault disintegrated, with Geoffrey's horsemen surrounded by enemy foot soldiers who hacked at their legs and saddles.

'Back!' Geoffrey yelled, hoping his men would remember what he had drilled into them the previous day. 'Fall back! Now!'

He was relieved when they obeyed, breaking off the attack and swinging around to follow him. He glanced behind and saw, as he expected, whooping raiders following, sensing a rout. He waited until they were strung out, then wheeled his horse around hard and bore down on them again, using a tactic that had proven successful for Norman armies in the past: feigning flight, so pursuers were scattered and unable to fight as a unit. The invaders stopped in horror when they saw that they had rushed into a trap. The few who tried to fight were quickly dealt with, and Geoffrey rode for the camp itself. One of the first people he saw was Caerdig, kneeling next to his servant Hywel. There was a gaping wound in Hywel's shoulder, which Geoffrey knew would be fatal. He saw Bale set off after the fleeing Welsh and yelled for him to come back.

'I can get more of the bastards!' cried Bale. He was smeared in blood from head to toe, and there was a ferocious gleam in his eyes.

'Not in the woods. They will drag you off your horse and kill you.'

Bale was pale in the dawn light. 'This is the first time I have taken a man's life. It feels ... unreal.'

'Yes,' acknowledged Geoffrey. 'I was sick the first time I engaged in battle.'

'I did not say I was *sick*,' said Bale. 'I said it is unreal. But it is not unpleasant, and I shall be happy to do it again.'

It was no place for such a discussion. Geoffrey turned to Caerdig.

'Stop this,' he said, when Caerdig looked up at him with an anguished expression. 'I do not want to fight, and neither do you.'

'We can defeat them!' yelled Corwenna, appearing from nowhere and grabbing her father by the arm, as if she intended to shake her courage into him. 'Most of our warriors escaped – we will win.'

'We will talk,' countered Caerdig harshly. 'Call off your attack, Geoffrey, before any more of my men are slaughtered.'

As soon as Caerdig indicated that he wanted an end to the skirmish, Geoffrey called his men to order. He feared that it might be difficult to stop such raw recruits from killing once they started, and he was relieved when they did as they were told. He left Helbye in charge, with orders to call him if the raiders showed signs of regrouping, then he went to Caerdig. Hywel was already dead.

'This should not have happened,' Geoffrey said, dismounting. 'What were you thinking?'

Caerdig shook his head. 'I knew it was a mistake.'

'Coward!' shrieked Corwenna, throwing herself at her father with flailing fists.

'She will see you all dead,' Geoffrey said to the men who hurried to restrain her. 'Lock her away where she can do no more harm.'

Still screaming, Corwenna was dragged off. 'Goodrich is doomed. You have not won.'

Geoffrey's blood ran cold when he understood what she was saying. He had been a fool to fall for such an obvious ploy.

'Baderon's men will attack our front while you assault us from behind?'

'It was a stupid idea,' said Caerdig bitterly. 'We are raiders, ill equipped to tackle Norman horsemen. You had better go and face him. I do not think his heart is in this conflict, either, but Lambert and Corwenna have recruited war-like villains from both sides of the border with the promise of loot and grain. They are a bloodthirsty, undisciplined rabble, strengthened with Baderon's professional troops. Together, they represent a formidable force.'

'Do I have your word that *you* will not fight again?' asked Geoffrey, reaching for his reins. 'You will go home?'

Caerdig nodded. 'We should never have left it in the first place.'

Geoffrey did not wait to hear more, knowing that Caerdig would not break his promise. Yelling for his men to follow, he climbed into his saddle and turned his back on the broken bodies in the clearing. One of his men had a cut arm, but they had otherwise executed a massacre with no loss to themselves. They rode fast towards Goodrich.

It was not long before the wooden palisade came into view, and he saw smoke issuing from inside. Fire arrows had been deployed, and he hoped the flames were being doused with the water and sand he had ordered to be placed around the bailey the previous day. Arrows showered in both directions, and it was obvious that the engagement had reached a stalemate: the attackers could not broach the walls, but the defenders could not drive them away.

'Into the trees!' he ordered his men. 'Quickly.'

'Will we attack?' asked Helbye doubtfully, surveying the enemy with a practised eye. 'Baderon's horsemen alone outnumber us three to one.'

Geoffrey's look silenced him – he did not want

the men thinking the odds were insurmountable. He led the party along a forest track until they reached the place where *he* would have launched an assault against Goodrich. It comprised a spit of woodland that swept close to the castle and afforded good cover. Now he was going to attack the attackers.

'Break off the moment I say,' he whispered, lining up his men. 'It is even more critical this time, because these are horsemen you are fighting, not foot soldiers.'

He waited until Baderon's men were engaged in a futile swoop against the palisade, then he launched his own charge, feeling his throat crack as he screamed his war cry. Then he was out of the trees and thundering towards the enemy. Geoffrey saw the enemy scatter in alarm, then realize too late that they needed to meet his attack in formation. Baderon tried to rally them, but they were slow to obey. Geoffrey's force slammed into them, and several went down immediately. Geoffrey engaged Lambert with a vicious blow to the chest, then swung hard with his shield, so the knight was forced to fall back. Then he recalled his men, watching with satisfaction as Lambert made the assumption that he was running because of inferior numbers. The enemy started to pursue with gleeful whoops.

He wheeled around when he felt Lambert's troops were sufficiently strung out, and the tight formation of his own riders cut through them like a knife through butter. Bale was riding hard towards Baderon, a savage smile on his face and a couched lance in his hand. Baderon fumbled for his sword, but Geoffrey knew he would be too late. Geoffrey spurred his horse forward, and managed to come between them, raising his own shield just in time. Bale's lance shattered under the impact, and so did Geoffrey's shield. The blow was so violent that Geoffrey was hurled from his saddle. He staggered to his feet, cursing his reckless chivalry – a knight on foot was heavily disadvantaged, and Baderon was riding towards him. Geoffrey met his eyes and prepared to fight.

'Retreat!' yelled Baderon, wheeling away. 'Back!'

And then the skirmish was over, leaving one of Geoffrey's men severely wounded, and a number of Baderon's dead on the grass. Those who had been unhorsed fled for their lives, while Geoffrey's men whooped as they harried them, stopping only to claim riderless ponies as spoils of war.

Geoffrey arrived in Goodrich to the adulation of its inhabitants, who were even more pleased when informed by Helbye that Geoffrey's military masterpiece was against a much larger force. Tempered by the knowledge that one of their soldiers was coughing his last and three archers had been wounded, elation was still the order of the day.

'It is not over,' said Geoffrey, his voice hoarse from yelling. 'Caerdig will not fight again, but Baderon and Lambert will.'

'They will not,' predicted Olivier confidently. 'They have seen what we can do. You should have seen Joan direct the archers on their first attack!'

Geoffrey winced. 'I should not have left you to chase raiders in the woods.'

'You should,' countered Joan. 'We can repel an invasion from one direction, but not two. Had Caerdig attacked at the same time as Baderon, we could not have coped.'

'We need more arrows,' said Geoffrey, quickly turning his thoughts to the future. 'Tell the children to retrieve as many as they can.'

'Man the gate!' a guard yelled. 'They are coming again!'

'Already?' groaned Geoffrey. He had hoped there would be more time.

'Twenty horsemen!' shouted the guard, as Geoffrey climbed to the main gate's fighting platform to see for himself. 'And they appear a damned sight better than the last lot.'

Indeed, they did. They carried lances and rode in a tight formation, suggesting they were experienced in battle, and their weapons and armour appeared to be well tended, even from a distance. Geoffrey's heart sank, thinking such a force would make short work of his amateurs. Then he saw the leading horseman, and his spirits soared.

'Open the gate,' he ordered. 'It is Roger.'

'When Helbye told me about Baderon's alliances, I thought things might turn nasty,' said Roger, clattering into the bailey, before dismounting and clasping his friend's shoulder. 'So I recruited a few men to lend us a hand. I came back as fast as I could.'

'You are just in time,' said Geoffrey. 'Is that why you left? To rally troops?'

Roger nodded. 'There was no point telling you, because you would have tried to talk me out of it – not wanting me bloodied in your war, or claiming you do not have the funds to pay twenty mercenaries. But I am a wealthy man – I have not told you yet about my "visit" to Normandy, have I? I can afford to be generous to a friend.'

'Where did you find them?' asked Geoffrey. Roger's warriors looked rough, cold and ruthless.

'Hereford. I tried Rosse, but it was full of farmers, so I was obliged to travel farther afield, which is why I was longer than intended. What do you think?'

Geoffrey nodded his approval, and for the first time he started to believe there was a chance of success. Then Roger noticed the battle-stained horses being rubbed down and the swords being cleaned of blood.

'We are too late!' he cried in disappointment.

'You are in time,' countered Geoffrey. 'We fended off one attack, but Lambert and Baderon will not make the same mistakes twice. They were over-confident, and we took advantage of them, but it will not happen again.'

'The news that a large force is gathering to attack Goodrich travelled all the way to Hereford,' said Roger. 'Lambert has amassed an army comprising not only half-starved, desperate Welshmen who have decided to test Baderon's declarations of friendship, but many mercenaries, too.'

'At least Caerdig is no longer among them,' said Geoffrey. 'His heart was never in it, nor is Baderon's.'

'It is Corwenna's doing,' said Joan angrily. 'Damn her ridiculous taste for vengeance!'

'If Caerdig keeps her under lock and key, the attack may lose impetus,' said Olivier hopefully. 'She is the one who is firing them up.'

'She and Lambert,' said Geoffrey. 'But Caerdig will not be able to keep her quiet for long.'

'This army you say has gathered,' Joan asked Roger, 'just how large is it?'

'Several hundred, by all accounts,' replied Roger.

'Baderon,' said Joan bitterly. 'You say he does not want to fight us – and he held his hand this morning when he could have cut you down – but he still has a lot to answer for. He paid Jervil to get the Black Knife, so it stands to reason that he had Jervil killed.' She shook her head, attempting to come to terms with the fact that the man who had been a guest in her home should now be trying to raze it to the ground. 'He and Henry are the cause of all these problems.'

'Why Henry?' Geoffrey asked.

'His arrangement with Baderon,' explained Joan. 'Peter the cook said he mentioned it to you, so there is no point in trying to hide it any longer. There is a rumour that Henry made a secret pact with Baderon – he was to marry Hilde, but then he reneged and went after Isabel instead. *That* is why Baderon has turned against us so bitterly.'

'But Peter and Torva said the arrangement was *not* a marriage,' said Geoffrey, recalling that Baderon had also hinted as much.

Joan sighed. 'They cannot know what it entailed – Peter witnessed the agreement, but could not read it. A marriage between Hilde and Henry is the only thing it *could* have been.'

Roger grimaced. 'Life is very complicated here. Things are so much simpler in the Holy Land.'

'Will you watch the castle, Roger, and direct the defence if another attack comes?' Geoffrey asked, walking towards his horse.

Roger nodded. 'But what will you be doing?'

'Trying to stop this at its source,' answered Geoffrey. 'I am going to speak to Baderon.'

Father Adrian applauded Geoffrey's determination to bring an end to the dispute, but he was the only one; Joan, Olivier and Roger believed he was needlessly risking his life. Geoffrey declined Roger's offer of company; although it would have been comforting to have a friend at his side, the northern knight's blunt tongue was a danger to delicate negotiations. He rejected Bale's offer for the same reason, and refused Olivier's because the man looked terrified. He rode out of the castle alone, taking Dun – he wanted to save his own warhorse lest he needed it later.

Geoffrey crossed the ford and rode north to the flat terraces near the river, where he imagined Baderon would be camped. He carried a white pennant on his lance, hoping it would prevent him from being shot at first sight. The forest was eerily quiet, which told him that men were hidden in the trees. Eventually, he reached the first of Baderon's patrols. The captain of the guard saluted him, before wordlessly leading him to the camp.

Geoffrey was horrified when he saw the size of Baderon's army. Roger had been right: there were several hundred men sitting round fires or tending shaggy ponies. Some were clearly Welshmen, exploiting the opportunity to acquire grain to feed their villages, but more had the slovenly, undisciplined appearance of men who sold their services for a few coins and the prospect of plunder. The rest were Normans, distinctive in their mail and conical helmets. Appalled, Geoffrey knew that Goodrich could not withstand such a force for long. The guard took him to a tent, shouting in Norman-French that a messenger had arrived. Geoffrey dismounted and waited.

'Have you come to surrender?' asked Lambert, emerging from the tent with a scowl. He gestured to his troops. 'You should: you cannot defeat us.'

'Where is Baderon?' asked Geoffrey.

The next person to emerge from the tent, however, was Corwenna.

'It is Geoffrey Mappestone!' she exclaimed, pulling a dagger from her belt. 'This is better than I hoped. We shall send his head back to Joan – that will show her what we think of her attempts to negotiate.'

'Tempting, but unwise,' said Lambert laconically. 'It is not how these things are done.'

'Hywel was killed this morning,' she hissed. 'And my father is a broken man, refusing to fight. Do not talk to *me* about what is right!' She spat on the ground at Geoffrey's feet, and there was a murmur of approval from those nearby.

Baderon emerged at last, with Hilde behind him. Hilde wore a mail tunic over her kirtle and a hefty sword strapped to her side.

'You should not have come,' Hilde said. 'You have risked your life for nothing, because there can be no peace. These men will not disperse until they have the spoils they have been promised.' She glared at Corwenna.

'It is true,' said Baderon hoarsely. 'Either their food supplies are low and they need an excuse to take cattle and grain, or they have been promised plunder in return for their services. Neither faction will agree to leave empty-handed.'

'They will be disappointed,' warned Geoffrey. 'Our livestock have been hidden, and there are men standing by to fire the granaries if we are overrun. And Goodrich has little to please mercenaries – it is not a wealthy estate. Tell your men that. It may make them less willing to squander their lives when they will have nothing in return.'

'I am in an impossible position,' said Baderon. 'I wanted alliances with my Welsh neighbours, but it has all gone sour. I do not understand—'

'We shall send Geoffrey's corpse to Joan,' interrupted Corwenna imperiously. 'Then we shall burn Goodrich and slaughter every one of its inhabitants. I do not care about cattle, grain and loot. I just want to see blood spilt to avenge my murdered husband.'

Geoffrey addressed Baderon. 'Corwenna's vengeance will cost you dearly. Many men will die – including those who should be planting crops for next year. Your people will take nothing of ours with you; Joan will see to that.'

'I am sure she will,' said Hilde. 'I would do the same in her position.'

'No grain?' asked one of the Welsh captains, struggling to understand the Norman-French.

'Every granary will be fired the moment you appear,' replied Geoffrey, speaking Welsh to ensure he understood. 'You will not have a single kernel.'

This caused considerable consternation, and Geoffrey saw the extent to which hunger drove some of them.

'He lies,' Corwenna said with contempt. 'Normans do not destroy grain.'

Geoffrey did not need to press his point: the Welshmen had understood him perfectly. He addressed them directly. 'We have corn aplenty, and we are prepared to share it with you – but only if you retreat by this evening.'

'Do not listen,' hissed Corwenna. 'He will wait until you have disbanded, then destroy you one by one. And you will see none of his corn. I know what the word of a Mappestone means.'

'Goodrich helped Llan Martin through lean times last year,' said one of the captains. 'And I trust Caerdig: if *he* will not fight, we should reconsider.'

Another leader agreed, pointing out the futility of fighting if there was no booty to take home. They began to argue, while Corwenna watched, aghast.

'They are going to back down,' she breathed.

'What were you telling them?' demanded Lambert of Geoffrey.

'He said he would pay each captain ten pieces of silver if they abandon you now,' said Corwenna before Geoffrey could answer. 'And another ten if they bring him your head and Baderon's on pikes.'

Lambert steamed across to the conferring Welsh and began to rail at them, while Corwenna 'translated'. Geoffrey tried to interrupt, but swords were drawn and he was ordered back. He closed his eyes in despair when Corwenna informed her countrymen that Goodrich intended to trick them: that Roger's recent arrival with mercenaries was evidence that they intended to attack Wales. Baderon watched for a moment, then ducked back inside the tent, his shoulders bowed.

'Did you offer them silver to back down, Geoffrey?' asked Hilde uneasily.

'Of course not,' said Geoffrey. 'Do you think me a fool?'

'I do not,' Hilde said softly. She was silent for a moment, then spoke in a rush. 'I have been thinking about the deaths of Hugh and Seguin, and I do not believe you are responsible.'

'I am glad to hear it,' said Geoffrey drily. 'It is a pity Lambert does not think the same.'

'You had no reason to want them dead,' Hilde

continued. 'If you had been willing to marry me, I might have assumed you wanted Hugh out of the way, but you do not. And you never let Seguin's ill manners bother you much, either. You are not their killer.'

'Well, despite all the evidence that points to his guilt, I do not believe your father killed my brother, either. He does not behave like a murderer, and the servants at Goodrich think there was a secret pact – a marriage contract, perhaps – between him and Henry, which makes it highly unlikely that your father is the culprit.'

Hilde sighed. 'They are right, in part. We *did* have an arrangement that only Henry and my family knew about, but it was nothing to do with him marrying me. I would never have agreed to that. It is a pity he was not you – I would not have minded you.'

'You are not so bad yourself,' said Geoffrey, feeling some sort of reciprocal compliment was in order. 'Better than the others.'

Unexpectedly, Hilde laughed. 'You have a silver tongue, Geoffrey Mappestone, there is no doubt about that!'

Geoffrey smiled. 'What was this arrangement with Henry, if it did not involve an alliance by marriage?'

'I did not say it was not an alliance by marriage. It was just not between him and me.'

Geoffrey looked confused. 'Who then?'

'Joan. To Hugh.'

Geoffrey regarded her askance. 'But Joan has Olivier.'

'Olivier had an accident last summer,' said

Hilde. 'He broke his arm, but Henry led us to believe it was more serious, and offered Joan for Hugh.'

Geoffrey stared at her. 'I do not think Joan would have appreciated that.'

'Neither would Hugh, whose heart was set on Eleanor. But it would have served its purpose: Henry could have had Isabel *and* secured an alliance with us. It would have united three Houses.'

'But Joan has not produced heirs for Olivier, so her marriage with Hugh would have been equally barren. How would it have benefited Goodrich?'

'Joan had children. Did you not know? Like Henry's, they were taken by fevers, and then Olivier had an illness that means he cannot ... well, *she* could provide heirs for a different husband.'

Geoffrey had not known about such children and realized, yet again, that there was a good deal about his sister and her life that was a closed book to him.

'Henry misled us over Olivier's broken arm,' Hilde went on. 'And we have since learnt he attacked the poor man, clearly intending to kill him to provide a wife for Hugh. But I would be obliged if you keep this to yourself – if Joan were to find out that we were even remotely associated with a plot that almost saw Olivier murdered, we would never have peace.'

'So that is why our servants think your father would not have killed Henry.' Geoffrey rubbed his head; then an unpleasant thought occurred to him. 'Are you sure Joan did not know about this?'

'Positive,' said Hilde firmly. 'If she had learnt that Henry had attempted to kill Olivier, do you think she would have murdered him by stealth? Of course not! She would have hanged him from the castle walls.'

Geoffrey glanced at Corwenna and Lambert, who were still trying to persuade the wary Welshmen against leaving. He started to move towards them, but swords blocked him a second time, and Hilde pulled him back with a surprisingly strong arm.

'Even if you do convince the Welsh that they are making a mistake, Lambert and Corwena will still have their Normans and mercenaries,' she said. 'Goodrich remains outnumbered by a considerable margin. If I thought you would listen, I would urge you to turn around and aim for the Holy Land, because there is nothing but death left for you here.'

'And leave my sister?' asked Geoffrey archly.

There was no more to be said, so Geoffrey went to his horse and mounted. Then there was a sudden blur of movement as Corwenna snatched a crossbow from a guard, and fired.

Geoffrey reacted instinctively, throwing himself to one side. Dun reared up in confusion and the bolt hit his chest. With a piercing whinny, the horse crashed to the ground. Hands dragged Geoffrey to safety, but he twisted away from them and knelt next to Dun, trying to stem the gush of blood with his fingers. It seemed a long time before the horse's desperate, agonized battle for life was over.

Geoffrey looked at the blood staining his hands and climbed slowly to his feet. The Welsh captains stood in a shocked, mute circle around him, while Hilde looked as angry as Geoffrey felt. He liked horses, and for his to have been killed by Corwenna was more than his temper could bear. He stalked towards her.

'Easy, man,' said Lambert uncomfortably. 'She did not mean to hurt the horse. She was aiming for you.'

Geoffrey was not sure why this was expected to make him feel better. Corwenna did not flinch when he reached her. Instead, she smiled, her eyes carrying an expression of intense satisfaction; she was delighted to see the death of the horse had touched him.

'You have a long walk ahead of you,' she said smugly. 'You had better start, if you do not want to be alone in the forest after dark. It is dangerous for those who are not welcome.'

Geoffrey had never before experienced such a strong urge to put his hands around someone's throat and choke the life out of them. But an enemy camp, where he was surrounded by hostile forces, was not the place for it. He allowed Hilde to tug him away.

'Take my horse,' she said. 'You can give him back when all this is over.'

Geoffrey did not trust himself to speak. He shot Corwenna a glare filled with loathing, then turned away, half-expecting her to launch another attack while his back was turned. He followed Hilde to where Lambert was already saddling up a sturdy pony, snatched the reins and rode out of the camp. He did not look back.

Bitterly, he saw that Roger, Joan and Olivier had been right: he had risked his life for nothing – and lost a good horse in the bargain. He had learnt of Henry's plans for Joan, but they seemed unimportant now. How many men would die because Henry had been a brute and Corwenna hated him for it? And could Goodrich hold out against such a huge horde, even if the Welsh captains did see sense and go home?

He was so engrossed in his thoughts that it was some time before he realized he had ridden farther than he should have, and the sun was on the wrong side – it was behind him, meaning he had travelled east instead of south. He was angry with himself as he wheeled around and rode back the way he had come. Then he reached a fork and turned westward, but the track soon doubled back on itself, and it was not long before he was lost.

While the sun was up, he knew which way to go, but with dusk came clouds and rain, and it was soon too dark to see. He was furious that he had been so careless and desperately hoped Corwenna would not attack Goodrich that night. Visions of Joan battling against the hordes drove him on, but the night was pitch-black, and he had no idea which way he was travelling. He knew he should stop and find shelter until dawn, but he could not rid himself of the notion that he would be needed. He dismounted when the pony stumbled a second time and continued on foot.

By now he was hopelessly lost, no longer even on a path. He stood still for a moment with his eyes closed, trying to let his innate sense of direction take over. It did not work, leaving him to move blindly through wet branches that scratched at his face, knowing he would not see a path if he walked across it. Then the ground suddenly disappeared from beneath his feet. He managed to release the bridle before he fell, so the horse was not dragged down with him, and slid down a slope thick with dead leaves. He started to skid faster, and then he was airborne, landing with a splash in agonizingly cold water.

Weighed down by full armour, with water soaking into his surcoat, his first thought was that he was going to drown, but his feet touched the bottom and he was able to stand. He saw that he should not have been impatient, and that finding shelter had been the right thing to do. Now, not only was he hopelessly lost, he did not even have the pony.

However, the place seemed familiar, and he suddenly realized it was the Angel Springs. He could just make out the flat stone altar. He eased towards it, but the objects that had been there on his previous visit had gone. Then his feet skidded on the rain-slicked rocks and he fell again. Cold, disgusted and with a nasty ache from a wrenched knee, he released a litany of oaths of the kind he never used in company, comprising a lot of Anglo-Saxon and a bit of very expressive Arabic.

'That is fine language for a knight,' came a

mocking voice from the darkness. 'It is a good thing I do not understand any of it, or we would both be heartily embarrassed.'

Thirteen

The voice made Geoffrey jump so violently that he almost lost his balance again. He fumbled for his dagger, cursing fingers that were numb from the cold. 'Who is there?'

'Eleanor, of course. Can you not see me? I am right above you.'

Geoffrey strained his eyes, and could just make out a figure standing on the bank. There was a sudden flare of light as she removed whatever had been covering her torch.

'Well?' she asked. 'Are you going to stand in the stream all night, or would you like to sit by my fire?'

Geoffrey scrambled after her, noting that she wore her red cloak and the veil still covered her face. He struggled to catch up, eager to accept her offer of warmth.

'Where have you been?' he asked breathlessly.

'I like to be alone,' she replied enigmatically. 'I thought I would have some peace when I returned from Normandy without being married off like some prize sow. But people started talking about weddings and alliances again, and it was worse than ever.'

343

'I know how you feel,' muttered Geoffrey. They reached the top of the hill and she led him to the little shepherd's hut, indicating that he should precede her inside. Reluctantly, he held back. 'My horse. I should—'

'I tethered it and removed its saddle,' said Eleanor. 'It is quite comfortable. Sit by the fire and drink this – and do not look suspicious! It is only a little concoction of my own devising.'

'That is what I am worried about,' said Geoffrey ungraciously, so she took the first sip behind her veil and handed him the rest. It tasted fairly pleasant, and he felt warmer after finishing it. He removed his sopping surcoat, which she placed near the fire, but he kept his armour on. He glanced at the ceiling and saw that the dead birds had been removed from the rafters.

'I heard Hugh is dead,' Eleanor said, following his look. 'So, I thought I had better hide any evidence that indicates I am still alive. I do not want to be accused of his murder.'

Geoffrey did not blame her. 'You have been here all the time?'

'Here or nearby. Few people linger at the Angel Springs, which is how I like it. Hugh followed me occasionally, but he was no trouble – and no one listened to him, anyway.'

Geoffrey remembered what Bale had said about the Angel Springs. 'You sharpen knives. My squire leaves them with a coin and thinks spirits hone them.'

She laughed. 'A number of folk have been obliging in that way, and a little money does not go amiss. I have none of my own, and neither

344

does my lover.'

'Your lover? Is that why you ran away after the fire? To be with him?'

Eleanor nodded. 'We did not see each other for months when I was in Normandy, so I escaped as soon as I could – the fire provided a useful diversion. However, I did not know murders had been taking place.'

Geoffrey thought about the woman kissed by the red-cloaked figure as they fled the fire. He reached out and tugged off the veil, revealing a face that was impish in its prettiness, and certainly not missing a jaw.

'Your lover is not a man, but a woman,' he surmised. 'That is why you have refused to marry – and have been to such pains to pretend you are disfigured. You do not want men to pester you.'

'You guessed that rather easily,' she said, frowning. 'How?'

'You do not speak as though you were minus a mandible, but it is certainly a disfigurement that would make most men think twice. Who is she?'

'She is Welsh, of noble birth – from one of the villages that declines to join Corwenna's assault on Goodrich. That wretched woman has de-stabilized the entire region, so I am removing any evidence of me being here, lest *I* am accused of causing the war by witchcraft. You know how people are – regardless of the victor, someone will look for a scapegoat.'

'And who better than a sorceress?' agreed Geoffrey. 'Do you know what happened to Hugh?'

'When he followed me after the fire, I went north and lost him. I thought he would find his own way home, but I was wrong. I am sorry he is dead. He was a stupid lump, but he did no harm – unlike those with more wits. Your brother, for a start.'

'Tell me about the dagger that killed Henry,' said Geoffrey, remembering what Olivier had seen. 'I know you cursed it, but who asked you for such a spell?'

'That I shall never reveal, because he knows the identity of my lover. If I tell, so will he.'

'But it is a man,' said Geoffrey, supposing he could cross Hilde off his list of suspects. 'Do you really believe that putting a spell on an object can imbue it with an evil life of its own?'

She nodded earnestly. 'Of course. And so do many others.'

'The Black Knife has killed both Seguin and Hugh since it dispatched Henry,' said Geoffrey. 'I locked it in my room, and the next night someone tried to set me alight.'

Eleanor shrugged. 'That is what Black Knives do. You must take it deep into the forest and bury it under an old oak – as old as you can find – with mistletoe growing on it. That should stop it in its tracks.'

'Lord!' muttered Geoffrey. 'Are you sure?'

'It would be even better if the person who ordered the curse were to do it, but I doubt that will happen.' Eleanor rummaged in a sack and handed Geoffrey a tiny pouch with a piece of twine attached. 'Wear this amulet. It will protect you while you do it. Bury it near the oak at the same time.'

Geoffrey was tempted to decline, thinking a Crusader should have more faith in his own God, but he was unsettled by the self-confessed witch, and decided to err on the side of caution. He put it around his neck, tucking it inside his surcoat.

'I wish you knew a spell to bring an end to this ridiculous fighting,' he said.

She gave a sad smile. 'You must pray to your God for something of that magnitude. I work on a much more modest level.'

Geoffrey and Eleanor sat in silence for a long time, listening to the rain and the crackle of the fire. His thoughts were of Goodrich, and his fears of a night attack. Hoping to distract himself, he decided to interrogate Eleanor about the murders he had been ordered to solve.

'I would like to ask you some questions,' he said. 'With your permission.'

Eleanor smirked, amused. 'How could I refuse such a politely worded request? Would that all men were so well mannered – then I might not have felt the need to secure a female lover.'

'Did Agnes ask you for poison while you were in Normandy? Mandrake, for example?'

Eleanor knew exactly why he asked. 'If she had, I would not tell you. It would make *me* an accomplice to the murder of the Duchess. But, as it happens, she did not need poison from me, because Walter had some mandrake of his own.'

'His phial has been empty for a long time. It was so dusty inside that I could barely smell what was once in it – and a book Mother Elgiva gave me said mandrake has a powerful aroma. I imagine Walter found an empty container and carried it for show.'

'He is a silly boy. I watched them carefully once I realized the Duchess' death would suit Agnes, but I never saw anything untoward. The only thing they ever gave her was a dish of dried yellow plums. Sibylla ate one, but declared it too sweet and passed the rest to her courtiers. The poison was not in the fruit, or they would have died, too.'

'You spied on Agnes and Walter? I thought they were your friends.'

'No, they were just after my spells: Agnes wanted the Duke to love her, and Walter wanted a charm to attract women. I told him to speak Italian, and he has been doing it ever since. He even tried to bed *me* with his nonsensical phrases. I clouted his ears.'

'So neither Walter nor Agnes asked you for mandrake?'

'They asked *about* it, but it is not a plant I use because it irritates my skin. Look what happened when I touched my lover's hand after she had sliced some.' Eleanor removed her glove to reveal a rash. It had healed somewhat since when Geoffrey had seen it at Dene, but it still looked sore. 'Mandrake does not grow readily in this part of the world, so I am not often exposed to it. However, my sensitivity exonerates me from giving any to Agnes – *if* Sybilla was poisoned, that is.'

'You think she may not have been?'

Eleanor shrugged. 'Her physicians say she died of childbirth fever – it happens to duchesses and paupers alike, so perhaps they are right.'

'What about the fire at Dene?' asked Geoffrey. 'Did your curses bring that about? I saw a picture of a burning house at the Angel Springs just hours after the blaze.'

Eleanor's face hardened. 'Agnes drew that. I was delighted when it started, because it gave me the chance to escape from my father and brother, but I am sorry people died.'

Geoffrey was thoughtful. The solution to at least one part of the mystery snapped into place as he thought about the people allocated rooms in the corridor where the fire had started. He just needed one or two more details.

'How well had the fire taken hold before you became aware of it?' he asked.

'Agnes had warned me that a fire *might* break out, so I was alert that night. However, she is full of talk and I was surprised when it really happened. Had I known the entire manor would go up, I would have tried to stop her.'

'It started at your end of the corridor, not near Giffard and me. In fact, I suspect it began in Isabel's room.'

'How did you guess that?' asked Eleanor, start-led.

'Because Isabel started it. I imagine Agnes told her to.'

Eleanor gave a wry smile. 'You are right: Agnes wanted the fire, and when her drawings at the Angel Springs did not work, she adopted another approach. She encouraged Isabel to start it, lest she herself was caught.'

'I suppose she contrived some nonsense about Ralph realizing his true feelings if Isabel were in danger – and poor Isabel was desperate enough to believe it. Meanwhile, Agnes would be rid of Giffard, who is keeping her from the Duke.'

'You are right in every detail. Nasty, is it not?'

'So why did you not expose them? Several servants died – and it very nearly claimed the King and Isabel herself.'

'Agnes made me promise to say nothing. I agreed because I did not think Isabel would have the courage to go through with it anyway, and also because Agnes agreed to stop trying to learn the identity of my lover if I complied. By the time I realized Isabel had not set a little fire but a raging inferno, it was too late. And the irony is that the whole ghastly business achieved none of its objectives.'

Geoffrey recalled seeing Agnes at the Angel Springs after the fire, doubtless destroying evidence of her involvement. The plan *had* failed spectacularly: Isabel had lost her house and several servants, Ralph had discovered an attraction to Agnes, and Giffard had escaped.

'It is a pity you have seen me,' said Eleanor eventually. 'It was more convenient for people to assume I died in the fire.'

'Leave your veil in the rubble, then,' Geoffrey suggested. 'You are never seen without it, so it may convince them.'

'But *you* know I am alive.'

'I will never reveal your secret.' Geoffrey studied her pretty face uneasily. 'You do not want me to drip my blood on chicken entrails to prove my sincerity, do you?'

Eleanor laughed. 'Do not be ridiculous! I do not have a chicken to hand, and it would be a terrible waste to kill one when I know you are a man of your word. To repay your understanding, at first light I shall lead you to your castle by a quicker route than you would find on your own. Until then, keep yourself warm by the fire.'

Despite sharing the hut with a witch, Geoffrey was so fatigued, he soon fell asleep. He woke at one point to find himself alone, but Eleanor glided back in and shot him a mysterious smile. He was ready to leave long before dawn and fretted impatiently until she deemed it light enough to travel. He urged her to move as fast as possible, sitting her on the pony and running behind it in his desire to reach Goodrich. They parted south of the castle, he to follow the main road to his home, and she to head west to her lover. She slid off the horse and gave it a pat.

'Be careful, Geoffrey. You have a turbulent time ahead. Do not be fooled by fair eyes filled with tears, and remember that women are just as ruthless as men. And do not forget the Black Knife, either. Get rid of it as soon as you can. Do you still have the amulet I gave you?'

Geoffrey fingered the bundle around his neck, his thoughts on Joan, Roger and the others.

'All is well at Goodrich,' she said kindly, seeing his concern. 'The wind is from the north, and we would smell smoke if it were burning. You will find your home still standing. And thank you for agreeing to be discreet – you have earned a friend.'

'So have you,' said Geoffrey.

Eleanor laughed, and Geoffrey was glad she would no longer wear her veil, thinking hers was a face that should be seen. 'But I mean it, Geoffrey. If you ever have need of a witch, just leave two sticks tied together by the well at Llangarron, and I will come.'

They parted, and when Geoffrey glanced behind him, Eleanor was already lost among the trees. He doubted he would ever see her again, suspecting he was unlikely to need the services of a witch. He urged the pony into a gallop, wanting to be home as soon as he could. He was reassured when he was challenged by one of the patrols he had organized, and soon found himself trotting into the bailey.

Roger rushed to meet him, sombre-faced and anxious, Olivier and Joan behind. Joan looked angry, and Geoffrey suspected his absence had given her an uneasy night.

'Where is Giffard?' he asked as they approached.

'In the hall,' snapped Joan. 'Where have you been? You promised you would return by dusk, and we were worried.'

'Where is Dun?' cried Olivier. 'If you traded him for this beast, you have been cheated.'

'Corwenna shot him,' said Geoffrey sadly. 'I am sorry, Olivier. God knows where I will find the funds to replace him.'

'Do not worry about that,' said Roger, while Olivier gaped at Geoffrey in dismay. 'We shall loot Baderon's estates when this is over, and then you will have enough.'

'If we win,' said Geoffrey soberly. 'There are at least five hundred men in Baderon's camp. We are heavily outnumbered.'

'Rubbish!' said Roger with characteristic optimism. 'Baderon and his rabble will not defeat two *Jerosolimitani*!'

There was a lot to do, and Geoffrey was busy for much of the morning strengthening the defences and checking the deployment of archers. He was grateful for Roger's company, and found Olivier surprisingly helpful, too. His brother-in-law's extensive theoretical knowledge made him an excellent strategist – he was just not very good at actual fighting.

There was a brief respite for the midday meal, which Geoffrey ate while inspecting a cache of ancient weapons Joan had discovered in a cellar. Some were usable, but most were not. Then, suddenly, everything was done that could be, and there was nothing left to do but wait. Waiting was the part Geoffrey hated, so he decided to go in search of Isabel, who had remained at Goodrich with her father, because Dene's garrison had been disbanded following the fire. No one had imagined fitzNorman would need his soldiers within a week, and the old veteran had been appalled to find a war bubbling and him powerless to prevent or join it.

Isabel smiled when Geoffrey spoke her name, although there was unhappy resignation in her face. He glanced across the hall and saw Ralph and Agnes in a nearby corner. Isabel knew they were together, and the horrible truth was finally becoming clear.

'He will never love me, will he?' she asked.

'No,' replied Geoffrey honestly. 'I am sorry.'

She fumbled for his hand, wanting him to sit next to her, but sensed his reluctance.

'What is wrong?' she asked. 'What have I done?'

'Agnes urged you to start the fire, because she said Ralph's anger would melt if he thought you were in danger. It might have worked, had there been any warmth in his heart, but there is not.'

'No,' Isabel sighed, not denying the accusation. 'There is not. I see now that he thinks only about himself and does not care for me. I suspect he never did.'

'Is that why you killed Margaret?' he asked softly. 'Because she told you the truth?'

Isabel gaped at Geoffrey, then forced a laugh. 'Has this battle unhinged your wits? Wait here, and I shall fetch a draught that is good for fevered minds.' She started to rise, but Geoffrey stopped her.

'Margaret told you on the night of the fire that Ralph did not care about you, but you did not believe her. In outraged fury, your killed her.'

Isabel was appalled. 'But Margaret died because she witnessed Jervil's murder. You said so yourself.'

'I was wrong. It was the other way round: someone killed Jervil *after* you strangled Margaret, probably in the hope that you would be blamed for both deaths.'

354

'But I am blind, Sir Geoffrey,' said Isabel earnestly. 'How could I kill anyone?'

'We were all blind that night. It was dark and there was smoke everywhere. Margaret could no more see you than you could see her. She told you about Ralph, and you grabbed her throat. But you squeezed harder than you had intended, and she died. She was not young and fit like you.'

'This is nonsense,' said Isabel. 'I shall tell my father about these ridiculous accusations.'

'He already knows,' said Geoffrey. 'Perhaps he saw something – or heard you and Margaret arguing – but he knows. Why do you think he threatened to kill me if I investigated? He even claimed Margaret was having an affair with Jervil, just so I would ask no more questions.'

Isabel's pale blue eyes filled with tears. 'He did that?'

'In order to protect you, he was prepared to let people think his beloved sister slept with servants. It also explains what he said when you asked him to fetch Ralph and he refused. He said, "He thinks you have Margaret. If only he knew." I did not understand what he meant at the time, because it did not occur to me that *you* would kill her.'

'It was an accident,' said Isabel, starting to cry. 'She said Ralph did not care for me, and that he ran away when he knew I needed him. I could not bear it – not when servants had died and the house lay in ruins. Agnes promised to douse the fire before it did any real damage, but it took hold so quickly.'

Geoffrey doubted Agnes had intended anything of the kind – at least not until the flames had reached the room where Giffard lay in his drugged stupor. But, of course, Giffard was not the only one who had been drugged.

'You added a sleeping draught to the honeyed milk you gave me,' said Geoffrey. 'But I do not think you wanted me to burn. I think you did it because I had been restless the previous night, and you did not want me to catch you with your tinderbox.'

Isabel's head drooped, confirming his theory. 'What will you do? I will hang if you tell the sheriff.'

Geoffrey did not know. Both Isabel and Agnes would end up kicking empty air at the gibbet if any of what he had learnt ever came to light.

'I told you once that I would sooner become a nun than marry anyone but Ralph,' said Isabel weakly. 'It is still true. I will ride to Gloucester today and ask Serlo to find me a remote convent.'

'Very well,' said Geoffrey, not wanting to be responsible for a hanging. 'But you cannot leave now: it is too dangerous.'

'But I must,' said Isabel tearfully. 'It pains me to be here. I can hear *them* laughing together, like lovers. I would rather be gone, to reflect on the harm love can bring. I have little to pack; most of my belongings were lost in the fire. I will leave within the hour. My father will escort me.'

Geoffrey saw that he would be unable to dissuade her and did not try. A short while later, he met fitzNorman, who was ready to leave. He looked old and tired, the fire gone from his eyes.

'Not even Baderon's mercenaries will attack a man and his blind daughter on a pilgrimage to Gloucester Abbey,' said fitzNorman when Geoffrey suggested he should delay their departure until the looming battle was over. 'But will you wait until tomorrow before telling anyone what you know? By then, Isabel will be safe.'

'What will *you* do?'

'I will see Isabel settled, and then return to Dene. I shall survive, although I am not sure you will. You could come with us and save yourself. I hear Baderon has an army of five hundred, and Goodrich cannot hold out against such numbers.'

'Time is passing, and you should leave,' said Geoffrey, ignoring the older man's suggestion. He was already having second thoughts about allowing a killer to go free.

He watched them ride away, before seeking Roger in the battlements. While talking, he fingered the charm around his neck, and found himself wondering if he had enough time to find an old oak draped with mistletoe. On a whim, he decided to collect the Black Knife, but to his horror, found it had gone. He sat back on his heels, wondering who might have taken it.

He was still thinking when Durand burst into the room, flopped on to the bed and began a litany of complaints about Joan assigning him to a group to defend the well. A man of his status and wealth should be exempt from such duties, he said.

'The Black Knife has gone,' Geoffrey interrupted.

Durand gaped at him, before turning recriminatory. 'I told you to get rid of it, and now someone else will die. Why did you not take it to Rosse, instead of attempting to parley with men determined to fight?'

'Who else knew it was here?' asked Geoffrey. 'Other than you?'

'The whole castle,' replied Durand. 'Roger found it while he was browsing through your possessions this morning and took it downstairs to quiz Joan about it. She made him put it back, but everyone knows where he got it from.'

'Damn!' muttered Geoffrey. He had forgotten Roger's disagreeable habit of rifling through Geoffrey's belongings to assess what was valuable. 'We must get it back before—'

He was interrupted by a series of shouts. Assuming they were under attack, he raced down the stairs and tore across the bailey. But the soldiers were not looking outside the castle, they were looking within. Geoffrey's dog had found something concealed behind several water butts. Pleased with itself, it wagged its tail and pushed its nose against what looked to be a leg. When Geoffrey pulled the dog away, he saw Ralph. The heir to Bicanofre had been stabbed in the chest.

'There is your Black Knife,' said Durand, peering over the knight's shoulder. 'And it does not require a great deal to work out who murdered *him*!'

'No,' agreed Geoffrey. He thought about

358

Eleanor's warning: Do not be fooled by fair eyes filled with tears. He should have paid more heed to what was very good advice.

'Is there any point in going after Isabel?' asked Durand doubtfully. 'She will be halfway to Shropshire by now, where she plans to live with a distant cousin.'

'Gloucester,' corrected Geoffrey. 'She is going to join a convent.'

'She told me York,' countered Joan.

'FitzNorman told *me* it was Normandy,' said Olivier. 'Or perhaps Anjou.'

Geoffrey shook his head in disgust.

The following morning, after a night in which every sound made him start into wakefulness, Geoffrey's head was still heavy with regret over Isabel's deceit. To make amends for his failure in one case, he determined to succeed in another, and decided to resolve the question of Sibylla's death once and for all. He thought he could do it, armed as he was with Eleanor's words, what he had read in Elgiva's book and his own suspicions.

He secured Roger's help, asking him to occupy Agnes and Walter. The big knight promptly gave Walter a lesson in swordplay, demonstrating to his alarmed mother that the boy had been exceedingly poorly trained.

Meanwhile, Geoffrey shut himself inside the chamber where the pair had slept and began a close inspection of their luggage. It was not long before he found what he was looking for: a small, heavy box with an Italian label brazenly claiming its contents to be mandrake. Inside were several dried fruits and a list of suggestions for their use, also in Italian. Geoffrey read it, then rubbed his chin. He understood the instructions perfectly, but was equally sure Agnes and Walter had not. He went in search of Giffard.

The bishop, wearing mail under his monastic habit, was talking to Father Adrian. Although he deplored violence, Giffard was a practical man and knew that Geoffrey had done all in his power to avert a catastrophe. He was willing to support his friend's cause, and carried a wooden staff, which he would use if necessary. Adrian was less pragmatic and had informed Goodrich's inhabitants that they would go to Hell if they fought – a statement promptly retracted when Giffard had quietly ordered him to desist or risk an early visit to Hell himself.

'I am sorry Isabel could not resist such an evil choice,' said Giffard. 'I suppose she accepted that *she* could not have Ralph, so decided no one else would, either. It is a pity – I could have told her Agnes would not have bothered with him for much longer.'

'Ralph still would not have taken Isabel,' said Father Adrian. 'Her adoration delighted him initially, but the incident with Henry showed him her affection was fanatical. Too much love can be suffocating.'

'Isabel did not kill Ralph,' said Geoffrey. 'That was fitzNorman. Isabel could not have hidden Ralph's body behind the water butts or found the Black Knife in my chamber – you need eyes to do both.'

'You are probably right,' said Father Adrian sadly. 'He will deny all when he returns, and she will be safely in her secret refuge. You will never prove what happened. Poor Wulfric. He has lost two children – Eleanor's veil was found in the rubble at Dene yesterday, and only one conclusion can be drawn: she is dead.'

Geoffrey thought about Eleanor's absence from the hut two nights before. She had taken his suggestion seriously, and would be delighted to know the ruse had worked.

'Come with me,' he said, indicating Giffard was to follow him outside. 'I want you to hear something.'

They walked to where Agnes was screeching at Roger to be careful, while Walter dashed in circles to avoid being nicked by the big knight's sword. Walter was furious at the humiliation, and his hand shook in rabid outrage as he pointed at Geoffrey.

'You have no right to make me fight such an ox! He might have killed me!'

'And he might have taught you something that will save your life,' said Geoffrey, grabbing Roger's arm before he took offence. 'His lessons will be far more valuable than the ones your mother taught you – about mandrake and lighting fires to kill those who stand in your way.'

Giffard regarded him uneasily. 'Isabel set Dene alight, to secure the affection of her lover. You told me she admitted it.'

'But someone put the idea in her mind and encouraged her to follow it through. And that person had her own motives. Do you remember

361

the wine you drank that night?'

Giffard shuddered, while Agnes' eyes narrowed into hard, spiteful slits. 'It was revolting stuff and made me ill.'

'It tasted salty – someone had added salt to make you thirsty, so you would drink more of it. But it contained more than wine and salt, did it not, Agnes?'

'I do not know what you are talking about,' she said coldly.

'Two days ago Mother Elgiva made me smell something. It was poppy juice, which had been given to Jervil to make him unable to resist when his killer strangled him. The scent was familiar, although I could not place it. But now I remember: it was in the wine you gave Giffard.'

'You are talking nonsense,' snapped Agnes. 'That wine was—'

'Giffard seldom drinks, so could not tell that your gift contained substances it should not have done,' Geoffrey cut in. 'Salt and a sleeping draught.'

'Why would I do such a thing?' demanded Agnes. 'Poppy juice syrup is expensive.'

'Because you did not want him to wake when the fire took hold. You wanted him to die.'

Giffard gaped at him. 'You must be mistaken!'

Agnes' red lips parted in a sensual smile, and she took Giffard's hand. 'Geoffrey is deluded! I *did* give you wine, but it was to soothe your ragged spirits. You seemed so sad.'

'That is right,' declared Walter. 'Only a fool would not notice salt in his wine.' He gave Giffard a patently false smile. 'And you are not

362

a fool.'

'He is not,' agreed Geoffrey. 'But he still does not know a good brew from a poor one. You were also ready to kill him later, in the confusion of the fire. I heard you. You saw me listening and promptly changed the subject.'

Agnes opened her mouth to protest her innocence again, but Walter was less skilled at dissembling. He sighed with impatient resignation, as if he had been caught cheating at dice rather than in a plot to kill his uncle.

'Well, we did not know what else to do. He will not let us do what we want, and he ruins our plans by interfering all the time.'

Giffard was aghast. 'You would kill me, when all I want is for you to live good, honest lives?'

Even Agnes saw that there was no point in denials now. 'You are tedious, Giffard, and your brother was the same. I do not want a "good, honest" life. I want to enjoy riches, power and lovers. Why will you not leave us alone to live as *we* see fit, not as you want us to be?'

Giffard's face was ashen. 'Then you may consider yourselves free of me, if that is what you want. I wash my hands of you.'

Walter was unashamedly delighted. 'We shall leave today,' he declared. 'Isabel and fitzNorman had the right idea: *I* do not want to stay here to be slaughtered, either.'

Roger had been listening to the discussion with open disgust. Suddenly, he stepped forward and grabbed Walter by the tunic, speaking in a low hiss that even Geoffrey found intimidating.

'The King does not like people murdering his

bishops, so you had better hope Giffard lives a long and happy life, boy. If he dies a day before he reaches his three-score years-and-ten, I shall tell King Henry *you* are responsible for his death.'

'But it might not be true,' said Agnes, alarmed. 'All powerful men have enemies.'

'Then you must join ranks against them,' said Roger coolly. 'The day Giffard dies is the day I tell the King *you* are responsible.'

Geoffrey agreed with Agnes that Roger's threat was unfair, but he did not care. If it prevented them from striking at Giffard in the future, that was fine with him.

'And what about the Duchess?' asked Giffard in a whisper. His face was grey with shock as the enormity of the betrayal struck home. 'Did you harm her?'

'They tried,' said Geoffrey, when Agnes opened her mouth to lie. 'And Walter provided the means. But they did not succeed, because they cannot read Italian.'

'What do you mean?' demanded Agnes, too startled to deny the charge. She glanced at her son, who seemed equally bemused. 'What does Italian have to do with it? Besides, Walter *does* read Italian.'

'He knows some phrases, but he does not understand the language – no matter what he tells you.'

'Lies!' shouted Walter. He took a deep breath. 'All cats love beautiful women when the moon is green.' He reverted to Norman-French. 'See? I speak it like a native.'

'Then tell me what I am saying now,' said Geoffrey, also in Italian. 'And prove it.'

'He is talking gibberish,' said Walter, appealing to Giffard. 'He is trying to make me look stupid when I am not. *I* speak Italian. He is just blathering with nonsense words.'

'Actually, he is not,' said Giffard. 'I know Italian myself – I learnt with the Pope in Rome. Geoffrey made sense; you did not. I warned you against lying before, Walter: not only will it stain your soul, but now you have been caught out.'

'I found this among your possessions,' said Geoffrey, showing the box of mandrake to the seething boy and his mother. Both looked shocked. 'Unlike most people on the night of the fire, *you* had time to gather your belongings, because you knew what was about to happen. It was a mistake: you should have left this to burn, so it would not be here to accuse you.'

'It is dried mandrake fruit,' said Agnes with a light, false laugh. 'What is your point? Many people own them, and in Italy they are considered a rare treat.'

'Eat one, then,' suggested Geoffrey, offering her the box.

She stepped away from it. 'I do not like the taste.'

'Walter?' said Geoffrey. Walter regarded him with sullen loathing, but made no move to take one.

'I will,' offered Giffard, reaching out to the box. 'I am partial to these, but they are rarely seen in England.' He swallowed it and took another.

'Have them all,' suggested Agnes eagerly. 'They are the finest money can buy.'

'Here,' said Roger, looking from Giffard to Geoffrey in concern. 'Should you be doing that? Mandrake is poisonous – even *I* know that.'

'Yes, it is,' agreed Geoffrey. 'But not all the plant is toxic. There are times when mandrake fruit, which look like yellow plums, can be harvested and eaten with no ill effects – as you would know, had you read the label on this box, and as Giffard is aware. But Agnes did *not* know: she told me that *all* parts are poisonous. She was wrong.'

'You gave Sibylla these, thinking to poison her?' asked Giffard, incredulously. 'Silly woman! Surely you know they are harmless when they are ripe? And even when they are unripe, they are not as toxic as the root. You cannot kill anyone with these!'

'Margaret and Eleanor both saw Agnes give the Duchess yellow fruit,' said Geoffrey. 'Sibylla ate one, but did not like it. She gave the rest to her courtiers, who ate them with no ill effects. Agnes and Walter fully expected Sibylla to die from their gift, but that was not what killed her.'

'Are you sure?' asked Roger uneasily.

Geoffrey nodded. 'Mandrake poisoning is characterized by gripping pains in the gut and purging. I have spoken to people who saw the Duchess in the final stages of her illness, and they mentioned no such symptoms: she slipped away peacefully. Agnes and Walter *wanted* to murder the Duchess, and even executed their

366

plan to kill her, but they did not succeed.'

Agnes shot Walter an accusing glare. '*You* told me—' she began, before realizing she should hold her tongue.

'He told you mandrake is poisonous,' finished Geoffrey. He held up the phial Durand had seen fall from Walter's bag after the fire. 'And he had this, which contained juice of mandrake root. Mandrake root is *very* toxic. However, he grabbed an empty pot from somewhere, and it was never full when you were with the Duchess.'

'You *told* me you tested mandrake and it worked,' Agnes snapped imprudently.

'I saw it work in Italy,' said Walter defensively. 'I stole the pot later, so I would remember its name.'

Agnes sighed angrily, before shooting Geoffrey a triumphant smirk. 'So, you have learnt the truth, but it means nothing. Our fruit did not harm Sibylla – as you have just proved – so we have committed no crime. We are innocent.'

'And Sibylla is still dead,' said Walter, contemptuous of Geoffrey's conclusions and their implications. 'And my mother will be duchess in her place.'

'She can try,' said Geoffrey. 'But the rumours that she is a killer – regardless of whether they are true – mean that will never happen. Despite his infidelity, the Duke loved his wife.'

'He did,' agreed Giffard. 'So do not be surprised if he declines your offer of marriage, Agnes.'

'Come, Mother,' said Walter loftily. 'We do not have to listen to this. We are leaving.'

'It is not safe,' warned Geoffrey. 'You are not

Isabel and fitzNorman, who know the area and evoke sympathy as a blind woman and an old man. You will be caught and treated as spies.'

'Well, I will not stay here,' said Walter defiantly. He glared at Roger. *'He* might try to stab me when Baderon attacks and pretend I was struck by the enemy.'

'Aye, lad,' said Roger. 'I just might.'

'Thank you,' said Giffard, as he sat with Geoffrey at the midday meal. The knight had little appetite, his nerves stretched taut from the imminent attack.

'For what?' he asked. 'Proving what you did not want to hear? That Agnes *did* try to kill the Duchess, and that Walter was not only party to the plan, but provided her with the means to do it?'

'You showed they did not succeed,' said Giffard.

'But they *wanted* to, and only failed because they used the wrong poison. That is almost as bad.'

'Perhaps,' agreed Giffard. 'But I feel happier now that I have the truth – living with uncertainty was far worse. I feel safe, too: they will not try to hurt me now. Not after what Roger said.'

Geoffrey nodded. 'But if they send gifts of yellow plums, you should not eat them.'

'I doubt they will send me presents,' said Giffard. 'I am going to ask the King to place Agnes in a convent, and Walter will not become a man of significance without her. Their brush with power is over.'

'You should eat something, Geoff,' advised Roger, who was himself enjoying a sizeable portion of meat. 'It is unlike you to refuse food. What is wrong?'

'This situation,' replied Geoffrey. 'God knows we have seen battles before, but there is something deeply wrong about this one. I barely know what it is for, other than that Corwenna wants it.'

'Do not dwell on it, or it will sap your concentration,' advised Roger. 'If the enemy is as numerous as we fear, then we need all the resources we can muster – including your wits.'

Reluctantly, Geoffrey accepted the bread Roger shoved into his hands, but he had taken no more than a mouthful before there was a shout. Geoffrey was on his feet in an instant, running across the hall and clattering down the stairs to the bailey, Roger at his heels.

'They are here!' called the white-faced man from the main gate's fighting platform. 'And there are thousands of them, stretching as far as the eye can see.'

Fourteen

'Hundreds,' corrected Geoffrey, scrambling up on to the fighting platform and trying to conceal his alarm at the size of the army Baderon had mustered. 'Not thousands.'

With Roger at his side, he assessed the troops massing just out of arrow range. They formed a vast inverted U, with horsemen on each side, and a huge company of foot soldiers in the middle. Behind, watching from the vantage point of a knoll, were Baderon and his commanders. The Lord of Monmouth sat astride a dark bay. Lambert was on his right, identifiable by the fair hair below his helmet, and Hilde was to his left, atop a white pony. Corwenna was well to the front, however, head bared to reveal her auburn mane. She was standing in her stirrups, yelling. Even from a distance, her voice was clear and strong, and her words met with cheers.

Meanwhile, Goodrich's defenders watched in horrified silence as rank after rank filed forward, armed with spears, battleaxes and shields. Just when Geoffrey thought the last had arrived, more appeared, until the fields around the castle gleamed silver with weapons and armour.

'Lord!' breathed Olivier. 'We cannot withstand

such a number. We shall be slaughtered.'

Roger clapped a hand on his shoulder. 'But you and I will take a few with us, eh? We shall meet in Paradise and exchange stories.' Olivier looked terrified, and Geoffrey suspected Roger's illusions about him were soon to be shattered once and for all.

'We are well defended,' said Joan firmly, although Geoffrey knew she spoke only for the benefit of the troops.

Geoffrey jumped from the platform and strode to where Bale waited with his warhorse. Durand was with him, dressed in something suspiciously like one of Father Adrian's habits. Geoffrey could not find it in his heart to condemn Durand for donning clothes he hoped might see him spared. He was caught in the middle of a battle that was none of his making.

'Remember what you promised me,' Geoffrey said to Joan. 'You cannot lead an attack yourself.'

She touched his cheek, her hand shaking. She was frightened, although her face betrayed no emotion. 'Dear Geoff. But go, and let us pray we live to see each other again.'

He took the reins from Durand. 'I am sorry,' he said to his old squire. 'You should not be here.'

'No, I should not,' agreed Durand fervently. 'I knew it was a mistake coming here. Violence follows you, but this time you have excelled yourself. I do not envy Bale for what you are going to make him do today.' He glanced at the squire. 'Although he looks more than eager to begin.'

Bale was armed with an axe and a sword. Both were honed to a devastating sharpness, and the dull light in his eyes indicated he was ready.

'You should hide,' Geoffrey said to Durand, watching Roger prepare his mercenaries to engage the masses outside. 'Remember the passage I told you about, which leads from my chamber to the woods? Go down it if we are overrun. Then tell the King what really happened.'

'Very well,' said Durand, terrified. 'But let us hope it will not be necessary.'

With a great whoop, the gate was flung open and Roger hurtled out, his warriors streaming behind him. They flew across the space separating the invaders from the castle and, when the enemy broke ranks to meet them, Geoffrey signalled for his archers to begin their deadly attack. Roger tore among the front ranks with his broadsword, men falling around him like timber. Baderon's troops fell back, and Geoffrey held his breath, half-expecting Roger to forget the plan in the heat of battle. But, still hacking at hapless stragglers, Roger yelled a retreat.

Geoffrey heard Lambert order his men to pursue Roger and watched as they obeyed, shields raised to fend off the deadly hail of arrows. As per his instruction, Roger veered to the right, towards Baderon's right flank. The speed of the change confused the enemy, and some scattered, getting in the way of others trying to press forward. Roger wheeled away again.

Geoffrey ordered the gates opened a second time and led his own men out, yelling for them to keep in formation and not break ranks. He made a feint at the horsemen on the left, who had seen what happened to their comrades and were ready. They surged forward, but Geoffrey abruptly changed direction and aimed for the swarming foot soldiers, making sure Baderon's left followed him.

Roger's identical manoeuvre was completed simultaneously, and suddenly there were four separate units of horsemen – Geoffrey's and Roger's, plus Baderon's left and right – converging on the hapless infantry. There was instant confusion, and more foot soldiers were crushed under the hoofs of friends' horses than were killed by Goodrich's men. Then Geoffrey's and Roger's forces met and formed a single unit, slashing with swords and axes.

With little room to move, and men behind pressing against those in front, it was sheer slaughter. Geoffrey lost count of the men who fell by his sword. The battle cries and horses' whinnies almost drowned the clash of weapons. His hands were slippery with blood, and the faces that swarmed towards him blurred as he fought on, standing in his stirrups and using both hands to swing his sword. The rich, earthy stink of blood was sickening. Then, as the yell came for Baderon's troops to retreat, a horseman appeared, aiming a series of heavy blows at Geoffrey.

'You brought us to this point!' screamed Lambert. His eyes were glazed and he was splattered with gore from head to foot. 'And you killed my brother!'

'On my honour, I did not raise my hand against Seguin!' shouted Geoffrey. 'Can we not, even at this stage, stop the slaughter and negotiate?'

'It is too late!' yelled Lambert bitterly. 'Baderon is not in control: Corwenna is, and she will not rest until Goodrich is destroyed. It is what happens when you make alliances with rabid dogs – and there are few more rabid than her. I wish I had never set eyes on the woman.'

Before he could say more, there was the crash of a battleaxe, and Lambert toppled from his saddle, blood erupting from a huge gash in the back of his head. Behind him, face split in a diabolical grimace, was Corwenna.

Her face was splattered with blood, and it was clear that she had been at the heart of the slaughter. Her eyes were wild, and she was more ecstatic than Geoffrey had ever seen her. She drove her horse forward and raised her axe, aiming for his head. He raised his shield and launched an attack of his own, jabbing hard under it with his sword. Corwenna gave a screech of outrage as the blade bit into her thigh, and brought the axe down with all her might.

Caught at the wrong angle, Geoffrey's shield split into several pieces, but before she could take advantage, several vicious swipes of his sword drove her back. With the heat of the moment compounding his mental exhaustion, he made an appalling blunder, jumping from his saddle to grab a replacement shield from a corpse. It was an inexcusable mistake that left him infinitely more vulnerable: no knight willingly left his horse during battle.

Corwenna, who was no match for him under normal circumstances, grinned her delight and came after him with a series of hacking swipes. Fortunately, it was easy to evade them, as she held her axe high up on its handle, restricting its reach.

'Why did you kill Lambert?' Geoffrey demanded, trying to make the crazed woman lose concentration.

'He was weak,' she snarled, swinging her axe, as he dodged away. 'Like Baderon, who does not fight, but directs the battle from where it is safe.'

Several of her men hurried to help, and soon three blades were stabbing at Geoffrey. Before they could skewer him, he ducked under the belly of Corwenna's horse and out the other side, grabbing one of her legs to haul her off. She fell, kicking and spitting. He ran to his horse and scrambled into the saddle. When her men saw Geoffrey remounted, they melted away, unwilling to face a Norman on horseback. Corwenna hesitated for a moment, but then followed them, also unwilling to pit her life against such unattractive odds.

'Back to the castle!' Geoffrey yelled. He and Roger had done all they could, and it was time to retreat before they started taking serious casualties.

'I can get her!' screeched Bale, his face smeared red and eyes alight.

'Her cavalry have regrouped!' Geoffrey shouted back. 'They will cut you off if you move forward, so retreat. Now!'

Most obeyed, although one man charged ahead regardless, guided by some primal part of his mind. Geoffrey saw him surrounded by foot soldiers, then dragged from his horse. He did not wait to see more. He wheeled his horse round and yelled for his men to follow. Baderon's riders, eager to avenge their losses, thundered towards them, and Geoffrey saw that it would be a close-run thing as to whether they reached the gate in time. But a rush of arrows drove back the pursuit, and Geoffrey and his men streamed through the gate unhindered.

'That worked,' said Olivier, his voice unsteady. 'But even though their dead litter the ground, we seem to have made no appreciable impact. There are still more of them than leaves on the trees.'

'There are not,' snapped Geoffrey, afraid the men would hear and lose heart. It was a hard enough battle, without the soldiers becoming demoralized. 'We have severely damaged their horsemen.'

But when he clambered up to the platform, he saw that Olivier was right. Although there were many dead and wounded on the battlefield, their loss had made no dent in the main fighting force. It was then that Geoffrey knew for certain that they would never win; the odds were simply too great. Roger came to stand next to him.

'I did not think my life would end somewhere like this,' Roger said. He also recognized a lost cause when he saw one. 'I thought I would die an old man, in bed with a vigorous whore on top of me.'

'You still could, if you took your men and rode south,' said Geoffrey. 'I doubt Baderon will follow. Take Joan.'

Roger sniffed. His face was splattered with blood and his surcoat was drenched in it. 'She will not leave. Durand would come, but he is the only one.'

'Have you considered surrender?' asked Walter weakly from behind, clearly appalled by what he had seen. 'They may spare our lives if you give them the castle.'

Roger laughed. 'You think they will let us give up now? You are a fool, boy!'

'I will offer them money,' said Walter desperately. 'Send Giffard to tell them I will pay handsomely for safe passage. I have a chest of coins.'

'Why would they spare you, when they can have the coins regardless?' asked Roger.

'Then I shall hide in the cellars,' said Walter, 'and come out when all the fighting is over.'

'If you do, you will burn when the castle is fired,' warned Geoffrey. He saw Durand nearby, his face white with fear. 'Collect the women and children – and Walter – and lead them down that passage. Keep them hidden until nightfall.'

'But we will be without protection,' objected Durand uneasily.

Geoffrey nodded. 'But we cannot win this fight, and it is only a matter of time before the enemy breach the walls.'

Durand swallowed hard. 'Very well.'

Geoffrey clapped him on the shoulder, aware

377

that his hand left a bloody streak on his habit. Durand asked a few questions about the tunnel, and what might be done to conceal it after they had gone, and then left. Geoffrey breathed a prayer for his success.

'Now what?' asked Olivier shakily. 'We cannot repeat your manoeuvre, because they have already adapted. I think the next attack will be in several places at the same time.'

'It is what I would do,' said Geoffrey. 'With a concentrated push to smash the gate. Then, once they are inside, we will have to retreat to the keep.'

'Here they come again!' yelled Roger. 'They do not want to give us time to recoup.'

'Aim for the rider on the piebald pony!' shouted Geoffrey to the archers. 'It is Corwenna.'

Fire arrows streamed across the walls, some falling harmlessly, some landing in places where they started to burn and others thudding into the people running to douse them. Men with ladders moved forward outside.

Geoffrey ran to the northern wall, where invaders were already swarming the ramparts. He snatched a bow from a dead archer and shot off several arrows, but the raiders were protected by the shields they held aloft, and they were too many to deter with bows. One of Geoffrey's archers yelled that they were almost out of ammunition, and a howl of enemy glee from the east told him the gate had been breached.

'So soon?' he whispered, appalled.

'It was opened from inside!' howled Roger.

'We have been betrayed!'

Yelling for everyone else to retreat to the keep, Geoffrey joined Roger and his mounted mercenaries in brutal combat with the first of the invaders to stream in. Gradually, the press of men forced the defenders back until they were in the narrow space between stables and kitchen. Geoffrey's foot soldiers rushed to aid them, and the bailey was a hive of skirmishes, ringing with war cries, screams of pain and the clang of desperately wielded weapons.

A group of enemy soldiers recognized Geoffrey's surcoat and launched a concerted attack to separate him from his troops. Slowly, they drove him into the kitchen. Geoffrey was tiring, but suddenly, Durand appeared. The clerk slipped a knife between one man's ribs and, with better odds, Geoffrey dispatched two more. The remainder fled.

Durand watched dispassionately as the man he had stabbed choked on his own blood.

'There,' he said, glancing at Geoffrey. 'I do not want you dead. Not yet, at least.'

Geoffrey dropped his hands to his knees and tried to catch his breath. Durand's words slowly registered in his fatigued mind. 'Not yet?' he gasped. 'What do you mean?'

Durand waved his arm outside the door. Recognizing the danger too late, Geoffrey moved forward, but Corwenna and half a dozen of her followers were already racing into the room. He could only gaze at Durand in horror.

'What have you done?'

'I have backed the side that will win,' replied

Durand calmly. 'I always do. You said yourself you could not defeat Baderon, so do not blame me for changing my allegiance. I am simply being practical.'

Geoffrey was dumbfounded by the enormity of Durand's betrayal. He saw his old squire regarding him with complete lack of emotion, and several facts came together in his mind as he watched Durand turn to Corwenna.

'There is a tunnel that leads from the keep to the woods. Geoffrey wanted me to smuggle his civilians down it.'

Corwenna's face curled into a gloating sneer. She beckoned to one of her men, ordering him to find the passage and kill anyone attempting to use it. Geoffrey felt sick.

'Now we shall make an end of this,' said Corwenna. 'I will take your head and show it to Joan. It will be the last thing she will see; then we shall be free of the Mappestone curse. My Rhys will be avenged, and I will dance on your grave, just as I do Henry's.'

Geoffrey thought about the fallen cross. 'I might have known.'

'Fight me, Geoffrey,' she urged, eyes glittering madly. 'Just you and me.'

He regarded her warily, wondering whether he had misheard. He was a trained knight, and there was no way Corwenna could defeat him, no matter how filled she was with hate. 'Just you and me?'

'Why?' she snapped. 'Are you afraid? I have waited a long time for this.'

She darted forward with her axe, but he

immediately went on the offensive, attacking her with strong strokes that forced her back against the wall. He was on the brink of cutting her down when her men darted forward and forced him back. It was clearly not going to be a fair fight, and he could see by her alarmed expression that she knew she had underestimated him.

'I will kill you,' he warned. 'I am not as easy as Henry.'

The mention of his brother re-lit her impetus, but blind fury was no replacement for skill, and he soon had her retreating again. He was obliged to keep a wary eye on her men, as they jabbed their blades at him if he went too close. He wondered what would happen when he killed her, certain that he did not have the strength to defeat them all, too.

'Hurry up, Corwenna!' snapped Durand. 'I have done what you asked, and I want my reward.'

'*You* opened the gate!' spat Geoffrey in disgust, thinking about the speed with which their defences had failed. 'How could you?'

'I did what was best for *me*,' replied Durand. 'I was promised a sack of silver for opening the gate, and another if I delivered you alive.'

'You should watch whom you trust,' Geoffrey said to Corwenna, as she retreated to the far side of the room and the temporary safety of her men. 'Durand killed Seguin.'

'I did not,' said Durand, a sudden tremor in his voice. 'Do not accuse me—'

Corwenna lunged at Geoffrey, and for a few moments his attention was concentrated on parrying her blows. Although delivered with great venom and strength, they lacked the requisite skill to break him. He held her at arm's length until the fury of her attack subsided, then kicked her legs from under her so she fell. Her men again stepped forward protectively, and all Geoffrey could do was step back and try to catch his breath. His sword felt slippery and heavy in his aching hands.

'Like the King, you saw Baderon pay Jervil,' said Geoffrey to Durand while Corwenna was recuperating. 'You are greedy and you gave Jervil drugged wine to celebrate his sale, then strangled him. You have strangled men before – you killed a monk last year in the forest near Westminster – and I should have seen immediately that you were the culprit.'

'You are speaking nonsense,' said Durand, glancing nervously towards Corwenna.

Geoffrey continued, noticing he had Corwenna's reluctant attention. 'I assumed Jervil died first and Margaret second, but I was wrong. Isabel killed Margaret, then fled, appalled by what she had done. But you had watched her, and it gave you an idea.'

'You cannot prove I killed anyone,' hissed Durand.

'Oh, the knife you planted on Jervil's body does that. *You* were the one who drew attention to it, but you could not have seen it from where you were standing – it was covered with straw. I was kneeling right next to him, and *I* could not see it. The only way you could have known was if you put it there yourself. And the knife was in his wrong hand. Only someone like you, who knows nothing about fighting, would shove a dagger in a right-fisted fighter's left hand.'

Durand glanced at Corwenna. 'Hurry, woman.'

'In my own time,' said Corwenna. 'I am interested in what he has to say about Seguin.' She heaved her axe on to her shoulder and indicated that Geoffrey should continue.

'Baderon thought the Black Knife was destroyed in the fire. But it had been stolen before that. I met Durand running from the guest house during the fire. But he should not have been there: he was supposed to have been with Abbot Serlo above the buttery – in the opposite direction.'

'Everything was in chaos,' said Durand dismissively. 'You could not tell where I—'

'He grabbed the Black Knife and was cut,' Geoffrey went on. 'He told me he had been burnt, but later claimed it was a gash. They are not similar injuries. That is why he gave me his gloves – the injury meant he could not wear them anyway.'

'All this is fascinating,' said Corwenna caustically. 'But I want to know about Seguin.'

'Durand killed Hugh before he murdered Seguin,' Geoffrey continued, trying to keep the exhaustion from his voice. 'He knocked him on the head to stun him, then strangled him. The Black Knife was thrust into his corpse to cause trouble between Goodrich and Baderon. It succeeded.'

'Seguin!' snapped Corwenna, growing impatient. 'Lambert said *you* killed him, because you thought he killed Henry.'

'Seguin did not kill Henry,' said Geoffrey. 'I have known for some time who did that, and it was not Seguin. Seguin *was* lured to his death, just as Lambert claimed. But not by me.'

'Shut up!' yelled Durand furiously. He turned to Corwenna again. 'Kill him, for God's sake.'

'Who carried the message to Llan Martin, telling Seguin that Hugh's body was at Goodrich and that Baderon wanted it collected?' asked Geoffrey.

Corwenna's eyes flicked towards Durand. 'He did.'

'I was *told* to give Seguin that message!' shouted Durand. 'And I was *told* Hugh was at Goodrich. You cannot blame me for passing on what I was ordered to say.'

'Think,' said Geoffrey to Corwenna. 'Why would Baderon tell Seguin to collect Hugh, when he was here himself? And why would he send for Seguin and not a servant? And why would Durand – who owns estates in Suffolk – allow himself to be used as a messenger by a man he despised?'

'*Geoffrey* told me to give Seguin the message!' cried Durand, eyes flashing. 'And now he is try-ing to make you think the murder was my fault. Who do you believe? The man who slaughtered Seguin? Or the man who opened the gate for you?'

When put like that, Geoffrey saw that he was not in a strong position. He hurried to resume his tale, hoping Durand would yet incriminate himself in his increasing panic. 'When Father

Adrian left to fetch Seguin some ale, Durand crept into the house and stabbed him.'

'How?' sneered Durand. 'Do I look like a man who could take on a strong, well-armed knight? Of course not! Nor do I stab folk as they sit at tables.'

'See?' pounced Geoffrey. 'How could he know Seguin was at a table unless he was the killer?'

'I saw the body,' snapped Durand. 'Later, after Father Adrian had raised the alarm.'

'You did not,' countered Geoffrey. 'You were outside the whole time, while Father Adrian was sick.'

'*You* killed Seguin!' shouted Durand accusingly. '*You* lured him to Goodrich by ordering me to fetch him, and *you* stabbed him because you thought he murdered Henry.' He looked at Corwenna, his face pale and covered in sweat. 'He told me so, late one night, when he had too much ale.'

'Do not worry, Durand,' said Corwenna, patting the clerk's shoulder. 'I believe you.'

'Jervil, Hugh and Seguin,' said Geoffrey to Durand. 'You tried to kill me, too – it was you who started the fire in the mattress. I probably even gave you the idea, since Bale saving me from the blaze at Dene was one of the last things we talked about before I fell asleep.'

Durand was disdainful. 'I saved your life, and now you accuse me of trying to burn you alive.'

'You woke me because Joan came. If she had not, you would have succeeded. But that was your second attempt. The first was with the damaged straps and the spikes in Dun's saddle. You hoped I would break my neck riding him in the forest.'

'I wish you had,' muttered Durand fervently.

'No more!' roared Corwenna. 'Fight me, Geoffrey, and stop blathering.'

'If I win, will you leave Goodrich?' he asked.

'You will not win,' she snarled, swinging her axe in a series of fancy manoeuvres that made the air sing. Geoffrey jumped out of the way, but stumbled when one of her men tripped him. Before he regained his balance, another kicked him in the knee. He barely avoided Corwenna's axe as it plummeted down, splitting one of the tables.

Geoffrey went on the offensive again, his blows forcing Corwenna back against the wall. Her men moved to help her, so he feinted left and reached out to grab her by the neck, dropping his sword as he did so. Then he her pulled close against him, his dagger at her throat. She struggled furiously, gouging his hand with her fingernails. He intensified his grip, pressing his knife into her exposed skin.

She sagged in defeat. 'I surrender. Let me go, you have made your point.'

'No!' cried Durand in horror. 'You cannot let him win! What will happen to me? I will hang for Seguin's murder and for trying to dispatch Geoffrey.'

Corwenna ignored him. 'You heard that worm, Geoffrey,' she said. 'He admitted murdering Seguin. Let us bring an end to this bloodshed. Let me go.'

Geoffrey lowered his dagger, although he did

not relinquish it. Corwenna eased his hand away from her neck.

'Thank you,' she said, darting away too fast for him to stop her. She glanced at her men. 'Well? What are you waiting for? Kill him while I fire the castle and rid us of Joan. Durand may have killed Seguin, but Henry killed Rhys, and his kin will pay the price.'

All Geoffrey could hear was Durand's mocking laughter as Corwenna left the room and her men moved forward. Other sounds began to pervade his consciousness – the roar of desperate battle as the defenders of Goodrich gave way inch by inch. Through the open door he could see arrows raining down from the battlements, and the ground was thick with dead and wounded men. He was so tired, he could barely raise his arms, let alone fight six fresh swordsmen, but his anger against Durand renewed his strength.

He launched a wild attack that took them by surprise and momentarily pushed them back, but they rallied quickly, and then it was he who was retreating.

'Is it true?' asked one of them – the captain. 'All you said? Remember you are about to die, and you will go to Hell for eternity if you do so with a lie on your lips.'

'It is true,' said Geoffrey, darting behind a table and waiting to see whether he should duck right or left to avoid the next foray.

'You said you know Henry's murderer,' said the captain, indicating that his men should hold back. 'Who?'

'Someone from Goodrich,' replied Geoffrey. 'Not Baderon, and not a Welshman.'

'Durand?' asked the captain.

'I never even met Henry!' cried Durand indignantly, snatching up a bag he had brought in with him.

'Caerdig is my cousin,' said the captain, ignoring him. 'He has always spoken well of you, and I believe you are telling the truth. You may go.'

'What?' exclaimed Durand, watching aghast as the captain sheathed his sword. 'And what will you tell Corwenna when she asks you whether you obeyed her orders?'

'And you can take him with you,' said the captain, eyeing Durand with distaste. 'I would kill him, but I do not want to soil my blade with the blood of a snake. Go.'

He stood aside, and gestured for the others to do the same. They hesitated, but did as he ordered. Geoffrey edged past them, anticipating a trick, but they allowed him to walk unharmed across the kitchen and into the bailey. What he saw there sickened him. Everywhere lay the dead and injured, some in silent agony, others screaming for friends, water or God. It was a sight he had seen many times before, but not in his own home. He swung round, a blind rage gripping him, but Durand was already running away, hugging his bag as he went.

'Save your sister,' said the captain, nodding towards the hall. 'Corwenna will kill her otherwise.'

'What will you do?' asked Geoffrey uneasily, inclined to resist the advice of an enemy.

The captain indicated his sheathed sword. 'Go home and take my men with me. My name is Rhodri of Llangarron, and you can remember it if you win this fight and have grain to spare.'

Geoffrey took a deep breath and raised his bloodied sword to battle through the mass of men at the foot of the keep. The staircase had been removed, but the invaders had piled ladders against the wall and some were already inside. Roger and his men were still mounted, striking furiously at anyone entering the bailey gate, but Geoffrey could see none of his own horsemen, except for Bale, who was trying to keep raiders out of the stables.

Geoffrey's armour and surcoat attracted the attention of many hoping to claim a knight among their kills, and it was some time before he reached the ladders. He was weak with fatigue, and one inferior swordsman came closer to skewering him than he should have. Finally, Geoffrey grasped the ladder and climbed, kicking out when someone grabbed his leg.

With sweat stinging his eyes, he reached the door. Joan's once-pristine hall was stained with blood, and there were bodies everywhere, suggesting that it had not been taken easily. Giffard was in a corner wielding his stave against two attackers, while Olivier crouched behind him, hands raised to protect his head. Geoffrey moved quickly, and made short work of both invaders.

'Joan?' he gasped.

Giffard pointed to the opposite side of the hall, then braced himself as another man launched an attack with a war-like screech. The howl ended abruptly when Giffard's stave met the man's skull. Seeing the Bishop could fend for himself, Geoffrey fought his way across the room. At the centre of a tight knot of skirmishers was Joan, meeting Corwenna's axe blows with a shield, while Baderon exchanged half-hearted swipes with Torva and Peter. Hilde, hair flying wildly about her face, was screaming at Corwenna.

'They will surrender now!' she howled. 'Put up your weapon!'

'Not until Joan is dead,' hissed Corwenna.

'Our fight is not with her!' shouted Hilde, trying to pull Corwenna away.

Corwenna spun round and turned on Hilde, swinging the axe towards her unprotected head. Hilde ducked, and Joan struck Corwenna hard with the shield, but the blow had little impact. She raised her axe again, and Geoffrey saw her smile as Hilde backed up against a wall with no way to defend herself.

Hilde met Corwenna's eyes without fear. The axe started to fall. Geoffrey snatched a shield from a corpse and hurled himself between them, feeling the force of the blow send agonizing tremors through his arm.

'You!' screamed Corwenna in fury, turning on him. Geoffrey lifted his sword, but before he could close with her, Joan stepped forward and brought down her shield on Corwenna's head with all the force she could muster. Corwenna dropped to the floor and jerked convulsively before going limp.

'Is she dead?' asked Giffard uneasily. 'God

knows I am not a man to wish death on another human being, but the world will be a safer place without Corwenna in it.'

'Oh, yes,' said Hilde, looking at the distorted shape of Corwenna's skull. 'She is dead.'

'I think enough of us have died for one day,' said Baderon loudly, dropping his sword and raising his hand to indicate Torva and Peter should desist their attack. 'This fight is over.'

Those inside lowered their weapons, and Baderon and a trembling Olivier went together to end the skirmishes outside. Word spread quickly, and the sound of fighting petered out until only the groans of the wounded could be heard. Inside, Geoffrey looked at his broken home. He removed his helmet and scrubbed hard at his face. His arms were so sore from wielding his sword that he felt he might never raise them again. The faces of the others showed they felt the same.

'Who won?' asked Torva. 'Them, because they managed to get into the hall? Or us, because we fended them off?'

'I do not think there are any winners here,' said Giffard soberly.

The silence that followed was broken by an urgent call.

'Geoff!' shouted Roger from the door. 'Come quickly!'

Afraid there was a pocket where the fighting continued, Geoffrey forced his weary legs into a run. He caught up with Roger – beckoning urgently – near the stables. When they rounded a corner, there was Durand, sitting against a wall and clutching his bag to his chest.

'Our traitor,' Geoffrey said coldly. 'What did you call me for? I want nothing to do with him.'

'He was asking for you,' said Roger. 'He is dying.'

Geoffrey crouched to examine the clerk and was startled to see blood pooling in his lap. Durand's face was ghastly white, although Geoffrey could see no injury. He tried to move the sack, but Durand clutched it tighter against him.

'No,' he whispered. 'You cannot have it while I am still alive.'

'I am looking for your wound, to stem the bleeding,' said Geoffrey. 'I do not want your silver.'

'You can have it after I have gone,' croaked Durand. 'I bequeath it to you, but only on condition that you buy masses for my immortal soul.'

Geoffrey thought Durand's sins were far too great to be tempered by prayers. 'Let go of the bag,' he ordered. 'I may be able to save you.'

'No,' said Durand, fiercely clutching the sack. 'You will steal it and leave me to die alone. I want you to hear what I have to say first.'

Feeling that he was betraying himself even being in Durand's presence, Geoffrey sighed. 'What? There are wounded men all over my bailey who need tending. I do not have time to chat.'

'Everything you said is true. I killed Jervil, I killed Hugh and I killed Seguin. And I twice tried to kill you. I did it because it is not fair that you have fine lands and a loving family, and I do not.'

'You have your demesne in Suffolk,' Geoffrey said. 'And it is better than mine – or so you have boasted on several occasions.'

'*Suffolk!*' sneered Durand. 'The King insulted me when he gave me that estate. It is nothing!'

'I do not understand,' said Geoffrey. 'Are you saying you committed your crimes because you are jealous of Goodrich?'

'I wanted you to give up living here and work with me. We could have had a glittering future – earned a great fortune. Besides, the King promised me a better manor if I could entice you back into his service. I tried asking politely, but you refused. You left me with no alternative but to deprive you of home and family to make you change your mind.'

Geoffrey was appalled. 'But it is not just me you damaged here. Baderon—'

'*Baderon!* The bastard who refused me appropriate respect. Your sister is no better. She did not even offer me the welcoming cup when we arrived. Everyone else was given wine, but not me.'

Geoffrey glanced at Roger, and saw that he was just as bewildered by the stream of invective. 'If all this was because you wanted me to work with you, why did you try to kill me?'

'I am not stupid.' Durand's voice was growing softer. 'I knew you would never seriously consider my offer – even after I helped you by lending you my gloves and giving you that phial Walter dropped. You have always despised me.'

'That is not true,' said Geoffrey, not entirely truthfully. 'I admire your intelligence and turned to you several times because I thought you were the best person to ask for advice.'

Durand's sullen expression lifted for a moment, but then collapsed again in obvious disbelief. 'So, being unable to bring you to my side, I decided to take away your happiness. I do not see why you – a brutal, cold ruffian – should grow old peacefully while I struggle.'

Geoffrey was baffled. 'Let me see your wound, Durand,' he said finally. 'We can talk about this later.'

'It is too late,' whispered Durand. 'I am dying. I should not have tried to destroy you, and I need your forgiveness before I meet my Maker, or I will never escape purgatory, and that would not be fair. You have to forgive me. I order it.'

Geoffrey recalled Durand's earlier monastic aspirations and that, despite his crimes, he believed what the Church said happened to sinners. 'You cannot order forgiveness. It must be freely given.'

'Then give if freely,' wheedled Durand. 'If you do, I will tell you another secret – the last one I have that affects you.'

'Forgiveness is not mine to grant,' said Geoffrey, thinking about the grief Durand's actions had brought to so many others.

'It was you I wronged,' said Durand weakly. 'So it is you who must forgive me. I am begging you, Geoffrey. And then I will tell you something important.'

Geoffrey hesitated for the briefest of moments,

but when he looked back, the clerk was dead. He removed the bag from Durand's limp hands and saw that the blade of a knife protruded from it.

Roger stepped forward. 'Baderon was dashing here and there to end the fighting, and Durand thought he was being chased. He ran away, and fell over in his haste to escape. He landed on his bag, and the knife he carried in it must have pierced his chest. But Baderon was *not* chasing Durand – he had no reason to, because he does not yet know that it was Durand who killed his son.'

Geoffrey inspected Durand's wound, then sat back on his heels. 'If he had let me see this, instead of assuming I wanted to steal his fortune, I *would* have been able to save him. The cut is not in his chest, but nicked a vessel in his groin. He bled to death from an injury that did not need to be fatal.'

'Then it serves him right,' said Roger. He nodded towards the bag. 'He left you whatever is in that. Will you open it?'

Geoffrey hesitatingly obliged and was astonished to find it packed full of silver coins and jewellery. 'There is a fortune here! Durand claimed to be envious of Goodrich, but he could have bought a manor three times its size with this.'

'He saw you were happy,' said Roger sagely. 'And, because he equates happiness with wealth, he assumed you were rich, too. But there is something else in the bag.'

Something light flopped to the ground when Roger shook the sack, but Geoffrey's attention was on the silver and he did not notice. Roger quickly shoved the bundle of documents in his surcoat before his friend noticed. Documents, he knew, would only bring trouble, and Geoffrey had endured more than his share of that at Durand's instigation. It was better he remained ignorant of whatever was written on the neatly tied parchments.

Oblivious to Roger's actions, Geoffrey shook the bag a final time, then jumped back in revulsion when the last object clattered to the ground. It was the knife that had killed Durand. The blade was still wet with his blood and the ruby in its hilt gleamed in a sudden burst of sunshine.

'It is the Black Knife,' whispered Roger. 'And it has just claimed its latest victim.'

'Its *last* victim,' corrected Geoffrey softly. 'Its reign of terror ends here.'

Epilogue

St Paul's Cathedral was full, and there was celebration in the air. Bells rang to announce the beginning of the ceremony, and, outside, crowds of Londoners gathered to watch the grand processions as the bishops of Winchester, Hereford and Salisbury prepared to accept their consecration from the Archbishop of York. People wore their best clothes, and ermine-lined cloaks, kirtles of expensive silk and jewel-encrusted shoes were everywhere. Geoffrey stood near the back of the church with Roger, wearing the new surcoat Joan had made for him. Its Crusader's cross was bright and sharp, and Bale had made his mail gleam.

The great west door was thrown open, filling the cathedral with light. Geoffrey gazed in admiration at the elegant lines of the clerestory and the thick, sturdy piers. Giffard was obliged to poke him hard with a bony finger to get his attention.

'I asked whether Goodrich was recovered.'

The Bishop wore his ecclesiastical finery – a cope of gold and a mitre on which precious stones were sewn. He carried a silver crosier,

397

and the holy ring on his finger was almost as large as his fist. Geoffrey smiled when he saw the hair shirt still in place under the handsome vestments. The occasion had not touched Giffard with vanity.

He nodded to his friend. 'And there is peace. We sent grain to Caerdig, and he has married Mother Elgiva – who, as a wise woman, is greatly respected in Llan Martin.'

'And you are betrothed to Hilde, to strengthen the truce,' said Giffard. 'That seems a major sacrifice.'

'Hilde is a fine warrior,' said Roger admiringly. 'They will produce strong sons who will be great soldiers.'

'Oh, good,' said Giffard acidly. 'More men spoiling war. But have you heard the news? Reinhelm of Hereford has declined to accept consecration today. He says he can only have it from the Archbishop of Canterbury. He has gone home.'

'That still leaves you and Salisbury,' said Roger, not understanding the Bishop's point. 'Two is not as good as three, but do not worry. We will still enjoy ourselves, especially at the feast tonight.'

'I was not thinking about your fun,' said Giffard irritably. 'I was thinking of my conscience. Reinhelm is right: York does not have the authority, and if I allow him to consecrate me, I tell the King that he can order me to do what he likes, even when Canterbury forbids it.'

Geoffrey was worried. 'But you have known this for weeks. I thought you were pleased that the King had found a way to consecrate you while he and Canterbury are locked in this row. Henry will be furious if you refuse now.'

Giffard swallowed. 'If I flout Henry today, he will be my enemy forever. He will send me into exile and I can hardly rule my see from Normandy.'

'Then do not flout him,' urged Geoffrey.

'And my conscience?' asked Giffard. 'It tells me something different. You follow yours, so do not tell me to ignore mine.'

'I would never do that,' said Geoffrey. 'I would always trust you to do what is right.'

Giffard was troubled. 'The King has already questioned some of my actions. He took Agnes from the convent I put her in and she is back at court. Look, she is there.'

Dressed in her ceremonial best, Agnes Giffard looked stunning, and triumph was in every line of her being. Next to her was Walter, wearing a sword to indicate that he had recently been granted his spurs; he was officially a knight.

'She told the King she was acting in *his* interests by trying to kill the Duchess,' Giffard went on. 'There is no question that Sibylla's death has damaged Normandy, and Henry says he believes her. I only hope he knows what he is doing.'

'There are many rumours that she killed Sibylla,' said Geoffrey. 'By bringing Agnes to his court, Henry is perpetuating them. She is basking in her perceived success and is unlikely to confess that she failed. Do you not see what is happening?'

Giffard frowned. 'I am so repelled by the whole business that I cannot imagine what Henry hopes to achieve by flaunting her sins.'

'He is taking attention away from someone who might have had an even greater reason to want the Duchess dead and Normandy weakened.'

Giffard stared at him. 'You think the *King* might have harmed Sibylla, and is using Agnes to obscure his guilt?'

Geoffrey shrugged. 'We will never know. But your ceremony is about to begin.' He caught the Bishop's hand as Giffard turned to leave. 'And smile occasionally. You are happy, remember?'

The grin Giffard shot him was sickly, and Geoffrey thought it would do more harm than good if seen by the masses. Giffard hurried to take his place in the procession, and with a flurry of horns, the magnificent event began. First a line of monks chanting a psalm, then a number of assistant bishops who were also to be consecrated, with Giffard and Salisbury bringing up the rear. The procession was an explosion of gold and white, jewels glinting in the sunlight that flooded through the clerestory. Geoffrey's ears rang from the exultant singing, and he did not think he had ever seen such a display of splendour.

The procession reached the high altar, and York began so speak, hushing even the rabble outside. More singing followed, then the heady scent of incense wafted up the aisles. In ringing tones, York invited the bishops to come before him and receive his blessing. Because Winchester had priority over Salisbury, Giffard went first. He knelt, then stood up.

'I cannot do this,' he announced. 'It is not right.'

He shrugged out of his cope and mitre, shoved his crosier at a startled monk and strode towards the door. For a moment, there was only stunned silence and the sound of Giffard's sandals slapping the flagstones. Then pandemonium erupted. Monks surged forward, as if to drag him back, while others pressed towards the altar. The ceremony quickly degenerated into a scene of confusion, with York howling for Giffard to return, some applauding Giffard's courage and others cursing him.

Geoffrey ran to Giffard's aid as people pressed around him. Tears coursed down the Bishop's anguished face. Walter snatched his uncle's arm and yelled that he was a traitor, and it was with some satisfaction that Geoffrey shot an elbow to the boy's nose. Roger helped Geoffrey beat back those who wanted to haul Giffard to the altar and have him consecrated by force. Word quickly reached the common people, and they cheered Giffard for his courage. Eventually, Geoffrey managed to spirit him away.

'Now you have done it,' said Roger nervously. 'The King will not be pleased.'

'No, he will not,' said Giffard with a serene smile. 'But my conscience is clear.'

A few hours later, Roger waylaid a royal clerk and offered him a silver coin to read the documents he had taken from Durand. Roger had an unpleasant feeling that Durand's 'final secret' had something to do with the parchments. He knew he should give them to Geoffrey, to make up his own mind, but Roger could not rid himself of the notion that they would bring more problems to his friend's door.

The clerk, a man called Eudo, was one of Henry's longest serving scribes. His kindly, honest features were a ruse: he was neither. However, he was absolutely and completely devoted to the King. He took the letters Roger proffered and began to read, making sure his face did not register the surprise he felt. They were missives sent from Prince Tancred to Geoffrey Mappestone, asking the knight to proceed to the Holy Land as soon as his business with King Henry was completed. Geoffrey's wise counsel was missed, Tancred wrote, and there would always be a place for him in his Holy Land kingdom, no matter how often family obligations forced him to visit England. The tone was brotherly and affectionate, and it was clear the two men enjoyed a strong friendship.

Then there were copies of other letters that Eudo's skilled eye told him were not written by the same scribe. They were forgeries, albeit clever ones. These railed furiously at Geoffrey for not returning when he had promised, and the last was a brutal severing of all further correspondence in a manner that could not have been more different from the originals.

There were also several missives signed by Geoffrey himself, apologizing for his tardiness in returning to his liege lord's service and explaining his reasons in a clear, orderly manner. It was obvious these had never been sent. Notes on a scrap of parchment, along with several words mimicking Geoffrey's writing, told what had been dispatched in their place – bald statements that verged on the insolent. Eudo was not surprised Tancred had professed himself concerned about his favourite commander's health in his later replies: the letters Tancred had received were a far cry from the originals.

Listening to Roger's explanation of how he had come by the documents, Eudo managed to piece together the puzzle: Durand had taken over the correspondence between knight and prince. Tancred now believed Geoffrey could no longer be bothered to fight his cause, and Geoffrey was under the impression Tancred would kill him for disloyalty if he set foot in his kingdom. Even Eudo would not have stooped to use such tactics, but it was done, and there was a chance that the King might benefit from the situation...

'You were right not to give these to your friend – or to show them to anyone else,' Eudo said to Roger, who was watching with troubled eyes. 'They outline a treasonous plot against the King, led by Durand and in which Sir Geoffrey was to play a significant role.'

'No!' breathed Roger. 'Durand might be that stupid, but Geoff has far too much sense.'

Eudo smiled his kindly smile. 'Then the best thing we can do is burn these and ensure they never fall into the wrong hands. It would be unfortunate if your friend was charged with treason, just because Durand penned some deranged thoughts of regicide.'

Roger nodded eagerly, and they both watched as the letters were consumed by flame. Eudo knew the King would be keen to hear of Durand's revenge on the two men he felt had tormented him. Their friendship was irreparably smashed, and neither was likely to write to the other again. Like other kings, Henry would soon have a *Jerosolimitanus* in his retinue.

'There,' said Roger, when the last letter was curled and black. 'Now he is safe.'

'We have taken a serious risk,' said Eudo sternly. 'If we tell another soul what we have done, we may be accused of treason ourselves – and your friend will be doomed for certain.'

Roger rested his hand on the Crusader's cross on his surcoat, and his face was grave. 'I swear, by this holy symbol, that I will never tell *anyone* what we have just done.'

'Good,' said Eudo, who could see Roger meant every word. Only Eudo himself and the King would know what had really transpired between Tancred and his faithful knight.

Goodrich, mid-summer 1103

A few days after Geoffrey's return from seeing Giffard board a ship into exile, he opened the chest in his room and removed the Black Knife. He knew he should have disposed of it sooner, but he had been too busy with castle repairs and trying to pay court to Hilde. Now, with Goodrich recovering, he could delay no longer. He put the charm from Eleanor around his neck and took the dagger in his hands. He knew it was his imagination, but he thought he sensed the thing vibrating.

He shoved it in a sack, asked Bale to saddle his horse and rode out of the castle. He headed west, in the direction Eleanor had taken when she had gone to meet her lover, because he held the inexplicable belief that the weapon might cause less harm if closer to her. He had travelled about three miles when he met Olivier, returning from an amble. Olivier frowned when he saw Geoffrey's preoccupied expression, and, when Geoffrey told him what he planned to do, turned his little pony to follow him.

They searched in companionable silence for a long time, and Geoffrey was beginning to despair of ever finding what he sought, when suddenly they stumbled on a tree meeting Eleanor's specifications. Geoffrey dismounted and stood beneath the oak. It felt strong and solid, and was a long way from any path, so he felt reasonably confident that the Black Knife would remain hidden until its evil powers had leached away. He fetched the spade he had brought and started to dig.

'That is deep enough, Geoff,' said Olivier, seeing a veritable chasm appearing. 'If you go much further, you may damage the roots.'

'Tell me what happened when Henry died,' said Geoffrey, still digging hard. He did not want rains to wash the dagger out or winter frosts to force it to the surface.

Olivier sighed. 'There is nothing to say that

you do not already know.'

Geoffrey straightened. 'No, there is not, but I would like to hear it from you. It was *you* who asked Eleanor to curse the knife, because it was you who killed Henry.'

Olivier stared at him, then sat down heavily. 'How do you know?'

'The bloody footprints around Henry's body were small, which led me to wonder if a woman might be involved, but they were yours. And there was the blood that was never cleaned away and the bird charms – you did that with Jervil's encouragement. It was why you always refused to enter the stables after the murder.'

'They felt haunted,' said Olivier in a strangled whisper. 'They still do.'

'Then there was Eleanor: she said the person who asked her to turn this dagger into a Black Knife knew her secret. That was why you both trusted each other.'

'I do not—'

'When you and I went riding the day Dun threw me, you said you would have asked Eleanor for a charm to calm his wild temper. That implies you had used her spells to good effect before. You also said she was "God knows where" after the fire, although everyone else thought she was dead. You knew she would be with her lover.'

'She does not have a lover.'

'She does; she told me herself. You need not pretend with me. You *did* witness the ceremony she performed on your knife – or rather on the knife Seguin gave Baderon – because you asked

406

her to do it. But how did you come to have it in the first place?'

Olivier hung his head. 'I do not ... I...'

Geoffrey did not need his confession. 'Actually, I know the answer to that, too: Henry stole it. He took it from Baderon's house on the Feast of Corpus Christi. Baderon said he had invited all his neighbours – including Henry – to celebrate.'

Olivier nodded slowly. 'Henry stole the dagger, and Eleanor told me a weapon that was already tainted with a crime would make a better receptacle for her curse. She was right.'

'I do not blame you, Olivier,' said Geoffrey. 'I know Henry tried to kill you, but he only broke your arm. And I know about his plan to marry Joan to Hugh as soon as you were dead. He might have succeeded, had you not killed him first. But why did you always insist he committed suicide?'

Olivier gave a short, humourless laugh. 'I doubt you will believe me, but when I saw his face in the moonlight, my nerve failed me, and I found I could not do it. I hesitated with the dagger at his stomach. But he lurched into me – straight at the thing. He died cursing every person who had ever crossed his path – especially Joan.'

'Jervil said he mentioned Joan specifically. I suppose he cursed her for marrying you – because you were the one who brought him his death. Henry always did have a twisted sense of logic.'

Olivier's face was white as he dredged up the

terrible memory. 'I thought his reign of terror would be over when he breathed his last, but he has continued to haunt us.'

'Eleanor said a Black Knife is best buried by the person who bought the curse,' said Geoffrey. He climbed out of the hole and removed the charm from around his neck. 'You must do it.'

It took considerable courage for Olivier to don the charm and climb into the pit. Geoffrey handed him the dagger, which he accepted with unsteady hands. He placed it carefully in the deepest part, then took the spade and covered it with the rich forest soil. When it was done, he spent a long time stamping the ground flat, while Geoffrey covered it with leaves to hide evidence of disturbance. Then Olivier placed the charm in a crevice under the roots. It was done.

'Will you tell Joan?' asked Olivier shakily.

'There is nothing to tell,' said Geoffrey, his hand on his kinsman's shoulder as they walked away. 'The story ended when you buried the dagger, and I, for one, do not want to talk about it again.'

Historical note

The early years of Henry I's reign were marked by his dispute with Anselm, the Archbishop of Canterbury. William Giffard, who had been given his ecclesiastical ring and pastoral staff by Anselm, was caught in the middle. He was still unconsecrated when Henry suggested the Archbishop of York should do the job, and Giffard agreed to the ceremony. To be consecrated with him were Reinhelm of Hereford and Roger of Salisbury. Reinhelm, siding with Anselm, declined to accept York and did not attend the ceremony, but Giffard did, and it was only in the middle of the service that he gave way to his conscience and walked out.

There followed a scene of violent confusion, and the festivities were abandoned. Many people applauded Giffard's courage in taking the side of the Church over the state in religious matters, but the King was less than pleased. He reacted with immediate and predictable harshness, banishing Giffard from England and confiscating all his property. Anselm tried to intervene, but Henry remained adamant. Anselm and Giffard grew closer, and when Anselm was exiled in 1103, Giffard accompanied him on his travels around Europe. We do not know when

Henry forgave Giffard, but he was back in England by 1105, and was eventually consecrated – by Anselm – in 1107.

Giffard thereafter introduced Cistercian reform into England and founded its first house at Waverley in Surrey. He founded a house of Austin Canons at Taunton and was instrumental in raising the Church of St Mary Overy in Southwark. It was near this church that he built a palace, for use by future bishops of Winchester while they stayed in London. Contemporary chroniclers give him a strong moral character.

It is thought that Giffard came from the same family as Walter Giffard, the Earl of Buckingham. Walter Giffard died on 15 July 1102, leaving a widow called Agnes and a son named Walter. On 25 October of that same year, Sibylla de Conversano, Duchess of Normandy and wife to Henry I's brother, Duke Robert, gave birth to a son, William (known as 'the Clito'). It is not clear what happened later, only that by 18 March 1103, Sibylla was dead. She was reputed to be intelligent and sensible – which the Duke was not – and it is generally agreed that her death was bad news for Normandy.

The chronicler William of Malmesbury blames the disaster on medical problems following the birth of her son, but the contemporary historian Orderic Vitalis (1075–c.1142) has a darker suggestion: that Duke Robert's mistress, one Agnes Giffard, poisoned her. The rumour may have been down to spite, because Sibylla was popular and the mistress was not, but we shall never know the truth. We do know that if Agnes did murder the Duchess, she did not gain from her crime. The Duke's realm began to fall apart, and he was far too busy quashing rebellions to marry his mistress.